Dear Friends,

Long ago I learned a valuable lesson as a writer, and that was the importance of listening to my readers. One thing I consistently hear from you is: "Please write more Blossom Street books." And so, my friends, here is the latest update from my heart to yours. You'll meet some new characters and visit familiar ones. Naturally, Lydia, from A Good Yarn, with her daughter, Casey, is front and center, as well as a handful of others.

You'll also meet Libby Morgan, who is becoming reacquainted with knitting after being laid off from a high-pressure job at a law firm. Wayne and I are familiar with what it is like to go through a long stretch of unemployment. The year our daughter Jenny Adele was born, Wayne, who worked as a construction electrician, was out of work nearly nine months. He made good use of the time and took classes at the community college while I cared for our older daughter and found a hundred different ways to stretch our unemployment check. In fact, Wayne was in Alaska looking for work on the pipeline in the early 1980s when I sold my first book. So you can see this story comes from a wealth of personal experience. Most of us have gone through similar situations at one time or another, and while it's never fun, there are lessons to be learned and truths to be discovered. I hope you enjoy meeting Libby and watching the world unfold as her eyes are opened and she discovers the meaning of friendship . . . and love.

As always, I welcome your comments and letters. You can reach me in a variety of ways. Old-fashioned snail mail still works. Contact me at P.O. Box 1458, Port Orchard, WA 98366 or through the guest page on my website at DebbieMacomber .com. I'm also on Facebook and have my own phone app. I'm connected just about everyplace there is to be plugged in.

Now sit back, turn the pages, and enjoy.

Warmest regards,

Debbie Macomber

Starting Now

DEBBIE MACOMBER

Starting Now

A Blossom Street Novel

DOUBLEDAY LARGE PRINT HOME LIBRARY EDITION

BALLANTINE BOOKS
NEW YORK

Published in the United States by Ballantine Books, an imprint of The Random House Publishing Group, a division of Random House, Inc., New York.

BALLANTINE and colophon are registered trademarks of Random House, Inc.

Grateful acknowledgment is made to Watson-Guptill Publications, an imprint of The Crown Publishing Group, a division of Random House, Inc., for permission to reprint one baby hat pattern and photograph from *Baby Beanies* by Amanda Keeys, copyright © 2008 by Amanda Keeys. Used by permission of Watson-Guptill Publications, an imprint of The Crown Publishing Group, a division of Random House, Inc. Any third party use of this material, outside of this publication, is prohibited. Interested parties must apply directly to Random House, Inc., for permission.

ISBN 978-1-62490-197-3

Printed in the United States of America

Title-page and chapter-opening illustration:
© iStockphoto.com

To Theresa Park

For opening doors
and broadening my perspective

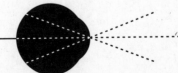

This Large Print Book carries the
Seal of Approval of N.A.V.H.

Starting Now

Chapter 1

This was it. Surely it must be.

The instant Libby Morgan heard her paralegal tell her "Hershel would like to see you in his office," she knew. Oh, there'd been rumblings around the office about layoffs and early retirements. Such gossip simply verified what she felt in her heart Hershel was sure to tell her. She'd waited for this moment for six very long years.

Libby had always wondered how she'd feel when she finally got the news. She longed to hold on to this sense of happy expectation for as long as possible. In retrospect, she must have intuitively known something was up because she'd worn her best pin-striped suit today, choosing the pencil skirt over her normal tailored slacks. And thankfully she'd had a salon appointment just the day before. Getting her hair cut was long overdue, but seeing how good it looked now, she felt it was worth every penny of the hundred dollars Jacques had charged her. A good cut did wonders for her appearance. She wore her dark brown hair parted in the middle in an inverted bob so that it framed her face, curling around her jawline. Jacques had mentioned more than once how fortunate she was to have such thick hair. She hadn't felt that way when he'd insisted she have her eyebrows plucked. But he'd been right; she looked good. Polished. Professional. She promised herself not to go so long between appointments again.

Libby didn't see herself as any great beauty. She was far too realistic and sensible, was well aware of her physical shortcomings. At best she was pretty, or at least Joe, her ex-husband, had told her she was. She knew she was probably no better than average. Average height, average weight; brown hair, brown eyes, with no outstanding features, but on the inside she was a dynamo. Dedicated, hardworking, goal-oriented. Perfect partner material.

Reaching for her yellow legal pad, Libby headed toward the managing partner's opulent office. Outwardly she remained calm and composed, but inwardly her heart raced and her head spun.

Finally. Finally, she was about to be rewarded for the hard choices and sacrifices she'd made.

Libby was in her sixth year of an eight-year partnership track. Hopefully she was about to achieve the goal that she had set her heart on the minute she'd been accepted as an associate in the Trusts and Estates Department at Burkhart, Smith & Crandall, a high-end Seattle-based law firm. She was about to be made partner even earlier than anticipated.

While she didn't want to appear

overly confident, it went without saying that no one deserved it more than she did. Libby had worked harder, longer, and more effectively than any other attorney employed by the firm. Her legal expertise on the complex estate-planning project for Martha Reed hadn't gone unnoticed either. Libby had provided a large number of billable hours and the older woman had taken a liking to her. Over the past month two partners had stopped by her office to compliment her work.

Libby could almost feel her mother looking down on her from heaven, smiling and proud. Molly Jo Morgan had died of breast cancer when Libby was thirteen. Before dying, Libby's mother had taken her daughter's hand and told her to work hard, and to never be afraid to go after her goals. She'd advised Libby to dream big and warned her there would be hard choices and sacrifices along the way.

That last summer her mother was alive had set Libby's life course for her. Although her mother wouldn't be around to see her achievements, Libby longed to make her mother proud. Today was sure to be one of those *Hey, Mom, look at me* moments.

Early on in high school Libby had set her sights on becoming an attorney. She was the president of the Debate Club and was well known for her way of taking either side of an issue and making a good argument. Reaching her goal hadn't been easy. Academic scholarships helped, but there were still plenty of expenses along the way. Funds were always tight. In order to support herself through college she'd worked as a waitress and made some good friends. Later on in law school she'd found employment as a paralegal in the Seattle area.

Her career path had taken a short detour when she married Joe Wilson. Joe worked as a short-order cook. They'd met at the diner where she waited tables while in college. When she moved from Spokane he willingly followed her to the Seattle area and quickly found another job, cooking in a diner. He was the nicest guy in the world, but their marriage was doomed from the beginning. Joe was content to stay exactly where he was for the rest of his life while Libby was filled with ambition to be so much more. The crux came when he wanted her to take time out of her career so they could start a family. Joe wanted children and so did Libby, but she couldn't risk being shunted off to the "Mommy Track" at the firm. She'd asked him to be patient for a couple more years. Really, that wasn't so long. Once she was established at the firm it wouldn't matter so much. But Joe was impatient. He feared that once those two years were up she'd want another year and then another. Nothing she said would convince him otherwise.

Hershel glanced up when she entered his office. He wasn't smiling, but that wasn't unusual.

"Sit down, Libby," he said, gesturing toward the chair on the other side of his desk.

One day her office would look like this, Libby mused, with old-world charm, comfortable leather chairs, polished wood bookcases, and a free-standing globe. Pictures of Hershel's wife and children stared back at her from the credenza behind his desk. The one of him sailing never failed to stir her. Hershel had his face to the camera, his hair wind-tossed as the sailboat sliced through the Pacific Ocean on a crystal-clear day, with a sky as blue as Caribbean waters. The sailboat keeled over so close to the water's edge she wanted to hold her breath for fear the vessel would completely overturn.

The photograph inspired Libby because it proved to her that one day, as partner, she, too, would have time to vacation and enjoy life away from the office. But in order to do that her work, her commitment to the law firm and her clients, had to be her sole focus.

Libby sat in the chair Hershel indicated and relaxed, crossing her legs. She knew the managing partner's agenda. What she hadn't expected was the deeply etched look of concern on his face. Oh, it would be just like Hershel to lead into this announcement circuitously.

"I've taken a personal interest in you from the day the firm decided to hire you," he said, setting his pen down on his desk. He took a moment to be certain it was perfectly straight.

"I know and I'm grateful." Libby rested her back against the comfortable padding. "It's been a wonderful six years. I've worked hard and feel that I'm an asset to the firm."

"You have done an excellent job."

Libby resisted the impulse to remind him of all the billable hours she'd piled up on a number of accounts.

"You're a hard worker and an excellent attorney."

Libby took a moment to savor his words. Hershel wasn't known to hand out praise freely. "Thank you." She sat up straighter now, anticipating what would come next. First he would smile, and then he would announce that after discussing the matter with the other partners they would like to . . .

Her projection was interrupted when Hershel went on to say, "I'm sure you're aware that the last six months have been a challenge for the firm." He met her gaze head-on, and in his eyes she read regret and concern as his thick brows came together. "We've experienced a significant decline in profitability due to the recession."

A tingling sensation started at the base of Libby's neck. This conversation wasn't taking the route she'd anticipated.

"I've certainly carried my load," she felt obliged to remind him. More than any other attorney on staff, especially Ben Holmes, she thought but didn't say. At six o'clock, like a precision timepiece, Ben was out the door.

Hershel picked up the same pen he'd so carefully positioned only a few moments before and held it between his palms. "You've carried a substantial load, which is one reason why this decision has been especially difficult."

"Decision?" she repeated as a sense of dread quickly overtook any elation she'd experienced earlier.

"The problem is your lack of 'making

rain,'" he said. "You haven't brought any major clients into the firm."

Meeting potential clients was next to impossible with the hours she worked. Libby had tried attending social functions but she wasn't good at "power schmoozing" the way others were. She felt awkward inserting herself into conversations or initiating them herself. With little to talk about besides work, she often felt inept and awkward. She hadn't always been this shy, this hesitant.

"Hershel," she said, voicing her suspicion, her greatest fear, "what are you trying to say? You aren't laying me off, are you?" She finished with a short disbelieving laugh.

The senior partner exhaled slowly and then nodded. "I can't tell you how much I regret having to do this. You aren't the only one. We're letting five go in all. As you can imagine this hasn't been an easy decision."

Libby's first concern was for her paralegal. "Sarah?"

"She's fine. She'll be reassigned."

Libby's heart slowed to a dull thud.

"We're offering you a generous severance package." Hershel outlined the details but Libby sat frozen, stunned, unable to believe this was actually happening. People she worked with, people she knew, were losing their jobs. She was losing *her* job. Why hadn't she sensed that? She didn't like to think she was so out of touch with reality that she hadn't picked up on it.

"I'd also like to offer you a bit of advice, Libby, if I may?"

The shock had yet to dissipate, and because her throat had gone dry she didn't respond. All she could manage was to stare at him aghast, disbelieving, shaken to the very core of her being.

"I don't want you to think of this as the end. This is a new beginning for you. One of the reasons I've taken a personal interest in you is because you're very much the way I was years ago. I felt the need to prove myself, too. I set my sights on making partner to the exclusion of everything else, the same way I've seen you do. I completely missed my children's childhoods. By the time they were in high school they were strangers to me. Thankfully, I've been able to make up for lost time. The point is, I sacrificed far too much, and I see you making the same mistakes I did."

Libby tried to focus but couldn't get past the fact that she was suddenly unemployed. She blinked a couple of times in an effort to absorb what was happening. It didn't help. The sickening feeling in the pit of her stomach intensified.

"I hope," Hershel continued, "that you will take this time to find some balance in life. Starting now."

"Pardon?" she asked, looking up and blinking. Some of the numbness had begun to wear off. All Libby could think about was the fact that she had given her life, her marriage, her everything to this firm, and they were about to shove her out the door.

"I want you to enjoy life," Hershel repeated. "A real life, with friends and interests outside of the office. There's a whole world out there ready for you to explore."

Libby continued to stare at him. Didn't Hershel understand? She had a life, and that life was right here in this office. She was passionate about her work and now it was being ripped away from her.

"Who will take over working with Martha Reed?" she asked. Surely this was all a big mistake. Martha Reed was one of their most important clients and she enjoyed working with Libby.

"Libby, you're not listening. The decision has already been made. The firm is being more than generous."

"Generous," she repeated, and gave a humorless laugh. Anger took hold then and she surged to her feet. The legal pad fell unnoticed to the floor as she knotted her fists at her sides. "This is a decision unworthy of you, Hershel. You're making a mistake. I thought you had my back . . ." She could feel the heat crawling up her neck, creeping into her face, and snapped her mouth closed. Arguing was pointless; as he said, the decision had been made, but by heaven she wanted him to know she wasn't taking this sitting down. Stabbing an index finger at his desk, she looked him hard in the eyes and said, "I hope you know I'll have another job before the end of the day."

"For your sake I hope you don't, but if that's the case then so be it."

"You're going to regret this, Hershel. I've given you and this firm *everything*." Without bothering to argue more, she whirled around and stormed out of his office.

With her heart pounding wildly, Libby approached her own small office. When Sarah saw Libby, the paralegal stood, her brown eyes wide and expectant.

"Well?" Sarah asked.

"I . . . I've been laid off."

Sarah's face went slack. "You're joking?"

A security guard came to stand just outside her door, watching as she packed up her things. Libby jerked open her desk drawer and started emptying the contents onto her desktop. "Does it look like I'm joking?"

Sarah wore the same stunned expression as Libby had only moments earlier. "But why?"

"Ask Hershel." Libby pinched her lips closed as she struggled to rein in her outrage.

"What . . . what about me?" Sarah sank into a chair as though her knees had given out on her.

"Not to worry, I already asked. You'll be reassigned."

"I can't believe this."

"You?" Libby choked out, now dumping the contents of her drawers into a tote bag she kept on hand.

"What are you going to do?"

"Do?" Libby repeated, as though the answer should be self-explanatory. "What else is there to do? I'll find another job. I'll be working for another firm before I'm out of the building. I told Hershel and I meant it. Jeff Goldstein has been after me for years." This was no exaggeration. Jeff had contacted her two or three times since she'd been with Burkhart, Smith & Crandall to see if she was happy in her current position. He was the first person she'd call. Already a list of potential firms was scrolling through her mind. Any number of law offices would consider themselves fortunate to get her.

Slamming the final drawer closed, she reached for her briefcase and dumped onto her desk the files she'd spent several hours working on at home the previous night. Next she hefted the bag containing the personal items from her desk drawer over her shoulder.

"Libby," Sarah said, eyeing the security guard.

Frankly she couldn't get away fast enough. "I don't think I could stand it here another minute."

Hershel had offered her fatherly advice, sounding so righteous and superior . . . so patronizing. Well, she'd show him. He would rue this day; he'd made a huge mistake and was about to see just how wrong he was. Throughout her life, Libby had faced challenge after challenge and proved herself again and again. This would be no different.

If her mother's death had taught her anything, it was that Libby should do whatever was needed to rise above setbacks. She'd survive. She had before and she would again. She'd lost her mother when she was far too young, and she'd gotten through her divorce. She'd weather this, too, just the way she had everything else.

Forcing herself to smile, she swallowed hard and looked at Sarah. "Keep in touch."

"I will," her paralegal promised. "You'll let me know where you land, won't you?"

"Of course." When she did, Libby would ask Sarah to join her. They were a good team. They'd worked together for so long that they'd become like running partners—keeping pace with each other, intuiting each other's needs and expectations. When she'd last spoken to Jeff Goldstein, Libby had insisted that if she ever were to join his firm he'd need to hire Sarah, too. Jeff had assured her it wouldn't be a problem.

Without a backward glance, Libby walked out of the office. She felt other staff members staring at her, but she chose to ignore them. Standing in the doorway to his office, Ben Holmes started to say something, but after one glaring look from Libby he apparently changed his mind. Good thing. Ben wouldn't want to hear what she had to say to him.

Her cell phone was in her hand even before she reached the elevator. After a quick call to directory assistance, she connected with Goldstein & Goldstein.

"Jeff Goldstein, please," she told the receptionist. "Tell him Libby Morgan is calling."

She was connected immediately.

"Libby, how are you?"

"Fabulous." She got directly to the point. "You called a few months back and asked if I was happy in my current position, remember?"

"Of course. But that was over a year and a half ago."

"That long?" Time had gotten away from her. "As it happens I'm free to come on board with Goldstein & Goldstein." No need to hint at what she wanted. Libby preferred the direct approach.

"Really?" his voice dipped slightly. "As I said, that was well over a year ago. We've had a sharp decline in business since then. Almost everyone has.

We aren't currently taking on any associates."

The news deflated her, but Libby wasn't discouraged. "Not a problem, Jeff," she said, continuing to walk at a clipped pace. She was outside the building now, joining the traffic on the Seattle sidewalk, her steps brusque and purposeful. The dark, overcast March sky was an accurate reflection of her mood. It was sure to start raining at any moment.

"I'm sure with your track record you won't have a problem finding another position," Jeff continued.

"I don't think I will, either," she said, making sure her voice reflected an air of confidence. "I wanted to give you the first opportunity since you've pursued me in the past."

"I appreciate that. If something comes up you'll be the first person I contact."

"Wonderful. Thank you for your time," Libby said.

"No problem. Keep in touch."

"Will do," she said, cutting off the words in her rush to end the call.

She regretted calling Jeff in an angry

flush. She should have given the conversation more thought instead of acting out of emotion and outrage. Even
now she was fuming, caught between
disbelief and indignation.

The walk to her condo took fifteen
minutes. The distance was what she
considered her daily workout. Her building was on a busy street and safe
enough for her to hoof it both early in
the morning and late at night. She
hoped she'd be able to continue to walk
to and from work at her new firm.

Shifting the load from one shoulder
to the other, Libby struggled to maintain her composure as she walked
through her front door. She'd been so
certain that this was it, so confident
that her hard work and sacrifices were
finally being recognized. To get laid off
instead was unbelievable.

Only now was the truth of it beginning to sink in.

Libby had always been driven to succeed. She'd been the valedictorian of
her high school class and had been in
the top ten percent of her class in both
college and law school. She had worked

hard for those grades; she worked hard for everything.

With her arms wrapped around her middle, Libby walked around the living room three times, her mind racing at a speed to rival any NASCAR engine. The sky had gone even darker and a drizzle splashed against the windows, weaving wet and crooked trails on the glass. This was March in the Pacific Northwest.

Libby needed to think. First things first: update her résumé.

She turned on her one-cup coffee-maker, brewed a mug, and carried it into her home office. Setting it down on a coaster, she looked at the picture of her mother that rested on the corner of her desk. Her mother's eyes seemed to focus directly on hers.

"I know, Mom. Don't worry. This is only temporary. All is not lost."

It was then that Libby noticed the plant next to her mother's framed photograph. She didn't even know what kind it was, but regardless: it was brown and shriveled now. It had withered with neglect.

Chapter 2

Four Months Later

With her briefcase clenched in her hand, Libby Morgan left her latest interview with the gut-wrenching feeling that she wouldn't get this job, either. The economy was killing her chances. Her résumé highlighted her professional qualifications; Hershel had written her a glowing letter of recommendation, and yet nothing had panned out.

Four months!

Finding another position shouldn't have been a problem; only it was. No one was hiring. No one was interested. Libby lost count of the number of firms where she'd applied, the number of interviews she'd sat through. She'd followed leads from friends, and still nothing. Oh, she'd come close any number of times, but up until now she'd always come in second . . . or third. Her ego was in the gutter and her self-esteem was dragging close to the seafloor. Libby had never been this depressed in her life. Having nothing to do with her time was slowly killing her. She desperately needed to work.

As she walked into her condo, she tossed her briefcase onto the sofa and sagged into the thick, cushioned seat. The middle button of her suit jacket had stretched to the breaking point. On top of everything else she'd gained weight. Ten pounds. Ten ugly pounds. She unfastened her jacket and let out a disgusted sigh. Nothing fit right. Nothing felt right. Not her life. Not her clothes. Nothing.

The phone rang, and thinking it might be a potential employer, Libby leaped for it.

"Libby Morgan," she said, doing her utmost to sound upbeat and positive.

"Libby, it's Sarah. How'd the interview go?"

Her shoulders sagged with disappointment. Who was she kidding? No one was going to call her about a job. "It's the same old story: there are at least forty candidates for every opening."

Even before the interview was finished Libby knew she wasn't a contender. In the months since she'd left Burkhart, Smith & Crandall she'd developed a sixth sense about her chances. Two or three times she knew she was in the running. Second and even third interviews followed, and yet it was always the same outcome. Sorry, another time. Close, but no cigar.

"How's the office?" Libby asked. Her one lingering hope was that Hershel and the other partners would recognize their mistake and ask her to return. Four months ago, if they had, she would've taken pleasure in laughing in their faces and telling them to take a flying leap into some cow pile. Over the last several weeks, though, her attitude had softened considerably. She wanted to work. She needed to work. She couldn't take this endless battle of building herself up for the next interview only to be dashed against the rocks of self-doubt and frustration.

"I was so hoping it would work out this time," Sarah continued.

Libby had been, too.

"Don't get discouraged," Sarah said.

"I won't." Yeah, like that was possible. She felt beaten down and defeated and it wasn't even noon yet.

"Gotta scoot."

"Bye." Her paralegal's calls weren't as frequent as they'd been the first month. In fact, these days it was usually Libby who contacted Sarah. The paralegal was busy and preoccupied, and their conversations were short. Libby knew that Sarah found it difficult working for Ben Holmes. She'd gladly follow Libby to another law firm given the opportunity.

What she needed, Libby decided, was a break. She hadn't been to Spokane since Christmas two years ago. Hadn't seen her father or stepmother in that long. Libby got along fine with

Charlene, the woman her father had married when she was a high school senior. Their relationship was warm. Charlene was pleasant enough, but she had no intention of mothering Libby, which was fine by her. Libby held on to the memories of her mother and worked hard to live up to the potential Molly had seen in her.

Unfortunately, Libby had never been particularly close to her father. He was a civilian working for the air force as a computer analyst and had always been distant. The small family had gotten their first emotional hit when Libby's older brother, Timmy, was killed while riding his bike when he was ten. A drunk driver had hit him and then sped away. Her father had taken the tragic death of his son especially hard. Although Libby was only vaguely aware of it, Timmy's death had put a strain on her parents' marriage. Then her mother had been diagnosed with cancer.

Robert Morgan seemed to close himself off from life after his son's death. In many ways that drunk driver had claimed more than her brother's life;

he'd destroyed their family. Her mother and father were never the same. Gone were the days when her father would laugh and tease her. As a child Libby had loved it when her father would pick her up and twirl her around and around. She couldn't remember him playing with her again after they lost Timmy.

When it was just the two of them, Robert and Libby rarely even spoke. The day she was admitted into the National Honor Society, her father hadn't come to the school for the presentation. He hadn't taken pictures of her and her date for the high school senior prom the way other parents did, and for her birthday and Christmas he gave her cash. He simply didn't seem to care. Still, he was family. Her only family.

It was her mother Libby missed— now more than ever. She longed to burrow into her mother's arms and be comforted by her warm embrace, just as she'd done when Libby was young and frightened. Her mother had always found a way to cheer her. In first grade, when Libby hadn't gotten an invitation to a birthday party, her mother had taken her to a fancy restaurant for tea. They'd worn special hats and gloves and dined on cucumber sandwiches. All these years after her mother's death, Libby still missed her hugs and the notes her mother used to write and tuck into her sack lunch.

Reaching for her phone, Libby looked up the Spokane number for her father on her contacts list, a sad commentary all on its own. Charlene answered on the third ring.

"Hello, Libby," she said, sounding pleased to hear from her.

They spoke for a few moments, exchanging pleasantries before Libby asked, "I was wondering if you and Dad have plans this weekend? I thought I might drive over for a visit."

Charlene hesitated. "Is everything all right?"

"Oh, sure. I just need a change of pace." What she needed was purpose, something to do other than sit around the condo and slowly go insane.

"You aren't working yet?"

"Not yet." The words nearly stuck in her throat. She felt like such a loser.

"What you need is a little TLC," Charlene murmured sympathetically. "Come visit and I'll make you comfort food. I've got a new macaroni and cheese recipe I've been meaning to try."

"I don't need macaroni and cheese," Libby cried on the tail end of a hysterical laugh. "I need cottage cheese."

"Oh dear, have you gained weight?"

"It's the ice cream," Libby lamented. Late nights with Jay Leno and the featured flavor of the month were the culprits. With no reason to go to bed, she was often up until one or two in the morning. Libby knew she should quit the nighttime snacks, but she couldn't discipline herself to do it. Her comforts were few. Until the last few months Libby had had no idea how consoling ice cream could be to a troubled heart and mind.

"Join a gym," Charlene suggested. "It'll help. Here's your father."

"Libby, what's up?" Robert Morgan asked. He'd never been a warm and fuzzy father, but after losing Timmy and

Molly, he wasn't entirely sure what to do with Libby at all.

"I'd thought I'd drive over to Spokane for a visit," Libby said. "It's been a while since I was last home."

"You mean to say you still don't have a job?" The question felt like an accusation.

"I'm trying, Dad," she said, fighting back a defensive response. It wasn't like she hadn't put effort into this job search. She'd run herself ragged, cheerfully subjecting herself to one rejection after another. It seemed the longer she was unemployed, the harder it was to interest a potential employer.

"Well, you're welcome to *visit*." Heavy emphasis was placed on the last word.

Visit. Not stay. Visit.

Libby exhaled, swallowing down yet another bitter lesson in humility. "Thanks, Dad."

That weekend Libby drove over to Spokane on Saturday morning and stayed until late Sunday morning. The *visit* was short and sweet. Charlene looked on sympathetically as her father found it important to ply her with unsolicited and unwelcome advice.

Don't be a quitter.

Try harder.

Don't be so picky.

Be willing to start at the bottom.

Prove yourself.

He said all these things as if Libby hadn't been trying.

Monday morning, following her stepmother's advice, Libby found a local gym on the Internet, stopped by for a tour, and at the end of the visit signed a twelve-month contract. She should be watching her pennies more closely, but at the rate she was gaining weight it would be cheaper to pay gym fees than it would be to purchase the entirely new wardrobe she'd need if she got too fat to fit into the one she already owned.

"Do I need special workout clothes for the yoga and Pilates classes?" she asked the perky girl who'd given her the tour of the facility. She'd introduced herself as Gina and she had a Miss Universe figure.

"Nothing special; just something loose and comfortable."

Libby snickered. "If I had anything loose I wouldn't be enrolling at the gym."

"Funny."

Libby didn't think it was all that humorous.

The next morning at eight, she arrived to find the gym packed. Every machine was in use, and the sound of whirling wheels filled the cavernous room. Libby had chosen to wear sweatpants and a T-shirt and felt incredibly out of place. The other women wore stylish color-coordinated outfits. Looking around, she was convinced she was the fattest woman in the room.

"You can have my machine," a tall, good-looking man around her age offered when she approached the row of treadmills.

"Thanks." She waited until he finished, stepped onto the base, and set the speed at a brisk pace to walk a mile and a half. Before she finished she thought she would throw up. Libby had no idea she was so badly out of shape.

Afterward, in an effort to catch her breath, she sat in the dressing room on the bench and bent forward, elbows on her knees. The wall clock told her it was nine. She would be at her desk right now if she still worked at the firm, and would probably have already put in two hours of hard work. Those days were gone. Now the rest of the day stretched out before her as a complete blank. At least now she was walking off the pounds she'd gained.

After showering and changing clothes she returned to her condo and spent the next hour on the computer in a futile job search. She broke for lunch, watched the noon news on television, and fifteen minutes of the soap opera that followed. When she realized she was getting hooked on the story line, she abruptly turned it off and headed back to the computer. A couple of days last week, she'd actually taken a nap. A nap in the middle of the day—it was outrageous. The mere thought of watching soap operas and taking naps horrified her. An unknown person was taking over her body and she had to find a way to stop this hostile takeover.

When she arrived at the gym the next morning, a professional-looking woman around her age opened the locker next to Libby's. She looked vaguely familiar. Then it hit her. She was an attorney at one of the bigger law firms in town. It took Libby a few minutes to recall her name. Megan . . . Maggie . . . no, Maddy Something. Why oh why hadn't she paid more attention?

Her father had offered one bit of good advice. He'd suggested that Libby needed to network more.

The problem was, Libby had been so intent on making partner that she hadn't invested a lot in professional friendships. It wasn't that she didn't have any friends. She made an effort to keep in touch with a few people from college and law school. Her problem was, she didn't know how to network. But she was willing to learn. At this point she was willing to do just about anything that might lead to a job.

Well, there was no time like the present.

"Hi," Libby said, closing up her locker. "It's Maddy, isn't it?"

Maddy turned to look at her, but her face was a blank.

"I'm Libby," she said, smiling. "Libby Morgan from Burkhart, Smith & Crandall." No need announcing she was currently without employment.

"Oh, hi."

It didn't look like Maddy recognized her.

Libby wasn't sure what to say next. "You come here often?" Oh dear, that sounded like a pickup line. "I just signed up . . . this is my first week and I have to tell you, this is hard work." She waved her hand under her armpit in a halfhearted attempt to be funny. Actually, she probably looked more pathetic than amusing.

"I'm here three mornings a week," Maddy said, and turned her attention to the friend on her other side. The two of them left the locker area and went into the gym.

Embarrassed, Libby looked away. She picked up a hand towel on her way onto the main floor and sought out a machine. The stair-stepper was available and she figured she'd give it a try. Thirty minutes later Libby felt like she needed to be resuscitated. Her lungs burned and her calf muscles screamed in protest.

Gina, the Miss Universe double who'd given her the tour of the gym, noticed, and while Libby sucked in shallow breaths, Gina made a number of suggestions about a physical fitness program, all of which sounded painful. From now on she'd stick with the treadmill.

When Hershel had first suggested she get a life, Libby had been offended; her life was just fine, thank you very much! She enjoyed her job and lived in a nice condo. Really there wasn't anything she wanted or needed beyond that—well, other than making partner.

In the weeks and months since, she'd come to realize he'd been right. If she was going to be honest, most of her friends were more like acquaintances. She felt completely inept at making new ones. Without a job she felt like a fish out of water.

Back at home, Libby reached for her phone and called Robin Hamlin, who was the closest of her school friends. The two had been study partners in law school. Robin worked as a prosecutor for the city of Seattle and was as driven and dedicated as Libby . . . or as Libby used to be. Ninety minutes later Robin returned the call.

"What's up?" Robin asked in her usual no-nonsense way.

"Can you meet me for lunch?"

"When?" Robin asked, sounding distracted.

"Any day this week." Or next, or the one after that, thought Libby.

"Thursday's open. Noon at The French Cafe on Blossom Street?"

"Sure." Libby didn't know The French Cafe or Blossom Street, but it would take only a click of her mouse to locate the restaurant.

"Good. See you then."

On Thursday, Libby had already claimed one of the few outside tables and ordered their lunches when Robin arrived ten minutes late.

"Sorry, I got here as soon as I could."

"No problem." Her friend looked good. Maybe a tad overweight, but Libby wasn't one to throw stones, especially since she couldn't button her pants. Robin wore a crisp navy blue business suit with a straight skirt. Her hair was shorter than Libby remembered it. Actually, she couldn't remember the last time they'd gotten together. They'd talked on the phone a couple of times since Libby had started her job search, but their conversations were always short. Brusque. Libby wondered if that was the way she'd appeared to others in the past. Probably. She was always rushing to finish a brief or late to a meeting.

"I ordered for us," Libby said. She'd known Robin would be late and short on time.

"What am I having for lunch?" Robin asked, laughing.

"Half a turkey sandwich with split pea soup and iced tea."

"Perfect." Robin pulled out the chair

and sat across from Libby. The umbrella shaded them from the July sun.

As soon as Robin was seated the server dropped off both lunch plates along with two tumblers filled with iced tea, and then left with the plastic order number Libby had placed on the table.

"How's the job search going?" Robin asked, as she reached for her half sandwich.

Libby hesitated, unwilling to admit how desperate she was fast becoming. "It's going."

"You found a job?"

Libby shook her head.

Robin paused with the sandwich halfway to her mouth. "You've got to be kidding."

"I wish I was."

Her friend shook her head. "I might be able to get you an interview with the city, working as a prosecutor."

Libby held up her hand. "I appreciate the thought, but no thanks." She'd seen how Robin had changed since she'd taken a job with the city. Being exposed to the criminal element day after day had given her friend rough edges, making her outlook more pessimistic.

"Remember how I told you Hershel Burkhart suggested I get a life?"

"The SOB."

Libby smiled. She'd gone back and forth between anger and lingering affection for her old boss. She was fond of Hershel, despite the fact that he'd done her a grave disservice. Robin apparently didn't share her opinion. "You know what?" Libby asked, forcing herself to own up to the truth. "I'm starting to realize Hershel was right."

"You have a life, Lib."

Libby shook her head. "I don't, not anymore. And I'm so miserable I hardly know what to do with myself. Oh, I joined a gym." That was one positive. "Actually, I felt like I had to do something and fast, after all the weight I've gained." Thankfully Robin hadn't seen fit to mention it. "I am so fat."

Robin nearly choked on her sandwich. "You are *not* fat."

"Am so. Look." She bolted to her feet and exposed her unfastened waistband. "I'm up ten pounds. Nothing fits."

"You are not fat," Robin insisted. "If anyone is out of shape, it's me. I've gained fifteen pounds in the last six years and can't seem to get rid of it."

Libby's eyes widened and she waved her hands excitedly as she finished chewing a bite of her sandwich and swallowed. "Come to the gym with me. We'll sweat off these excess pounds together."

Automatically, Robin shook her head. "Like I have time to work out."

"You need to make time."

Robin hesitated and then shook her head again. "If you saw my caseload, you'd understand."

"There will always be cases that need your attention. It's time to take care of yourself. I walked to work every morning and thought I was in shape. All it took was a mile and a half on the treadmill to prove how wrong I was. Exercise is important for both your physical and your mental health. If you don't take care of yourself no one else will." Libby repeated the words of the sales pitch she'd gotten from Gina. It'd worked on her. Maybe it would with Robin, too.

Her friend frowned and set her soup-spoon down on the table as though giving the idea serious consideration.

Libby was prepared to argue the benefits of exercise. She needed a gym buddy. Miss Universe had urged her to bring a friend, telling her it would help with motivation.

"If you'd told me six months ago I'd be spouting off the advantages of an exercise routine I would have taken your temperature," Libby added. "But working out will do us both good, and I've already lost three pounds." Libby didn't expect Robin to take her up on her offer, but she felt she had to try.

Robin lowered her drink to the table. "You've lost weight? Already?"

Libby nodded. So she'd exaggerated a little, but she was down a couple of pounds. It wasn't enough to make a difference in how her clothes fit, but every little bit helped. What she didn't mention was that it felt like she'd chis-eled off those miserable pounds one ounce at a time. They hadn't come off easily.

"How often do you go?" Robin asked, slowly taking another bite of her turkey sandwich.

"Me? Right now, every day." She had the time, so why not? It'd actually helped her mental outlook, and while she hadn't made any friends, she saw a number of the same people every day. They nodded at one another as they traded off machines.

"I can't do every day."

"I'll meet you on the days you do go," Libby promised.

"I'd have to be out of there by seven-thirty."

Libby would need to change her time. No problem. She still knew how to set her alarm. "Great." She hadn't expected it to be this easy to recruit Robin, but she knew it would do her friend good.

Then, as if she suddenly remembered she had limited time, Robin glanced at her watch. "I've got an errand to run before I head back to court," she said, pushing her plate aside. "My mom's living in Florida now and she asked me to pick up a skein of yarn for her."

Debbie Macomber

"There's a yarn store close by?" Libby asked, looking around.

Robin motioned her head across the street. A shop called A Good Yarn was directly opposite The French Cafe. When Libby was a young girl, her mother had taught her how to knit. She'd enjoyed it until her mom had died, and then there hadn't been anyone to help her fix her mistakes or explain how to read the patterns. In all the years since, Libby hadn't picked up her knitting needles.

"I'll come with you."

Chapter 3

A cat snoozed in the window of the yarn store, next to a wire mannequin wearing a knitted sleeveless top. A neatly lettered sign indicated that it was crafted in Morning Glory, a cotton-blend yarn. The ribbing was done in cable. Libby recognized the cable stitch from when she was a kid. The project she'd been knitting when her mother died had a cable in it. Libby had never completed the sweater, and she didn't know what had happened to it. No doubt her father or stepmother had gotten rid of it long ago.

A bell rang above the door when Robin entered the store. Libby felt drawn inside. Two steps into the shop and she paused as a warm sensation settled over her, a welcome. She could still remember the last time she'd been inside a yarn store. She'd been with her mother. Wool was displayed against the wall in bright white bins. Everything was organized by color, creating a fascinating mosaic. Just seeing the red, green, yellow, and blue tones and textures mesmerized her.

Instantly, Libby was brought back to her early teen years, sitting with her mother, doing her best to learn as much from her as she could. Her mother had been so ill and so brave. In the last weeks of her life, her mom had spent every available minute with Libby, until her strength gave out.

While Libby had refused to believe her mother wouldn't survive, Molly had known the truth. She had done her best to impart a lifetime of wisdom to her only daughter. Libby had listened intently, remembering everything she could, even writing some things down so she wouldn't forget. Her mother's final instructions had become Libby's mantra.

Take charge of your life.

Don't be afraid to pursue your dreams.

Work hard and don't listen to anyone who says you can't, because you can and you will.

A deep sense of loss filled Libby. All these weeks of being unemployed had eaten at her self-esteem, chipped away at the very foundation of her belief in herself. She wanted to feel her mother's reassuring arms around her, encouraging her, giving her fortitude to move ahead and not be disheartened.

Libby glanced around the shop. A number of knitted samples were artfully displayed throughout. Toward the back of the room was a long table, presumably for classes. Two girls, probably around thirteen or fourteen, sat there and appeared to be deep in conversation. One seemed to be helping the other.

Robin, with no time to spare, walked directly up to the counter. The woman who waited on her greeted her by name and inquired about Ruth, Robin's mother. The two chatted briefly while Robin paid for her mother's yarn. The purchase took less than three minutes and then Robin turned to leave.

"I'll join the gym on my way home from work and give you a call tonight," Robin told Libby just before she reached the door. She glanced at her watch, grimaced, and was gone.

Libby remained rooted to the spot.

"Can I help you?" the woman behind the counter asked.

Libby realized she was making something of a spectacle of herself. "Oh, sorry. I didn't mean to stand here like a flamingo in the middle of a pond. It's just that I haven't been inside a yarn store in years—not since I was a kid."

"You're welcome to take a look around."

"Thanks, I will," Libby said, feeling foolish and a bit self-conscious. She wandered over to one of the display cases next to the wall and picked up a fire-engine-red skein of yarn. Reading the label, she was surprised to discover the yarn was made from corn silk.

"That just recently came into the store," the clerk told her. "My name's Lydia Goetz, by the way."

"Libby," she said, "Libby Morgan." She set the yarn back in the bin.

"We have yarn made from soy, too. And there's a new yarn made from milk."

"Do people still knit with wool?" With all this alternative fiber, Libby had to wonder. Maybe real wool had become passé.

Lydia smiled. "Oh, yes. The vast majority of the yarn we carry is made from wool. There are lots of blends, though. The world of knitting has changed drastically in the last several years. You'd be amazed."

"I already am."

Lydia automatically straightened out a bin, restacking the skeins. "If you need any help just say the word."

Libby nodded and started toward the back of the store where the two teens sat.

"Hi," one of the girls said. "I'm Casey

and that's my mom. She owns the shop."

"Hi, Casey." Libby smiled at the girl. She realized Casey wasn't knitting but crocheting.

Casey appeared to notice Libby's interest. "I'm much better with a crochet hook than I am with knitting needles. This is my friend Ava; I'm teaching her to crochet."

Ava glanced up briefly, but didn't make eye contact.

"What are you making?" Libby asked the two.

Casey was friendly enough but Ava appeared shy and preoccupied.

"We're working on preemie caps. Mom and the other knitters and crocheters make caps for the babies in the hospital. Seattle General. It's right up the street."

Libby knew it well. "It looks like you're doing a great job."

"Not me," Ava said, her head lowered. "Mine looks like crap."

Libby knew exactly how she felt. Her own first attempts had been pretty bad. "I learned to knit when I was your age and my first pieces looked horrible. You know what my mother said? She told me I had to knit all the ugly ones before I learned how to make them pretty." Several times Libby had wanted to quit and throw her scarf away, but her mother's simple words had helped her stick to it. She'd been right, too. By the time she'd finished her third or fourth project, Libby had noticed a difference in her stitches and the tension. When she'd first started knitting the stitches were so tight she could barely get the yarn to move on the needles. Gradually she'd relaxed. By then she'd knit a scarf, a dishcloth, another scarf, and had started on a vest. The vest hadn't turned out half bad and she'd worn it with pride.

"My mother died last year," Ava whispered. She looked up then with eyes that were rimmed with sadness.

Libby's throat thickened. She wanted to tell the girl she'd lost her mother at the same age, but she rarely spoke of her mother. And yet the words tumbled from her lips. "I'm sorry; I know what it's like to lose your mother," she whispered. "Mine died when I was about your age, too."

"Ava hangs with me," Casey said, covering the awkward silence that followed. "Otherwise Ava's stuck with her older brother and he can be a real . . ."

"Casey," Lydia called out to the girl. "Why don't you show Libby the hat tree?"

"Okay, it's over here." Casey set her work down on the tabletop and led Libby to the opposite side of the store. What looked to be a tall coatrack with a number of short, stubby hooks was nearly completely covered in impossibly small knit and crocheted caps. "These are all for the preemies," the teenager explained.

Libby removed one of the hats and examined it.

"Would you like to knit one?" Casey asked.

The question took Libby by surprise. "I . . . I don't know. It's been a long time since I last knitted."

"It won't take you long to relearn."

Libby was amused by the girl's enthusiasm.

"You should do it," Casey said and then returned to her friend.

"Maybe I will."

Libby made her way up to the front of the store, where the owner was busy helping another customer. She walked over to the display window and gently pet the cat, who purred and then stretched his front legs out in front of him, yawning. Giving the shop one last look, Libby reached the door and stepped outside. It was warm and getting warmer.

Then, thinking Robin might back out of joining the gym, she grabbed her phone to send her friend a text. Only she'd need to be subtle. Grinning, Libby typed out FAT and pushed the "send" button.

Not a minute later Robin returned her text with FAT. FAT. FAT.

Libby laughed and sent her fingers flying. FATTER.

Seconds later Robin returned with FATTEST.

It wasn't until Libby looked up that she noticed the flower shop next door to the yarn store. It was called Susan-

nah's Garden. Buckets of freshly cut
flowers lined the sidewalk. On impulse
Libby bought a mixed bouquet of white
and yellow daisies and laughed for no
reason other than that the silly exchange
with Robin had greatly lifted her mood.
She carried the daisies back to her
condo and to her dismay realized she
didn't own a vase.

After cutting the stems, she placed
the flowers in two tall water glasses.
She set one on her desk next to the
plant she was nursing back to health
and the other in the middle of her
kitchen table. It surprised her how much
the afternoon out had lightened her
mood.

Until recently her home had been little more than an office away from her
office. The sofa could use some throw
pillows, and most of her walls remained
bare. How sterile the condo looked. It
certainly wouldn't hurt to brighten the
place up a bit. She could buy a paint-
ing or two. That was a start. Looking
through magazines for ideas might
help, too.

She stopped in the middle of her living room and her pulse accelerated. This was the first time that she'd returned home without immediately rushing to check her messages. When she saw the red light flashing, her heart started to pound hard and fast. It could be a request for a job interview.

Pushing the button, she discovered it was Robin. "All right, all right. I got your message. I'll be there Monday at six-fifteen. Seeing as how you're the one who talked me into this, I expect you to be there, too. And," she added, "I am fatter than you and that's the end of it."

Libby grinned. Well, at least now she'd have a friend to work out with.

Libby slept better that night than she had in weeks. She wasn't sure why, other than the lunch with Robin and the visit to the yarn store.

The yarn store . . . something about the place had deeply affected her. Libby realized what it was. She had felt closer to her mother while in the store. As soon as she'd entered the shop she'd experienced a sense of comfort. The ugly negative voices she struggled to keep at bay had faded to a mere whisper.

Friday morning, after her visit to the gym, she followed her usual routine, surfing the Internet seeking job information. Then she called Sarah to check in. The firm had laid off five more staff and Sarah felt fortunate to still have a job. When Libby inquired about the others, she learned that two of her colleagues had been picked up by other firms. Her self-esteem took an immediate nosedive into a deep, dark pit of doubt.

Frankly she couldn't understand why the others had gotten jobs and she hadn't. No one worked harder or longer hours than Libby. No one. She was an asset. Okay, fine, she hadn't brought in any major clients. That wasn't her gift; she was still a hard worker—her billable hours proved as much.

At ten, Libby showered and dressed. She planned to return to the yarn store and purchase yarn if Lydia had time to reacquaint her with the basics. It wouldn't take long. She figured she'd pick up on the knit and purl stitches without much effort; it was casting on and off that she'd forgotten. Having a goal, a purpose to help fill the time between interviews and job searches, appealed to her. She could knit.

When Libby arrived at A Good Yarn, the cat was warming himself in the window. Apparently he was something of a fixture in the store. She walked in and was surprised to find that Lydia wasn't there.

"Can I help you?" The woman who greeted her looked busy and wasn't nearly as welcoming or as friendly as Lydia.

"I was here yesterday," Libby explained. "I met Lydia and Casey and another girl. I think her name was Ava."

The other woman stared at her and didn't offer a return comment.

"Lydia offered to help me relearn knitting."

"My sister is a good teacher."

"Lydia's your sister?" Although both had the same dark brown hair and eyes, they were about as different as any two women could be. In addition to the obvious differences in personality, Lydia was tiny and delicate and her sister was large and big boned.

"I'm Margaret, and I get that quite a bit."

"Get what?"

"That look of surprise when people find out Lydia and I are related. She had cancer as a kid and I think it stunted her growth."

"Oh."

"She took our mom to a doctor's appointment this morning. We take turns helping Mom."

Libby walked over to the display for the preemie hats. "I was thinking I could probably knit one of these, but I'd need a bit of guidance getting started."

"I can help you with that." Margaret came out from behind the counter. "Sorry if I seemed brusque, Lydia's much more of a people person than I am. Do you have needles?"

"Ah . . . no. Actually I'll need everything."

"No problem." Walking at a brisk pace, Margaret went from one end of

the store to the other collecting items.
"What color yarn do you want?"

"Ah . . ."

"Pink, blue, neutral?"

"Neutral, I guess." Libby had trouble
keeping up with the other woman. Margaret grabbed a peach-colored ball of
yarn.

"The pattern Lydia prefers is for knitting in the round, but she has another
for straight needles." She paused and
looked at Libby.

Libby blinked, unsure what the question was. "I don't know that I've ever
knit anything in the round."

"Not a problem," Margaret said, and
grabbed a pair of straight needles off
the case. "In addition to yarn and needles, you'll need a measuring tape and
scissors."

This charity project was quickly adding up. "Exactly how much is this going
to cost me?"

"Less than you'd think. Lydia gives a
discount when knitters buy yarn for
charity projects."

"Okay." While Margaret tallied everything up, Libby withdrew her debit card. "Will you be able to help me this morning?" Now that she had the yarn and needles, Libby was eager to get started.

"Sure thing."

Someone else stepped into the store and Margaret greeted her by name. Libby settled down at the back table where she'd met Casey and Ava the day before and waited for Margaret to join her. It didn't take long. The customer knew exactly what she wanted, made her purchase, and was gone.

Margaret joined Libby. "I usually crochet," she explained, "but I knit, too. It'd probably be best to do a knitted cast-on." She handed Libby the pattern, which was on a single sheet of paper. The picture of the hat had faded from repeated copying, but Libby didn't think that would matter.

"Ah . . . sure . . . whichever cast-on you think would be best."

"You might want to read the instructions all the way through first," she suggested.

"Okay." Libby reached for the sheet.

They were actually pretty easy to understand.

"You finished?"

Libby nodded.

Margaret made a single loop and slipped it onto the needle. It only took watching Margaret cast on two stitches before Libby picked up on how it was done. Another customer dropped by and Margaret stepped away from the table. By the time she returned, Libby had the required number of stitches on the needle.

"I suggest you make a couple of the hats in stockinet stitch, which is knitting one row and purling the next. Once you're comfortable with that, Lydia can show you how to knit in the round with either double-pointed needles or two circular needles."

This sounded a bit like Greek to Libby, but she nodded as though she understood.

Libby had her first hat finished by the time Lydia returned. Casey was with her and the teenager broke into a huge grin as soon as she saw Libby. She hurried to the back table.

"You came back."

Libby smiled at the girl's enthusiasm. "You inspired me."

"Ava's coming by later. Can you stay?"

It wasn't like Libby had anyplace else to rush off to. "Sure."

"I'll sit with you if you want." Casey pulled out a chair and sat down next to Libby. She took her project from her backpack and started to work on it.

After a few minutes Lydia joined them.

"Libby, I'm glad you decided to come back. I see Margaret got you set up."

She nodded. "The stitches aren't that even . . ."

"Remember what you told Ava," Casey reminded her. "It really helped. She was ready to quit and then you said she had to crochet all the ugly ones before she could do anything pretty. She's still waiting for the pretty ones, but I told her they're coming."

"Apparently I have a few ugly ones left in me, too," Libby said, and smiled. Casey smiled back.

Chapter 4

Bright and early Monday morning, Libby waited in the gym lobby for Robin. They'd continued to text over the weekend, but her friend hadn't mentioned the gym again.

"I wasn't sure you'd show," Libby admitted when Robin walked through the gym door.

Robin, who'd never been much of a morning person, growled back, "Me either, but I'm here." She'd brought along a change of clothes, which told Libby her friend intended to head straight to the office after their workout. It was what Libby would have done if she were employed, not that she needed a reminder that she was without a job. By living frugally, her severance package and unemployment benefits had carried her financially up until now, but it wouldn't be long before she had to dig into her savings. The thought of that terrified her.

"Let's get started," Libby said, eager to show Robin the ropes. They found lockers next to each other and headed onto the floor. At this time of the morning the gym was even busier than at Libby's usual time. They put their names on the waiting list for the treadmills and walked the track on the second-floor level until the machines were free. Runners raced past them as if Libby and Robin were standing still. Libby took delight in reminding Robin that the tortoises always beat the hares. Robin grumbled an incomprehensible reply.

"I'm tired already," Robin complained as they reached the main floor for their turn on the treadmills.

Libby remembered how sore and out of shape she'd felt after her first week, but said nothing. No need to discourage Robin before she got started.

Libby stepped onto her machine, set the program, and started walking. Her pace the first few minutes was slow and easy, working up to a fast clip, gradually increasing the angle. The instructor set up Robin's machine and left after a few encouraging words.

"This isn't so bad," Robin said as she started walking.

Libby smiled, knowing what was coming. "I'm glad you decided to join me."

Robin glanced her way and muttered, "Fat."

Libby laughed. She was glad Robin had followed through. It would have required an act of Congress to tear Libby away from the office for something as trivial as exercise.

"This . . . will help me to . . . lose weight . . . right?" Robin already sounded winded and she wasn't five minutes into the routine.

"Yeah. I'm down another pound." Again, it would have been less painful to melt the weight off with a blowtorch, but she wasn't telling Robin that. Her friend was about to discover that for herself. Still, she wondered why it'd been so easy to convince Robin to work out with her. "What made you decide to do it?" Libby's pace had increased and she worked her arms at her sides.

"What?" Robin gasped.

"Join the gym."

"Oh . . . I don't know."

Libby frowned. She knew Robin, or thought she did. The two of them were cut from the same cloth. Robin didn't do anything without a reason, without knowing the end result. Then it hit her. There was more going on than sweating off a few extra pounds. Robin was doing this for a man.

"You dating anyone?" Libby asked, hoping to sound casual.

Robin jerked her head toward her so fast she might have injured her neck. "No. What makes you ask?"

"No reason." Libby wasn't sure Robin believed her. The machine had her half-running now and at an angle that made talking impossible. She kept her gaze focused ahead instead of looking at the timer that flashed the minutes left in her program. Directly in front of her several men lifted weights, their upper arm muscles bulging. Frankly, they were just the distraction she needed. Eye candy.

Robin and Libby finished at the same time. Libby grabbed a towel and wiped the sweat from her face. Robin looked about the same as Libby had her first day—as if she were ready to vomit.

"You okay?"

Robin stared back at her. "You know CPR, right?"

Libby smiled. "Yeah, I got certified in high school."

They entered the locker room and sat down on the bench to collect their breath.

"When was the last time you went on a date?" Robin asked.

Libby had to think about it. Following her divorce she'd basically avoided relationships. Getting involved hadn't seemed like a good idea until she made partner, if she wanted to avoid the pitfalls of her failed marriage. Their conflicting schedules certainly didn't help.

Joe cooked the dinner shift while Libby maintained a normal daytime work schedule, so they rarely saw each other. By the time she was home from the office, he was already at the diner. After a while they became more roommates than lovers. As the months progressed their worlds seemed to grow farther and farther apart.

Libby vividly remembered the day she'd arrived home to discover that Joe was at the apartment instead of the diner. At first she'd been thrilled to see him, but then she realized why he was there. He was packing up to move out.

"Joe?" she'd asked, hardly able to believe this could be happening. Even now she felt her stomach tightening at the memory.

Her husband refused to look at her. Instead he continued collecting his clothes and personal items almost as if she wasn't in the room.

"What are you doing?" she asked.

"It should be obvious." He continued to avoid eye contact, intent on carting his shirts from the closet to the suitcase he'd spread open atop their bed.

"Nothing's going to change, Libby. You have your life and I have mine. You don't want to admit it, so I will. You've got dreams, and that's great. You're the best, but I'm a regular Joe, no pun intended. I don't want anything more than a wife and a few kids."

"But I thought we agreed—"

Joe cut her off. "I can see the writing on the wall. There's never going to be a convenient time for you to have one baby, let alone two or three."

She opened her mouth to argue, but he continued.

"A family would hold you back. I'm not angry, Libby, really I'm not. I want you to have the things you want. But I have dreams, too, and my dreams clash with yours. It's time we recognized we aren't both going to be able to have the things we want . . . at least not together."

He was right, and deep down Libby had recognized the truth of it. After a few weak arguments she let him go. It'd broken her heart to watch him cart his suitcases out the door.

Their divorce was probably one of

the most amicable ones in history. Once it was final, they met for lunch and hugged afterward. Libby cried against his shoulder and Joe held her close and tight. Then they broke apart, walking away in separate directions. He'd remarried within a year, a waitress from the diner. Although they were no longer in contact, she wished Joe love and happiness.

That was three years ago. Three long years. She regretted her failed marriage, and afterward had thrown herself into her career even more. Following her mother's advice had sustained her through the loneliness and the sense of loss that accompanied her breakup with Joe. Perhaps she could look back at that painful period after this morning and feel that it had all been worth it.

"A date," she repeated. "It must be more than a year ago now. What makes you ask?"

Robin shrugged.

"What about you?"

"Longer."

Libby sympathized. "Anyone interested?" Clearly Robin had a reason for bringing up the subject again.

"A man interested in me?" Robin repeated. "Not that I've noticed."

"Anyone you find interesting?" Libby asked.

Robin popped up like a jack-in-the-box and headed for the shower. "I've got to get to work."

So that was it. Robin had a crush on someone. Well, well, well. Good for her. And they were enough alike that Libby understood the problem: Robin didn't have a clue what to do about it. Libby wouldn't have had, either. Relationships were often complicated, and getting involved could get sticky. It must be someone in Robin's office. Although it was tempting, Libby didn't pry. Robin would tell her when she was ready.

Libby grabbed her towel and followed her friend into the shower room.

She was dressing when Robin joined her. "I went back to that yarn store," Libby mentioned casually, hooking up her bra.

"Oh? Are you knitting a project?"

"Yeah."

"What are you knitting?"

"Preemie hats for Seattle General. I knit ten Friday night and ran out of yarn so I went back on Saturday to buy more. I knit another twenty over the weekend."

Robin laughed. "As compulsive as ever." She grabbed her workout bag. "See you Wednesday."

"See ya," Libby echoed.

Libby returned to A Good Yarn that same morning only to find a sign on the door indicating that the store was closed on Mondays. Seeing movement inside, she peered through the front window, her nose pressed against the glass and her hands at the sides of her head to block the reflection. She saw Casey and Lydia inside the shop.

Casey noticed her and hurried to the door, unlatching it. "We're closed."

"So I see. I came to drop off the hats I knit," Libby explained. "I'll come back tomorrow."

"Come in," Lydia invited, joining her daughter. "I was just doing some paperwork and Casey and Ava were going to walk over to Seattle General to deliver the hats."

"If you'd like, I'll go with you," Libby said. She wasn't sure what made her volunteer, but she could see from the way Lydia reacted that she was glad that she wouldn't need to send the girls off without an adult.

"That would be great."

"My pleasure." She had the time, so why not?

Ava avoided looking at her, but when she did, she offered Libby a shy smile.

"We have over two hundred hats," Casey announced proudly. "The hospital goes through them real fast."

"I think they share the hats with a number of other facilities in the Puget Sound area," Lydia explained.

Casey and Ava divided the load between them, carting it in two plastic bags.

"Deliver the hats directly to Sharon Jennings on the third floor," Lydia instructed. "Have reception notify Sharon and she'll make sure you get passes." Lydia walked them to the door and saw them out.

The three started down the sidewalk past the flower shop. As an adult, Libby had never spent much time with kids and wasn't sure how to start a conversation. She needn't have worried—Casey liked to chatter.

"Did you know I'm adopted?"

"I didn't," Libby said.

"I was twelve and came as a foster kid. Lydia and Brad wanted a baby but they got me instead. I have a little brother; he isn't adopted—he's from Brad's first marriage. I have a real brother, too. He's in jail right now. I write him and he's happy that I'm part of a family."

"Oh. Does he need an attorney?" asked Libby, only half-joking.

Casey laughed, apparently finding the offer amusing. "It's too late for that. Lee's getting out soon and is thinking about joining the army if he can. Brad told me the army has high standards these days and they might not take him."

"You have a brother, too, don't you, Ava?" Libby asked, wanting to draw the other girl into the conversation.

Ava nodded.

"He's two years older and a real pest," Casey supplied. "Ava lives with her grandmother and her grandmother works."

"So you're alone most of the day?" Libby turned it into a question, looking down at the young teen.

Ava nodded. "She doesn't get home until late, so I cook dinner."

"I bet she appreciates that." After her mother died, Libby had taken over the responsibility of meals for her and her father. Her repertoire of recipes had been limited, but her father rarely commented or encouraged her. Perhaps that was why Libby never enjoyed spending time in the kitchen. No need, considering what an excellent cook Joe was. He'd done the majority of the cooking. Following the divorce she missed his home-cooked meals almost as much as she missed him.

"Grandma doesn't eat much," Ava added. "After work she goes to the tavern to unwind with her friends."

"Oh." Libby wasn't sure what to say. This bit of information spoke volumes, and she had a sneaking suspicion that Ava's home life wasn't all that wonderful. "Where's your father?"

Ava shrugged. "Don't know. I haven't seen him since I was a kid."

But she was still a kid.

The hospital sat at the crest of a hill in a district known as Pill Hill, just north of downtown Seattle. The last couple of blocks were a steep climb. Either Libby was in better shape than she realized or the hats were heavier than they looked because Ava seemed to have a difficult time keeping up with her and Casey.

Seattle General's front entrance came into view. "Do you know Sharon Jennings?" Libby asked.

Casey nodded. "I went with Mom once when she dropped off the hats. I didn't talk to Sharon, but I know what she looks like."

"We'll find her," Libby said confidently.

The hospital's glass doors automatically glided open as they approached. The information desk was just a few feet inside the entrance. Libby led the way and waited until the woman behind the counter finished her phone conversation.

"How can I help you?"

"We're here to deliver preemie hats to Sharon Jennings," Libby explained.

The receptionist took their information and then contacted Sharon.

"Third floor," she said, as she handed them visitor badges. "Take the elevator on the right-hand side."

"Thank you." Libby led the girls to the elevator, pushed the button, and waited.

It arrived and they stepped inside. Just before the doors glided shut a physician entered. He glanced at the buttons but didn't push one—he was apparently headed to the same floor they were. He looked at Libby and then the girls and then back at Libby. His gaze narrowed slightly before he looked away.

Libby recognized him immediately. She'd seen him before, but she couldn't recall where. Perhaps that look, or whatever it was, had been one of recognition, and he was trying to figure out where he knew her from.

"I know you," he said.

"I recognize you, too."

He frowned again, with a faint look of disapproval.

What an unfriendly man, Libby mused. Well, it takes all kinds. Then she remembered where she'd last seen him. He was the eye candy she'd been studying at the gym that very morning. "You work out at Frankie and Johnny's," she said. As soon as she spoke, Libby wished she'd kept her mouth closed.

He clearly recognized her now, too, but apparently she must have irritated him in some way. He didn't smile or comment.

"What's the matter, did I take the machine you wanted?" she asked, bristling. He probably thought she was fat. Seeing how perfect his body was in practically every way.

He ignored her question.

"You know Libby?" Casey asked him, apparently oblivious to the tension between them. The girl didn't have a shy bone in her body.

"I've seen her at the gym," the doctor said, and grinned at the young teen. It was a really nice smile, and one he hadn't bothered sharing with Libby. The sad part was that she wished he had. Now she was certain it was those extra pounds, or maybe he somehow knew she'd been unemployed for months. Libby crossed her arms protectively and then, realizing what she'd done, promptly dropped them again and squared her shoulders. She certainly didn't need his approval.

"I'm Casey and this is my friend Ava," Casey continued brightly, all smiles.

Ava gave him one of her timid looks.

"Phillip Stone," he said.

Libby noticed how his gaze lingered on Ava and a frown briefly brought his brows together before he turned his attention back to Libby. It seemed like he was about to say something when Casey spoke.

"We're delivering preemie hats for the babies from the yarn store."

"Did you knit them yourselves?"

"Not all of them," Casey said, "but some."

Dr. Stone ignored Libby entirely. "That's a terrific thing you've done. It's important to keep the preemies warm. A lot of heat escapes through their heads, so the hats are very much appreciated."

"That's what Mom said."

Phillip's gaze went to Libby and once again he frowned. Libby was about to ask what his problem was when the elevator stopped and the doors slid open.

Without another word, he stepped out and disappeared down the hall.

Libby watched him go. What an unpleasant, egotistical man. He didn't even know her and he'd managed to make her feel like scum.

Perhaps he assumed she'd been hitting on him at the gym. That was ridiculous, although she had to admit that she'd used him as a distraction. She hadn't been obvious about it; at least she hoped she hadn't.

Libby willingly admitted he was easy on the eyes, but that didn't mean she was interested in him as anything more than a diversion. He'd seemed likable enough. Until now, that is.

Watching the other men, Libby could tell some were there to amaze everyone else with how many pounds they could lift. They weren't even subtle about it. Libby hadn't caught the doctor glancing at himself in the mirror, nor did he appear to be a show-off. He was there to work out, just as she was. Nevertheless he'd been cute enough to attract her attention.

Now that they'd met, she'd look elsewhere.

"Hello, girls," said the woman at the nurses' station. "Lydia phoned to tell me you were on your way."

"Sharon Jennings?" Libby asked.

"That's me." Sharon was a middle-aged woman, dressed in a flowered smock and white pants. Her smile was ready and warm. "I see you met Dr. Stone."

"What's his problem?" Libby asked, unable to hold back the question.

"We call him Heart of Stone around here," Sharon said, laughing.

"I can see why," Libby muttered. "He's about as friendly as a rattlesnake."

"But he's cute," Casey countered, eager to defend the physician.

"Yup. Real cute," Sharon concurred. "And a great doctor."

"Why do you call him Heart of Stone?" Casey asked.

Frankly, Libby was curious to know herself. Clearly he wasn't the warmest person, but it sounded like there was more to it than that.

"He breaks hearts. Plenty of women who work here have set their sights on Dr. Stone, but he isn't interested. I suspect he had a bad experience with someone and avoids hospital relationships."

Apparently, he was looking to avoid relationships altogether, if his reaction to her was typical. The nerve of the man. Rarely had Libby taken a dislike to anyone the way she had old Heart of Stone. From the look of it, the feeling had been mutual.

"We brought you more hats," Casey said.

"That's wonderful." Sharon took the two plastic bags and set them behind the counter.

"I'm Libby Morgan."

"Glad to meet you, Libby."

"Can we look at the babies?" Ava asked.

"Of course." Sharon led them to the window that overlooked the nursery. "The newborns are here but the preemies are in a separate section."

The babies were lined up in neat rows in small cribs with the surnames posted on the headboards. Each one was swaddled in a blanket of either pink or blue.

"They're so cute," Casey said, staring at them through the window.

"That one is crying," Ava said, pointing to the baby with the name Wilcox printed above his head. "Shouldn't someone see what's wrong?"

"Crying is good for their lungs," Sharon explained. "But we're also short-staffed. We rely on volunteers to come in and rock the babies."

"Could I volunteer?" Casey asked. "I love babies."

"Sorry, sweetie, you have to be over twenty-one."

Libby noticed the rocking chair in the corner.

Sharon must have followed her gaze because she looked at Libby and said pointedly, "Like I said, we could use a few more volunteers."

"Don't look at me," Libby said, pressing her hand over her chest. "I don't know a thing about babies."

"You don't need to," Sharon insisted. "All that's required is to hold the baby and rock. You'd be amazed how comforting it is. I swear the rockers get as much out of it as the rockees."

Comforting? Babies? Libby had given up her marriage because she'd insisted on delaying having children until her career was at the right point. Seeing these newborns stirred awake a long-buried desire. She couldn't help but wonder what might have happened if she'd given in and had Joe's baby. Well, it was a moot point now. Still, the thought lingered.

"You might consider volunteering," Sharon urged softly.

The most astonishing thing happened to Libby—her breath caught in her throat as the suggestion took root. She'd taken up knitting, and now after only a few minutes in the hospital she was actually considering becoming a volunteer. Was this what Hershel meant when he suggested that she get a life?

Chapter 5

Phillip Stone stood and escorted the young couple to the door of his office. Friday morning he would be operating on their three-pound son, who had been born ten weeks prematurely. Baby Blaine had a defective heart valve, a not uncommon defect. Over the course of his career Phillip had done this same procedure more times than he could remember.

Still, he'd never performed it on their son, and both parents looked as if they were about to cave in from anxiety and fear.

"I'll see you Friday," Phillip said in his most reassuring voice.

The wife paused and held his look. Her own eyes were rimmed with tears. "Dr. Stone, do you pray?"

He debated on how best to answer. When he was a kid, he'd memorized the prayers his mother had taught him. She was Catholic and his father, well, his father wasn't much of anything. His grandmother had given him a Bible for his high school graduation. He still had it . . . somewhere.

"Annie." The husband urged his wife toward the elevator.

"This is our first baby," the young mother said, her voice quivering. "He means the world to us."

"I pray," Phillip said, after a lengthy pause. He hadn't recently, but there'd certainly been times over the last thirty-nine years when he'd called upon God. Not always in the politest of terms, or in ways that might technically constitute prayer, but it was as close as he got.

"Then pray on Friday," she urged,

before turning away and joining her husband.

The couple entered the elevator. The husband placed his arm around his wife's slim shoulders. Phillip noticed how she leaned into him, as though the love and strength of her mate was the only thing that could keep her upright.

Their baby's chances were good; Phillip didn't anticipate complications. The boy would do fine . . . God willing.

He spent the next hour doing paperwork and was surprised when he glanced up and saw that it was already after seven. He'd meant to leave earlier. Old habits die hard, harder than he realized. Finding balance in his life had demanded discipline and restraint. It was much too easy to fall back into the trap of staying late at the hospital and completely immersing himself in his work.

He saved lives, and these babies needed him. What he'd discovered, though, much to his chagrin, was that he wasn't much good to anyone if his entire focus remained in the hospital. After he and Heather split, he'd realized the problem was his. At the time, he'd felt she wanted more of him than he was willing to give.

After the breakup another realization had hit him. Working such long hours, he'd completely lost sight of himself. Every day at the hospital he became enmeshed in the life-and-death drama of what was happening around him, taking no time to reflect on or absorb the impact of these events. He needed to get away, think, make time for himself and for a life outside the hospital.

Since then, he'd given a lot of thought to his tendency to be so completely single-minded and focused on his work. He realized there was more to this personality trait of his than just pure dedication. Self-analysis wasn't comfortable or especially easy, but he knew that if he was ever going to find fulfillment in life outside of work, then he was going to need to change. It struck him that he was the kind of person who found rigorous self-discipline and accomplishment actually easier than relaxation. He hadn't gotten to the point where he was comfortable lowering his guard, but he was working on that.

One of the first things he'd done was set a hard-and-fast rule that he had to leave Seattle General before seven o'clock. For a while, he'd cast about to find something other than work to occupy his time. That was when he'd stumbled upon the idea of sailing. He enjoyed the water, and being on either Puget Sound or Lake Washington looked exhilarating. So after much research and a series of sailing lessons, he'd bought his own sailboat and made a friend in the bargain. Phillip got along well with his sailing instructor, and the two often went out together for a couple of hours. They weren't bosom buddies, but it felt good to hang out with Fred.

Phillip spent many a summer evening on Lake Washington, soaking in the sunshine and the warm breeze. Recently he'd been invited to join a poker game with a group of other physicians. He'd accepted and enjoyed the camaraderie. Cards had never been his forte and he'd lost far more than he'd won, but being able to laugh with the guys was all the compensation he needed. The funny part was that despite the fact that he always enjoyed himself, he often had to talk himself into going. At heart, he was still a loner.

He logged off his computer, ignoring the long list of emails requiring his attention. They could easily wait until morning. Most evenings he grabbed a quick meal in the hospital cafeteria. The food wasn't half bad; it was tastier than anything he could make himself and it was a damn sight more nutritious than anything he could pick up at a fast-food place.

As he headed down the wide corridor he recognized several nurses. Since he'd started at the hospital a few of them had made it clear that they wouldn't be opposed to seeing him outside of work. Rule number one in Phillip's book was not to get involved with anyone in the medical profession. That was a lesson he'd learned early on in his career, and it'd stuck.

Every now and again he wondered about Heather. They'd met in medical school, fallen in love, moved in together, and decided to marry when they finished their residencies. That was the original plan. But they both worked crazy hours and they barely saw each other. With so little time together it felt like they slipped out of sync—they practically had to start at square one on the rare days they both had off at the same time. He knew they were drifting apart but he didn't realize how far until one day he returned to the apartment only to find it empty. Heather had moved out. He tried to talk to her, to reason things out, but she hadn't listened.

Fine. Whatever. He played it cool for a month or so, gave Heather space, and waited for her to come to her senses. Only she never did. The next thing he heard, Heather, the love of his life, had married another doctor and moved out of the state. Just like that.

It took him six months to get over the shock of it. He dated again, but the results were mostly the same. Marsha Lynch, a reporter who worked for *The Seattle Times,* and Phillip had dated for almost a year before she called it quits. It'd shocked Phillip because he thought their relationship was going along just fine. Sure, he worked long hours, but that was to be expected with his profession. They'd actually discussed marriage at one point. When Marsha walked out she claimed marriage was out of the question. With tears in her eyes, she told him he was remote and too hard to get close to. She said he worked ridiculous hours, but she could live with that if he wasn't so closed off when they were actually together. The ugly scene had lingered in his mind for months afterward.

His problem, Phillip had reasoned, was that he didn't understand women.

It took almost eight months for Phillip to realize that Marsha had pretty much hit the nail on the head. Phillip was married to the hospital, but there was more to it than that. He hadn't viewed himself as remote or distant. He'd never been one to share his troubles or wear his heart on his sleeve, but that didn't make him emotionally inaccessible, as both Heather and Marsha had accused. And yet his tendency to keep his thoughts and feelings to himself seemed to be a problem. His friends were few, but that was the way he liked it. Life shouldn't be a popularity contest.

After Marsha he'd more or less sworn off dating for a few years. With determination he'd started building a life outside the hospital, but it was a constant struggle not to revert to old habits. Every so often he longed for a woman to hold, but he honestly felt as if he just didn't know where to start or if it was in him to give what they all seemed to want and need. When it came to romantic relationships, he was at a loss as to how it should be—the baring of souls, the shared intimacies—all that seemed beyond him. For someone others considered smart and intelligent, he was having a difficult time figuring this out.

This evening was a good example. The Blaines had entrusted their son's life to him, and they were relying on his skill to correct their infant son's heart. If he succeeded, the boy had a good

chance of living a normal life. He admired the way the parents leaned on
each other. They were partners, friends,
lovers. Phillip wanted that kind of relationship, too, a wife and family of his
own, only he didn't know if it was possible for him. At thirty-nine he was set
in his ways.

The trouble was that most of the
women he met came with baggage. Either they were divorced and embittered,
with two or three kids, or they were like
him, married to their careers.

On Thursday morning, Phillip woke to
the sound of his alarm. He stumbled
into the kitchen and got a cup of coffee
brewing while he grabbed his workout
clothes.

He was at the gym lifting weights
when he saw the woman he'd met Monday in the hospital elevator. The one
who'd arrived with the two girls and the
preemie hats.

She was alone this morning; apparently the friend she usually worked out
with didn't make it today. They made

eye contact and she stiffened and
looked away. Phillip figured he deserved
that. He'd taken one look at her daughter and recognized trouble, and he'd
probably been a bit brusque as a result.

He didn't envy . . . oh, what was her
name again . . . Lesley, Lindy . . . no,
Libby. He wondered if she knew her
daughter was pregnant. He doubted it.
In fact, she seemed completely oblivious. Unfortunately, the girl couldn't be
much older than thirteen or fourteen.
He might have misread the situation,
but he doubted it. He'd been around
pregnant women far too long not to
recognize the symptoms. The teenager
wore loose clothes but they couldn't
hide what he found obvious. He gave
her high marks for being clever, though.
He suspected she was six to seven
months along; she hid it well. His guess
was that Libby didn't have a clue. It
was unfair to blame the mother, but
clearly she wasn't paying nearly enough
attention to her daughter.

Well, Libby was in for a shock. And
the girl probably wasn't getting the

medical attention she needed, either. This could be a formula for disaster. He'd toyed with the idea of saying something right there in the elevator but had changed his mind. He didn't want to overstep his bounds. This wasn't his business. Still, he was concerned for the young teen and the possible consequences for her and her baby.

"Hey, Phillip, you coming tonight?"

Distracted from his thoughts, Phillip turned to face his friend, pediatrician Michael Everett. He set the weight down while his mind unscrambled his friend's comment.

"Poker. We're meeting at Ritchie's place. You coming or not?"

"Coming, and this time I intend to win my money back." Ritchie was Michael's brother-in-law from his first marriage. Hannah's brother. Michael had taken his wife Hannah's death hard. For months the pediatrician hadn't been himself. He'd holed up completely, refusing invitations and doing only what was necessary. Grief had crippled him. His staff and friends had worried he would never recover, and then, a year or so after Hannah's death, Michael had met Macy.

Michael slapped him across the back. "Good. See you at Ritchie's at seven."

"See ya."

Ritchie and Michael routinely worked out together, and Ritchie stood next to him with a weight in each hand. Ritchie laid down the weights. "Did you hear?" Michael asked Phillip, grinning sheepishly. "Macy's pregnant."

Phillip slapped his fellow physician across the back and experienced a twinge of envy. "Congratulations."

Michael nodded, looking pleased with himself. "Yeah, we just found out. See you tonight."

"Tonight," Phillip echoed. He was happy for his friend. Michael was a good man and a wonderful doctor, popular with the staff and respected. Phillip had met Macy once and rather liked her. Really, it was difficult not to. She was like a beam of sunshine. He'd met Hannah, too, and felt she would have approved of Michael's choice.

When he finished his regular workout, Phillip headed back to his condo. He didn't need to be at the hospital for another hour. He showered, got dressed, and decided on a second cup of coffee. He took a fresh mug from the cabinet and noticed the flower on his windowsill. He'd brought it home from the office because it'd looked sad and unhealthy. He'd hoped the sunlight would help if he placed it in his kitchen window.

Instead it had withered completely. It had died from neglect.

Chapter 6

The job situation looked bleak. Libby didn't have a single prospect on the horizon and was getting more depressed by the day. She'd knit so many baby hats that she knew the pattern by heart. At the rate she was going, she'd have two hundred hats completed by the end of the month.

Sharon Jennings, the nurse she'd met on Monday, had mentioned that volunteers were needed in the nursery. She'd also said that rocking the babies was comforting. Libby needed something, anything, that would soothe her troubled spirit.

Finding inner peace appealed to her, and rocking newborns was a whole lot cheaper than buying a bunch of books on the subject. What she found difficult to explain was the draw she felt toward these babies. She certainly hadn't felt a twinge of it when her ex-husband had been cajoling her to get pregnant. But now the pull felt magnetic. She longed to hold an infant in her arms. It was so completely counter to what she knew about herself, but there it was.

Well, she didn't have anything better to do with her time; she might as well give it a try. Thursday morning, after working out at the gym, she decided to stop off at the hospital and fill out the application. The form was lengthy, and it took far longer than she'd expected. Most job applications were shorter than this. She was fingerprinted as well. Apparently a complete background check had to be done and submitted before she could be approved.

Sharon Jennings phoned the following Monday morning to tell her she'd been cleared to volunteer at the hospital.

"Oh, great, thanks." Libby had assumed there wouldn't be a problem. She didn't have so much as a jaywalking ticket.

"When would you like to start?"

"Ah . . ." Libby wasn't sure. In the few days since she'd submitted the application she'd had time to think about it, and she'd realized that being with the newborns might not help. While she craved the comfort and peace Sharon had promised, she was afraid being around newborns might make her long for a child of her own. She was already past her prime childbearing years, although it was common these days for a woman to give birth in her late thirties or even her early forties. But with no man in sight, it wasn't likely to happen for her.

Rocking infants could very well be dangerous to her mental well-being. Doubts had already gnawed away at her self-confidence. What she didn't need was a constant reminder of what she'd given up with the divorce. How different her life would have been if she'd given Joe what he wanted. She didn't need to add guilt or regret.

If Libby was going to volunteer for a worthy cause she should consider working at a legal clinic. The problem was that most people who walked into a free clinic weren't interested in setting up estate planning, trust funds, or foundations, and that was her expertise.

"Could you be here at noon?" Sharon wasn't taking no for an answer.

"Ah . . ."

"We could really use your help."

"Sure," Libby capitulated before she could stop herself. Oh dear, what was she thinking?

Sharon's gratitude was immediate. "Wonderful; I'll see you then."

At precisely twelve o'clock, Libby arrived at the nursery. Sharon had her put on a hospital gown over her street clothes, and then she brought her into the nursery.

"Pick up an infant and start rocking" was all the instruction Libby was given.

The nursery was a cacophony of

squalling babies. The noise was deafening. "Which one?" Libby asked, not knowing where to start. She hadn't even begun and she was already in over her head.

"Whichever one you like."

Libby chose the closest baby: a fat, healthy, eight-pound baby boy with a thatch of dark brown hair. The surname was Burzotta. Italian, she suspected. Libby carefully lifted the infant from the soft bed and settled into the wooden rocker. The baby cried all the louder until Libby started rocking. The heated red face relaxed and the baby's lower lip trembled as he gradually settled down.

Libby didn't know any lullabies and so she softly sang the only song she could think of, which was a Rick Springfield hit from the eighties. It might not have been Brahms, but her low voice appeared to do the trick. Within minutes Baby Boy Burzotta was sound asleep in Libby's arms.

She placed the infant back inside his crib and reached for another little boy. He was downright angry, his face twisted into a scowl. "You've been fed, young man," Libby whispered, rocking gently. "The chart tells me your mother fed you no more than thirty minutes ago. It's naptime." Baby Jassin wasn't as easily appeased as Baby Burzotta had been.

Libby rocked and softly sang to him as well, easily slipping from one rock song to another, from Springfield to Springsteen. It surprised her that she remembered so many of the words. As a teenager, after her mother died, Libby had drowned her grief in music, listening to her cassettes, and later CDs, for hours on end. That had been long before iPods. She'd lie in bed, immersed in the songs that helped drown out the world and her loss. Her father never complained about the volume. He seemed to know she needed it loud. When he married Charlene that had changed. Charlene had claimed Libby would damage her hearing and it wasn't good for her.

Libby had dutifully turned down the music.

It took the equivalent of an entire CD

of songs before Baby Jassin fell asleep in her arms.

Nurse Jennings was right. Even in the midst of a dozen wailing infants, Libby felt a sense of peace, a sense of rightness. A calm washed over her, and all she did was rock babies. The worries that had weighed her down since she'd lost her job seemed to slowly fade away. It was as if she'd entered another world. A welcoming island where all that mattered was holding a baby in her arms and singing softly.

"Now, now," she said gently, picking up a third baby. "The world isn't such a bad place. Your mommy and daddy are going to love you so much." She placed the newborn over her shoulder and gently patted his back.

Sharon returned sometime later. "So how'd it go?"

"Great." The nursery was almost silent. "What time is it?"

Sharon glanced at her wrist. "Three. I'm surprised you stuck around this long."

Libby blinked. "I've been here for

three hours?" Sharon had been in and out. Libby had noticed her several times but hadn't paid her much attention.

"Three hours," Sharon repeated.

Unbelievable. Libby had no idea where the time had gone.

"You did a great job," the nurse said, and gave Libby's shoulder a reassuring pat. "I hope you'll come back."

"I will."

"There's a sign-up sheet on the other side of the door. We'd love to have you return soon."

Libby filled her name in on the clipboard and then left. Walking back to her condo she had the urge to talk to someone. She knew Robin would be busy, but she reached for her cell anyway.

"Prosecutor's office," her friend answered curtly.

"It's Libby. I just finished rocking babies at the hospital."

"What?" Robin demanded impatiently.

"I told you this morning I was going to volunteer at the hospital, remember?"

The line went silent. "You rocked . . . babies?"

"Yeah, for three hours. It didn't seem nearly that long, and it was so . . . so peaceful."

Again the line went silent. "Let me get this straight. You spent the last three hours rocking newborns."

"I loved every minute."

Robin snickered. "I'm worried about you, Libby. Very, very worried."

Chapter 7

Libby arrived to volunteer again at the Seattle General nursery a couple of days later on a Wednesday afternoon. She slipped on the drab blue gown just before Sharon stepped into the room.

"I'm so glad you're here," the head nurse said. "The morning volunteer canceled and I've had my hands full."

Sharon definitely looked like she could use a break. "By the way, did you see Dr. Stone?" she asked. The question had an expectancy to it, as if Libby was supposed to have met up with the good doctor.

"No." Libby noticed that he hadn't shown up at the gym the last couple of mornings, either, which was fine by her.

"He asked about you this morning."

"He asked about me?" Her stomach tightened with a sense of dread. If Dr. Heart of Stone sought her out it couldn't be for anything pleasant.

The last time she saw him at the gym she'd purposely looked elsewhere for fear that he would assume she was watching him. He'd ignored her, too, and she'd been grateful.

In fact, Libby and the physician hadn't spoken once since their awkward encounter in the hospital elevator. As far as she was concerned he had issues. Yet in Libby's mind she'd built it up to so much more. She didn't want to think of him, but she found that he often occupied her thoughts, which irritated her no end. She couldn't imagine what she'd done to cause him to be so curt with her.

"Dr. Stone asked when you were going to volunteer next," Sharon said.

Libby wasn't sure what the inquiry

meant, but clearly it was not a good sign.

Sharon looked away and appeared slightly uncomfortable. "I might have mentioned you were on the schedule for today—hope that's okay."

"Oh."

"I hope you don't mind."

"I . . . no, that's fine." If he wanted to clear the air then perhaps it was best to do it now.

"Usually I keep that sort of information to myself," Sharon continued, "but it's so unusual for Dr. Stone to express interest in someone here at the hospital that I was taken aback."

Maybe the negative vibes coming off him hadn't been directed at her.

Already Libby's stomach was in knots. She had such little experience in male/female relationships that she wasn't entirely sure what to make of this. Although she was in her late thirties, she felt so socially inept sometimes, and this was definitely one of those times.

Robin hadn't given her any clues about her new love interest, either. The two of them were quite the pair. Libby suspected that was what made them such good friends. Robin had also been married, but her marriage had failed a couple of years after she learned that her husband had a gambling problem. She never spoke of Kyle or any of the relationships she'd had since the divorce.

"If I see Dr. Stone, you wouldn't mind if I mentioned you're in the nursery, would you?" Sharon asked.

Libby hesitated, unsure she was up to a showdown.

"What's the matter with you two?" Sharon demanded. "The minute I mentioned his name you tensed up. What gives?"

"I'm not entirely sure. He doesn't like me."

Sharon frowned. "Don't be ridiculous. He wouldn't be asking about you if that was the way he felt."

"Then by all means, tell him." Libby rubbed her open palms together, incapable of hiding how nervous she felt.

"He does this, too, you know?" Sharon said.

"I'm sorry. Does what?" He'd intimidated other women?

"Every now and again Dr. Stone comes to the nursery and rocks the babies. Not on a regular basis. He would rather I didn't say anything about it. He's like that; it's almost as if he's afraid someone might find out he's got a soft heart, but I've seen him with these families with infants at risk. He's patient and gentle. Watch him for yourself and you'll see what I mean."

Dr. Heart of Stone rocked the babies? Were they discussing the same man? It seemed highly unlikely.

As though she felt the need to build him up in Libby's eyes, Sharon shook her head and continued. "Every woman here would give her eyeteeth to grab his attention, which isn't any big surprise. He's handsome as sin, successful, and beyond that, he's an incredible doctor and human being. That's a combination that most women can't resist."

Libby might have been too hasty in judging him.

Sharon patted her on the shoulder.

"It's encouraging that he asked about you."

Libby wasn't the least bit encouraged. Her head buzzed as she entered the rows of hospital cribs. A nurse was there the same as before, walking back and forth, taking the newborns in to be with their mothers.

Settling down in the rocker with a fussy infant, Libby soon forgot about Dr. Stone. She took pleasure and delight in watching the baby gradually fall asleep in her arms.

Sharon had been right about how peaceful it was to rock these little ones. Crooning softly, Libby sang another medley of soft-rock hits while brushing her hand over the top of the baby's bald head. She told herself this baby boy would one day grow into a strong young man who'd steal hearts. He stretched twenty-two inches at birth, which told her he would be tall one day. Libby suspected both his parents were tall, but then that was pure speculation on her part.

As she rocked one infant after another, she couldn't help wondering what their lives would be like. What potential she saw in each one. It felt good to hold these babies. Good in ways that were difficult to explain. Libby idly wondered at the emotions her mother had experienced holding her for the first time.

Then she sensed someone standing behind her. At first she thought it was the nurse, but no . . .

Dr. Stone.

"It's Libby, isn't it?" he asked when he realized she knew he was behind her.

"Yes. Dr. Stone, right?"

He walked around and stood in front of her, looking tall and muscular, looming over her like a black storm cloud. Libby found it difficult to swallow, let alone talk normally.

"Phillip," he offered.

So they were to be on a first-name basis. That was good to know, and probably some sign a twelve-year-old would be more adept at deciphering than Libby.

"I thought that was you behind me," she said, hoping to sound cool and un-

ruffled. She doubted that she'd succeeded. Far be it from her to let him
know how easily he intimidated her.

"I apologize if I startled you. I heard
you've been volunteering for the nursery."

"Yes . . . I find I have time on my
hands." She didn't mention the reason
and regretted even saying that much.
Being unemployed was hard enough
on her ego. Admitting it to anyone else
was even more so. The fact that she
hadn't found another position after all
these months made it worse.

"I see . . ."

"I'm an attorney," she blurted out.

"Oh. Okay."

Libby couldn't seem to shut up. "I
specialize in trusts and estates . . .
things are a bit slow at the moment.
Bet that doesn't happen to physicians,
though, right?" she asked, half choking
on the question, which she knew was
ridiculous.

Thankfully he ignored it.

The infant in her arms squalled. For
an instant Libby had completely forgotten she was holding a baby. She

thanked God the newborn hadn't fallen from her embrace and tumbled onto the floor. Her grip tightened slightly. She realized she should probably say something, but her mind went blank. In fact, she had become totally incapable of managing a single word.

"You've apparently been around babies before," he stated conversationally.

"Ah . . ."

"You seem at ease with them."

At ease? Her? With babies? The truth was that until last week she couldn't remember the last time she'd even been close to a baby.

Six years ago. She remembered with clarity now. Juliette, one of the paralegals, had taken maternity leave. After her baby was born, Juliette had stopped by the office with her daughter in tow. Libby wasn't even clear on how it had happened, but the baby was thrust into her arms and she'd held her for several minutes. When Juliette had taken her daughter back, Libby had been relieved.

Yet here she was volunteering at Seattle General to rock infants. Libby wasn't sure what had changed. Could it possibly be her? Since she'd been let go—she cringed even thinking about Burkhart, Smith & Crandall—she'd lost a sense of what and who she really was.

"I'd like to speak to you privately," Phillip said, breaking into her thoughts.

Taken aback, she stared up at him blankly, wondering what he could possibly have to say to her. "Why?"

He ignored her question. "Although the cafeteria isn't an ideal location, it will do."

She blinked. "What's this about?"

"There's a matter I wish to discuss," he said, as if his answer was all the explanation that was required.

Libby frowned. Perhaps something had shown up on her volunteer application, but that seemed unlikely because she had already been approved.

"It'll only take a few minutes."

She hesitated.

"It's important."

"All right," she agreed, with some reluctance. "I finish at three."

"That's what Sharon said."

She realized she was staring, and that he was waiting for her reply.

"Three," she repeated. "The cafeteria."

Without another word he left. As soon as the nursery door closed, Libby released a breath she didn't realize she'd been holding. Phillip Stone was abrupt and demanding. What irritated her most was the fact that she'd let him intimidate her. Just because he was some hotshot doctor didn't make him any better than anyone else. Yet she couldn't help wondering what he found so important that he had to talk to her privately about it.

Sharon returned a few minutes later. "Was that Dr. Stone I saw in here?" she asked. The smile that curved up the edges of her mouth said she couldn't be more pleased by this unexpected turn of events. She all but rubbed her hands together with glee.

"Yeah, he stopped by." Libby tried hard to hide how uncomfortable the physician made her.

"Well?" Sharon continued, her dark brown eyes wide and expectant as she eagerly awaited the details of their short meeting. "Are you going to make me torture it out of you? What did he want?"

"He said he had something private to discuss with me," Libby said, thinking Sharon might know what this was all about.

Sharon's look of surprise told her the nurse was in the dark as much as she was. Then gradually a smile came into play. "I thought he might be romantically interested in you and I was right."

"I don't think so." Libby didn't know where Sharon had come up with that idea, but she sincerely doubted Dr. Stone was in any way attracted to her.

Sharon's smile didn't waver. "Mark my words."

Libby rolled her eyes. "Oh, please," she said, "I don't think you should make more out of this than necessary. I'm sure he probably has some innocuous question or something he wants to ask."

"Think what you like, dearie."

At three, Libby removed the hospital gown, and then spent the next few minutes repairing her makeup and comb-

ing her hair. If she was going to confront the devil then she wanted to look
her best. The fact that she cared irritated her all the more.

Grabbing her cell on the way to the
elevator, Libby waited until she was in
the lobby and texted Robin. DR. STONE
ASKED TO SPEAK TO ME PRIVATELY.
DON'T KNOW WHAT THIS IS ABOUT.

After pushing the "send" button Robin's message came back within seconds. DR. HEART OF STONE?

Libby texted back. FROM THE GYM.
HOT STUFF.

Libby scowled back at the text message. She didn't know what women
saw in Phillip Stone. Oh, sure, he was
easy on the eyes, but he had the personality of a snapping turtle.

Walking into the cafeteria, she
dropped her cell into her purse and
then paused in the doorway, drew in a
calming breath, and looked for Phillip.

He sat in the back of the room in an
area that would grant them privacy.
Libby started toward him with all the
energy and enthusiasm of a condemned
prisoner heading toward the hangman.

Her one optimistic thought was that he was probably on his break and didn't have long. She noticed the two cups of coffee on the table.

She managed a half smile as she pulled out a chair and sat down. No way was she going to let him know how badly he intimidated her.

"I wasn't sure how you took your coffee," he said, and handed her a mug.

"This is fine. Now what's this about?" Libby gripped the mug with both hands.

He glanced at his wrist as if to say he didn't have much time, which was great by her.

"Mainly I wanted to know about the baby."

"The baby?" she repeated. "The one I was holding when you were in the nursery?" She couldn't imagine what she could tell him other than the sex of the child and his parents' surname.

"No, no." He frowned and shook his head as if irritated with her for not being a mind reader. "When is the baby due, or do you even know?"

Did he seriously think she was pregnant? It wasn't humanly possible for her to be pregnant at this point. She hadn't been with a man since . . . well, there was no need to drag up that frustrating subject.

"No way am I pregnant," she said, speaking distinctly and clearly. "And if I were, let me assure you that it wouldn't be any of your business."

His eyes flared and he stretched out his arms and gripped the mug. Neither of them had even tasted their coffee. "I'm not talking about you."

Libby stared at him blankly. Frankly, he wasn't making any sense, but nothing about him had from the beginning, so she wasn't surprised.

"You're right . . . this isn't my business and I hesitated to say anything, but then felt I should. I realize I might well be out of line even bringing this up."

She raised her right hand, at a complete loss. "I'm sorry, but I don't have a clue what you're talking about."

"Your daughter," he snapped.

"I don't have a daughter." She flattened her hand against her breast. "I'm not even married." Not that being married was a prerequisite for having a child. Oh dear, she couldn't seem to speak coherently around this guy.

"The girls who were with you the other day when you dropped off the preemie hats."

"Casey and Ava?"

"One of them is pregnant."

Libby automatically shook her head. "You're wrong." He had to be. "They're just thirteen."

His face tightened and he grew more insistent. "I strongly suspect the dark-haired one is pregnant."

That bit of information wasn't the least bit helpful. "They both have dark hair."

"The one who wore jeans, then."

"They both had on jeans."

He shook his head. "Okay, the one on the right."

Libby blinked and searched her memory, trying to remember where they'd stood in the elevator. "Your right or mine?"

"Yours. No, mine."

An announcement came over the public address system asking for Dr.

Stone to return immediately to the neo-natal unit.

Phillip stood. "I've got to go. I'm sorry I can't be more helpful. I felt I should mention it because that girl needs to see a physician. She needs proper health care for her and her baby. I wish I could be more specific about which girl it was. If you aren't the mother"— he hesitated and then shook his head as though he was frustrated and regretful—"I apologize that . . . I assumed. Well, never mind, I'm sure you'll do what you can."

Having said that, he hurried out of the cafeteria.

Chapter 8

He was there. Robin Hamlin bit into her lower lip and did her best to quell her stampeding heart. Judge Roy Bollinger had attended the annual fund-raising dinner held by the local Legal Aid Society. Naturally she'd hoped to see him, but she'd had no way of knowing if he would participate or not.

Robin had admired Roy years ago when they worked together on an election campaign. Recently she'd learned that his wife had died two years ago. To the best of her knowledge he wasn't dating. She didn't dare ask for fear one of her colleagues might question her interest. Up until now, all she'd done was admire him from afar. Roy was decent and honest, loyal and kind. They shared many of the same political views as well.

Oh, she definitely had a crush. But Robin intended to keep it cool. Nonchalant. A blatant approach wasn't her style. She would need to play her hand carefully, keeping her cards close to her chest. Normally she would have mailed in a generous check to the Legal Aid Society and avoided the dinner. Her sole reason for showing up was the off chance, the hope, that Judge Bollinger would be there.

The doors to the dining room hadn't opened. He stood in line at the bar at the cocktail reception. She was three people behind him. The two people who stood between her and Roy were a married couple she didn't recognize, and they were chatting away animatedly. Just then Roy turned and looked past her. Perhaps he was searching for someone. He might have a date for the night. The only way to tell was if he purchased one drink or two. Robin held her breath and waited.

One drink.

He turned away, caught sight of her, and smiled.

Robin smiled back and wondered how it was that her heart could pound this hard and fast and not explode. Her hands trembled as she looked down at the program she'd been handed when she'd walked into the reception. The words blurred as she struggled to hide her reaction.

"Good evening, Counselor," Roy said as he paused next to her. He held a glass of red wine. Pinot noir, if she guessed right. Robin enjoyed wine as well and was particularly fond of the Willamette Valley pinot noirs out of Oregon.

"Judge Bollinger," she said, hoping to sound causal. He wasn't a striking man. They were close to the same height, about five-eight. His hair was completely gray and his hairline was receding. He carried himself well, and although he was ten years her senior he remained vibrant and healthy. Robin was strongly drawn to him.

She'd never been in his court. He didn't try criminal cases, although their courtrooms were in the same area of the King County Courthouse. They sometimes saw each other between sessions.

"I don't believe I've seen you at one of these functions before," Roy said, pausing to chat.

"I . . . I don't often attend, although I support the cause." Robin had never been much of a social butterfly. Like her friend Libby, she'd been married to her job for so long that she didn't have much of a life outside the courthouse. Family and friends had warned her that the criminal cases she tried had affected her personality. How could they not? Dealing with the criminal element was bound to impact her. She felt powerless to change her way of thinking and yet she needed an outlet . . . some way or someone to center her. Someone to take her mind off the ugliness she confronted every day in court. Someone who would help her remember there was goodness and beauty and love in this world. She remembered laughing with Judge Bollinger and how lighthearted she'd felt after spending time with him.

"It's good to see you."

"You too." She thought about mentioning his wife, telling him how sorry she was to hear of Mrs. Bollinger's passing. Thankfully she stopped herself. It had happened two years ago, and it was long past the time for condolences.

Roy wrapped his hand around the stem of the wineglass. Robin stared at his hands. They were good hands, she thought. Not large or thick. Just average, nice hands. He'd never touched her and she wondered what it would feel like to have his fingers slide across her bare skin. Oh, what a fanciful imagination she had. Still, the thought intrigued her and she couldn't banish the image from her mind.

He started to move away and Robin went on a desperate search for a reason to detain him. Then it came to her.

"Judge Bollinger?"

"Roy."

"Roy," she amended. That was how she thought of him, but it would have been presumptuous of her to address him by something other than his title. "I have a friend, a very good friend, who's seeking a position in trusts and estates. I was wondering if you know of any firm with an opening?"

"Where did your friend work before?"

"Burkhart, Smith & Crandall."

"Ah yes, I heard they had to let go some excellent attorneys. Unfortunate."

"Very," Robin agreed. "My friend is Libby Morgan."

His brow creased as if he was trying to place the name.

"Elizabeth Morgan," she corrected, although most everyone called her Libby.

"I've heard of her. She has a good reputation. A hard worker."

"She's the best."

He nodded and raised his hand to his face, a habit she'd noticed about him. He did that when he was thinking, mulling over facts in his head. "Let me check around and I'll get back to you."

"I can't tell you how much she'd appreciate that . . . and I would, too, of course."

"It's good of you to look out for your friend."

"Thank you." Robin felt more than a little guilty. The sole reason she'd asked was to delay him.

Her turn had come and she ordered a glass of pinot noir.

Roy had been about to leave, but he hesitated. "You enjoy wine?"

"Very much, especially from the Willamette Valley."

He cocked his head to one side. "So do I." He looked like he was about to ask if she'd tried a certain winery when she heard someone say his name.

Roy excused himself. She paid for her drink and drifted away, although it felt as though she was walking on air.

The dinner seemed to take hours. The speeches droned on forever. Robin knew she wouldn't be able to recount a single word. Roy liked wine; she liked wine. She wondered if he worked Sudoku puzzles or was interested in chess. Keyed up from their short exchange, she found it impossible to eat. The woman next to her, the wife of an attorney she knew only fleetingly, attempted to make conversation but soon gave up. Robin's mind was preoccupied with her brief conversation with Roy. She kept thinking about all the things she could have said . . .

Robin left the dinner as soon as she could, and hurriedly made her way outside. It was still light out, and as she walked toward the parking garage, she reached for her cell, and scrolled down until she found Libby's number.

"Hi, what's up?" Libby wasn't one who enjoyed talking on the phone. For that matter Robin wasn't, either, but they'd been chatting more often since she'd joined the gym.

"I've been putting the word out for you," Robin said.

"You have?" Her friend sounded hopeful.

Robin didn't have an inkling if this would amount to anything. "I talked to Judge Bollinger."

"I've heard of him," Libby said.

Her friend's excitement made Robin

feel more than a little guilty. "You know Judge Bollinger?"

"Yes . . . I think so." Libby hesitated and seemed to put two and two together. "How do you know him?"

"From court . . . his courtroom is just down the hall."

"You're in criminal law."

This was a statement of fact and not a question.

"Do you want me to tell him to forget about it?" Robin snapped. She regretted saying anything to Libby now. It had been a mistake, but she hadn't been able to stop herself. What she really wanted, Robin realized, was to tell Libby that she'd finally talked to the man she'd been secretly longing for all these months.

"You went to the fund-raiser?"

Robin had mentioned it that morning at the gym. Libby had seemed surprised that she'd opted to attend. Like Robin, Libby usually mailed in a donation and left it at that.

"I was there," Robin murmured, wishing she'd kept her mouth shut.

"How was it?"

"Like I expected. Chicken and frozen peas for dinner, long speeches, major push for donations."

"I'm surprised you went."

Robin let the comment hang, unwilling to admit her real reason for attending.

An uncomfortable silence followed and Robin was about to end the conversation when Libby spoke.

"Can I ask you something?" Her friend's voice dropped several decibels as though she was troubled.

"Depends on what it is." If Libby intended to drill her about Roy, then the subject was off-limits. No one knew how strongly attracted Robin was to the judge. No one needed to know. It was her business and no one else's.

"Remember I texted you about Phillip . . . Dr. Stone . . . asking me to coffee?"

"Hot stuff," she joked.

"Well, it wasn't for the reason I thought."

"Oh?" Robin hadn't heard the outcome and had frankly been curious, but she'd assumed Libby would volunteer the information when she was ready. Libby tended to be as private as Robin was herself.

"He . . . wanted to tell me he thinks that one of the girls from the yarn store is pregnant and hiding it."

"An employee?"

"No . . . it's either Lydia's daughter or her friend."

That gave Robin pause. "They're just kids." She remembered seeing them and thinking it was inspiring to see two young teens taking up knitting.

"They're thirteen," Libby told her.

Thirteen? Well, it was young, but it wouldn't be the first time she'd heard of someone that age being pregnant. "He didn't identify which girl?" Robin asked.

Libby sighed. "No, he got called out of the cafeteria on an emergency. He seemed to think I should know, but I don't. I like Lydia a lot, but I don't know if I should say anything."

"Would you want someone to tell you if it was your daughter?"

Her friend hesitated. "I asked myself the same question and decided I probably would. He seemed a bit uncomfortable bringing up the subject. I'm sure it weighed heavily on his mind or he wouldn't have mentioned it."

"That's your answer then," Robin told her. "If Dr. Stone felt compelled to bring it up, he did it out of concern for the teenager."

After a moment, Libby agreed. "He was worried she wasn't getting proper medical care. After thinking about it myself, I wonder if she even knows she's pregnant."

"You could be right," Robin said, and then added, "You need to talk to Lydia."

Her friend exhaled audibly. "I know . . . but this isn't any of my business. It's awkward, especially since I don't even know which girl he meant."

"And to think the girl is only thirteen . . ."

Robin tried to think of what she'd been like at that age—quiet and shy, withdrawn and studious . . . in essence, a dork. If the two girls in the yarn store were anything like she was then, they didn't have a clue about what was happening to their bodies.

A few weeks ago Robin had been in court with a pregnant eleven-year-old girl. She and her stepbrother were being charged with drug crimes. The eleven-year-old had come to the courthouse to testify against her stepbrother, claiming he was the baby's father and she'd been raped. The stepbrother insisted that the girl had "wanted it" and had offered him her body in exchange for drugs. Hooked on crack, pregnant, and only eleven years old. These were the types of abysmal situations Robin faced daily as a prosecuting attorney. Was it any wonder she'd developed a cynical view of life? It was impossible to avoid, working the cases she did.

"I don't know if I'm the best person to handle this," Libby mumbled.

Robin, caught up in her own thoughts, lost track of the conversation.

"If not you, then who?" she asked, and then quickly tagged on a second question. "How well do you know Lydia?"

"Not well . . . some, I guess," Libby amended.

"I'd do it myself, but I hardly know

Lydia," Robin offered. "The only time I go into the yarn store is when Mom needs me to pick up yarn for her. Half the time I think it's an excuse."

"An excuse?" Libby asked.

"Yes, my mother thinks if I hang around the store enough I'll catch the knitting bug. Trust me, I'm immune. It's fine for you and my mother, but I wouldn't go near a pair of knitting needles if my life depended on it."

Robin's mother had recently married her high school sweetheart and moved to Florida. Apparently good yarn stores were few and far between in the Sunshine State. Perhaps this was Ruth's way of reaching out to her.

Robin knew she'd taken her mother for granted. It wasn't until Ruth had moved away that Robin realized how much she had liked having her mother around.

Christmas had been awful for her. Her only family in the area had been her twice-divorced brother. Grant had invited her to join him at his son's place for dinner, but she had declined.

Her mother, Robin had realized too late, was her anchor. Libby had lost her mother when she'd been a young teen. From conversations they'd had in college, Robin knew that when Libby's mother died, Libby had been cast adrift, lost on an emotional storm-tossed sea. The only time she felt safe was when she immersed herself in a book, or listened to her music. Both had helped her to escape the pain of having lost her mother, of being a motherless child.

It was shortly after that bleak Christmas Day that Robin had started thinking seriously about her future. She didn't want to be alone again. Like Libby, Robin longed for roots: a husband, children, a purpose.

"I hope I'm not putting you on the spot," Robin said. She didn't envy her friend this task. "But it's obvious you're going to have to say something to Lydia about all this."

"I guess you're right," Libby mumbled, sounding as though she would do just about anything to get out of it.

Robin reached her car and stood outside the vehicle while she considered the best way for Libby to approach the yarn-store owner.

If the situation was reversed and she was the one to talk to Lydia, what would she do? The memory of the eleven-year-old played in her mind. If this thirteen-year-old was pregnant it was more than the health issue involved. The question of whether the father was of legal age played into the equation. This could be rape. Charges might need to be filed. It could be a legal question as much as an ethical one.

"I plan to get to the bottom of this. If someone took advantage of this girl . . . she needs help," Libby said.

"I thought of that, too," Robin whispered.

"I imagine you did," Libby murmured. "Oh, Robin, what is our world coming to?"

Chapter 9

Libby thought long and hard about how best to approach Lydia Goetz.

It would have helped if Phillip had showed up at the gym the following morning. But he hadn't, so she didn't get the chance to question him further. Robin urged Libby to stop by the yarn store as soon as possible and talk to Lydia. Easy for her to say. She wasn't the one who had to face a woman she barely knew with this potentially devastating news.

As she mulled all this over, Libby was filled with dread. She paced the living area in her condo, checking her watch every five minutes until ten o'clock, when A Good Yarn opened.

She left the condo at around 9:45 a.m. and decided to walk, hoping the exercise would inspire her on how best to approach the subject. She needed just the right words—if there was such a thing. "Lydia, your thirteen-year-old daughter might be pregnant." How did anyone say that?

Wanting to delay the conversation, Libby stopped in at Susannah's Garden and aimlessly wandered around. The scent of flowers didn't lift her mood as she'd hoped it would. Instead she found herself thinking of all the flowers that family and friends had sent for her mother's funeral. There'd been so many bouquets that her father had given several away. Libby left the flower shop without making a purchase.

The bell above the door chimed as she entered the yarn store. Lydia's face brightened with a welcoming smile. She was such a warm, kind person, and Libby feared this news would devastate her.

"Libby, it's good to see you. Are you having any problems with the baby blanket you're working on?"

"No . . . no." She glanced around the shop. Lydia was alone. Either her sister, Margaret, was with their mother, or else she would arrive later.

"I was hoping the two of us would have time for a chat," Libby said, avoiding eye contact. Her voice was low and, despite her best efforts, filled with trepidation.

"Of course, Libby." Her friend led the way to the back of the shop and automatically poured them each a cup of coffee.

"Black, right?"

"Right." Oh, how she missed that half-and-half, but she'd given it up as part of her plan for dropping those extra ten pounds.

Lydia handed her the mug and they both sat down at the table.

"I hesitate to say anything," Libby said, staring into her coffee. "I wouldn't if it wasn't a health and legal issue and, well . . ."

"A health and legal issue?" Lydia repeated. Now she, too, seemed alarmed.

"I think it might be best if I start at the beginning," Libby suggested. She'd tried to think of the best way to lead into the subject with some finesse and hadn't come up with a single idea. The only way, she resolved, was to be as direct as possible.

"Yes, please, start at the beginning." Lydia held on to her coffee mug with both hands as if she needed to cling to something solid.

"Remember when I went to Seattle General with Casey and Ava about a week and a half ago?"

"Of course. You dropped off the preemie hats."

"Right. While we were there we met Dr. Stone in the elevator."

"Oh, yes." Lydia brightened somewhat. "The girls were impressed with the handsome Dr. Stone."

"He recognized me because we work out at the same gym."

"So the girls said."

Apparently Libby had said more than

she'd realized. "He recently asked to speak to me . . . privately."

Lydia smiled knowingly. "Really?"

"Don't get the wrong impression. I can categorically tell you that Dr. Stone isn't the least bit interested in me personally."

"Oh, Libby, are you disappointed?"

"No, not at all." She shook her head, not wanting to get sidetracked. "The thing is, he felt it was important we talk because . . ."

The bell above the door chimed, indicating that Lydia had a customer. Libby groaned inwardly and forced herself to sit back. Her entire body felt coiled, like she was a warrior going into battle. Her senses were on full alert; adrenaline was pumping hard and fast through her veins.

While Lydia dealt with the customer, Margaret arrived. Libby had grown accustomed to her brusque ways and knew not to take offense. She suspected that beneath that gruff exterior was a gentle soul. Libby knew that Margaret was fiercely protective of her sister, and she wished she could continue her conversation with Lydia in private. Margaret wouldn't take kindly to her upsetting Lydia.

"Hello, Libby," Margaret said, as she put her purse inside the small office. She returned with a mug of coffee.

Lydia finished with her customer and almost immediately someone else stepped into the store. Hesitating, Libby wondered if it might be best for her to return another time. Then she decided it was now or never—otherwise she might lose her courage.

Lydia seemed to feel the same way because she asked her sister to help the next customer. "Libby and I are having a bit of a talk here. Could you cover for me?" she asked.

"Sure thing." Margaret set aside her coffee and headed to the front of the store.

"Okay," Lydia said, reclaiming her seat. "You were about to say?"

Libby inhaled and briefly closed her eyes. "Dr. Stone asked to speak with me because after meeting the girls in the elevator he was convinced one of them is pregnant."

"What?" Lydia's shock echoed through the store.

Margaret stopped short and so did the woman she was helping.

"Everything all right back there?" Margaret asked.

"It's fine," Lydia murmured. Her eyes held Libby captive. "This is a joke, right?"

Libby shook her head. The sick feeling in the pit of her stomach returned. "I wish it was."

"Is . . . is it Casey?"

"I don't know if it's her or Ava." She wanted to slap Phillip for not being clearer. He had assumed she would remember the girl on his right, or was it her right? Her gut reaction told her it was Ava, just from the way the girl behaved, but she couldn't be sure. She almost said so but changed her mind. She simply didn't know.

Lydia had gone pale. She brushed the soft brown hair off her forehead and held her hand there. "Brad caught Casey trying to sneak out of the house the other night . . . it wasn't the first time. We don't know where she goes and she won't tell us."

Libby's stomach twisted into a giant knot. Maybe she was off base. "What about Ava?"

"She's a sweet girl and all, but from what I've seen of her grandmother, well, let's just say the living situation isn't ideal. It could be her."

"Dr. Stone said that Casey or Ava might not even know about her condition."

"How can he tell? Really, it's only speculation, right?" Lydia seemed to be clinging to the possibility that it wasn't true and this was all a big mistake.

Her shock and disbelief mirrored Libby's own response when Phillip had approached her. Surely this was pure speculation, misguided concern, or misunderstanding. The girls were both so young and naive. Pregnant? At thirteen? It shocked and angered her. Still, Libby couldn't ignore what she knew, couldn't pretend he was off base. He was the physician, not her.

"I'm not entirely sure how he knew.

Dr. Stone didn't say, but he was concerned enough to approach me. I wish I could explain this further . . . Phillip . . . Dr. Stone and I only spoke for a few minutes before he was called away for an emergency. I haven't seen him since to ask."

Perhaps it would have been better to wait, but this entire matter had weighed so heavily on her mind that Libby couldn't ignore it any longer. Ever since her meeting with Phillip, she'd slept fitfully.

Lydia's hands started to shake. If Libby knew her better she would have reached across the table and gripped hold of the other woman's forearm. She wanted to comfort her, to offer Lydia reassurances, but she had none to give.

"Why did he bring this to you?" Lydia asked.

"He assumed the girl was my daughter."

"Oh."

The bell chimed as the customer left the store. Within seconds Margaret joined them.

"What's going on back here?" she demanded.

Libby left it up to Lydia to respond.

Lydia glanced blankly up at her sister and remained silent. "Something I need to look into . . . I need to talk to Brad."

With narrowed eyes, Margaret studied Libby suspiciously. After a few uncomfortable moments she left the two of them alone again.

"My husband and I wanted to adopt an infant," Lydia whispered. "We had a wonderful social worker and then one night we got a phone call. It was an emergency situation and she needed a place for a young girl just for a couple of nights."

Libby nodded. She remembered Casey telling her that she was adopted.

"We fell in love with Casey. Brad, Cody, and I decided to make her part of our family." She paused and it looked as if she was about to break down and weep.

Libby wanted to say or do something to help but didn't have a clue how she could.

"The day we stood before the judge

to finalize the adoption, Casey was so happy and excited she ran up and hugged the judge." A tear spilled out of the corner of her eye and scooted down the side of Lydia's face. "But Casey came with a lot of baggage . . ."

Libby could only imagine.

"The last six months haven't been easy, adolescence, and all the hormones have kicked in . . . Casey started her period." Lydia's mouth snapped closed and she pressed her fingertips over her lips. Her eyelids slammed shut. She inhaled and seemed to be holding her breath. More tears rolled down her face.

"Lydia?" Libby felt helpless. She would give anything to take all this back. The last thing she wanted was to hurt her new friend or bring problems to her front steps.

Lydia swallowed tightly and then whispered. "I . . . I don't know if Casey had a period last month."

Libby's stomach clenched. "One of the reasons I decided I had to say something is because of the legal issues involved."

Lydia stared at her blankly. "How do you mean?"

"If . . . if Casey is pregnant, you'll need to find out who the father is. If he's over eighteen then it's statutory rape. Criminal charges will need to be filed. Do you know if Casey has a boyfriend?"

Lydia nodded. "She does."

"How old is he?"

"I . . . I don't know. I think they're about the same age. He's in junior high; they're in the same class."

"Thirteen?" Libby didn't know if it was possible for a thirteen-year-old boy to father a child—she was utterly inexperienced when it came to such matters.

"Children having children . . ." Lydia whispered.

"What are you going to do?" It wasn't her business, Libby realized. If she were the one facing this delicate situation, Libby would be at an utter loss as to how best to handle it.

"I . . . don't know. I . . . I need to talk to my husband."

A partner in life, someone to share

her burdens, someone to cry with and laugh with. Libby had relinquished all of that, and for what? On the other hand, during the last six months of their marriage all Joe and Libby had seemed to do was disagree. She worked hard all day and often after hours as well, and when she got home she was tired. Joe was far more sociable than she. Coming from a large family, he was accustomed to being around people. Then there was the matter of starting their family. The timing had been all wrong for her. Nonetheless, she still thought about Joe now and again. She sincerely hoped he was happy, and she was pleased that he'd moved on in life. "Brad will know how best to handle this."

"I'm sure he will," Libby whispered.

The bell continued to chime and Lydia looked up at the same time as Libby. The shop had a number of customers.

"Margaret needs my help."

Libby nodded and left soon afterward. She returned to her apartment but couldn't settle down. She wanted to apologize and tell her friend how sorry she was to be the bearer of bad news. Instead of feeling better she felt ten times worse. She hoped Lydia and her husband would find out what they needed to know and then deal with it in a way that best suited Casey. Then again, it might be Ava.

Her cell chirped and she retrieved it from her purse. It was Robin.

"So did you talk to Lydia?"

"I did."

"How did it go?"

Libby wasn't sure what to say. It'd been horrible. She hurt for her friend and felt responsible even though she'd tried her best to help. "She was shocked, of course."

"I'm sure she was."

"She's going to talk to her husband first and then to Casey."

"You did the right thing," Robin assured her.

Libby believed that, too, which made her appreciate how difficult it'd been for Phillip to seek her out.

Even more depressed than usual, Libby sat down in front of her computer and checked the job sites she'd been searching. She didn't know why she bothered.

Her cell rang again. She checked the caller ID and saw that it was Sarah. They hadn't talked in a couple of weeks now. Libby wasn't sure she was up to chatting.

Their conversations had grown shorter as the months had passed. Outside the office they had little in common. Libby felt compelled to put on a good front, convincing both Sarah and herself that it was just a matter of days before she found another position. It was becoming more and more difficult to continue the lie.

She answered on the fourth ring just before the call went to voice mail.

"Hello."

"Libby," Sarah whispered as if she feared being overheard. "Mrs. Reed was in this afternoon."

Martha Reed. Libby had worked extensively on setting up the older woman's estate, creating a number of trusts. She liked and admired Mrs. Reed.

"She's not happy," Sarah continued,

keeping her voice low. "I heard her complaining to Hershel. She asked about you and said Ben Holmes isn't half the attorney you are. She said she's thinking of moving her business."

"She said that?" Libby instantly perked up.

"She doesn't like Ben working on her foundation business."

"What did Hershel say?" Libby was all ears. This was the first bit of encouraging news she'd had in weeks.

"Just that she was one of the firm's most important clients and he would do whatever it took to make Mrs. Reed happy."

Libby sincerely hoped that meant he would consider hiring her back.

At one time she would have taken a great deal of pleasure in turning him down, refusing him and walking away with her head held high. That was then, and this was almost five months post employment. If Hershel were to phone she'd swallow her pride, sincerely thank him, and show up chipper and happy with her briefcase in hand.

Chapter 10

Lydia Goetz couldn't hold still. The conversation with Libby Morgan had upset her terribly, and while she tried to hide it from Margaret, her sister knew something was drastically wrong. She tried several times to get Lydia to talk, but she remained tight-lipped and agitated the rest of the afternoon.

Casey pregnant? She couldn't stop thinking about what that would mean to their family, and how she and Brad would deal with the situation. When they'd decided to adopt Casey they'd accepted that this wouldn't be a smooth road. While their daughter was thrilled to be part of a family, she continued to have issues, but this was far and away more than either Lydia or Brad had expected. Pregnant at such a young age. It just didn't seem possible, and yet . . .

At home it didn't take Brad long to discern that something or someone had deeply distressed Lydia. No more than ten minutes after she walked in the door, Brad asked, "What's up?" He followed her into the kitchen and leaned against the doorjamb with his arms folded.

"We need to talk," she whispered for fear he would hear the tremble in her voice. She removed the roast cooking in the Crock-Pot and placed it on a serving dish, and then grabbed hold of the counter, afraid she was about to burst into tears.

"Okay, when?"

"Not now. After we eat."

"You sure you want to wait that long?" he asked.

Fearing she might break into tears if she answered, Lydia nodded.

Mealtime was a miserable affair. All

through dinner, Lydia could barely look at Casey. Her mood seemed to be contagious. She caught Cody and Casey exchanging looks. Cody shrugged as if to say he didn't know what was wrong. Casey didn't say a word after the first few minutes. When the teenager finished her meal, she helped with the dishes and then quickly retired to her bedroom.

"What's up with everyone?" Cody asked after Casey left the room.

"Nothing," Brad told him.

"Why do parents always say that?" the youth muttered under his breath. He shook his head and then went outside to play baseball with his friends.

As soon as Cody was out the door, Brad turned to Lydia. "All right, what gives?"

Lydia sat across from her husband and covered her face with both hands, unsure if she could get through this.

"That bad?"

"Worse."

"Then let's deal with it together." Brad reached for her hand and gave her fingers a squeeze. "Is it . . . did you get a report from the doctor you're not telling me about?"

It was only natural her husband would assume this distress was related to her problems with cancer. Twice she'd been treated for cancerous brain tumors. Treated. The word discounted the torment she'd endured. Her first go-round took place when she was only sixteen. The tumors returned again later when she was in her early twenties. Lydia had nearly died both times.

Although she'd been cancer-free for almost fifteen years, there was always the fear that the tumors would return. Lydia had learned far earlier than most people do that life holds few guarantees. Every day was a precious gift. She'd opened the yarn store as an affirmation of life, determined not to allow fear to dominate whatever time she had left.

"This doesn't have anything to do with cancer," she assured him.

The relief in his eyes spoke of his deep love and concern.

"I . . . I had a customer come in this morning first thing. I might have mentioned her. She's the attorney who has been unemployed for a few months now."

"The one who knit like thirty preemie caps over one weekend?"

Smiling briefly, Lydia nodded. "That's the one. Her name is Libby. She went with Casey and Ava to drop off the donation from the knitters to Seattle General."

Brad's brow furrowed. "I think I remember you telling me about that."

"The girls were perfectly capable of going on their own but I was grateful to have an adult with them." Lydia paused and bit into her lower lip. "While they were at the hospital Libby met a doctor she knows from the gym where she works out. He asked to speak to Libby privately afterward."

"And what did he say?"

She looked down at her hands, which were clenched together so tightly that her nail beds were white. "He assumed one of the girls was her daughter and . . . and he felt it was important to tell Libby that he suspects one of them is . . . pregnant." Lydia could barely get the last word out of her mouth.

Brad bolted up off his chair, knocking it over. "You've got to be joking." His shocked, disbelieving reaction mirrored her own.

"I wish I was."

Brad's gaze narrowed. "How would he know?"

"I don't know . . . but he is a physician. He wasn't sure, but he was concerned enough that he felt he should mention it. His fear was that the teen didn't even realize she was . . . pregnant." Again she nearly stumbled over the word.

Brad picked up his chair and sat down again, wiping his hand across his face as if he needed time to assimilate what she'd told him. It had taken a few minutes for Lydia to understand the ramifications of this news, too. His eyes flickered about the room as though searching out something to focus on that would help him digest this situation.

"Could it be . . . Casey?" he asked after several tense moments. Clearly he didn't want to believe it any more than she did.

"We don't know everything she does," she reminded him. They had yet to learn where Casey had been going when they found her sneaking out of the house at midnight.

"You had the . . . talk with her, right?"

Lydia nodded. It had been uncomfortable because Casey probably knew more about the subject of sex than Lydia did. The kid had seen more in her thirteen years than Lydia had in a lifetime. Casey had been patient and had even asked a couple of questions after Lydia had explained the basic facts of life to her.

To her chagrin, Lydia hadn't brought up the subject of disease or teenage pregnancy. She'd figured that a little information was better than none and she could fill in the gaps later . . . as it turned out, she might have been too late.

"It could be Ava," Lydia offered, and immediately felt bad for wishing it was the other girl rather than her own daughter. Casey's motherless friend was shy and vulnerable. Lydia had been pleased when Casey befriended her and brought her to the yarn shop. Ava and her older brother were left alone all day while their grandmother waited tables at a local cafe. And at the end of her shift she apparently didn't feel any compulsion to hurry home. From what Ava said, her grandmother spent part of each night in a neighborhood tavern, leaving Ava and her brother to their own devices.

Brad squared his shoulders and said, "We need to talk to Casey."

Lydia agreed.

"You can talk to me now." Casey stood in the doorway leading to the kitchen. Her face was blank and her eyes were focused on the floor.

"Come sit with us," Lydia said. She stood and wrapped her arm around her daughter.

Casey shrugged her off and moved to the chair at the far end of the table. She lowered her head and looked down, avoiding eye contact. "I know what this is about," she said.

Brad and Lydia exchanged looks.

"You want to get rid of me, right? Send me back to foster care."

Lydia gasped. "Casey, no, never."

"What would make you even think such a thing?" Brad demanded angrily. "You're our daughter. We brought you into our family and that's for good."

"Casey, don't you know how much we love you?" Lydia asked, because clearly she didn't.

Casey's shoulders started to shake and tears fell from her eyes, splashing onto the tabletop. Irritated, she wiped them away as though the weakness embarrassed her. "I thought you didn't want me anymore. I thought you wanted me to leave."

Casey so rarely cried that when Lydia saw how upset her daughter was tears formed in her own eyes. She stood and wrapped her arms around Casey's shoulders. Leaning down, she pressed her head next to Casey's, hands on her shoulders, and together the two of them sobbed.

It wasn't long before Brad joined them, wrapping his arms around the two of them. He left momentarily and returned with a box of tissues.

Lydia blew her nose and so did Casey.

After taking a moment to compose herself, Lydia sat back down and scooted her chair closer to Casey and then reached for her hand. "You need to know something important," Lydia whispered. "Brad, Cody, and I asked you to be part of our family. We made this decision together because we realized that this is where you belong. You are our daughter and nothing could ever change that."

"What . . . what if I did something terrible?" she asked.

"Nothing," Lydia repeated. "No matter what it is, we'll deal with it together as a family. You need to understand that while I might not have given birth to you physically, you are a part of me. A part of my heart."

Casey sniffled again.

"Don't even think that your mother and I would make you go back into foster care," Brad said. "It's not going to happen."

"I might rebel when I get older. Lots of kids do."

"We might not always agree, Casey, but whether you share our views or not you will always remain our daughter."

"Always and forever," Lydia reiterated. "We're a family."

Casey blinked as if the concept was beyond anything she had ever imagined. "You will always love me . . . no matter what I do?"

Lydia heard the skepticism in her daughter's question. "Parents love their children. We might not always approve of the things you do, we might not like your friends, and cringe at some of the choices you make, but that doesn't change our love."

"You'll love me no matter what?"

Brad looked to Lydia and then answered. "No matter what."

Casey frowned as if she found that difficult to believe. "You love me as much as Cody?"

"Without question," Lydia said.

Casey relaxed against the back of the chair. "Wow."

They gave her a few moments to let

their words soak in before continuing the conversation.

Brad broke the silence. "Can you tell us where you were going the other night when you tried to sneak out?" he asked.

Casey stared down at the table. "I'd rather not. It wasn't bad, though, I promise."

Lydia felt she had to trust her daughter.

"We need to ask you something," Brad said. He, too, had nudged his chair closer to their daughter.

Casey's hand tightened around Lydia's.

"Okay," she said, looking and sounding unsure. She wiped her index finger across her upper lip and sniffled.

Lydia handed her another tissue.

"Your mother talked to a friend today," Brad said. "She was with you and Ava when you went to the hospital."

"You mean Libby?" Casey asked, looking up for the first time.

"Yes. She knows the doctor you saw in the elevator."

"Dr. Stone. He's hot."

Brad grinned.

Lydia was grateful Casey had lightened the mood, although they had yet to broach the subject of the pregnancy, if there even was a pregnancy. Perhaps it was wishful hoping on her part, but Lydia still found it difficult to believe that either Casey or her friend Ava could possibly be pregnant.

"Dr. Stone told Libby that he suspected one of you girls is . . . pregnant."

"Pregnant?" Casey repeated slowly, frowning. "No way."

"If you are pregnant," Lydia said, wanting to be sure Casey understood that she shouldn't be afraid to tell them, "then Dad and I are here to help you. The most important thing is to get you to a doctor. The baby . . . well, we'll deal with that subject when the time comes. What's important is that you know you can come to us with anything."

"You seriously think I'm pregnant?" Casey asked, her head rearing back.

"We don't know," Brad told her. "That's why we're asking."

"It's not me."

"You're sure? One of the things Dr. Stone said was that you might not even know you're carrying a baby."

"It's not me," Casey insisted. "No angel came to see me and I'm not giving birth to Jesus."

Lydia smiled in spite of herself.

"Could it be Ava?" Brad asked.

Casey shook her head. "No. Dr. Stone is wrong. How would he know, anyway? We were only with him a few minutes."

This was the same question Lydia and Brad had both asked.

"Libby said one of the reasons she came to me is because there might be a legal issue involved."

"I'm still . . . you know." She seemed embarrassed to say the word.

"A virgin," Lydia supplied.

"Yeah."

"Good," Brad said forcefully. "Keep it that way."

Casey blinked several times. "I won't always be, Dad. I'll get married and have kids one day, you know."

"No problem." Brad raised his hands

as though surrendering. "But I want
you to wait until you're at least thirty."

"Dad!"

"Just kidding."

Lydia rubbed her thumb over the top
of Casey's hand. "I think I should probably call Ava's grandmother," she said,
thinking out loud.

"Don't," Casey urged. "Her grandmother isn't there half the time anyway.
Ava thinks having them with her makes
her sad because her daughter died and
now she's stuck with them."

"But her grandmother needs to know
so she can talk to Ava."

Casey considered that for several
moments, gnawing on her lower lip.
"Let me do it."

"Casey, I appreciate the offer but I
think I should be the one . . ."

"Mom, I can help Ava. I know I can.
Ava trusts me. The other night when I
snuck out of the house?"

"Yes," Brad said.

"I was helping Ava . . . I brought her
food. I have a few times now. Her grandmother said she's getting fat and would

only let her eat salad for dinner and she got really hungry. So I took her some food." They both fell silent as the implication that Ava was "getting fat" sank in.

"Oh, Casey . . ." Lydia hardly knew what to say. "I appreciate that you want to talk to your friend, but there are a lot of factors involved in this."

"Let me be the one," Casey pleaded. "If you do it then I doubt she'll ever come back to the yarn store. She might open up to me, but she would never with you."

Brad placed his hand on Lydia's arm. "Maybe you should let her."

Lydia reluctantly agreed. She liked Ava, but it was true that the girl hardly said a word whenever she was around. Ava seemed to draw deep into herself when she was at the store, and Casey had taken the other girl under her wing. But it went against Lydia's better judgment to put this on Casey's shoulders. "Let me think on it, okay?"

Casey nodded and then brightened. "Maybe Libby should be the one."

"Libby," Lydia repeated.

"Ava likes Libby a lot," Casey volunteered. "She told me so."

"That's a possibility," Lydia repeated slowly.

"Libby's mother died when she was the same age as Ava. She talked to Ava, too, when we went to the hospital. Ava didn't say much but I could tell she really likes Libby. She'd listen to her; I know she would."

That was the answer, Lydia mused, as a huge sense of relief filled her. She'd ask Libby to talk to Ava. If the girl liked and trusted Libby, then perhaps she would open up to her.

Chapter 11

High on enthusiasm, Libby's steps were lighter as she walked into Seattle General. When it rained it poured, as the proverb went—and it was just as true of good news as bad. First Sarah had phoned to say that Martha Reed was unhappy with Ben Holmes's working on her account. Libby didn't mean to gloat, but she knew she was ten times the trust and estate lawyer Ben Holmes was.

The second bit of positive news came as a complete surprise. Just that morning Robin had ever so casually mentioned that a friend of hers might have a line on a job for Libby. When pressed, Robin had been reluctant to say much more, but she'd told Libby that she'd give her details when she had them.

Although Robin had refused to answer questions, Libby suspected this friend was the very one the prosecutor had set her sights on. Every time Robin mentioned her contact she looked away, as though she was afraid Libby might read more into it than she intended.

Libby couldn't stop smiling. It wouldn't be long now. Intuitively she sensed this long dry period was about to come to an end. An oasis was in sight.

Sharon saw her and smiled. It was the same smile she'd had the day she'd insisted Dr. Stone was interested in Libby. Little did Sharon know the real reason he'd asked for a private word.

"Did Dr. Stone find you?" the nurse asked as soon as Libby entered the nursery.

Libby frowned. "No."

Her smile grew to the size of a

Cheshire cat's. "He asked about you again."

"Oh, goody." If he had more news along the lines of what he'd shared last time they spoke, she'd rather not see him, she mused wryly. Then again he'd been on her mind almost nonstop since the day they'd met in the elevator, and then later when he'd asked her to coffee. No matter how many times she tried to keep him from her thoughts, he was there. It'd been a long time since she'd been this strongly attracted to a man. It irritated her that she felt drawn to Phillip Stone. She didn't even like him. He was arrogant and rude and yet . . . yet he'd cared enough about a young girl to risk approaching Libby with his concern. That couldn't have been easy.

"He . . . he hasn't been to the gym in a while. If he wanted to talk to me, all he had to do was show up there," Libby said, thinking out loud.

"That's easily explained," Sharon said. "His rotation for the operating room changed at the first of the month. He assisted last week, so if he hasn't been following his regular workout schedule, that's probably why."

"Oh." She hated to admit it, and she would not to anyone, not even Robin, but the fact was that she'd missed seeing him. She'd wanted to tell Phillip how she'd handled the situation with the girls and get his reaction. And truth be told . . . she was looking to feed this attraction. Yes, he had a great body and he was good-looking. Robin called him "hot stuff" and that was all well and good, but it was more than that. She appreciated what he'd done, and gradually her opinion of him had started to change. She'd heard from Sharon and other nurses how deeply Dr. Stone cared for his tiny patients and their parents. Despite herself, Libby found herself wishing she would run into him.

The last time Libby had felt like this was in college, when she first met Joe while waitressing. Joe's personality was completely the opposite of Phillip Stone's. Joe was funny and outgoing; he was the kind of guy everyone wanted at their party simply because he was so likable. Part of his charm came from his large, chaotic family.

After Timmy was killed, Libby had been raised as an only child. She'd been fascinated by the bantering exchange between Joe and his siblings. Family gatherings were noisy, chaotic affairs, with babies crying and children madly racing through the house. The men gathered around either the television or the barbecue, and the women congregated in the kitchen, exchanging recipes or housekeeping tips. Libby had felt completely out of place, and she'd often sat in the corner on her visits to his house, unaccustomed to the noise and pandemonium. Still, she'd loved it, and she missed spending holidays with his family even more than she missed Joe.

"Well, Dr. Stone wants to see you," Sharon said, looking pleased with herself, as if she was solely responsible for matchmaking the two.

Rather than continue this unsettling conversation, Libby looked at the newborns lined up in neat rows in the nursery. There'd been a full moon, and

Sharon had warned her that there were
always more births at such times. The
nurse had been right, because Libby
had yet to see this many newborns at
one time. But then again she'd been a
volunteer for only a short while.

"You've very good, you know," Sharon
mentioned, reaching for a chart.

Libby paused. "With the babies?"

Sharon set the chart down and
looked at her. "You're a natural. I've
watched you. The first couple of times
I could tell you weren't accustomed to
holding an infant." She smiled, as
though reliving the memory. "It was almost as if you were afraid they were
going to break, and then after a while
you relaxed and started to sing. The
transformation in you was amazing.
Really amazing."

Libby was too tongue-tied to respond
right away. "I remember my mother
singing to me." The memories were
fleeting. She'd been sick with strep
throat, Libby recalled, and her fever had
raged for two days. It had hurt so much
to swallow. Back then test results took
twenty-four hours. Now, from what she

understood, it took only minutes to diagnose strep, but when she was young it'd taken time to grow the culture.

Her mother had sat on the edge of Libby's bed, under the pink canopy, and gently brushed the wet hair from her fevered brow and sang her to sleep. If Libby closed her eyes she could almost hear her mother's melodic voice.

Sharon's words meant a great deal. "Thank you," Libby whispered. The nurse was right. In the beginning it had felt awkward to hold these tiny babies. This morning as she walked to the hospital, Libby realized how eager she was to spend time with the precious newborns.

"Do you have children?" Sharon asked.

Libby looked away and shook her head.

"You should. You'd make a wonderful mother."

Her throat thickened and she moved toward one of the cribs rather than let her friend know how deeply the words had touched her.

"Well," Sharon continued at the end

of a sigh, "I better get busy. I'll be back in a few minutes."

"Okay." Her voice sounded strange, Libby realized, and she was grateful when Sharon didn't comment.

Libby picked up a seven-pound baby girl with the surname Knight. She had a small pink bow clipped to a tiny patch of hair. Kissing the infant's brow, Libby settled into the rocker. As if the infant was aware of everything taking place around her, Baby Knight stared up at Libby. She sang a medley of Barry Manilow hits until the baby yawned and her eyelids drooped closed. After several minutes Libby replaced her in the tiny bed.

The baby directly across from Baby Knight let out a lusty cry, as if demanding her attention. Libby turned and looked at him, and smiled when she saw that his surname was Wilson.

She picked him up and gently cradled him in her arms as she returned to the rocking chair. He wasn't easily comforted, and he arched his back, screaming at the top of his lungs.

"My, my, aren't you a hotheaded

one," she whispered. Placing him over her shoulder, she rubbed his back and sure enough he burped. Libby laughed softly and continued to rock him.

Holding these babies in her arms, her head and heart flooded with regrets. She wished she'd worked harder at saving her marriage. In the end, Libby had been convinced she and Joe would never be happy together; each of them wanted the other person to be something they were not. At the time it had just seemed best to walk away. Now, holding these babies in her arms, Libby was left to wonder what might have happened if they'd stayed together, gone to counseling, worked out their differences. If she had, perhaps the infant in her arms would be her own. Their baby. That would never happen now, and sadness filled her heart. If she could turn back time, Libby realized, she might have made different choices. The divorce seemed like an easy way out for what had become a strained and difficult relationship.

With these thoughts circling in her mind Libby glanced up and froze. Her heart shot to her throat and remained lodged there as she locked eyes with the man on the other side of the nursery window.

Joe. Joe Wilson, her ex-husband.

How was this possible? Had her imagination conjured him up? He looked real. In fact, he looked as shocked as she did.

Standing, she replaced the little boy in his crib and walked out of the nursery. Joe stood by the door when she opened it.

"What are you doing here?" he asked, frowning. "That's my son."

"I . . . I volunteer here at the hospital. I had no idea he was your baby."

He paced the area in front of the window. "You volunteer at the hospital?" he asked, as if he found that unbelievable.

"Two or three days a week."

"What happened with Burkhart, Smith & Crandall?"

"They laid me off." It hurt to admit it, but Joe deserved the truth.

"Laid you off?" His voice registered

shock. "You've got to be kidding me. No one worked the hours you did."

She didn't say anything.

"You didn't make partner?"

She shook her head. "I don't think I even came close."

He frowned, as if to say he found that unbelievable and then shook his head. Libby knew what he was thinking . . . because she'd had the same thought herself just moments before. It went without saying that she'd given up a whole lot for very little return. All she needed to do was look inside the nursery at the baby she'd held so briefly in her arms to realize the sacrifices she'd made.

She felt numb and her head was buzzing. A tight constriction gripped her throat, but she managed to squeak out, "Congratulations on your son."

He nodded. "Maureen and I feel very blessed."

She swallowed against the knot in her throat. "I'm happy for you . . . I really mean that."

"I know you do." Joe's eyes held hers and he offered her a gentle smile, and then reached out and squeezed her shoulder.

"I . . . I better get back," she said in a rush, for fear she was about to break down in front of him.

"Yeah . . . I . . . ah." Obviously he was as much at a loss as she was.

"It was good to see you, Joe," she said, opening the door. Her hand shook so badly she had a difficult time getting her identification badge into the slot so the door would open.

"You too," he said.

Once inside, Libby leaned against the wall. She hung her head and drew in a couple of deep, stabilizing breaths in order to get ahold of herself. This was so unlike her. Both levelheaded and patient, she was known for her ability to deal with a crisis without allowing her personal feelings to get the best of her. Well, they had the best of her now. Or the worst, she wasn't sure which. To her acute embarrassment, she realized that if something didn't happen quickly she was going to dissolve into tears.

Libby was not a crier. She couldn't

remember the last time she'd wept in public. High school? She planted her hand over her mouth and walked blindly into the nursery, pausing at Sharon's desk. Thankfully the other woman was out of the room. Libby grabbed hold of the edge, struggling, gritting her teeth, not breathing, determined to get a grip.

The nursery door opened and she stiffened. Just her luck, Sharon was back. She wasn't about to let anyone see her like this and she looked toward the ceiling.

"Libby."

It wasn't Sharon. It was Dr. Stone. Why, oh why, did it have to be him?

"I was hoping to have a chance to talk to you," he said from behind her.

Libby refused to turn around. "Another time." Somehow she managed to eke out the words. All she wanted was for him to leave. He was the last person in the world she wanted to speak to right now.

"Okay."

But he didn't leave. Instead he stayed right where he was. Libby wanted to shout at him to go away. Why did he linger when she so badly wanted him gone?

"I have a feeling something's wrong here."

She wondered sarcastically if all men were this intuitive. "Please, would you just go?"

Instead he stepped closer.

"Leave me alone," she demanded between gritted teeth, fire in her words and in her spirit. Then to her absolute horror the dam broke and she burst into tears. She whirled around, intent on leaving the nursery. If he insisted on staying, then fine. What she didn't realize was how close he was behind her, and she abruptly bumped into him. That was all it took. Unable to stop herself, she buried her face in his chest and cried. The room filled with the sound of her heart-wrenching sobs. Her entire upper body shook with the force of her tears.

"Ah . . ." Phillip's arms remained at his sides. Then he bounced his hand against the top of her shoulder a couple of times. "I'm sure it isn't that bad."

The words sounded stiff and awkward, as if he didn't know what to say.

Unable to hold back the sobs, the grief, and the profound sense of loss, her knees started to give way. She might have collapsed to the floor if Dr. Stone hadn't caught her.

He wrapped her in his arms; Libby tried to break away but he held her fast against him and his voice turned soft and kind.

"It'll be all right," he whispered. "Whatever it is will work out." Anything else she might have been able to resist, but not gentleness.

Phillip held a sobbing woman in his arms. He didn't know what had happened to cause this meltdown, and Libby was in no condition to tell him. Through the years he'd dealt with plenty of emotional women, but the context was completely different. He'd had on his doctor hat and they were mothers worried about their children; he would hand them tissues and say what he could to reassure them, filling in the medical details they needed to know.

He would never embrace them, not the way he was holding on to Libby.

She clung to him, her arms around his waist and her face buried in his chest, as she released what appeared to be years of stockpiled tears. She sobbed as violently as if it were the end of the world, as if there was nothing left for her to live for, and she'd lost everything that would ever be precious. The need to comfort her overwhelmed him and he pressed his cheek to the crown of her head.

It'd been awkward at first, seeing her cry like this. He'd had his chance— she'd asked him to leave, and by all that was right he should have taken his cue and vacated the nursery. Instead he'd found it impossible to walk away.

He wasn't good at this. He didn't know what to say, and had only managed a few hackneyed words that he doubted she'd even heard. That was probably for the best.

"Shh, shh," he whispered, rubbing his hand over the back of her head, wanting to comfort her, needing to comfort her.

"My . . . my ex-husband," she said, the words muffled against his chest.

"He was here?" Phillip was beginning to imagine what might have happened.

She nodded, her forehead rubbing against his shirt.

"I . . . I held his . . . son."

"You're still in love with him, then?"

"No." The lone word was nearly shouted.

"Okay, sorry, you aren't in love with him."

"He's married . . . he has a son."

Phillip tried to follow her, knowing he wasn't always the most intuitive man around.

"I'm sorry," she blubbered, breaking away. "I have to go. Really, I need to go." Abruptly, she turned away from him and nearly stumbled.

Phillip would have stopped her if he'd known what to say. But before he could think clearly Libby had grabbed her purse and was gone.

Chapter 12

Still shaken, Libby returned to her condo, sank into her sofa, and buried her face in her hands. It felt as if her entire world had crumbled at her feet. Seeing Joe and his son had been devastating, bringing into stark reality every single regret she'd been struggling with lately. To make everything ten times worse, Phillip Stone had witnessed it all. To break down in front of him . . . of all people. Libby wanted to crawl into bed, pull the covers over her head, and hibernate for the next ten years.

Phillip Stone was a complete enigma. On the one hand he was both rude and arrogant, and on the other he'd been gentle, caring, and kind. As far as Libby was concerned, he was the perfect candidate for intense, deep emotional therapy. He was a doctor, all right. Dr. Jekyll and Mr. Hyde . . . two completely different people. The first was infinitely easy to dislike and distrust and ignore. The second made her want to bury herself in the comfort of his arms and let him hold her for the next twenty years. Just thinking about the way she'd melted down in front of him caused her acute embarrassment. She'd never be able to look him in the face again.

This couldn't be happening; it just couldn't.

Only it was.

Sucking in a deep breath to center herself, Libby sat upright and squared her shoulders. She reached for her knitting. She'd discovered that holding the needles and yarn calmed her. Although her hands trembled and she was forced to catch a sob or two, she managed to complete an entire row without an error. The baby blanket pattern was the most difficult project she'd tackled. She wasn't even sure why she'd chosen to knit it. It'd seemed like a good idea at the time. No shaping, no need to sew it together once she'd finished. Lydia had one knitted up for display, and Libby had been drawn to it. The progression from the preemie hats to a blanket had seemed natural enough—like the hats, the blanket would most likely be given to a charity.

After knitting for an hour, Libby's nerves had relaxed, but only a little. Every time her mind took her to an uncomfortable place she forced her thoughts in a different direction. She refused to entertain a single flashback of her failed marriage or what had happened with Phillip that afternoon. To do so would only upset her more, and she was distressed enough. What a mess she'd made of her life . . .

Her doorbell chimed, interrupting her musings. It was so rare to get company that all Libby did was stare at the front door. By the time she stood, the doorbell had rung a second time. Apparently whoever was on the other side was impatient.

"Hold on," she said. Checking the peephole, she gasped and rolled away from the door, flattening her back and her hands against the wall.

Phillip Stone.

"Libby," he called. "I know you're in there. Open up."

Biting into her lower lip so hard she almost broke the skin, she twisted the deadbolt and opened the door.

"What are you doing here?" she demanded with great bravado. Her heart felt as if it was about to explode. At this rate she would never need to exercise again. All she needed to raise her pulse was Phillip Stone.

"Nice to see you, too. Are you going to invite me inside?"

Keeping her hand on the doorknob, she reluctantly moved out of the way.

Phillip walked three feet into her condo, paused, and looked around. "Nice view."

Libby was fairly certain he hadn't stopped by to gaze at the Seattle skyline.

"You can close the door now, if you'd like."

He was bossy, too. Libby shut the door and then leaned against it, needing its support. "Why are you here?" she asked a second time.

"To be perfectly frank, I haven't figured that out myself." He walked over to the couch and sat in the very spot she'd so recently vacated.

"As you can see, I'm fine . . . I apologize for that emotional display, but I'm in control now."

"Good." He hesitated and then commented, "When I get upset I usually have a shot of good whiskey."

"Not my thing," Libby told him, cringing at the thought. She had a bottle of wine in the refrigerator, but frankly she wasn't in the mood.

Not knowing what to say, Libby claimed the chair across from him and pressed her two hands between her knees. The silence felt awkward and strained. She was content to wait him out. Eventually he'd get bored and leave. At least that was what she hoped.

Finally Libby couldn't stand it any

longer. "Did you stop by to embarrass me even more?"

He arched his brows as though her question surprised him. "No. I came to make sure you made it home all right."

"As you can see I . . . did."

That didn't appear to satisfy him. "You want to tell me what happened back there?"

"No." Libby had no intention of explaining what had led to that dreadful scene. She'd embarrassed herself enough for one day and wasn't looking to repeat the performance. Besides, she'd blurted out more than she'd intended earlier. "I believe I already told you everything . . ." Actually she'd told him more than she was comfortable admitting.

Leaning forward, he set his elbows on his knees and rubbed his palms together.

"I'm not normally like this," Libby blurted out. Naturally, she'd been upset before. Losing her position with the law firm had been traumatic, too. But it hadn't caused her to throw herself into a man's arms and sob her heart out.

"Let me put it this way. I am usually able to control my emotions; today was an exception."

"Good to know."

She'd been on the verge of calming down when Phillip Stone had arrived. Her pulse had returned to an even rhythm, and she'd managed to herd her thoughts away from the keen embarrassment. Now all her emotions threatened to burst free again. "I was doing just fine until you came along." Her voice wobbled slightly before she regained control.

"I see. Then it's all my fault."

"Yes, exactly." She smiled in spite of herself. He really was the most surprising man.

He smiled back. "I was worried about you," he said, speaking low.

"I . . . I'm okay now."

He leaned forward and reached for her hand. His touch felt cool against her heated skin.

"How did you know where I live?" she asked without looking up. Her phone number was unlisted.

"I asked Sharon. She had your volunteer form on file."

He'd been a bit bold about tracking her down. And Sharon already seemed to think there was something romantic happening between them. Her nurse friend had probably been eager to share the information.

"Do you regret your divorce?" he asked.

Libby debated how best to answer that. "What I regret was that I didn't try harder to save the marriage. We were both so eager to give up on each other. Joe wanted a family and I felt we should wait. Then seeing his baby today . . ." She paused as her throat started to tighten, and she found she couldn't complete the sentence.

"We all have regrets, Libby. I have my share, too. I let someone I loved go; a woman I'd hoped to spend the rest of my life with. I just stood back and let her walk away."

Libby looked up, amazed that he was willing to share something so personal with her.

"What happened today was clearly

painful," he continued, "but you seem like you're willing to own your part in what caused the divorce. Don't make the mistake of beating yourself up, especially now. You don't have anything to feel guilty about."

"You didn't have regrets after your breakup?"

He laughed softly. "Oh, I had plenty. It took a while for me to realize that I had lost perspective. I assumed the hospital would fail to function if I wasn't there to overlook every detail."

"I've heard Sharon say that several of the physicians on staff have pretty big egos."

"It happens," he agreed, and smiled.

Libby returned it with a wobbly smile of her own.

He released her hand and straightened his posture. "Have you ever been sailing?" he asked out of the blue.

Libby remembered the picture on Hershel's credenza—the one of him on the sailboat—and the feeling she'd had each time she caught a glimpse of it—that sensation of being free and enjoy-

ing life. "No, but I would like to someday."

He stood. "No time like the present."

"Now?" She nervously clenched her
hands. She had no experience with
boats, let alone boating. After the
trauma of the afternoon, staying in-
doors and licking her wounds appealed
to her more.

"Why not?" Phillip asked.

Nibbling on her lower lip, Libby held
his gaze, uncertain but tempted.

Reading her indecision, he added,
"When I need to think things through, I
head for the marina. Being on the water helps clear my head and relaxes
me."

That was incentive enough, or it
should have been. "I'm not sure I should.
I've never sailed before and . . ."

"You'll feel better with the sun on
your face and the wind at your back,
while you're gliding through the water."

He made it sound so magical. Libby
felt a smile coming. Really, what did
she have to lose at this point? Nothing
about the way she'd been living her life
seemed to be working. Maybe it was

time to stop listening to her first im-
pulses. The decision made, she looked
up and met his gaze. "Okay, let's do it."

An hour later they were on Lake
Washington aboard his twenty-four-foot
sloop. When they'd first arrived at the
marina, Phillip had gotten busy bringing out the sails, tying them up to the
mast, and getting everything ready to
take them onto the lake. He moved
gracefully, comfortably, about the boat.

Once they'd motored out of the marina, he set the course and raised the
sails. Within moments the main sail and
the jib filled with wind as the Challenger
7.4 sliced effortlessly through the dark
green water.

Phillip had been right. The sun felt
good on Libby's face, and as the wind
whipped about her it seemed to take
with it the pain and regrets of that afternoon. She understood now what
Phillip had meant when he said he went
sailing when he needed to think something through. Sailing had a calming effect on her, too.

Phillip seemed completely at ease at
the helm. He was confident and sure of

himself. The wind ruffled his dark hair, blowing it back from his face. He looked boyish and happy; Libby found it difficult not to stare at him. When he caught her watching him, he grinned. It hardly seemed possible that just that morning she'd thought of him as brusque and unpleasant. The transformation was amazing.

"What do you think?" he asked.

She didn't know what to say. "It's everything I thought it must be. I can't wait to tell Hershel."

A frown briefly marked his brow. "Who's Hershel?"

She didn't need to stop and think. "A . . . friend," Libby said, although she had only recently come to think of him as one. "Hershel has a picture of his sailboat on his credenza and I'd always wondered why he loved it so. Now I know."

The lake had plenty of water traffic, sailboats galore, and motorboats, too, their engines roaring as they sped past.

A section of Lake Washington had been cordoned off for swimming, and the cheers and shouts of youngsters taking advantage of the sunshine rang through the late afternoon. Even with all the busyness of the lake, Libby felt a strange sense of intimacy with Phillip. In the close confines of the boat, her feelings were stronger than ever. While there was sound all around them, the sailboat was surprisingly quiet, making conversation easy. She wondered if Phillip felt the connection, too, and assumed he must, although neither of them spoke of it.

Filling the silence, he talked about the sailing classes he'd taken and his search for just the right boat before he decided on the Challenger 7.4, which he kept docked at the marina.

After a few minutes Libby relaxed, and they shared a companionable silence. She closed her eyes and turned her face toward the sun and relaxed, really relaxed. Her tears earlier had been cathartic—they'd drained all the tension out of her, leaving her free of recriminations.

The main sail caught the wind and

the Challenger sliced through the water like a hot knife through butter. Surprised by the sudden burst of speed, Libby grabbed hold of the side and held on.

Phillip laughed and motioned for her to come sit by him. "Come here by me," he urged. "I'll teach you to sail."

"Ah . . ." The desire to learn outweighed her reluctance to take over the helm. She settled close to his side, but he had her sit in front of him, wrapping his arms around her and letting her take hold of the wheel. He explained basic sailing theory to her but the words made little sense. Although she did her best to pay attention, she couldn't ignore the fact that she was basically in his arms. Her mind was spinning at an incredible speed, trying to take in how quickly her feelings for him, and apparently his for her, had changed.

"You're doing great," he assured her. His hands rested on her shoulders as she held on to the wheel.

"This is great." Turning her head, she smiled up at him.

"You're a natural."

She laughed softly and then after only a short pause, Phillip leaned down and pressed his mouth to hers. It was a gentle, exploratory kiss that quickly deepened. This man could kiss. Libby strained up toward him; her position was slightly uncomfortable, but she didn't care. She continued to hold on to the helm with one hand and slipped her free arm around his neck. The sail went slack and the flapping noise of the canvas was barely discernible to Libby, but apparently not to Phillip. Gradually, he broke off the kiss and lifted his head. He took over again, but when Libby went to move, he stopped her.

"I like having you here."

Still flushed and a bit light-headed, she leaned against him and sat in his embrace for an hour, perhaps longer. Neither of them felt the need to speak. Being this close to Phillip felt incredibly good. Every now and again he'd rest his hand against her shoulder or lean down and kiss the side of her neck. When he did Libby would close her eyes, unable to believe that within the space of a few hours she had gone from one of the lowest points of her life to such supreme joy. The transformation had happened because of Phillip.

Eventually they headed back to the marina.

"Being on the water always makes me hungry," Phillip said as he motored into his marina slot. "How does fish and chips sound?"

"Wonderful. I'm starved."

"I am, too."

He helped her off the boat, and they worked together to get the gear down and properly stored. When they started to leave, Phillip placed his arm around her shoulders.

"Be careful now, these docks get slippery." He slipped an arm around her waist, as though he needed an excuse to keep her close.

"Especially in July," she teased, noticing how dried out the wood seemed in the summer sunshine.

"Especially in July," Phillip echoed, chuckling.

She looped her arm around his waist

and together the two of them walked toward his car.

This day had certainly been full of surprises.

Chapter 13

***

Friday morning Libby could hardly wait to get to the gym to see Robin. She would have phoned or sent a text, but her time with Phillip was something she wanted to discuss in person.

They'd sat at the picnic tables outside the fish and chips stand and talked for two hours straight. He was completely different from what she'd expected. Her emotional collapse seemed to have made him willing to share deeper parts of his life with her.

Libby had never been the chatty type. Yet she found it so incredibly easy to talk to Phillip now that she'd gotten past his seemingly reserved exterior. They discussed a dozen different subjects, from popular music to books, politics, and religion.

He seemed genuinely interested in her opinions, some of which he agreed with and others of which he didn't. She learned that he'd been badly burned in his last relationship. What she found remarkable was his honesty and willingness to acknowledge his part in the breakup. As one workaholic to another, she identified with him on a number of different levels. Afterward she felt buoyed, encouraged, and inspired.

At the end of the evening, he walked her up to her condo and kissed her good night. It wasn't a simple peck on the cheek. It was a heated exchange that rocked her to the very core of her being. It'd been difficult to break away from each other, and when they did his breath was as ragged as hers.

The attraction she'd felt on the boat had exploded. Phillip felt it, too. Libby could see it in his eyes. He looked as shocked as she felt, as if he wasn't sure this should be happening. They'd both been gun-shy because of previous relationships, and while what they felt was new and exciting, it was scary, too.

She could hardly sleep; she was that happy. Her entire being was filled with a hopeful expectation that was unlike anything she'd experienced in a very long while.

Libby was at her locker when Robin flew into the dressing room. Her friend's face lit up the instant she saw Libby.

"I've got news," Robin said, gripping Libby by the forearms.

Libby reached for her friend's arms at the same time. "Me too."

"Let me go first."

"Okay," Libby acquiesced. She was too happy to argue about anything so trivial.

"I talked to Roy and he mentioned a position would be opening with the city as a junior prosecutor. I know it's pretty much a starting position, but I think you'd quickly rise through the ranks, so please don't be turned off by that."

Libby frowned. While grateful for any

job opening, she wasn't keen to be a prosecutor.

"It's for the department dealing with tax fraud and financial crimes."

This was an important component of estate work, with which Libby was well acquainted. This was promising, very promising. "This is big," she whispered.

"You're telling me?" Robin joked. "This is huge, and right up your alley."

"Oh, Robin, thank you." She briefly hugged her friend. To do something like this for her was outside Robin's comfort zone.

"I've got the information. You need to call first thing this morning," Robin told her.

"Done."

"Interviews are next Wednesday."

"Perfect." She hoped she could arrange for hers to take place in the afternoon, as she was scheduled to volunteer at the hospital in the morning. Nevertheless, if asked to come in the morning Libby would. Sharon knew she could be called away at any time for work—finding a new job was her priority.

"Okay," Robin said, looking pleased with herself. "What's your news?"

Libby barely knew where to start. "I saw Joe."

"Your ex?"

Filling in the blanks, she described her emotional breakdown and how Phillip had shown up unexpectedly at her condo. She mentioned the sailing lesson, and although she felt a little like a gossiping schoolgirl she told Robin about the amazing kisses they'd shared.

"Wow," Robin whispered when she finished.

"He asked to see me again tonight."

"Dinner?"

"Phillip suggested going out on the sailboat again, but that depends on the weather. I checked out the forecast, and it's supposed to rain." Frankly, Libby didn't care what they did, as long as she was with him.

"Roy has a boat," Robin murmured wistfully.

"Roy . . . Judge Bollinger told you about the opening in the prosecutor's office?"

"Yeah." Robin immediately changed the subject.

Apparently the judge was strictly off-limits. Well, well, so Libby had guessed right. It was Roy who had captured her friend's attention.

After her workout, Libby returned to her condo. She was changing clothes before heading to the hospital when her cell chirped. Thinking—actually, hoping—it was Phillip, she didn't bother to look at caller ID before answering.

"Hello." Her voice was elevated, happy.

"Libby, it's Lydia Goetz from A Good Yarn."

Libby tensed. She hadn't been in the yarn store since dropping the bomb.

"Oh, hi," she said, hoping she sounded casual.

"You haven't been by lately. Did you find a job?"

"No, but I have a line on one. How is everything with you?"

"Actually I'm calling because I wanted you to know how grateful I am that you came to me with your concerns."

Lydia was grateful? The situation had felt like a heavy, wet blanket weighing down on her shoulders. She'd feared Lydia might have taken her interference the wrong way. If she hadn't been concerned for the young mother's health, Libby wouldn't have said anything. Phillip had felt the same obligation.

"We're convinced it's Ava," Lydia continued. "When I saw her last, I took a good look and I realized that Dr. Stone's right. Ava is pregnant. She does a good job of hiding it, wearing loose clothes. Casey told me she barely has anything that fits her anymore."

"Oh, my." The poor girl.

"I thought I would talk to her myself," Lydia continued, "but Casey suggested that it would be better if you did it."

"Me?" Libby barely knew the girl.

"Casey told me Ava likes you. She asked about you yesterday when she stopped off at the shop. Would you mind terribly?"

Libby hesitated for only a moment. Stepping outside her comfort zone seemed to be the order of the day, and if this girl needed help . . . "Of course

I'll talk to her," she agreed. "When will she be in next, do you know?"

"Could you come by on Monday? The shop will be closed, which might work well."

"Of course. I'll make sure I stop by," she said.

So it was Ava who was pregnant— the motherless girl who so reminded Libby of herself at that age.

Chapter 14

Libby sat at the table in the back of the yarn store, working intently on the baby blanket while Lydia sat in her office paying bills. Casey and Ava were busily knitting and crocheting with Libby. If the fact that she was in the store when it was technically closed surprised them, they didn't say. She certainly didn't want to introduce the subject of Ava's pregnancy in front of Casey, and so she anxiously waited for the right moment when she could speak privately to the young teen.

Phillip had kindly offered a few words

of advice and she was grateful for his help, but no matter what anyone suggested, confronting Ava wouldn't be easy.

At least she didn't need to worry about carrying the current conversation. Casey easily took on that responsibility, bouncing from one subject to the next as if she were playing verbal hopscotch.

When Casey took a short breath, Libby asked Ava a couple of questions and Casey, bless her dear heart, didn't leap in to answer, allowing Ava to respond.

"I've decided I wanted to learn how to knit, too," Ava announced, focusing her attention on her knitting.

When they'd first met, Casey had been teaching her to crochet. Lydia seemed to think it was Libby's influence that had shifted Ava's interest to knitting.

"Knitting really isn't difficult once you get the hang of it," Libby assured her.

"That's what Lydia said. I'm knitting a dishcloth." Ava laid it on top of the table and smoothed it out for Libby to see. "I've made a bunch of mistakes, but no one is going to be wearing it, so that shouldn't matter, right?"

"Right." Ava had done a really good job, especially for a beginner. Libby told her so, and the teenager beamed with the praise.

Out of the blue, Casey scooted her chair out and stood. "I'll be back in a few minutes."

Libby wasn't sure if this was her cue to broach the subject of the pregnancy with Ava, but either way she decided to seize the opportunity.

"If you'll remember, I was about the same age as you when my mother died," Libby reminded her while studying Ava's knitting.

Ava glanced up from her knitting, and her hands went still. "How did your mother die?"

"She had cancer. In fact, I originally learned to knit sitting with my mother when she was in bed. She taught me, but after she died I set it aside and didn't start again until just recently."

"Why did you stop?" Ava asked. She returned her attention to the needles and the yarn, her tongue darting in and out of her mouth as she concentrated on creating the stitches.

"After my mother died, I didn't know anyone else who knit and there wasn't anyone I could go to for help if I had a question or made a mistake." Recognizing this as the perfect opportunity to lead into the pregnancy, Libby continued. "I wonder if you feel the same way about some things now that your mother is gone."

Ava responded with a slight shrug of her shoulders. "My mom worked a lot . . . she didn't have time to spend with me or Jackson, knitting or anything else. My dad left us and Mom had two jobs."

"I'm sorry." Libby remembered Casey telling her that Ava's mother had died in a car crash. Apparently she'd fallen asleep at the wheel. A single mom, working two jobs—it's no wonder the poor woman was so tired.

"I'm not your mother, Ava, but if you have any questions, you can always ask me."

"About knitting?"

"About anything."

The tentative smile returned and she held Libby's gaze for longer than she had before, and then nodded as though to say she would. Seeing her gratitude made Libby realize how incredibly young Ava was. Her heart ached for the girl, having experienced the same loneliness herself.

Libby tried a new angle. "After my mother died, I was alone after school every day." She remembered how empty the house had felt without her mother. It hadn't completely hit her that her mother would never return until several weeks after the funeral when she was struggling to find something easy to cook for dinner. Her mother would never be able to tell her how to cut down a recipe. She wouldn't be able to teach her how to hem her pants, or shop for a special dress with her.

"Jackson and I are alone a lot, too, because Grandma works so many hours."

"Sometimes I did things I knew would get me in trouble if my father knew about them." Libby had given a lot of thought to how she should broach the subject and hoped to lead into it naturally.

Ava's fingers slowed. "Like what?"

"I phoned my grandmother in Colorado. Long-distance calls cost money. She said I could talk to her anytime I wanted, but the minute my father saw the phone bill he blew up and put me on restrictions."

"Grandma gets upset about money, too. I know she misses my mom because she doesn't like me to talk about her. It makes her sad; it . . . it makes me sad, too."

Libby still had her mother's picture on her desk. For years she'd kept it on her nightstand for fear she would forget what her mother looked like. "Do you have a special boyfriend?" Libby asked, unwilling to get sidetracked.

"Not really."

"Is there a boy you like more than anyone else?" she tried again.

Once more Ava shrugged. "My brother is friends with Peter. He lives next door, but he can't come over because my grandma doesn't like us to have anyone in the house when she isn't there. She's afraid someone might take something. Peter wouldn't but she said we couldn't break the rules for him."

"So you don't see Peter much."

"Not so much," she said, and looked away.

"Is he cute?"

Ava grinned. "I guess."

Libby felt completely inept at this. She'd hoped the conversation would lead naturally into boyfriends, and that she could transition into the topic with a lot more ease and finesse than this.

"Does your grandmother ever take you to the doctor?" she asked.

Ava looked up as though the question surprised her. "I went to the dentist earlier this summer."

"What about a physical? Don't you get one every year for school?" Oh dear, this was going badly.

Ava shook her head. "Not really. You do if you're playing sports, so Jackson has an appointment, but I don't. I'm not any good at sports. I like to sing. I was in the choir at school and sang a solo once. Do . . . do you sing?"

Libby shook her head and then remembered how much she enjoyed singing to the babies, but that was different. "I didn't have many interests in school. I always had my face in a book, studying."

"Did you get good grades?"

Libby nodded. "My mother wanted me to graduate at the top of my class. She convinced me I was the smartest girl in school. She said that because she knew she wouldn't be around to see me grow up and graduate from high school and college. She said it every day because she wanted me to believe it, too. Sometimes she would close her eyes when she talked about me going to college."

Ava cocked her head to one side. "Why did she do that?"

"I asked her that, too, and she said she was using her imagination to see me excelling in everything I tackled."

"Did you?" Ava asked.

Libby blinked until she realized what the thirteen-year-old was asking. "Yes.

I wanted to get good grades for my mother." Libby rarely spoke of her mother to anyone. Those last few months with her mother, before she went into hospice, had been special. The memories had lingered in Libby's mind through the years.

"Did you have a boyfriend?" Ava asked.

"No . . . not until college."

"College?" Ava repeated, as though she was shocked Libby had waited so long.

Casey returned and her eyes instantly went to Libby, who quickly looked away. She hadn't gotten very far into the conversation and now that Casey was back everything would change.

"Where'd you go?" Ava asked her friend.

"I ran over to see Alix at The French Cafe."

"Oh . . . damn . . . darn it." Ava exhaled and thrust her knitting at Libby. "I dropped a stitch."

"I'll get it for you." Libby reached for her notions bag and brought out her crochet hook. Once she'd snagged the rebel stitch she handed the dishcloth back to Ava and showed her how to weave it back into place and slip it onto the knitting needle.

Casey continued chattering away. "Alix is the one I was telling you about who bakes those yummy buttery croissants."

"Lydia bought me one this morning," Ava explained.

"Alix and my mom are good friends," Casey went on. "Mom taught her how to knit, too. Before she got married she went to cooking school and then she started working at The French Cafe."

Libby had tasted those incredible croissants herself and they were every bit as good as Casey claimed. She had to avoid them altogether or her workout sessions at the gym would be for naught.

Looking up from her knitting, Libby discovered that Ava was watching her. Immediately the girl's gaze dropped as though she was embarrassed.

"I was thinking of getting some lunch. Do you girls want to join me?" Libby asked.

"Casey and I already have plans," Lydia said as she approached the table.

"We do?" Casey looked surprised.

"Would you like to come with me?" Libby asked Ava, realizing Lydia had given her an opening for the two to spend time together.

Ava hesitated and looked to Casey as if she needed her friend's approval.

"It's all right with me if you want to have lunch with Libby," Casey said, although she didn't look all that pleased about it.

"Okay," Ava said softly, glancing up at Libby and offering her a shy smile.

"Where are we going?" Casey asked her mother as Lydia drew her daughter away from the table.

"I thought we'd meet Margaret," said Lydia.

"Can we have Chinese food?" Casey asked hopefully, then looking over at Ava, she added, "It's my favorite."

"I'll call Margaret and suggest that she meet us at China West."

Casey's face lit up with a huge smile. "Great!"

"What kind of food do you like?" Libby asked Ava as she started picking up her things.

Ava shrugged.

"There's a really good soup and salad place a couple of blocks from here." What Libby liked best was the outdoor dining. They would have some privacy . . . she hoped.

"That sounds okay. I like soup."

"So do I." Most people thought of it as a winter lunch but Libby could easily eat soup every day.

Ava and Libby left the shop together. While heading toward the cafe, Libby did all the talking. Drawing Ava into the conversation was difficult. When they reached the small restaurant, she chose an isolated table and hoped it would stay that way.

The waitress arrived with filled water glasses and two menus tucked under her arm. "The soup special today is butternut bisque."

"They have a wonderful crab salad if that interests you," Libby suggested to Ava.

Ava studied the menu as if Libby was

going to give her a test on its contents. "I like tuna fish."

"You can order whatever you'd like." Her own stomach was in knots. Everyone was counting on her to help Ava. Good grief, she knew nothing about teenage girls, let alone pregnant ones. What she did know was what it was like to be a motherless daughter. That was her main connection with Ava and she prayed it would be enough.

The waitress returned a couple of minutes later.

"I'll have the soup special," Libby said, handing the other woman her menu.

Ava continued to study the page. "Do you have peanut butter and jelly?"

"Sorry, no," the waitress informed her.

"Can I have a tuna sandwich, then?"

"On wheat, sourdough, rye, pumpernickel, or white bread?" she asked, her hand poised over the order pad.

"Ah . . ." Ava's gaze shot to Libby, as if the question had overwhelmed her.

"Wheat," Libby said, answering on her behalf.

"Lettuce and tomato?"

Ava nodded.

"Mayo?"

Ava smiled. "Yes, please."

The waitress finished penning the order. "One tuna sandwich on wheat with lettuce, tomato, and mayo, plus a bowl of butternut squash bisque coming right up."

Libby waited until their food arrived and they were both eating before she made another attempt to broach the subject that needed to be addressed.

"After my mother died, I felt lost and alone," she told Ava. "Have you felt that way?"

"Sometimes. Do you ever dream about her?"

As soon as Ava posed the question, the memory of a vivid dream played back in Libby's mind. She set her water glass down but kept her hand folded around the cold glass. "About a month after Mom's funeral I dreamt that I was in a rowboat on a big lake. It was foggy and I couldn't see the shore. I was scared and I kept calling out for my mother, until I remembered she couldn't hear me. I woke up shaking and crying."

When she stopped speaking, she found that Ava had abandoned her sandwich.

"Do you ever dream about your mother?" Libby asked.

"I did earlier this summer. She was going to the car and I tried to stop her, but she wouldn't listen. I kept telling her that if she got in the car she was going to die, and she said she didn't care if she died because her life was hell anyway."

"Oh, Ava, that must have been horrible."

The teenager shrugged and reached for the second half of her sandwich.

Libby stiffened and dipped her spoon into the bright orange bisque. It was now or never.

"Sometimes when we don't have our mothers to watch over us, things happen," Libby said.

Frowning, Ava looked up and seemed confused.

"What I mean is," Libby added, leaning forward until her stomach pressed against the edge of the table, "we find ourselves in situations we probably never would be in if our mothers were alive."

"Did you?"

Libby nodded, although for the most part she'd focused on her studies and strived to be the daughter her mother had wanted her to be. Thankfully, Libby hadn't gotten involved with boys or drugs. The thing was, she could understand how that might have happened for Ava.

"As motherless daughters we often look for someone to step in and love us, and we do what we can to be worthy of that love." Libby sincerely hoped Ava understood where she was leading the conversation without her needing to spell it out chapter and verse.

Ava just stared at her as though she was completely lost.

Beneath the table Libby bunched her hands into tight fists. The only thing left was to ask Ava outright.

She inhaled and held her breath for several seconds. "Do you remember when you met Dr. Stone in the elevator that day in the hospital?" she asked.

Ava smiled. "You like him, don't you?"

"I do," she admitted.

"Casey said the two of you are dating."

This wasn't the direction she wanted to take their conversation in. "Dr. Stone and I have gone out a couple of times on his boat. The reason I mention him is because . . ."

"He's cute."

Libby agreed.

"Does he really have a heart of stone?"

"Not once you get to know him."

Not knowing what else to do, Libby stretched her arm across the table and gently set her hand on Ava's forearm.

"Ava, I realize you don't know me very well, but I hope you will count me as your friend."

"Okay," the girl mumbled.

"If you are ever in any kind of trouble, I want you to know that you can come to me or talk to me about it."

Ava lowered her gaze to her empty plate. "Okay."

Libby reached inside her purse for a small notepad and a pen and wrote out her cell number. "You can phone me anytime, day or night, understand?"

Ava looked away.

"Now I'm going to ask you something and I don't want this to embarrass you."

Ava continued to stare down at the table.

"Could you be pregnant, Ava?"

The girl's eyes shot up. "No . . ." She stood and tossed her napkin on the plate. "I have to go now."

Libby tried to stop her, but Ava darted away in the opposite direction of the yarn store. She would have raced after her, but Libby had yet to receive the bill for their food. All she could do was watch helplessly as the teenager made her escape.

Chapter 15

"Are you all set for your interview?" Robin asked Libby Wednesday morning on her way out of the gym.

"You're joking, right?" Libby had such a good feeling about this job opportunity. She couldn't be more prepared to meet the deputy district attorney. Not only was her résumé up to date, and her references top-notch, but Libby had had a gut feeling about this almost from the moment Robin had mentioned it.

She might have blown her talk with Ava, but this was familiar ground for

Libby. Her résumé was impressive, even if she said so herself. Robin had made a point of talking her up at the office, too. Nothing would please Libby more than to inform Hershel—if he were ever to want her back—that she already had another job and it was too late. But then, she'd been confident before and gone down in flames. One minute she was riding high and the next she was batting down doubts.

Robin wasn't the only one to offer her advice.

"Morning," Phillip said, meeting up with her in the gym foyer. Clearly he'd been waiting for her.

"Hi." She held on to her gym bag with both hands.

"I wanted to wish you good luck with that interview this afternoon."

"Oh, thanks. I might be overly confident, but I have a good feeling about this one."

"You'll do great. Call me afterward, okay?"

"Sure." They walked out together. Just outside Phillip glanced over his shoulder and when he apparently didn't see anyone, he bent down and gently pressed his lips against hers in a long, slow, lingering kiss.

"For luck?" she asked.

He grinned. "You don't need luck. You're going to wow that deputy district attorney."

His encouragement was better than a weekend's worth of motivational seminars.

All at once, Phillip frowned. "That deputy is a woman, right?"

"As a matter of fact, yes."

His brow relaxed. "Good. If you're going to wow any man I want it to be me."

"I'll take that under consideration."

"Do that, Counselor."

With that he was off and so was she.

Libby arrived at the hospital an hour later. When she reached the nursery Sharon told her Abby Higginbotham from HR had asked to speak to her.

"Should I phone or go down to Abby's office?" Libby asked, wondering if there was something wrong. She'd been approved as a volunteer already and couldn't imagine why the head of HR would want to speak to her.

She'd best find out. Riding the elevator downstairs, Libby realized that she'd found a second home at Seattle General. Over the last few weeks she'd met several physicians and nurses plus other volunteers. Word had gotten around that she was dating Phillip Stone and people seemed to be curious about her and went out of their way to make an introduction.

Human Resources was on the first floor. Libby stepped into the office and spoke to Abby's assistant.

"Abby asked to speak to me. I'm Libby Morgan."

"Oh, hi. If you'll wait here a moment."

"Of course." Libby sat and reached for an outdated magazine while the assistant went into Abby's office.

She emerged a few moments later and said, "Abby will see you now." She held the door open for Libby, who walked into the office. Abby stood up behind her desk and extended a hand. "Sit down, please."

Libby did as requested.

"Can I get you anything to drink?"

"I'm fine, thanks." Libby was more curious than thirsty.

Abby looked uncomfortable. "I asked to speak to you in order to apologize."

"Apologize?" Libby repeated. "Whatever for?"

"I understand that Sharon Jennings gave Dr. Stone your personal information. Phillip can be quite persuasive when he wants to be." The corners of her mouth quirked just slightly with the beginnings of a smile. "According to hospital regulations Sharon should have contacted you first for your approval. I heard about it later and wanted to be sure there isn't a problem . . ."

Libby held up her hand. "No problem whatsoever."

Abby's gaze held Libby's. "You're sure."

"Positive." Libby stood, eager to return to her babies. "Is that all?"

"That's it," Abby assured her.

Abby escorted her to the door, opening it for her. "We have a huge fund-raising dinner coming up soon. I hope you'll be able to attend." She mentioned the date and time.

"I'll look forward to it," Libby told her.

When she arrived back at the nursery, Libby realized she was humming. She enjoyed singing to the babies. While knitting calmed her, she'd discovered that time with these newborns inspired and invigorated her. If anyone had told her as little as eight months ago that she'd be rocking newborns and singing Bob Dylan songs to quiet them she would have laughed them out of her office.

Times, they were a-changing.

When Libby entered the nursery she noticed Sharon looking harried. "Two sets of twins being born," she told Libby. "We've got our hands full."

"Not to worry, I'm here."

"I thank the good Lord for that."

Every nurse on staff was in full gear. The first set, a boy and a girl, arrived in the nursery and the flurry of activity continued as the next set arrived less than an hour later. This time it was two boys, identical twins. All too soon Libby

had four screaming and angry newborns demanding her attention.

"Make that three multiple births,"
Sharon said, stopping only long enough
to take a short break. "This has never
happened in all the years I've worked
at the hospital. Three sets of twins born
the same day."

Libby loved it. The babies filled the
nursery and she was just as busy,
showing off the newborns to proud
grandparents and family members. One
grandmother was so excited she started
to weep, and when her husband hugged
her, Libby saw tears in his eyes, too.
This was pure undiluted joy . . . happiness that could be expressed only
through tears.

Libby found out from Sharon that the
last set of twins had been born six
weeks premature and there were multiple complications. Phillip was called
in and the three-pound girls were sent
to NICU, the neonatal intensive-care
unit.

Once the flurry of activity finally
slowed down, Sharon stepped into the
nursery and nearly collapsed at her

desk. She looked completely exhausted. "Oh, my, I can't remember a morning like this in years."

Libby laughed. "There were some pretty excited family members here as well." She looked up and happened to catch a glimpse of the wall clock. Twelve fifty-five. What? That time couldn't be right. It just couldn't.

"Tell me that clock is fast," Libby begged as she hurriedly untied the back of her hospital gown. Her heart was already in a panic. If she was late for this interview she'd never forgive herself. Robin wasn't likely to forgive her either.

Sharon glanced at her watch. "No, it's right."

"My interview is today at one," Libby cried. She raced out of the nursery and was halfway to the elevator before she realized she'd forgotten her purse. Her head and her heart were in total chaos as she tore back down the hallway and grabbed it. Unwilling to wait for the elevator, she took the stairs, racing down them as fast as her legs would carry her, bouncing from one step to the next with such speed that it jarred her teeth.

Once outside she managed to flag down a cab, only to get caught in a funeral procession that ate up an additional five minutes. It seemed everything that could go wrong had or would. While in the taxi, Libby brushed her hair and freshened up her makeup. She'd intended to change clothes but it was too late for that now. Her hand shook so badly that it was a wonder the lipstick didn't get smeared across her entire face.

Once at the King County Courthouse, she paid the driver and told him to keep the change. Libby was breathless by the time she raced up the multiple sets of stairs that led to the inside of the building.

Getting through security seemed to take a lifetime and then she was forced to wait for the elevator. She was late, so late. Libby couldn't believe this was happening. Robin was going to be furious, but no angrier than Libby was with herself. Babies. She'd gotten so caught up with the newborns that she'd simply lost track of the time.

Once she was on the right floor, Libby raced down the corridor and paused only long enough to take in a deep, calming breath before she opened the door. Her only hope, her one chance, was if no one noticed how late she was.

"Hello," she said, giving the woman at the desk her biggest, most charming smile. "I'm Elizabeth Morgan. I'm here for my interview."

The receptionist looked down at the clipboard in front of her. "Your appointment was at one. I'm afraid you'll need to wait, as another applicant is with Ms. Rabe at the moment."

Libby groaned inwardly and glanced at the wall clock. She was fifteen minutes late. "I apologize for being late."

"Take a seat, Ms. Morgan, and I'll call you when Ms. Rabe is free." The receptionist disappeared.

Despite the receptionist's instructions, Libby remained standing at the desk, too nervous to sit down. She turned expectantly when the other woman returned a few minutes later.

"Ms. Rabe will see you now." She led Libby down a hallway and into an interview room.

The deputy district attorney stood with her back to Libby when she entered the room.

"Thank you so much for seeing me," she said, doing her best to sound calm and professional, although her heart rate felt like it was racing at double time.

"You're not exactly starting off on the right foot, are you?"

"No, and I apologize. The fault is entirely mine." Libby was willing to accept responsibility; she had no one to blame but herself. She couldn't even attribute the multiple births to a full moon. One thing was crystal clear: Ms. Rabe didn't want to hear excuses.

Unfortunately, the interview didn't go well. Libby wasn't able to regain the ground she'd lost by showing up late. She did her best to impress the deputy DA but it was clear that she'd blown it from the moment she walked into the room. She had as much chance of getting this job as a donkey did of winning the Kentucky Derby.

With her head filled with self-recrimination, Libby left the building. Her cell phone rang a few minutes later. When Libby glanced at caller ID she groaned.

Robin Hamlin.

"Hello." She was tempted not to answer, but she might as well get this over with now and be done with it.

"So," Robin asked, her voice bright and excited, "how'd the interview go?"

"Not so good."

Robin sucked in a deep breath, or that was what it sounded like to Libby.

"Why not?" her friend demanded. "You're a perfect fit. I talked you up and so did Roy—"

"I was a little late."

"You?" Robin cried. "You're never late. What happened?"

"I was at the hospital."

"The emergency room? Are you okay?" Her voice softened considerably.

For just an instant Libby was tempted to make up a wild story that would excuse her and at the same time garner

Robin's sympathy. If she were a better liar she might have attempted it. Anything not to have to listen to Robin's irritation . . . not that she blamed her.

"I was with the babies and they had three sets of twins born this morning. Time got away from me and—"

"Hold on," Robin said, cutting in. "Are you telling me that you were late for the interview because"—she paused as if she found it so unbelievable that she couldn't even say the words—"because you were rocking babies?"

No way to deny it. "Yes."

A shocked silence followed and then just as Libby was about to speak, Robin said, "I don't know you anymore, Libby. I don't know what happened to the woman I once knew, but that person isn't you. Listen, I have to go, and frankly it's a good thing." Having said that, the line was disconnected.

Libby stared down at her cell phone and wanted to crawl into the nearest gutter and disappear. Not only had she let her friend down, she was deeply disappointed in herself.

Libby decided to walk home. It was well over a mile, but the physical exertion was bound to help. If ever she needed endorphins it was now. Unfortunately, the only thing the walk did was give her a blister on the heel of her left foot.

Limping into her condo she headed for the kitchen and poured herself a glass of iced tea. She called Phillip, and when he didn't answer, she left a message on his voice mail.

"I . . . I didn't get the job. I lost track of the time and arrived late for the interview. Robin is furious with me but no more so than I am with myself."

The day she'd run into Joe had been traumatic, but losing the opportunity of this job was almost as harrowing. Her once orderly life felt unfamiliar and completely out of control.

She wanted to cry and shout at the walls. Stamping her feet was out of the question with that blister. Her throat felt parched and her head throbbed. Her friends were few and she feared she was about to lose one she really needed.

Her knitting sat on the coffee table

but Libby was too agitated even for that.

What she needed, what she wanted, Libby realized, was . . . her mother.

Chapter 16

Robin paced the confines of her compact office with such determination that she nearly walked straight into the wall. In all her years as a prosecutor she'd never asked for favors from anyone, but she had gone out on a limb in order to help Libby. And now her friend had squandered the opportunity.

Libby had lost track of the time because she was rocking babies? Unbelievable. She'd noticed the subtle changes in her friend over the last several months. It was as though Libby's priorities had gone askew, as if she had lost sight of what was important. Although they hadn't spoken of it, Robin feared Libby's finances weren't in the best shape. Now this. Nothing added up.

Then there was Libby's budding relationship with Dr. Stone. Perhaps the root cause for these subtle changes had nothing to do with the hospital, after all. Perhaps this was what romance did to a person. Romance . . . oh, the two of them were such dorks when it came to men. Libby's prospects were certainly looking up, while her own were stalled. With her arms folded around her middle, Robin looked for a way to vent her frustration.

Roy had been wonderfully helpful in connecting Libby with his contact, but she hadn't heard from him since and wasn't sure what her next move should be, especially given what had just happened.

Because she was due in court in a few minutes, Robin did her best to concentrate on the case before her. It should be a slam dunk but she needed to stay focused and let go of her irritation with herself and with Libby. Otherwise, she might easily make a mistake, and in her job, a mistake could mean a defendant got off scot-free.

On her way to the courtroom, she passed Judge Bollinger. His face lit up in a smile when they walked by each other in the hallway. He appeared to be leaving for the day. She longed for an excuse to speak to him, but she couldn't think of a solitary thing to say. Thankfully, he didn't stop to ask how the job interview had gone for Libby. Robin wouldn't have known what to tell him. The fact was, she didn't know how to let Roy know she was interested in him, and she feared any attempt would only embarrass them both.

It didn't help that every time he was close she grew so tongue-tied she could barely speak. Put her in a courtroom and she was never at a loss for words, but with Roy, she felt like a schoolgirl all over again.

Like Libby, Robin had dedicated her entire life to the law, so much so that she had little experience with men. Over the years there had been an affair or

two, one in college and another following her divorce. But both had ended
badly and left her determined not to repeat her mistakes. With Roy it was different. She'd admired him from afar for
a long time, fearful of making a move.

Robin had joined the gym, hoping to
lose a few pounds and make herself as
attractive as possible. She thanked
Libby for that. Without her fellow attorney spurring her on, Robin would have
dropped out long ago. When they first
started exercising together they'd been
casual friends. Gradually Robin had
grown closer to Libby, but not so much
that she felt comfortable sharing her
feelings about the judge. Still, she could
tell Libby had guessed there was a man
behind Robin's interest in losing weight.

Over the last two months, Robin had
come to think of Libby as a close friend.
Friend enough that she'd been willing
to help Libby find employment. It'd
been grossly unfair for Libby to be laid
off in the first place. Despite the generous severance package, being unemployed had been hard on Libby in a
number of different ways. Her ego had

been badly bruised—and after so many months without work, her confidence was wounded, too.

Robin had sympathized and wanted to help. She saw much of herself in Libby. Both were hardworking, determined, goal-oriented, and focused. Robin couldn't imagine what she'd do if she were to lose her job. No doubt, like Libby, she'd assume she'd find another one without a problem. But would she?

Back in her office after the hearing, Robin sat down at her desk and braced her head in her hands. Embarrassing as it was, she felt she needed to connect with Alice Rabe and apologize for bringing Libby to her attention. She'd given Libby a glowing personal recommendation and apparently Roy had as well. By showing up late, Libby had made not only herself look irresponsible, but Robin, too.

Reluctantly she reached for her phone and was connected with the deputy district attorney in short order.

"I take it the interview with Elizabeth Morgan didn't go well."

Alice snorted.

So it'd been that bad.

"That's putting it mildly. Your *friend*," Alice said with heavy emphasis placed on the word *friend*, "arrived in jeans."

Robin squeezed her eyes closed. Could this get any worse? "Although this isn't an excuse, I believe she was at the hospital."

"I didn't give her a chance to explain. To her credit she did apologize."

Alice could be brusque, but Robin knew her to be fair.

"Not only did she arrive almost fifteen minutes late but she seemed completely unprepared for the interview, flustered, unfocused, and overly nervous."

"Let me assure you that Libby isn't normally like that."

"So you've talked to her?"

"I have," Robin admitted.

Alice hesitated. "You said she was at the hospital?"

Robin regretted mentioning it. "It wasn't an emergency . . . she volunteers there."

"Oh?" This appeared to interest the deputy district attorney.

Robin squared her shoulders as she realized she might as well say it. "Libby is generous and caring."

"What does she do at the hospital?"

Robin tucked her arm around her middle. "She rocks the newborns."

"That was why she was late?"

"Apparently they got terribly busy this morning." Talk about weak excuses.

"So she didn't have time to change her clothes?"

"Apparently not." She wanted to ask Alice how Libby's résumé read. Robin had gone over it herself, helped Libby fine-tune it, hoping a fresh pair of eyes would help.

"It goes without saying that I won't be hiring your friend."

"I understand," Robin murmured, and then because she felt obligated, she added, "I wanted to call and apologize. I feel terrible that this happened."

"It isn't your fault," Alice was kind enough to say. "Anyway, I appreciate the call," she continued, "but I believe I've already made my choice."

"I understand perfectly." Robin disconnected the line and then exhaled deeply.

A couple of days later Robin planned to work late, like she did most nights. It was Friday and she didn't have a single plan. That said a lot about her life—her job was her life. Seeing what had happened to Libby made Robin decide she was in no frame of mind to remain at the office. Grabbing her briefcase, she headed out of the courthouse. Her pace was hurried, although she didn't have anyplace special to go or anyone to meet.

She was heading toward the parking lot when she heard someone call her name. When she turned to see who it might be, she saw Roy . . . Judge Bollinger. Instantly she felt her pulse accelerate. Her mouth went dry.

"Robin, my goodness, you move like a speed walker." He was breathless and his round face appeared flushed.

"Sorry, I didn't realize you were behind me." If she had she would have slowed to a snail's pace. They hadn't spoken in several days and she'd despaired that they ever would again.

"I understand the interviews were held the other day for the position I mentioned. How did your friend do?"

Robin immediately looked down. "Not well, I'm afraid." When she glanced up again she found that his eyes had warmed with sympathy.

"I'm sorry to hear that."

"I am, too." Thankfully he didn't know the details, and she wasn't about to tell him.

"I know you've probably got plans this evening—"

"I don't," she blurted out, interrupting him.

He smiled briefly. "Would you care to join me? I generally have a glass of wine on Friday evenings. My wife and I . . ." He hesitated at the mention of his wife.

"I'd enjoy that very much." The dear man had no idea how she'd been hoping for such an invitation.

"There's a nice bar in the Four Seasons," he suggested. "Shall I meet you there?"

"Sure." He could have suggested they rendezvous on the moon and she would have found a way to get there.

"Shall we say," he paused and glanced at his watch. "Thirty minutes?"

"Perfect."

He turned away then, and Robin waited until he was out of sight before she broke into a dance, thrusting her arms into the air and turning around in a complete circle.

Chapter 17

Saturday morning, with bright sunshine streaming into her bedroom window, Libby glanced at the digital readout of the clock next to her bed and groaned. Her eyes stung from lack of sleep. Tossing aside the blankets, she crawled out of bed and brewed herself a cup of strong coffee.

Phillip had called three times. She hadn't answered her phone or listened to the messages. He was a great guy and she enjoyed his company, but he was a distraction. After her last disastrous job interview, Libby had decided she needed to focus.

The interview with Alice Rabe kept playing through her mind. It showed like an old-time silent movie, the frames flickering before her. No way around it, she'd blown her best chance at getting a job. After waiting for months for an opportunity like this she'd sabotaged herself. Libby no longer knew who she was. The determined, dedicated attorney or the volunteer who loved babies but couldn't make it to an interview on time. Libby wondered what her mother would think of her now.

And she could only imagine the damage she'd done to her relationship with Robin.

After standing under a cold shower for several minutes, she was awake enough to face the day. With errands to run, she left her condo at eight, determined to finish as quickly as possible and be back before noon. She needed to talk to Phillip, and explain, difficult as it was sure to be, that she couldn't be involved with him.

At ten she stopped by the yarn store.

Libby hoped Lydia would be able to update her on what had happened since she'd taken Ava to lunch. She hadn't managed to get through to the young teen, but perhaps Lydia had succeeded where she had failed. The more Libby thought about Ava, the stronger the urge was to take the girl under her wing and help her. She was so young and vulnerable. Libby couldn't help worrying about what would become of her. Apparently her grandmother was completely oblivious.

Both Lydia and Casey were at the yarn store when Libby arrived. She hadn't brought her knitting because she feared that, too, had become a distraction from her job search.

"Hi, Libby," Casey called out, exuberantly waving her arm from the back of the shop.

Already the shop was crowded with customers, and both Lydia and her sister, Margaret, were preoccupied. Libby walked to the back of the room to join Casey.

"You're certainly in a good mood,"

Libby said when Casey beamed her a huge smile.

The teenager patted the chair next to her, welcoming Libby's company.

"Mom's taking me school shopping tomorrow. I'm using the money I earned helping in the shop."

Libby sat down next to her. "Have you seen Ava lately?"

Casey nodded. "Yeah, she was here yesterday."

"Did she say anything?"

Casey set aside her crochet project. "About the talk you had with her?"

Libby nodded.

"Not really. How'd it go?" Casey leaned forward, eagerly anticipating the details, it seemed.

"We did talk a little, but unfortunately not much."

"When I asked her about it all she said was that she enjoyed lunch."

That was only somewhat encouraging.

"Did she mention when she'd be visiting the shop again?" Libby could casually drop by at the same time. If she continued to develop the relationship, she might be able to convince Ava to make a doctor's appointment. She could accompany the young teen and pay for the visit. If Ava was willing, Libby would even offer to go with her when she told her grandmother about the pregnancy. The point was, Ava couldn't ignore the obvious for much longer. Decisions had to be made, and Libby wanted to be Ava's advocate, wanted to help her deal with the complexities of her situation. Besides, someone needed to find out if Ava continued to be sexually active and warn her that there could be other consequences.

The bell chimed as someone either left or entered the shop. Libby didn't pay much attention until Casey said, "Libby, isn't that your doctor friend?"

Libby whirled around. Sure enough, Phillip was inside A Good Yarn, looking about as uncomfortable as a man in a shop full of women could get. His gaze shot straight to her. His eyes narrowed as he made his way to the back of the store.

Even if it meant winning the Washington State lottery, Libby couldn't have spoken a word. Her mouth was as dry as a sand dune. She wanted to know what he was doing here. It soon became obvious he'd come looking for her. She groaned inwardly; she wasn't quite ready to face him.

"Did you turn your cell phone off?" he asked, pulling out a chair and sitting down.

"Ah, I might have." She knew darn well that she had. Fishing inside her purse, she made a show of looking and then dropping it back inside.

"I left you several messages," Phillip told her.

"I . . . I wasn't in the mood to talk." Maybe he'd take the hint that she wasn't ready now, either.

"I tried phoning this morning," he said, and then noticed Casey. "Hello again," he added, apparently remembering her from their elevator ride together.

Casey was all smiles. "Libby, you're worse than my grandma. She has a cell phone, too, but she always forgets to turn it on."

"Where's your friend?" Phillip asked Casey.

He was concerned about Ava, too.

"I asked her to come this morning, but she said her grandmother wouldn't let her. She has to clean the house."

What was it about a handsome man that prompted women to divulge information? Libby had asked about Ava, too, and Casey hadn't said a word about her grandmother keeping her home for chores.

Phillip looked back to Libby. "Have you had lunch?"

Other than her early-morning coffee and a glass of orange juice, Libby hadn't eaten solid food all day. She wasn't the least bit hungry, but they needed to talk and the sooner she got this over with the better. "Not yet."

"Good."

"Have lunch at The French Cafe," Casey urged. "The food's fabulous, especially the croissants and the soup. Mom orders the soup almost every day."

"Sounds good to me," Phillip said.

As if connected to a puppet's string,

Libby automatically stood and followed him out of the store, pausing only long enough to say good-bye to Lydia and Margaret.

"Have you tried The French Cafe before?" he asked conversationally, placing his hand on the small of Libby's back as they crossed the street.

"A time or two. Casey's right, the food's great."

"Then let's go there. It's close and convenient and I'm famished."

Once inside the cafe, Phillip ordered a club sandwich, a small side salad, and two large peanut butter cookies. Libby ordered a cup of the ginger-carrot soup.

"That's all?" he asked when she completed her order.

"I . . . I don't have much of an appetite."

He paid for their food and then they carried their number to one of the empty tables outside the restaurant, where they could eat alfresco.

Until they sat down at an umbrella-covered table, Libby hadn't noticed what a glorious day it was. Late July in the Pacific Northwest generally had nice weather. A breeze blew off Elliot Bay, and even though they were several blocks from the waterfront, Libby smelled a hint of salt in the air. The waterfront would be crowded with tourists. Two or three large cruise ships were in port, adding to the bustling activity. A plane flew above them with a banner that advertised a life insurance company.

"I apologize for not answering your calls, but like I said, I wasn't in the mood to talk," she said, keeping her hands in her lap. She avoided eye contact, too.

Phillip reached for his iced tea and took a deep swallow. Completely relaxed, he leaned against the back of the chair and crossed his long legs. "I wanted to hear about the interview."

"I was late . . . and frankly, it couldn't have gone much worse. Now Robin is avoiding me . . . although I doubt that she's tried to call." Curious, she reached for her cell and scrolled down the list of recent calls. Robin's name didn't appear, but that didn't surprise Libby.

"She's upset with me, but then I can't really blame her."

"So what happened?"

"The twins . . ." She stopped and shook her head. Really, what was the point of trying to explain? Bottom line: she'd gotten sidetracked. Even now Libby couldn't believe she'd allowed that to happen.

"I know all about the three sets of twins," Phillip said. "I want to know what happened at the interview."

Just thinking about it made her chest tighten.

"That bad?"

"Worse. Time got away from me and I didn't have any choice but to show up in what I was wearing. After arriving late, I never got my balance back. I was flustered and inarticulate. It was dreadful." Even telling him embarrassed her tenfold.

To his credit, he did look sympathetic. "It might be little comfort to you now, but thank you for your help in the nursery. It was like a madhouse. Three sets of twins. Frankly, I don't know what we would have done without you."

Libby managed a weak smile. His appreciation did little to console her. "It should never have happened. This interview was important; this is my livelihood. I don't know what's happened to me over these last few months. I hardly know who I am any longer. I missed an important interview because I was rocking babies? That's insane. I'm spending half my time in a yarn store, knitting? In the meantime I'm going through my savings at an alarming rate. I need a job."

"You'll find one." How confident he sounded.

"Not at this rate I won't. I've allowed far too many distractions into my life." She bounced the side of her hand against the tabletop. "That's got to end. I have to focus on what's important and get back on track."

"Libby, you're being too hard on yourself." He leaned forward and gently squeezed her upper arm. "It isn't as bad as all that. It was just one interview."

She pulled back. Phillip might think he was helping, but he wasn't. He didn't

know her well enough to realize this irresponsible behavior wasn't normal for
her. Nor did he appreciate how angry
she was with herself.

Their lunch arrived and Phillip immediately reached for his sandwich. It was
cut into fourths, each secured with a
fancy toothpick with a frilly, colorful cel-
lophane top. Elegant for a cafe, Libby
mused.

She tasted her soup and it was deli-
cious. Well, at least her taste buds
hadn't gotten depressed along with everything else. Libby had about as much
zip as a slug. Her head throbbed, and
she longed to curl into a tight ball and
sleep. What she would give to put all of
this behind her and simply sleep.

Phillip had eaten half of his sandwich
before he paused. "I didn't get dinner
last night and was starving." He looked
down at his plate and then at Libby's.
"All right, why the glum face now? I get
that you messed up, but you need to
pick yourself up and move on. Right?"

If she'd had more sleep and her wits
about her she might have been able to

sidestep the question. Frankly she didn't have the energy.

"I don't have a lot of friends, and after the stunt I pulled with the botched interview I'm afraid I've lost a good one."

"Stop beating yourself up."

"Don't you understand?" she cried, losing patience with him. "This was exactly the wake-up call I needed."

"What do you mean?" Frowning, he pushed the empty plate aside.

She exhaled and decided the best way to deal with him was to be straightforward. He was the type of man who appreciated the truth.

"I think it might be best if we don't see each other for a while."

He stared back at her blankly, as if he hadn't heard a word she'd said.

"Is that what you want, Libby?" he asked after several moments.

She didn't know anymore so she avoided the question. "I'm not the woman I used to be and the woman I'm becoming is frightening me."

"What's that got to do with you and me?"

"Everything. Don't you see? I can't be seeing you . . . A relationship is a distraction I can't deal with right now. I've got to find work. I love being an attorney and I'm good at it. Getting back to work has got to be my focus."

He stared at her long and hard. "If you're having trouble finding work, why not set up your own practice? Why does it have to be with a big firm?"

Libby started to argue and quickly closed her mouth. All these months and not once had she considered opening her own practice. Actually, that was an excellent idea, and worthy of consideration. Still, it didn't change matters between Phillip and her.

"You're a very nice person . . ."

"But you aren't interested," he finished for her. "No problem, I get the message. In other words, thanks but no thanks."

That wasn't it at all, but she didn't want to argue with him.

"It's not you, it's me, right?" He grinned but his face lacked any hint of amusement. "Not the most original line, but it works." He scooted back his chair and stood. "Best of luck to you, Libby. I enjoyed being with you, but I think you're probably smart to end it now before either of us invests any more time in this relationship."

She started to say something, but he walked away. Libby longed to call him back but swallowed the words. He was right: it was best to end this now. That didn't explain why she longed to race after him and tell him she'd made a mistake. For a long time she sat, staring into space, and wondered what she'd just done. Already her heart was telling her that she would regret it.

Unsure how much time had passed, Libby reached for her purse in order to leave, then paused, thinking about Phillip's suggestion. All morning she'd been telling herself she needed to focus, and there was no time like the present. Reaching for the small notepad inside her purse, she quickly compiled a list of what she would need.

Such a venture would be expensive. It wasn't like she was rolling in cash.

When she was first laid off she had had a hefty savings account, mainly because she spent all of her time at the office. Only rarely did she take the opportunity to shop, and when she did, it was mostly online.

Her severance package had carried her for a while, but now she was digging into her savings, which were going fast. Soon she'd be forced to sell some of her investment stocks, and with the market so low she would suffer a loss.

If she set up her own shop, the first person she would hire would be Sarah, her paralegal. She'd need someone organized and efficient, and Sarah was certainly that. The two of them made a great team. Maybe it was possible. Certainly it was worth considering.

Her mother used to say that everything happened for a reason. Maybe she was meant to be late for that interview. As soon as she was home, she'd contact Robin and bounce the idea off her.

Libby's shoulders slumped forward. She debated whether to contact her friend or wait. She decided to wait. If she didn't hear from Robin by Monday morning, then Libby would have her answer as to how pissed off her friend actually was.

Chapter 18

"Stop eating so much. You're getting fat."

"Yes, Grandma." Ava hung her head, not wanting to look her grandmother in the face.

"Did you do the list of chores I left you?"

Keeping her eyes downcast, Ava nodded. Her grandmother had been in a bad mood all day. She left the table and took the dirty dishes with her. Jackson carried his own plate to the sink and sent her a sympathetic look. Their grandmother wasn't normally home on

Sunday afternoons. She was usually with her friends at the VFW club or the local tavern. Most of the time she left mid-afternoon and didn't return until just before dinnertime. Ava wished her grandmother was still with her friends instead of being out of sorts and snapping at her and Jackson.

That morning Jackson had gone to church with Peter from next door. Jackson said it would be all right if she wanted to go, too, but Ava didn't feel well. She didn't most days. She'd known something was wrong nearly all summer, but until her lunch with Libby she hadn't known what it was.

There was a baby inside of her.

A baby. Ava didn't know what she was going to do. If her grandmother found out, she'd be a whole lot more than cranky. According to their grandmother, Ava's mother had been a problem child. She wanted to be sure that Jackson and Ava were good students and grew up to be decent individuals. Ava didn't know what was required to be a decent individual, but she had a fairly good idea that it didn't mean having a baby when she was only thirteen.

While Ava washed the dishes, her grandmother lit a cigarette and sat in front of the television set and watched a Mariners baseball game. Ava wiped down the countertop and put the leftover food away.

Jackson was outside playing basketball with Peter, who had a hoop in his driveway. She watched them through the kitchen window for a while and when she finished cleaning up she went into her bedroom. It was quiet there. She didn't really care about watching the Mariners.

Ava needed to think. She didn't know what she was going to do about the baby. Her grandma thought she was eating too much. Ava had seen pregnant women, and some of them got really big up front. She didn't know what would happen if the baby grew that big inside of her.

Lifting the edge of her mattress, Ava reached for the piece of paper Libby Morgan had given her with her phone number written on it. She pulled out the folded slip and stared at it for several minutes. Libby had told Ava she could phone her anytime. Maybe Libby would know what to do. Maybe she could help her.

Her grandmother's voice echoed down the hallway. "Stupid Mariners."

The local team was losing and her grandmother's mood would turn even worse if they did. Ava decided it would be best to stay in her bedroom. Sitting on top of her bed, she raised her knees and buried her face there. The baby in her stomach was probably the reason her ankles had been swollen most of the summer.

"I'm going out for a while," her grandmother called.

Ava relaxed. If her grandmother went to the VFW, then she wouldn't be upset about the Mariners. She'd probably be gone until it was dark or even later.

About ten seconds later the front door closed.

Ava waited a few minutes more and then crept into the kitchen where the phone was. It was an old-fashioned one that was attached to the wall. After looking at Libby's phone number for so long she'd memorized it, she returned the sheet to its original hiding place.

It took her several minutes to gather up the courage to phone Libby. Finally she punched in the phone number, closed her eyes, and waited.

"Hello."

Just the sound of Libby's voice panicked her and Ava slammed down the receiver. Her grandmother had something on her phone that canceled their phone number on caller ID, so Ava didn't need to worry that Libby would try calling her back.

Her heart raced and she broke out in a cold sweat. Ava really did feel sick to her stomach. Her grandma said she was getting lazy and Jackson said she wasn't any fun because all she did was stay in her room. He would, too, if he felt the way she did.

She knew pregnant women went to see a doctor, but Ava didn't have the money for a doctor's visit. Even if she did, there was always the chance her grandmother would find out. She couldn't risk her grandmother learning about the baby inside of her.

Having a baby was dangerous. She might even die. She pressed her hand over her stomach and bit into her lip. Another thirty minutes passed before she found the courage to dial Libby's phone number a second time.

"Hello."

Ava didn't speak. She couldn't. Her throat had closed up on her and when she tried to talk nothing came out but a squeaking noise that sounded like a baby bird or something else small and helpless.

After a moment Ava replaced the receiver. She liked Libby. Libby had taken her to a sit-down restaurant. It had been Ava's first time ever in a restaurant where you didn't order off a menu on the wall and the waitress came right to the table. Only she hadn't told Libby that.

Returning to her bedroom, Ava laid down on the top of her bed, with her arms wrapped around her stomach. She wanted to close her eyes, but if she went to sleep now she'd wake up in the middle of the night and she hated that. It was at nighttime that she missed her mother the most.

Ava's mother had been a lot like her grandmother, only younger. What Ava really missed was the apartment where they'd lived before the car accident. She'd had friends and neighbors she knew and trusted. Since moving in with her grandmother, Ava had begun attending a new school. The only friend she had was Casey.

After a while Ava got up and went outside. She sat on the porch and watched her brother and Peter shoot baskets. Both boys ignored her. Peter's mother came out with a plate of cookies. Peter was an only child and Jackson said he was spoiled. Her brother was jealous. Ava didn't blame him. For once in their lives they would like for someone to spoil them. No one had ever baked cookies for her and Jackson.

"You okay?" Jackson asked, wandering over to her.

She shrugged. "Yeah."

Peter's mother walked across the

yard to Ava. "Would you like a cookie, Ava?" she asked.

"She can't," Jackson answered for her. "Grandma says she's getting fat."

"You're not fat," Mrs. Armstrong insisted. "One cookie isn't going to hurt you."

"Okay." Ava reached for the cookie and held it. She didn't eat it right away, but she would later. She would take tiny bites and savor each one.

Mrs. Armstrong returned to the house and the boys went back to playing basketball. Peter was on the junior high team and Jackson wanted to be, too. Tryouts weren't for a long time yet, so he had plenty of time to practice.

After a few minutes Ava went inside the house again. She stared at the phone on the wall and couldn't decide if she should talk to Libby or not. Instead she got out her knitting and sat down with it in front of the television.

Grandma couldn't afford cable so all they could get were the local channels. The reception wasn't good, but they watched it because it was all they had.

Nothing good was on anyway so Ava concentrated on her knitting.

She wondered if Casey would still be her friend if she found out about the baby. When school started everyone would think she'd gotten really fat over the summer. She hoped no one would guess she was pregnant.

On second thought, maybe she wouldn't go to school. Maybe she'd wait until her grandmother left for work and then come back to the house. She'd rather do that than have the kids tease her about being fat.

After knitting several rows, Ava set the knitting aside. Before her courage left her, she reached for the phone again and dialed the number Libby had given her.

Instead of saying hello this time, Libby said, "Ava, is that you?"

Her eyes widened. Libby knew it was her phoning.

"Please don't hang up," Libby pleaded.

"Okay," she managed to whisper.

"Are you all right?"

"Yes." She felt crummy, but she always did, so it wasn't different from any other day.

"Good." Libby sounded relieved.

"I'll be at the yarn store on Tuesday," Ava told her.

"So will I," Libby promised.

That was all the reassurance Ava needed. Libby would help her. She could trust Libby, Ava was sure of that. Libby would know what she should do.

Chapter 19

Libby was already on the treadmill when she saw Robin enter the gym. Her friend was fifteen minutes later than usual. Libby suspected she'd purposely arrived late to avoid chatting with Libby in the locker room. Still, Libby was encouraged. At least Robin had shown up. That was a good sign. The treadmill next to her was empty and she hoped Robin would claim it.

Ten minutes after she arrived, Robin stepped out of the locker room in her workout gear. She glanced briefly in Libby's direction and when she caught

Libby eyeing her, she quickly looked away.

So that was the way it was to be.

Robin stepped onto the treadmill next to Libby and started her regular routine. She pretended not to notice Libby, but that was to be expected.

Libby glanced at Robin and after carefully weighing how best to handle this, she decided to test the waters. "Morning."

Robin muttered some unintelligible reply. Then, as if she'd forgotten them, she inserted her earbuds into her ears and turned on her iPod, tuning Libby out completely.

Libby had an iPod, too. She hadn't brought it to the gym because she generally chatted with Robin while working out. If Robin had decided to ignore her completely, then perhaps Libby would bring her iPod in the future. Recognizing that there wasn't anything more she could do, she returned her concentration to her workout, increasing the treadmill speed in order to work out her frustration.

Libby tried not to think about Phillip,

but despite all her efforts he continued to pop into her mind at the most inconvenient times. She missed his small encouragements, the chats they'd shared while on his sailboat. And she missed having his arms around her and their kisses. Every time she thought about Phillip, and that was nearly constantly, her heart ached. He'd inspired her, and had been her devoted cheerleader before the interview. He'd been good to her and for her. In her frustration and anger she'd done the one thing that she knew would hurt her most, and broken off their relationship.

And yet Phillip had been the one to give her the idea of her own office. When she opened her door for business, Libby decided, she would hold a small open house and invite him.

No, that probably wouldn't work. If she knew anything about Phillip, it was the fact that he had his pride. Even if she did invite him he wouldn't come.

Besides, she needed to concentrate, needed to work out a business plan. The one person she wanted to talk to more than ever was Robin.

They'd never had a falling out before. Sure, over the years they'd drifted apart, but Libby remembered how they had helped each other as study partners while they were in law school. They'd gotten close again and she'd hate to lose that. She just didn't know how many times she could say she was sorry.

High on newfound energy, Libby almost wasn't ready for the treadmill to slow to a more sedate pace. She was raring to continue, to conquer new goals, to venture into territory she'd never thought to explore.

To Libby's surprise, Robin removed her earbuds.

"I'm still upset with you," she said, looking straight ahead.

"Are you speaking to me?" Libby asked.

"I shouldn't."

"But I hope you do. I miss you."

Robin muttered again so low Libby couldn't make out what she was saying.

"I *am* sorry," Libby said. If nothing else, she wanted her friend to understand how deeply she regretted disappointing her.

"Of course you're sorry . . . You should be." Robin deliberately slowed the pace of her treadmill to match Libby's.

"I realize how much you put yourself out for me and I don't want you to think I don't appreciate it."

Robin glanced at her and snickered. "Some appreciation."

"You're the best friend I have."

More muttering. "You're my best friend, too, and that's what makes it so hard to stay mad at you."

Libby looked away in order to hide a smile. She continued walking, going past the time allotted by the treadmill program. She was definitely earning exercise brownie points.

"Is there anything I can do to make this up to you?" she asked.

"I don't know." Robin continued walking, speeding up her pace. "Let me think on that."

"I'll buy you breakfast," Libby suggested. "I'll get two buttery croissants

at The French Cafe and personally deliver them to the courthouse."

Robin hesitated, clearly tempted.
"Too fattening."

"Oh, right. I forgot we're both trying
to lose weight." She thought to mention that she was down another two
pounds, but if Robin hadn't lost that
much it would be like rubbing salt in an
open wound.

"How about a fruit smoothie?" Libby
offered.

"That's a possibility."

The woman on the treadmill on the
other side of Libby shook her head as
though disgusted with the two of them.
"What's with you two?" she demanded.
"You sound like you're in third grade.
Whatever it is, get over it."

Libby was too stunned to speak.

Not so with Robin. "Mind your own
business."

"Gladly, only I can't help overhearing
the two of you, and you sound like
you're both eight years old. Good grief,
grow up."

"Don't talk to my friend like that,"
Libby snapped. The woman could say

what she wanted about her, but Robin was off-limits.

Hearing the exchange, a trainer came over to their section of the gym. "Is there a problem here, ladies?"

"Not at all," Libby said, and glared at the other woman.

Libby finished her time on the treadmill and headed toward the dressing room. Robin followed her. The instant they were in the locker room, Libby burst out laughing.

"What's so funny?" Robin demanded.

"Us," Libby said, shaking her head. "We were ready to come to blows defending each other to that woman."

"She was rude and obnoxious to you. I'm not putting up with that."

"But you're angry with me, remember?"

"I was . . . I am," Robin admitted as though she'd forgotten. "But you're still my friend."

"Oh, thank you, thank you." Libby resisted the urge to throw her arms around Robin and hug her. "Can you find a way to forgive me?" she pleaded. "You're my best friend in the world and it would crush me to lose you."

Robin appeared to be considering her request while walking back to her locker. Deep in thought, she twisted the dial on her lock. It took her three tries to get it to open. When she finally did, she sighed expressively and said, "You ever pull a stunt like that again and I swear, Elizabeth Morgan, I will personally hunt you down and beat the snot out of you."

"I won't, I promise."

Robin shook her head as though disgusted. "Rocking babies?"

"I know, it sounds crazy, but the hospital had three sets of twins born within a four-hour period. It even made the evening news."

"It's nuts. You're nuts."

"You ought to try volunteering in the nursery sometime," Libby suggested.

"Not me," Robin insisted. "I'm not the type."

"Did you ever think I would be the type?"

Robin grabbed her towel and headed

toward the shower. "Can't say that I did."

"Me neither, yet it's the most peaceful, wonderful thing to sit with those newborns and sing them Bob Dylan songs."

"Bob Dylan?"

"And the Righteous Brothers and the Bee Gees and—"

"Poor things. They haven't even left the hospital and already you're twisting their young minds."

Libby laughed and followed her friend into the shower room. "I'll probably give it up soon. If nothing else, what happened with the interview showed me how far I've slipped lately. I need to get back on track."

It wasn't until they were dressed and ready for their day that Libby mentioned opening her own office. She hesitated and waited for her friend's reaction. She could trust Robin to be straight with her. If this was a foolish idea, she wouldn't hesitate to tell her so.

Robin seemed to take a long time mulling it over.

"Well? What do you think?" Libby

hated to be so obviously anxious, but she valued her friend's opinion.

Slowly Robin nodded. "If anyone could make a go of it, it would be you."

"Thank you," she whispered, embarrassed by how badly she needed encouragement and approval.

"Are you sure you can get Sarah?"

"Positive. She says the morale of the entire law office is in the gutter. Everyone is afraid of being the next one cut. The workload has doubled and the staff is expected to keep up this killing pace without a pay raise. Sarah told me they're all supposed to just be grateful they have jobs."

Robin frowned. "It's the same with the city. It's been a nightmare with budget cuts. You won't believe what they did last week," Robin said, and exhaled. "They called it amnesty day."

"Amnesty day?" Libby repeated, perplexed.

"Yup. If you return office supplies within a twenty-four-hour period . . . rubber bands, pencils, paper clips, the things that somehow inadvertently got taken home, then the city won't prosecute."

"You've got to be joking," Libby said, and shook her head, aghast. If it weren't so ridiculous, she would cry.

"I wish I was. Now, let's get back to you setting up your own practice."

"Okay." Libby was open to any advice her friend was willing to give her.

"Where will your office be?"

"I'm not sure . . . I'll think about that later."

"You don't want to work out of your condo," Robin said. "There are probably restrictions on setting up any kind of business that uses your condo as an office. Plus you'll want to get away at the end of the day and 'go home.'"

Libby had already thought of that. "I'll need to find a space to rent."

"It won't be cheap and you'll be required to sign a lease."

Libby had taken that into consideration as well.

"That's the bad news, but there's good news, too. There are complexes that come with a receptionist and all the necessary equipment, copy machine, fax, that sort of thing."

"But I have Sarah."

"You think you have Sarah," Robin reminded her.

"I have her," Libby insisted. Whenever they talked, Sarah spent half the time complaining about all the changes at the firm and relaying the latest gossip. The rest of the time was spent telling Libby how much she had come to hate her job now that she'd been assigned to work with Ben Holmes.

"Call Sarah before you contact a realtor," Robin advised. Dressed for work, she headed out of the locker room.

Libby stopped her and shocked them both by briefly hugging Robin.

"What was that for?" Robin asked, clearly taken aback.

"Because you're my friend and I'm so grateful."

Robin straightened her jacket front and adjusted her sleeves. "Well, get over it."

Libby smiled. She hurried back to her condo and settled down on the sofa before she reached for her cell.

She knew the direct number to Sarah's desk and was able to sidestep the receptionist entirely.

"Sarah," Libby said anxiously when her friend picked up. "Happy Monday morning."

"I've got news," Sarah said, cutting her off.

"What's up?" Libby was all ears.

"I meant to call you over the weekend but didn't get around to it. Mrs. Reed has left the firm. Ben dropped the ball on something and she said enough is enough and told Hershel she was through. This would never have happened if you were still working on her account."

"Mrs. Reed has left?" That meant that Libby had to move fast. The first thing she intended to do was phone the older woman—probably this afternoon—and set up an appointment with her. She thought of Mrs. Reed as the grandmother she barely remembered. Well into her eighties, the widow had been frugal and wise with her money her whole life and she was wealthy now. While demanding, she'd been wonderful to work with and Libby had missed her. No one was going to pull the wool over this wise woman's eyes.

"Yes, and Hershel isn't happy about it, either."

Libby could only imagine. Mrs. Reed was a major client and Hershel had decided to keep Ben instead of Libby even though Ben wasn't half the attorney she was. His one attribute, and apparently most important asset, was that he'd brought in two big clients to the firm. The clients Libby had brought in were small potatoes by comparison.

She had to know, had to ask. "Did my name come up?"

Sarah hesitated. "Sorry, no."

Well, Libby couldn't be too disappointed. She had her own plans now and they were big.

"I'm calling with news, too," Libby said, doing a poor job of disguising her eagerness.

"You found a position," Sarah guessed.

"No." And then she quickly added, "I've decided to open my own practice."

Sarah's reaction was immediate. "Libby, that's wonderful."

The paralegal's confidence in her was reassuring.

"I would like to offer you the position of my personal assistant and my paralegal."

"Two jobs?"

"Just in the beginning." Libby didn't think it would be long before she could hire a second person and she told Sarah as much. "I need to get on my feet first, but it will only be a matter of a few months."

"You're sure you could manage all that in such a short while?"

"Positive. What do you think?"

"Do you have an office?"

"Not yet. I phoned you first, but my next phone call will be to a real estate agent. I'm really going to do it, Sarah. I haven't been this excited in months."

Sarah hesitated. "What about clients?"

"Well," she said, lowering her voice. "I have a line on a new one already."

"You do?"

It surprised her that Sarah hadn't figured it out. "Mrs. Reed."

"Oh . . . of course."

"You'll need more work than that," Sarah mentioned, as though Libby hadn't already figured that out for herself.

"I know and I'll get it." She thought about all the people she'd met at the hospital. She'd have business cards printed and hand them out at the gym, too. Why, just the other day, Lydia had asked Libby a question regarding getting a power of attorney for her mother. My goodness, Libby should have realized it then, the answer was obvious. She should set up her own practice. This was going to be fabulous.

"Are you on board?" Libby asked Sarah.

"I'll need time to think about it and I'll need to talk it over with Vaughn."

"Of course." Libby had understood that Sarah would want to discuss the job offer with her husband.

"I'll get back to you soon."

"Perfect," Libby said.

At that moment life felt exactly that

way. Perfect. Hopeful. Yet even in her excitement and enthusiasm, something was missing—or, rather, someone.

Phillip.

Chapter 20

"Mom, we've got to do something to help Ava," Casey pleaded while Lydia started dinner preparations on Monday evening. Ava and Casey had spent most of the afternoon together in Casey's bedroom.

"Ava's been crying all afternoon. She's going to have a baby and she doesn't know what to do."

Lydia wanted to weep herself. The poor girl desperately needed help. "Does she have a caseworker?" If Ava's grandmother was her legal guardian, then the state might have assigned the children someone from Social Services.

"I don't know and I doubt that Ava does, either." Casey looked as if she was ready to break into tears, too. Although she would quickly deny it, she had a sensitive heart for the pain of others. It wouldn't surprise Lydia if Casey decided on a career in the medical field. She seemed to be drawn in that direction. "Ava's afraid of what will happen once her grandmother finds out about the baby."

Lydia had met Ava's grandmother only once, and it hadn't been a pleasant exchange. She'd gone to the Carmichael residence to pick up Ava. The girls were going to a movie together and she'd thought it was time to meet the young teen's guardian. Darlene, who'd just returned from work, had been short-tempered with Ava and her brother. She made a point of complaining about the cost of the movie. Lydia had assured her she'd pay for the girls. The older woman had gruffly thanked her, but didn't seem interested in chatting. Lydia had left after a few minutes.

"Let me talk to Ava first," Lydia said as she placed the tomato on the cutting board.

"Mom, she doesn't want to talk to anyone, especially about the baby."

"Where is she?"

"She had to go home in case her grandmother came back to the house after work. If Ava and Jackson aren't there, her grandmother gets upset. She doesn't want them roaming the neighborhood."

Lydia wasn't sure what she could do to help and said as much.

"Ava's coming to the yarn store with me in the morning. She told me Libby would be there, too."

Good. Ava trusted Libby. Maybe the attorney would know how to handle this situation. Lydia felt at a complete loss.

"I think Libby wants to take Ava to the doctor," Casey continued, "but I don't think Ava will go because she's afraid her grandmother will find out. Someone has to tell her grandmother and she's too afraid to do it."

"Mrs. Carmichael will know soon enough." Lydia wasn't sure how Ava had been able to hide the pregnancy for this long.

"You need to be the one to tell her, Mom," Casey insisted.

"Me?" Lydia would rather do anything than be the one to tell Ava's grandmother her thirteen-year-old granddaughter was pregnant. Darlene Carmichael had already had to deal with the loss of her daughter, and she'd taken on the responsibility of rearing her grandchildren, and now this. It was too much.

"Then Ava will have an excuse to go to the doctor."

"Sweetheart . . ."

"Her grandmother needs to know. Sure, she'll be mad, but she'll get over it soon enough. It's wrong to leave something this important up to chance. How would you feel if something happened to Ava because no one would help her tell her grandmother about the baby?"

Her daughter made a good case. That was what Lydia got for letting her hang around with Libby a few afternoons a week. Casey could argue like an attorney. Maybe she'd choose law over medicine.

"Ava's frightened, Mom. Wouldn't you be? But I told her she'd be better off dealing with this now instead of letting it upset her so much. Crying this hard isn't good for her or the baby."

Lydia agreed with Casey that it was time for Ava's grandmother to learn the truth. What she dreaded was being the one to tell her. Mrs. Carmichael was sure to be upset, but at least she'd be able to help Ava deal with the pregnancy. The girl needed medical attention, and her family needed to make a decision about the baby.

"Will you talk to her grandmother for her?" Casey asked again.

Lydia realized she was probably the best choice. At least Mrs. Carmichael had met her before.

"Let me talk this over with your father first."

After the dinner dishes were cleared from the table, Lydia brought it up with her husband. Casey went outside for a few minutes with her brother and by the time she returned, Brad and Lydia had decided that Lydia should approach Darlene Carmichael.

No time like the present.

On the drive over, Lydia thought long and hard about the best way to break the news to the other woman. Ava wouldn't be happy with her, but the girl's physical and mental well-being was a far more important concern.

As a peace offering, she brought along a plate of oatmeal cookies she'd baked with Casey that morning while it was still cool. Hopefully the cookies would help sweeten the older woman's mood.

When she pulled up in front of the house, Jackson, Ava's older brother, was outside by himself, playing basketball in the next-door neighbor's driveway. He didn't seem to notice her.

Standing on the front steps, Lydia rang the doorbell. Her stomach was in knots and she whispered a silent prayer, asking God to give her the right words. The front door opened and Darlene Carmichael stood on the other side of the screen. Her eyes narrowed until she saw the plate of cookies. The screen had a giant rip in the bottom half.

"Hello again," Lydia said. "I'm Lydia Goetz, Casey's mom. We met a couple of months ago."

"I remember."

Lydia remained standing outside the screen door. "Would it be all right if I came inside for a few minutes?"

The older woman hesitated before unlatching the door, pulling it open for Lydia. When she stepped into the house the smell of cigarette smoke was overpowering. Mrs. Carmichael led the way into the living room and plopped herself down in a recliner. There was a beer can on the end table next to the chair.

The sofa was covered with what looked like an old bedspread. Something had been spilled on it and left to dry. Setting the plate of cookies down, Lydia sat at the far end of the sofa as close to the edge as she dared.

Ava's grandmother concentrated on the television screen, which was tuned to a Hollywood gossip show.

"I apologize for stopping by unannounced." Lydia nervously smoothed her hand over her knees.

"I hope Ava hasn't been making a pest of herself."

"Not at all," Lydia countered quickly. "I've enjoyed Ava tremendously. She's a charming girl."

Mrs. Carmichael's gaze left the television screen and a hint of a smile came and went from her eyes. "She looks a lot like my daughter. Sometimes . . ." she hesitated and then continued, "sometimes when I look at her I think it's Gaylene and then I remember that Gaylene is gone. I miss her, you know." She had a hoarse smoker's voice that quickly turned into a cough. Grabbing the ashtray next to the can of beer, she stabbed the cigarette butt several times into the glass. "I quit smoking two years ago and only started back after we buried Gaylene . . . I plan to quit again although I keep putting it off. I know it's bad for me and not a good example for Jackson and Ava, but for now I need these cigarettes."

She coughed again, so deep that for a moment Lydia thought she might need to slap the older woman across the back. Once the coughing subsided, Lydia said, "Ava and Casey have spent quite a bit of time together this summer."

"So I understand. Ava knit a couple of dishcloths; they aren't half bad." Her gaze remained focused on the television set. "She said you gave her the yarn." The last part was added as if the older woman was afraid Lydia was going to ask her for payment. Lydia had no intention of seeking reimbursement.

"I did . . . it's leftover yarn from other projects I've done. I'm glad to see it put to good use." Lydia smiled, proud of all that Ava had accomplished over the last few weeks. "Ava's learned how to crochet, too. She is actually a very quick learner." She resisted the urge to jabber away rather than discuss the reason for her visit.

A door opened; the sound came from the hallway that led off the living room. Ava came out and stopped cold when she saw Lydia. From her position, her grandmother couldn't see her, which was a good thing because Ava's eyes widened. It didn't seem possible that she could go any paler, but she did.

Lydia looked away. "Ava was over this afternoon and she mentioned that you've been concerned because she's gaining weight."

Ava took two steps forward and made a cutting motion with her hands while shaking her head.

Lydia ignored the girl as much as possible.

Ava came all the way into the room. "Hello, Mrs. Goetz," she said.

"Goetz is your surname?" Darlene asked, looking away from the television screen.

"My married name."

Ava stood almost directly in front of Lydia, her eyes begging her not to mention the pregnancy.

"Do you know Ronny Goetz?" Darlene asked.

"No, I'm sorry, but I can ask my husband if you'd like."

"Do. Ronny borrowed fifty bucks from me and never paid me back. Haven't seen him in six months. I should have known better, but he had a sob story, and fool that I am I fell for it."

"Ah, sorry, I haven't heard Brad ever mention any relation named Ronny."

"Goetz is an unusual name. If your husband's related, I'd appreciate a phone number. I'm not the only one Ronny owes, so I'd like to get to him before anyone else does."

"I'll mention that to Brad."

"I'd appreciate it."

"Getting back to what I was saying earlier . . ."

"Can I get you anything, Grandma?" Ava asked, breaking into the conversation.

"A beer. What about you?" She motioned to Lydia.

"No thanks."

Ava hesitated.

"Don't stand there like a bump on a log; get me another beer." The older woman glanced sheepishly at Lydia. "Another bad habit. I plan on cutting back on drinking, too. I only have two a night. That's my limit; really can't afford any more than that."

Ava hurried into the kitchen and returned with a beer can. She handed it to her grandmother.

"You could open it for me, you know," Mrs. Carmichael complained, as she took the aluminum can out of her granddaughter's hand. "I've got arthritis in my hands. I wish you'd learn to be more thoughtful."

"Sorry, Grandma."

Darlene Carmichael mumbled under her breath. She handed the empty can to Ava and took a deep swallow from the full one before setting it down next to the ashtray.

"I was saying that Ava looks like she's gained weight over the summer," Lydia said. "And I—"

"I've been telling her the same thing," Mrs. Carmichael said, interrupting her. "I tried to put her on a diet but it doesn't seem to be helping."

"I believe I know the reason for Ava's weight gain," Lydia said, speaking quickly. She refused to be deterred. Either she forged ahead or lost her nerve.

"So do I."

Lydia straightened. "You do?"

"She doesn't get enough exercise.

Ava spends half the day in her bedroom, and she steals snacks out of the kitchen. I swear Ava and her brother eat me out of house and home. They think money grows on trees, apparently. Last week alone I spent over a hundred dollars on groceries. I can't afford that and now they need new school clothes. Jackson wants to play sports and he had to get a physical. Those doctor visits don't come cheap." She shook her head as though overwhelmed by it all.

"I think the weight gain might be due to more than snacks between meals," Lydia suggested.

"Oh?" Darlene Carmichael frowned.

"I'm afraid Ava might . . ." Lydia paused and gathered her courage. "Actually, I believe Ava might be pregnant."

"Ava, pregnant?" The old woman laughed as though this was a bad joke. "No way. She's only thirteen."

"I know. She needs to see a physician."

Darlene rose to her feet, paused just long enough to take another drink of her beer. Then she shouted for Ava, who'd recently left the room. "Ava, get in here!" Her shrill voice rang through the house like a foghorn.

Nothing.

"Ava!" she shouted again, more threatening this time. "Get in here. Now."

The bedroom door opened again and Ava slowly made her way down the long, narrow hallway. Her grandmother met her halfway and grabbed her by the upper arm, practically dragging her into the living room. She brought her to stand in front of Lydia. Ava hung her head.

Lydia wanted to shout for Darlene to release the girl but knew it wouldn't do any good.

"Are you pregnant?" Darlene Carmichael demanded of her granddaughter.

Tears streamed down Ava's ashen face. "No, Grandma."

Darlene let go of Ava's arm as if that was all the proof she needed. "What did I tell you?" she stated calmly. "The girl eats too much. Isn't that right?" The question was posed to Ava.

"Yes," Ava whispered, keeping her head lowered.

"Now I think you should know that I don't appreciate you coming into my home and making accusations. I take care of my own, and my granddaughter doesn't sleep around."

"I didn't mean to imply—"

"I know you probably mean well," Darlene said, cutting Lydia off. "But I don't appreciate you butting your head into my family business. Ava says she's not pregnant and I believe her. I don't know what makes you think my granddaughter is having a baby, but that's the most ridiculous thing I've ever heard. Now I'd appreciate it if you left my home."

"I . . . I . . ."

Darlene walked to the front door and held open the screen door. "You listen, Ms. Goetz, if I hear any rumors about my granddaughter sleeping around I'll know where they got started. So you better not be saying anything about my Ava, understand?"

"Of course . . . I wouldn't."

"Now it's time for you to go."

Lydia reached for her purse and stood. "I understand. I apologize; I didn't mean to upset you, Mrs. Carmichael."

"I've met busybodies like you before, sticking your nose into everyone's business, pretending to be all neighborly," she said, frowning all the while. "Bringing cookies . . . well, you can take that plate back home with you. We don't want them and we don't need them. Most likely Ava would eat the whole plate herself and then you'd be telling me she's giving birth to twins."

Lydia walked out of the house. She paused and turned around and saw that Darlene was still standing in the doorway as if she wanted to be sure Lydia didn't linger.

"Mrs. Carmichael, if you . . . if you find out differently about Ava, please feel free to call me. I want to help."

Darlene's scowl deepened. "I believe you've already done more than enough."

With a heavy heart, Lydia drove back to the house. Both Brad and Casey were waiting for her when she walked into the kitchen.

"Well?" Casey asked.

"How'd it go?" Brad asked.

No need to sugarcoat the truth. "It was dreadful, just dreadful," she whispered. Lydia had felt sorry for Ava before, but now that she'd seen her home life, she felt like weeping. Tuesday she'd talk to Libby and see what the two of them could do to help poor, sweet Ava.

Chapter 21

Libby walked into A Good Yarn fifteen minutes after ten. She didn't want to appear overly eager but she was excited about talking to Ava. It had taken real courage for the teenager to contact her. While progress had been slow, she could see that they were making headway.

"Morning," Libby greeted as she entered the store. Her gaze automatically went to the back of the shop, where Casey and Ava generally hung out. The table was empty.

"I'm so glad you're here early," Lydia

said, coming around the front counter and taking Libby's hands in her own. Dark shadows appeared under her eyes as though she hadn't slept well.

"Lydia, what happened?"

The other woman looked like she was about to break into tears. "Oh, Libby, I think I made a terrible mistake." She started toward the back of the store and into the office where she kept a microwave. She filled the teapot with water and set it inside, then pushed the button to heat the water.

"I'll feel better with a cup of tea." She automatically brought down two cups.

"Where are Casey and Ava?" The pregnant teenager had told Libby she would be at the yarn store on Tuesday and now there was no evidence of either girl.

"I know, I know. Ava was at the house yesterday afternoon," Lydia explained. "She stayed in Casey's bedroom most of the day, crying her eyes out."

"Why, what happened?" Libby was immediately alarmed.

"I think your talk with her . . . the day you took her to lunch . . ."

"Yes. Did I do anything to upset Ava?"

"No . . . no, it wasn't anything you did. Frankly, I don't think Ava realized she was pregnant until you told her."

"I was afraid of that." Clearly Ava was several months along. In discussing the matter with Phillip, he thought she might even be heading into her eighth month. The baby must be growing and moving.

"And now she's frightened to death. Her biggest fear isn't for her own well-being or even that of the baby. She seems most concerned about what her grandmother will do once she finds out."

"Oh, no." Libby felt dreadful and wondered what she could do to help.

"Casey pleaded with me to go over to Ava's grandmother's house and talk to her," Lydia continued. "Casey was convinced that once Darlene Carmichael knew about the baby the worst would be over. She thought Ava could then get the medical attention she needs. All the poor girl could do was worry about hiding the pregnancy from her grandmother."

Libby already knew what was coming. "You told the grandmother, didn't you?"

"I tried. It wasn't a job I relished. I talked it over with Brad and we both felt I should probably be the one. Ava trusts you but you've never met Darlene Carmichael and we thought she'd probably take the news better from me than from someone she'd never met."

Libby agreed. "How'd it go?"

The microwave beeped and Lydia shook her head. "I doubt it could have gone much worse."

"Oh dear."

Lydia removed the teapot and then added two tea bags, which she allowed to steep. Carrying the ceramic pot to the table, she set it down next to the empty cups.

"Oh, Libby, you can't imagine how awful it was," Lydia said. "I brought a plate of cookies and if I hadn't I don't think Darlene would have even let me in the house. Ava mentioned that her grandmother is upset because she thinks she's getting fat, so that was the way I approached her."

Libby nodded, hoping to encourage her.

"When I suggested there was a reason Ava had gained all that weight and what I suspected, she dragged Ava into the room and asked her outright if she was pregnant or not."

"What did Ava say?"

"She denied it. Really, who could blame her? I probably would have done the same thing."

"In other words the grandmother refused to believe it?"

Lydia nodded, her brown eyes round and sad. "She claimed Ava was just fat and that I was a busybody . . . and she basically threatened me if I started spreading rumors about her granddaughter sleeping around."

"Oh, Lydia . . ." Libby felt dreadful for her friend, and for Ava, too.

"I don't think that's the worst of it, though."

"What do you mean?"

Lydia sat down and poured them each a cup of tea. The steam rose from the cups. Her hand lingered on the teapot as she set it back down on the table. "This morning Casey phoned Ava to tell her we were on our way to pick her up so she would be ready when we got there."

"And?" Libby feared she already knew what was coming.

"Ava said she couldn't come. Her grandmother won't let her have anything more to do with me or Casey."

At first Libby was at a loss for words, but as Lydia had said, Ava trusted her. "Maybe I should stop by her house this morning," she suggested. Perhaps if she talked to Ava, reassured her that everything would work out, then the teenager might agree to let Libby pay for a visit to the doctor. She'd talk to Sharon first and get a recommendation for a female obstetrician from her. Libby's own was male but she felt Ava might be more comfortable with a woman. Normally she would have asked Phillip. He was the first person who popped into her mind, but she couldn't— wouldn't—allow herself to do that. Still, he remained constantly in her thoughts.

"Would you be willing to go see Ava?"

Lydia asked. "I'd feel so much better if you did."

"Of course." She sipped her tea and brought out her knitting. When Libby was this upset putting her hands to work calmed her. She wasn't sure how this newly developed habit would play out in the office when dealing with a client, though. The thought of her reaching for her knitting in the middle of a legal discussion produced a smile.

"I feel just terrible," Lydia murmured, elbows at her sides, holding her teacup with both hands.

"You did what you could," Libby assured her. "I doubt it would have gone any better no matter who told Ava's grandmother. While she might choose to deny that Ava is pregnant, she'll be forced to acknowledge the truth soon enough."

"But what happens until then?"

The teenager was Libby's biggest concern as well. "I'll do what I can to help her."

"I'm so grateful."

The bell above the door chimed, announcing a customer. Lydia helped the knitter, who was looking for alpaca yarn. She rang up the sale and then returned to the table.

"Where's Casey today?" Libby asked. She liked talking to Lydia's daughter. Perhaps she could learn something from her.

Lydia reached for her own knitting. "She's with my mother. Casey and my mother have a special bond. Our daughter never knew any of her grandparents before we adopted her and she loves listening to my mother's stories. She simply enjoys spending time with Mom, and it's good for my mother, too. I do worry, though . . ." She let the rest fade.

"Worry?"

"My mother's health is failing and I can't help being concerned how Casey will deal with the loss once Mom . . . dies." Her voice cracked as the last half of the comment came in a whisper, as if she had a difficult time facing the possibility of life without her mother.

"Don't borrow trouble," Libby suggested. This was something her own mother had told her. "There's enough to handle for today; we don't need to take on the worries of another day."

Lydia's hands rested in her lap. "You're right."

The back door that led to the alley where the staff parked opened and Margaret came into the store. She smiled when she saw Libby. After greetings all around, Margaret tucked her purse away, grabbed a cup, and joined them at the table. Soon the three were chatting, occasionally interrupted by a customer.

After hearing about the events of the night before, Margaret offered Lydia her own words of reassurance and basically said the same thing Libby had. It wouldn't have mattered who delivered the news, Darlene's reactions would have been the same.

"Ava will listen to you," Margaret assured Libby. "She looks up to you."

Libby appreciated the encouragement. She needed it.

Libby remained at the store until lunchtime. "I'll get something to eat and take it over to Ava's with me," she said. She would bring a green salad and fresh fruit. As she gathered her knitting and her purse, she experienced a wave of affection for these two women who had become her friends.

For Libby to have spent two hours in a yarn store, visiting with Lydia and Margaret, would have been completely unheard-of only a few months ago. Once her law practice took off, she probably wouldn't find the time to do it often.

She hadn't taken a lot of time in the last ten years to cultivate friendships. There simply weren't enough hours in a day to work as hard and long as she did and still have time for a social life. Her new friends gave her a sense of belonging, and community. Libby knew she could discuss her troubles with Lydia and Margaret and they would listen, really listen, because they cared and wanted what was best for her.

Making friends hadn't happened overnight, but gradually, as she extended herself, she found connections with others. By being open she'd been the one to receive this precious gift of friendship. There was Sharon Jennings from the hospital, and Libby had connected with Abby Higginbotham in HR, too. They'd met for coffee in the hospital cafeteria a couple of times and had laughed together.

Phillip, too.

Her spirits faltered as she thought about him—not that he was ever far from her mind.

Phillip had been another surprise, but instead of appreciating him for the gift he was, she'd blown it, which was fairly typical of most of her relationships with men. She had no one to blame but herself, but this time she felt deep regret, and an even deeper sense of loss. She couldn't help wondering if it was too late to make things right with him. She'd like to try but was afraid.

On her way out the door of A Good Yarn, Libby checked her cell to be sure she hadn't inadvertently missed Sarah's call. The paralegal had said she'd get back to her about the job offer after she'd spoken to her husband. Libby expected her to phone at any time.

No calls. Surely she'd hear from Sarah by the end of the day.

After stopping by The French Cafe for two take-out lunches, Libby got into her car and checked the address Lydia had given her for Ava's grandmother's house. She followed the tin voice from the navigational guide to Jefferson Street, and parked in front of a plain white house.

The first thing she noticed was that the yard needed mowing. Where once there'd been flowerbeds, there was now nothing but tall weeds. The contrast between this house and the one next to it was striking. The lawn next door was well groomed, with vibrant flowers hanging from baskets across the porch. Two boys sat on the front steps of the neighbor's house, one holding a basketball.

Libby opened her car door and climbed out. She walked down the cracked cement walkway leading to the front door and rang the doorbell. No one answered right away, so she knocked against the wood.

One of the boys from the house next door ran across the lawn toward her.

"Whatever you're selling, we aren't buying."

Libby smiled at the youth, who looked to be fifteen, maybe slightly older. "I'm here to see Ava."

"What for?" he demanded. He tucked the basketball under his arm and regarded her suspiciously.

"I'm a friend of hers. Just tell her Libby is here."

He broke into a smile, revealing slightly crooked teeth. "Are you the lady who took her to a restaurant lunch the other day?"

"That's me."

He relaxed right away. "Oh, hi, I'm Jackson."

"Ava's brother."

"That's me," he said. "Come on in. I'll get Ava for you." He opened the front door and led the way into the house. "Ava!" he shouted. "You've got company."

Libby stood in the middle of the living room and looked around. A couple of empty beer cans sat next to an overflowing ashtray by a recliner. Her attention went to the kitchen. The table still had dirty breakfast dishes on it—crusted bowls and a cereal box, plus an empty milk container that was on its side. The sink appeared to be filled with unwashed dishes.

The bedroom door opened, and Libby saw Ava walking toward her. Ava broke into a smile as soon as she saw her. "Libby, what are you doing here?"

"I thought we were going to meet up at the yarn store?"

The teen's face went slack. "Grandma said I can't go there anymore."

"Oh dear, then I guess that means I'll just have to come to you. Have you had lunch yet?"

Ava shook her head.

Jackson spoke. "She didn't eat breakfast, either."

Instinctively Libby knew why. If Ava stopped eating she'd lose weight and her grandmother might not guess she was pregnant. "Oh, Ava, you need to eat."

"Grandma says she's getting fat and she is," Jackson muttered. "Doesn't seem right, though, because she barely eats anything."

Libby resisted the urge to hug the poor girl. She wanted to help Ava, to protect her, but her options were limited.

"Would you like to go out for a while?" Libby asked. "To the park or the waterfront?"

Ava's eyes brightened and then just as quickly she dropped her gaze. "I can't. Grandma grounded me."

"What did you do?"

"Nothing," she insisted.

"She was mad because Casey's mom came to visit and she took it out on Ava," Jackson explained. "I told her that wasn't fair, but then Grandma grounded me, too."

A hint of a smile showed in Ava's eyes. "Only Jackson ignored her."

"Grandma's at work; she won't know if I go over to Peter's or not, right?" He looked to Libby for confirmation.

"My father always knew," Libby said. "I don't know how he did, but he did."

"Spyware," Jackson said. "But Grandma can't afford anything like that."

Libby wasn't entirely sure what he

was talking about, but she could guess spyware had to do with hidden cameras watching every move she made. Libby doubted her father had had access to that type of technology when she was a teenager. "Maybe," she said. "I did bring lunch, though. Are you hungry?"

From the way Ava's eyes responded, Libby guessed that she was. "Salads," she said, "with dressing on the side."

"I guess that would be all right." Ava moved into the kitchen and started clearing off the table.

"I'll get our lunch and then we can talk, okay?"

Ava glanced toward her brother.

"Don't worry, I'll be with Peter," Jackson said.

Ava visibly relaxed. "Okay," she whispered, locking eyes with Libby.

Lunch was only semi-successful. Ava was more frightened than ever. More so of her grandmother's reaction than what she called "the baby in her stomach." No matter how persuasive Libby tried to be, she couldn't get Ava to agree to see a doctor for fear that her grandmother might find out.

"Do you know what you're going to do once the baby is born?" Libby asked.

Ava's answer was to hang her head. She didn't have an answer because she didn't know.

"Will the father be able to help you?"

"No." Her response was immediate and flat, indicating this was a subject she didn't want to discuss.

Up until this point Libby had avoided the subject of the baby's father, wanting to build up trust before she brought him into the situation. "If he's older than eighteen I need to know," Libby said gently.

Ava stood and backed away from the table. "I think you should go now before my grandmother comes home."

"Okay."

Libby realized it was an excuse to avoid the subject. She hesitated, wishing she hadn't brought up the subject of the baby's father so soon. A number of important issues needed to be discussed, including whether Ava continued to be sexually active. She packed up the lunch leftovers, afraid that if the girl's grandmother saw the take-out boxes she'd guess someone had stopped by the house.

The next time they met, Libby was determined she would broach the subject more carefully.

Chapter 22

"So what did Sarah tell you?" Robin asked as the two sat at the Smoothie Bar just outside the exercise room at the gym.

This was a rare treat. Robin usually rushed out of the gym and headed for her office in the courthouse the minute she'd showered and changed clothes. Her suggestion that they get a fruit smoothie together had come as a pleasant surprise.

"I haven't heard from Sarah," Libby told her.

"What?" Robin's gaze narrowed as if

she had been afraid of something like this.

Libby was surprised herself. She'd expected Sarah to jump at her offer to get away from the oppressive atmosphere of the office. As she'd told Lydia, Sarah didn't appear to be the friend Libby had once thought she was.

"Then write her off," Robin advised.

Libby had more or less already done so, although she couldn't help thinking Sarah would have a change of heart. What was it people said about the eternal optimist? Libby didn't remember, but she couldn't help but hold out hope that Sarah would seriously consider the job offer. If it wasn't in the cards, then so be it. While it'd be great to work with Sarah again, Libby would do fine without her. Still, it stung.

Really, all Sarah needed to do was pick up the phone and tell Libby she just didn't feel she could make the change. It wouldn't have been difficult. But to not call her back really said it all.

The gal at the counter delivered their smoothies and Libby took her first sip. She wasn't sure what to expect after reading the ingredient list. In addition to fresh fruit, the smoothie had a bunch of healthy, veggie-type goodies added: flaxseed, wheatgrass, and a couple of other items Libby had never seriously considered eating until now.

"Hey, this tastes good." Robin sat back on her stool and cocked her eyebrows with a look of surprise. "Never thought I'd see the day I'd voluntarily eat raw spinach."

"Me neither," Libby agreed. If she got any healthier she would sprout grass on top of her head.

"So . . ." Robin said, stirring her smoothie with her straw. "How's everything between you and Phillip?"

Libby froze. Up until now she'd managed to avoid the subject of Phillip. He hadn't been at the gym, either. Her shoulders sank and she admitted, "I'm not seeing him anymore."

Robin's face revealed her shock. "When did this happen?"

"A week or so ago . . . after the interview. I told him he was a distraction."

"You did what?"

"I know, I know." Libby had been kicking herself ever since.

"Is that why he hasn't been at the gym?"

Libby wasn't entirely sure. "Either he's avoiding me or he's on surgery rotation again." She'd heard through the hospital grapevine that Phillip planned to attend a charity tennis benefit to support a good friend of his who was the organizer, another doctor named Scott Busbee. Libby had debated attending the function and finding a seat close to him. The temptation was strong but she hated to be so obvious.

She hadn't seen him since that fateful afternoon. She was sorry she'd acted so impulsively, and now she wasn't sure if it would be possible to repair the damage. She'd come so far, only to back away when it mattered most.

"The two of you had been seeing a lot of each other, hadn't you?"

They'd found an excuse to be together almost every day. Well, no longer. "Yeah."

"You're sorry?"

"Oh, Robin, how could I have been so foolish? I feel dreadful."

"Then tell him that. Eat crow if you have to, but do it—otherwise you might regret it for the rest of your life."

"I'll think about it," Libby promised, and she would. Eventually she would run into Phillip. Either he was doing a masterful job of avoiding her or the fates were conspiring against them. She supposed she could pick up the phone, too, but she held back. Fear had made her break it off with him in the first place, a fear that she couldn't embrace new things and be a success. And also fear of being hurt again when so much of her life was up in the air.

Robin went silent and kept her head lowered as she drew circles with her straw in the thick drink.

Libby sipped her smoothie. She'd noticed lately that people tended to ask the very questions they wanted others to ask them. It made her wonder what exactly was going on between Robin and Roy. Robin only rarely mentioned the judge, and it seemed like she was

afraid of what Libby might say if she
did.

"What about you and . . . what's his
name again?" Libby asked, playing
dumb. "Roy, isn't it?"

Robin's head shot up.

Bull's-eye.

"What makes you ask?"

Libby played it nonchalant and
shrugged. "No reason."

Robin stirred the smoothie with increased energy. "I see him nearly every
day."

"Fabulous."

"Yeah, it's fabulous all right," Robin
muttered sarcastically, and set her drink
on the counter before she slid off the
stool. "Listen, I need to run. See you."
She scooted off the stool.

"Will I see you Friday?" Libby asked.

Robin nodded.

Libby didn't know what had happened between Robin and her judge,
but apparently something must have
for her friend to react that way.

*   *   *

Phillip wasn't at the gym the rest of the week. Friday morning, after working out with Robin, Libby showered and changed clothes, and headed to the hospital to rock babies. While she exchanged chitchat with Sharon, she kept an eye out for Phillip, hoping she'd see him. Gathering her resolve, she planned to talk to him, tell him she'd made a mistake, and ask for a second chance.

He didn't stop by.

Until today she'd always felt better after spending time with the newborns, but her nerves were on edge and the babies quickly picked up on her tension.

"Have you seen Dr. Stone this morning?" Libby gathered her courage and asked Sharon when she couldn't stand it any longer.

Sharon shook her head. "Dr. Stone hasn't stopped by all week, and frankly, that surprises me."

It didn't surprise Libby.

"He generally finds an excuse to visit the nursery on the days you're here."

At one time that had been true, but

Libby suspected that it wouldn't be any longer.

After leaving the hospital, Libby returned to her condo. She didn't bother with lunch. She sat with her knitting for a short time as she sorted through her feelings. After a while she decided she was too numb and upset to feel much of anything other than sadness over the loss of a promising relationship—a relationship she'd single-handedly ruined.

Phillip Stone wasn't the only person on her mind. Libby decided to try contacting Sarah one last time. She used the number for the direct line, only it wasn't Sarah who answered.

"Hello, this is Libby Morgan," she said. "Is Sarah available?"

"I'm sorry; Sarah is out for the day."

"All right, thank you." Libby hung up the phone. She had Sarah's cell number, but she'd need to dig out her address book to locate it.

After taking a couple of moments to compose her thoughts Libby punched out the number for Sarah's cell. It rang four times and then went to voice mail.

"Hello, Sarah," she said, doing her

best to sound upbeat and enthused. "I haven't heard back from you. If I don't get word by Monday morning I can only assume that you aren't interested in the job offer, which is completely fine."

She disconnected and then sat down. It felt as if she were struggling to swim upstream during a winter thaw.

Sarah was a huge disappointment, but Libby would do fine without the paralegal. Her life was moving along just fine—actually, more than fine.

She had friends.

She had prospects.

She had a bright future and Libby was determined to make the most of it.

She looked down at her knitting once more and reached for it.

Little did Sarah Matto realize that she had just walked away from the opportunity of a lifetime.

It'd taken courage to call Sarah. Now all she had to do was find the nerve to reach out to Phillip.

Chapter 23

Libby's doorbell chimed and she leaped off the sofa and hurried to open her front door. Robin stood on the other side, looking as sad and depressed as Libby herself felt. Friday night and the rest of the world was out partying and laughing while the two of them were alone. No men. No dates. No fun.

Robin was dressed in an old college sweatshirt and jeans. Head hanging low and shoulders slouched forward, she looked like she'd lost her best friend. She had a sack in her hand.

"I brought some DVDs . . . old movies," she muttered.

Libby shook her head. She refused to fall prey to feeling sorry for herself. She still hadn't run into Phillip and hadn't yet worked up the courage to contact him directly. Robin was in the dumps, too, although she wasn't open about her reasons. But Libby was smart enough to read between the lines. "We are not going to sit at home and have a pity party."

"We're not?"

"No way." Libby had a plan. "We're finished indulging in ice cream. We work way too hard to burn calories to give in to that sort of self-destructive behavior. I've seen every sappy chick flick a dozen times and I'm sick of watching other women get the guy while I'm lonely and depressed."

Robin's mouth sagged open as if she wasn't sure she recognized the woman in front of her. Seeing her friend's response boosted Libby's confidence. "We are not going to sit here and feed each other tissue after tissue while we lament the sorry state of our love lives."

"We aren't?"

"No," Libby insisted, spreading her feet apart and planting her hands on her waist, elbows jutting out.

"Okaaay," Robin returned, sounding apprehensive.

"What's the wildest thing you can think of doing? I mean something that would be completely out of character for both of us?"

"Ah . . ." Robin's face scrunched up as she gave the question some deep thought. "I . . . I don't know. Pick up men in a bar?"

Libby shook her head. "No; men don't interest me at the moment."

"Well, other than one man," Robin corrected.

She held up a hand, stopping her fellow attorney. "I don't want to think about Phillip, or deal with any other men, either. You know what the craziest thing I can think to do would be?"

Robin was barely in the front door. "I'm afraid to ask."

"Don't be. I want us to go out and get tattoos."

Silence followed and then Robin blurted out, "Are you nuts?"

"Yes. I want us to get tattoos."

"No way."

Libby wasn't taking no for an answer. "It doesn't have to be anyplace that shows."

"You want to get a tattoo on your butt?"

"Or the small of my back," she said, thinking out loud.

"Not me," Robin argued, shaking her head for emphasis. "You can if you want, but there is no way I'm letting anyone repeatedly poke me with a needle."

Libby could see Robin wasn't game. "Okay, fine, but I need you to come with me."

"You're serious?" She seemed to find it hard to believe Libby would actually do something like this.

It was out of character, but Libby was more than ready for something different, something that would crack open this shell she'd been living in for the majority of her life. Straightening slightly, she announced, "I'm doing it with or without you."

Robin's eyes rounded.

"Don't let me down now," Libby pleaded. "The least you can do is come with me."

"Okay, I'll watch, but that's all I intend to do."

Libby grabbed her purse and took her friend by the arm, resolutely leading her outside. They found a tattoo parlor next to a porn shop. Despite its location, it looked clean. Robin hesitated and Libby had to practically drag her along.

"You need to think this through more carefully," Robin warned.

"I am finished being the nice girl," Libby countered, sidestepping her friend.

"The shop next door is selling sex toys . . ."

"Good, we might learn a trick or two."

Robin snorted. "Like that's going to do either of us any good."

"Your point is well taken, Counselor." Undeterred, Libby entered the parlor. The tattoo artist, a woman, could see that they were both nervous. After a few questions, the artist suggested they take time to think it over.

"See," Robin whispered heatedly. "Even the tattoo lady recognizes we aren't her usual customers. You need to consider this very carefully."

Libby had already made up her mind, but she wasn't going to do anything rash. They took the other woman's advice and found a nearby bar.

"A bar is no place to make this kind of decision," Robin argued, nearly shouting to be heard above the loud music.

"Sure it is," Libby said. "It isn't like there's a church in the neighborhood."

Three tequila shots later Robin was convinced that they each needed a tattoo.

"You're sure about this?" the woman artist asked when they staggered into the parlor an hour later. "Both of you? I thought it was only one of you earlier."

"I want one, too," Robin insisted, holding up her index finger. "Only I don't know of what."

The woman grinned. "Okay, ladies, you got it."

Libby went first. The tequila had done the trick. She chose a lovely butterfly for the small of her back, gasped at the price, and paid it anyway. What she didn't anticipate was the pain. A needle repeatedly jabbed in such a sensitive area was a whole lot more uncomfortable than she'd ever imagined. Libby resisted the urge to shout out "I'll talk, I'll talk" for fear of frightening off Robin. Actually, her friend surprised her. She'd never thought Robin would be game for this.

"How was it?" Robin asked once Libby was through.

She smiled weakly and joked, "I should have had four tequilas."

Robin didn't seem to take nearly as long as Libby. She hadn't shown Libby her design, and when she came out Libby was shocked to discover that Robin had had the tattoo placed on the inside of her wrist. In plain view. It wasn't a picture but a Chinese character.

"What does it mean?" Libby asked

her friend, staring down at the rather elaborate symbol.

"It's . . . private."

"Private," she repeated.

"I didn't ask you about yours."

"Okay," Libby said. She'd respect Robin's privacy.

They walked back to the condo, and almost against their wills they discussed how impossible it was to understand men. The males of the species were the fickle ones. Women simply had a bad rap.

Once inside the condo they sagged onto the sofa. Libby had cried on Robin's shoulder about Phillip and she knew her friend was deeply discouraged by her own relationship even though Robin hadn't filled her in on the details.

"You know what?" Libby said, slouching forward on the sofa because her back continued to pain her. Thankfully she hadn't been able to see the needle.

"What?"

"It seems to me that if I'm a good enough friend for you to get a tattoo with, then you should be willing to share your tale of male woe."

Robin hesitated and then shrugged. "You're right."

Libby sat up straighter. "Sing it, sister," she said, slurring her words ever so slightly. She hadn't eaten much, and the liquor on an empty stomach had gone straight to her head.

"You probably know how I feel about Roy Bollinger," Robin whispered, almost as if she were afraid to say his name aloud.

"Judge Bollinger?"

"Go ahead and say it," Robin muttered.

"Say what?"

"That I'm wasting my time and that he's out of my league and that I'm acting like I'm still the high school nerd pining after the star quarterback."

"How well do you know him?" Libby asked.

"Not at all, really. We worked together on a political campaign years ago and have been on a couple of committees together through the years. His courtroom is down the hall from mine. He always makes a point of greeting me, and not long ago we met up at a fund-raiser and . . . we had drinks one night. I told him what happened with you at the interview and . . . I haven't talked to him since. Well, other than in passing."

If Libby felt miserable before, hearing this made her feel even worse. Could it be that the disastrous interview had also blown Robin's budding romance with Roy? It hardly seemed possible that a man would lose interest in a woman over something that trivial.

"Oh, Robin, I feel terrible."

Again Robin shrugged as if it wasn't any big deal. "I don't think that was it . . . apparently he just isn't interested enough in me to call me."

"You say you chatted with him at the fund-raiser?"

"We were in line for the bar when we talked. It wasn't like he sought me out or anything."

"What about when you went to have drinks with him?"

"That was it. We both ordered a glass of wine and chatted briefly and that was all there was to it. He hasn't called me since. I think I scared him off."

Libby sincerely doubted that. "What did you do?"

Robin looked as if she was about to cry. "That's just it. I didn't do anything. I was almost afraid to talk for fear of putting my foot in my mouth. The thing is . . . I like him so much and I . . . I'm uptight around him and probably send all the wrong messages."

Libby chewed on her bottom lip. "Okay, let's reason this out."

"You think I haven't tried?" Robin asked, her voice high-pitched and panicky.

"What do you have in common, other than the fact that you're both attorneys and you both work in the same building?"

Robin rubbed her palms together. "Well, we both like the same wine—pinot noir."

Libby tapped her finger against her lips.

"What are you thinking?" Robin asked.

"Did you thank him?"

"Thank him?"

"For finding a job lead for me?"

"Well, sort of . . ."

"Wouldn't a bottle of really wonderful pinot noir be appropriate? I mean, he did you a huge favor. The least you could do is show your appreciation."

"Yes, but . . ."

"In fact, why don't I buy the wine? My treat for everything you've done for me."

Robin's eyes rounded and then went back to normal. "You really think I should give him a bottle of wine?"

"Why not?"

Robin cocked her head from side to side as she mulled over the suggestion. "Okay, I'll do it."

"Phone him," Libby insisted. She stood and retrieved the portable phone she kept in the kitchen.

"Now? It's after nine!"

Libby thrust the receiver at her friend. "Trust me, he's still up. Do you have access to his home number?"

Looking a bit chagrined, she nodded.

Libby was on a mission now. She had the feeling this was going to work out nicely for Robin, very nicely indeed. If only one of them could find love, she wanted it to be Robin, especially after what Libby had done to mess things up for her friend.

Robin retrieved her purse, which she'd left by the front door, and brought out her cell. "I have his information listed under my contacts."

"That's positive thinking," Libby said, and gave her a thumbs-up.

"Wishful thinking, you mean." After pressing the button on her cell, Robin immediately disconnected the line. "I can't."

"Robin," Libby pleaded, gesturing with her hands. "You can and you will or I'll call him myself."

"You wouldn't dare."

"Don't test me, Robin Hamlin," she threatened.

Swallowing tightly, Robin tried again, this time turning her back on Libby as she waited for the line to connect. "Oh, hi," Robin said. "This is Robin . . . Oh, you recognized my voice . . . Of course, we do talk now and again. Fine, fine, thank you for asking. And you?"

Libby could only hear one half of the

conversation but she found even that half highly amusing. Robin barely sounded like herself. Clearly she was tense and nervous and out of her element.

Her friend walked to the far side of the condo and looked out the picture window. She seemed to think that if Libby couldn't see her face, she couldn't hear her, either.

"I wanted to thank you," Robin continued. "Oh, please, it would be my pleasure . . . No, I insist . . . Unless of course you'd rather I . . . Okay, sure. I was thinking about a bottle of wine. I could have it delivered."

Libby tossed her arms in the air. The point was for her to take the wine to him herself. Apparently Robin needed even more coaching in relationships than she did. Libby hadn't realized how much she'd learned over the past few weeks.

"Yes, how thoughtful. Yes, I'd enjoy that. Okay, where would you like to meet? Yes, I know where that is." She glanced down at her watch. "See you then." She ended the call and then very calmly turned around. "He suggested we meet for drinks."

"When?"

"Tonight . . . at nine-forty-five at this bar close to the courthouse. I've never been there but I know about it."

Libby regarded her friend. "Aren't you excited?"

"I'm terrified."

"Robin, just be yourself. Now go home and change clothes and then call me first thing in the morning."

She'd assumed her friend would want to dash home and dress up in something sleek and gorgeous. Instead Robin remained rooted in the middle of the room, looking lost and confused. "I . . . I don't know that I can do this."

"Robin, do you want to get to know Roy or not?"

Her friend sighed and covered her face with both hands. "Libby," she whispered. "I'm terrified. I really like this man. I mean really, really like him, and I don't want to blow it and I'm so afraid I will."

"But Robin . . ."

"Come with me."

Libby shook her head. "You've got to be kidding. Bringing me along isn't going to help your chances with him. If you show up with a friend in tow that will only confuse him!"

"No, I mean it. I need you with me."

"Sorry." Robin had to do this alone. "Besides, does he really want to meet the person who screwed up the job interview he arranged?"

Robin's mouth thinned. "I don't think he'll make the connection," she said, "and you owe me big-time."

"Oh, all right," Libby muttered, "but I need to change clothes."

"Hurry, we don't have all night."

"Okay, okay."

The next thirty minutes passed in a blur. Libby changed into slacks and a light sweater and then they rushed to Robin's apartment, where she went through three-quarters of her closet before she decided on a peach-colored outfit that suited her beautifully.

"It's the first time I've worn it," she

confessed on their way out the door. "My mother gave it to me for Christmas one year and I tossed it in the closet. It was Mom's way of telling me to get a life."

"Look at you now," Libby teased. "You have a life. I have a life." A semi-life, anyway. They were out on the town. Robin had a date, although she was determined to pay for the wine and was so nervous she needed Libby there to hold her hand. Baby steps. That's what this was. Baby steps.

They arrived a few minutes after the agreed-upon time and poor Robin was nearly in a panic. Judge Bollinger already had a table. He stood as they approached, otherwise Libby wouldn't have known who he was.

A high school football hero? That was the way Robin viewed the judge? He was short, a little pudgy, and balding. Beauty was definitely in the eyes of the beholder, she decided.

"This is my friend . . ." Robin said, offering an introduction. "I hope you don't mind that she joined me."

"Libby Morgan," Libby supplied and extended her hand.

He shook it, seeming unperturbed. "The more the merrier. Ladies, please sit."

Robin nearly collapsed into her chair.

The waitress stopped by the table and took their order. Two glasses of pinot noir and one glass of sauvignon blanc for Libby.

"This is my first time here," Robin confessed.

"Actually it's mine, too," Roy said and then added, "since they changed the name. The business has been sold a number of times through the years."

"My first time, too." But Libby could see that neither one was listening to her.

"Sally and I . . ." He hesitated. "Sally was my wife. I lost her to colon cancer a couple of years ago."

"I am so sorry," Robin whispered, her voice quivering.

Libby swore Robin was about to burst into tears. The poor girl really had it bad.

Their wine arrived and Libby took a

few sips. She glanced at her watch. "I don't mean to rush off but . . ."

Under the table, Robin grabbed Libby's knee and squeezed so hard that it demanded all of Libby's strength not to cry out in pain.

"I . . . suppose I could stay a while longer," she said from between gritted teeth.

Robin thanked her by mouthing the words.

Libby was glad she did stay. Over the next hour, Robin started to relax. The second glass of wine helped. When Libby next suggested it was time for her to leave, her friend didn't object.

"Talk to you tomorrow," Libby said as she reached for her purse and stood.

"Right," Robin said.

Libby planned to phone Robin first thing in the morning.

Because it was a beautiful evening, as it often was in August in the Pacific Northwest, Libby decided to walk to her condo. Her lower back ached from the fresh tattoo and she felt lonely and wished she could be with Phillip. If she wasn't able to set matters straight, she supposed she'd get over him and move on with her life. But she really hoped it wouldn't come to that. What she felt for him, even after not seeing him for so many days, was unlike anything she'd experienced before. It was scary to think about losing him. If nothing else, this long period of unemployment had taught her she was a survivor.

As she walked past the downtown area known for its nightlife, she looked into several lounges. She'd never gone into these places before, but maybe she should start . . . then again, maybe not. This wasn't exactly the best place to meet potential clients.

No sooner had the thought formed than Phillip Stone stepped into the night. Libby saw him from across the street and she stopped and stared. He was alone. Her heart skipped several beats. This was the opportunity she'd been hoping for, the chance to tell him she was sorry and that she missed him dreadfully.

Before she could catch his attention the door opened again and a tall, beautiful blonde stepped out, wrapped her arm around his waist, and smiled up at him.

Libby stopped cold in her tracks. It certainly hadn't taken him long to find someone else.

Chapter 24

Libby woke Saturday morning to the ringing of her phone. She pried open one eye and noted that it wasn't even eight yet. Apparently Robin was so excited she couldn't wait until a decent hour to call and update her on her evening with Judge Roy Bollinger. The stud. The football hero. The man of Robin's dreams.

"You better have had the time of your life to be calling me this early," Libby grumbled into the receiver.

"Libby?"

Libby bolted upright, tossing the

sheet aside as soon as she recognized the caller. "Ava?"

"Did I wake you up?" The girl lowered her voice as if she was afraid of being overheard.

"Not really. I was just lying here thinking I should get up." Saturday was the one day of the week when Libby allowed herself to sleep in. Even then she rarely slept past eight. She'd tossed and turned for several hours last night, unable to get the picture of Phillip and the woman he was with out of her head. Pounding her pillow hadn't helped, and watching late-late-night television hadn't done any good, either. As far as she could tell, she hadn't fallen asleep until sometime around four.

"I'm sorry, but if I didn't call you early then my grandma might have woken up and heard me."

"What's wrong?" Libby knew it must be important for Ava to risk phoning.

"A lady from Social Services contacted Grandma . . . she told her that she wants me to go to the doctor and is making an appointment as soon as she can. Grandma told her I was just fat, but if the state wanted to pay for a visit to the doctor she didn't care. But she wanted it understood that she wasn't paying because she couldn't afford it after Jackson went in for his physical so he could play sports."

Libby didn't dare tell her that she and Lydia Goetz were the ones responsible for contacting Social Services on Ava's behalf. The sooner Ava got medical attention the better. No one knew when this baby was due. Probably not even Ava.

"Grandma got really upset and made me tell her again that I wasn't pregnant. I stayed in my bedroom all day Friday, afraid she would ask to see my stomach. She thinks I was the one who called the lady and she got upset because she's afraid the state might think she's not taking good enough care of us and will send us to a foster home. That won't happen, will it?"

"Oh, Ava, I'm so sorry. No, I'm sure the authorities will want you to stay with your grandmother. But, sweetie, your grandmother will need to know the truth sooner or later. Sooner is better. You won't be able to hide the pregnancy much longer . . . other people will notice."

"I . . . I don't go outside much anymore. It's better that way."

Libby had worried that that was the case. The girl was locked up in her room most of the time anyway. This couldn't be mentally healthy.

"Can you come see me on Monday?" Ava asked.

"Absolutely."

"Oh, thank you."

"Are you taking the vitamins I gave you?" Libby asked.

"Yes, and I'm not adding salt to my food, either."

"Good."

"I try not to eat much at all."

"Oh, Ava, you need to take in enough food to make sure you and your baby are healthy." The fact that she was so afraid of eating was another worry. "Is there anything I can bring you?" She'd gotten Ava a book on pregnancy and some magazines to read. Ones she knew the teenager would enjoy. Casey had sent along a few books, too. Apparently Ava spent most of her time in her room reading.

"Could you get me some books from the library?" she asked, again in a hushed voice.

"Of course. I'll be by after ten." Ava's grandmother was sure to have left for work by then.

"Thank you," the teenager whispered, sounding close to tears.

"Ava," Libby said, feeling she needed to offer the girl some reassurances. "Everything will work out. Don't worry, okay? We'll talk more on Monday, but until then know that I'm your friend and I'll do whatever I can to help you."

"I miss you and Casey and . . ." Ava started to cry and then abruptly cut the connection.

Libby felt dreadful for the teenager. Poor Ava. Contacting Child Protective Services had been the only way Libby could think to help her. Ava needed to see a doctor. It astonished Libby that the girl's grandmother couldn't see that she was pregnant. The pregnancy was becoming more obvious all the time despite Ava's attempts to hide it.

Libby wondered if Ava's brother had figured it out, but he seemed far more interested in playing basketball than he was in his sister. And then there was the neighbor boy. Libby grew more and more suspicious that he was the baby's father. It certainly made sense. Ava seemed to care for whoever had fathered this child and was intent on protecting his identity. Anytime Libby brought up the subject, the young teen clammed up.

Libby's Saturday started off with an unexpected phone call, and the one she expected didn't come until much later. At ten, Libby got tired of waiting and phoned Robin's cell. The phone instantly went to voice mail. Apparently Robin had been out late. Really late.

She tried again at noon and got the same result. Well, okay. She'd wait for Robin to get in touch with her. That didn't happen until almost six o'clock Saturday night.

"It seems like you and the judge had a great time," Libby teased.

"It was all right." Obviously Robin was determined to play it down.

"What time did you get home?" she asked.

"Early. Eleven or so."

Libby had left at about ten-fifteen, ten-thirty, so Robin and Roy must not have stayed much longer.

"We talked a little." Robin didn't sound all that enthused. Perhaps the judge had been a disappointment, but that surprised Libby. He seemed charming and likable.

"Are you seeing him again?" Libby was unsure how much to pressure Robin for information. Naturally she was curious, but she didn't want to appear overly nosy.

"I . . . I don't know."

"He didn't ask?"

"No."

"Oh." Maybe the evening hadn't gone as well as she believed. "Do you want to get together for a movie tomorrow?"

"Maybe. Can I call you?"

"Sure." Libby couldn't help but wonder what had happened. Clearly something was up, but she couldn't imagine what. "If I don't hear from you, then I'll see you at the gym on Monday."

"Oh, yeah, right. See you Monday."

Robin sounded terribly depressed, and frankly Libby wasn't in the best of spirits herself. She longed to ask what had gone wrong but hesitated, not wanting to overstep. "Do you want to talk?" she asked, hoping a little encouragement would help Robin to open up.

"Not now," her attorney friend muttered. "Maybe later, all right?"

"Of course. I'm here if you need me." Libby understood. She wasn't in the mood to discuss the fact that she'd seen Phillip with some gorgeous woman draped all over him. She tried to guess what might have gone wrong for Robin and her judge and suspected that Robin had frozen up again. The poor girl had it bad.

Libby didn't hear from Robin on Sunday and she didn't show up at the gym on Monday morning, either. Phillip did, but Libby pretended not to notice. She caught him looking at her once but she quickly looked away, determined to ignore him. Clearly he'd moved on and pride demanded that she give the same impression.

At ten sharp Libby was parked outside of Ava's house. As soon as she turned off the engine, Ava appeared in the doorway. She raised her hand in greeting. Libby climbed out of the car and brought in the bag of books and a fruit smoothie from the gym. She'd kept it in the freezer at home before driving to Ava's so it was still cold.

To her surprise, Ava hugged her tightly once they were inside the house. The dear girl trembled and buried her face in Libby's shoulder. They sat down together so close their knees touched.

Libby reached for Ava's hands and held them in her own. "I don't want you to be afraid of seeing the doctor. You need to do this if you're going to have a healthy baby. It's for you, too, Ava. This is important."

"I know. But Grandma will be upset and I . . . I just can't do that to her."

"But she needs to know, Ava," Libby told her, not for the first time.

That apparently wasn't the only problem that worried Ava. "What if the lady from the state makes me tell her who the father is? I don't want anything to happen to him . . . We were . . ." She didn't finish the sentence and shook her head, indicating she was unwilling to say anything more.

Knowing how resistant Ava had been regarding the baby's paternity, Libby didn't feel she could pressure her. Again she suspected the boy next door, Jackson's basketball friend. Beyond Peter, she couldn't imagine, didn't want to imagine. Libby was fairly certain that Ava would tell her if she'd been raped or abused, but then, maybe not.

"Why don't we cross that bridge when we need to, okay?"

Ava sucked in a deep breath. "Okay, but I'm not telling. No one can force me to tell, right?"

"Right." Libby decided to let it go for the moment. The girl was terrified enough as it was. "Why are you so afraid of letting anyone know the name of the father?" she asked.

Ava hung her head low. "Because he might go to jail and . . . and I don't want that to happen."

"The sex was consensual?"

"If that means we both agreed, yes,

then it's that word you just said." Blushing, Ava looked away.

Identifying the father wasn't important for now. Libby would let the social worker get the answers to the difficult questions.

"Will you go to the doctor with me?" Ava asked.

"If that's what you want." Libby had offered to be with her once already. She assumed the caseworker would also be present, but Libby didn't know that for a fact.

"I don't know if I can do this if you aren't with me." Ava squeezed her hand. "I don't like needles and I don't want anyone touching me . . . there. I feel . . ." She paused and her lower lip trembled as she struggled not to cry. "I'm afraid, Libby."

"I know, but I'll make sure you aren't alone." Libby wrapped her arms around the teen and hugged her tightly. "Don't you worry. Everything will turn out all right. Do you know how far along you are?"

Ava sniffled and nodded. "Eight months. Maybe a week or two more. It

could be more. The book said the baby
is ready to be born after forty weeks."

"Yes, and the closer you carry the
baby to full term the better it is for the
health of the baby."

Ava nodded. "But I feel sick almost
all the time."

"That's one reason why it's so important for you to see a doctor."

"Okay, but what will happen to him
after he's born? Or she. I hope it's a
she. Is that wrong?"

"No, not at all. As to your questions,
you have a couple of options. You could
let a family adopt the baby."

"Adoption," Ava repeated. "Would
anyone want my baby?"

"Oh yes. There are families on waiting lists who would take your baby and
love him or her so much. Some women
are unable to have children for a number of reasons and they want a baby
badly. They often turn to adoption agencies. They would love your baby, Ava."

She smiled. "But what if I want to
keep the baby?"

"Then that's another option." Warning bells rang like a tornado warning

system in Libby's head, but she didn't want to say or do anything to sway the girl's decision. This was one Ava would need to make on her own or with her grandmother.

"Grandma wouldn't want me to do that; we can't afford to feed anyone else."

From everything she'd heard about the older woman, Libby had to agree finances were a major concern. Darlene Carmichael already had more than she could handle with Jackson and Ava.

"What about, you know, an abortion?" Ava whispered, lowering her voice.

"It's too late for that, Ava. Can you feel the baby move?"

She nodded.

"That's a real person inside of you."

"I know."

Libby had strong feelings on the subject, but she left it at that. Again, it was better to keep her opinions to herself.

"If I decide to let one of those families who can't have children adopt my baby, how will I do it?"

"The state has an adoption agency and there are private agencies, too. They would help guide you through the process. They will take care of your medical expenses, too."

"They will?"

"Yes. And you can meet the parents, if you want."

Her eyes widened. "Would I be able to visit the baby, too?"

"You could, if that was what you wanted. They call that an open adoption. You could have contact with the parents, receive pictures and updates on the child, and . . ." The sound of a door closing came from the area of the kitchen.

"Jackson?" Ava called, her voice trembling slightly.

No answer.

"If it's Grandma . . ."

Jackson walked into the living room holding a glass of water. "Hi," he said, and looked at his sister. His eyes seemed to say Ava was in deep trouble if their grandmother ever found out about Libby stopping by.

"I brought you something," Libby said.

"Oh?"

She pulled out a package of protein bars. She'd seen them advertised at the gym by a pro basketball player. She couldn't remember his name now and she wouldn't have recognized it even if she had. Basketball wasn't a game that interested her. Jackson, however, seemed to love the sport. The bars weren't something his grandmother could afford.

"Max Williams power bars," Jackson repeated as if she'd presented him with a ten-pound box of solid gold. "Wow, thanks."

"Libby's my friend," Ava whispered.

"I know and you don't need to worry; I won't say anything to Grandma about her coming to see you."

Jackson took the box into his room and then went back outside with two of the bars clenched in his hand.

Ava lowered her head. "He doesn't know about the baby."

Libby had suspected as much.

"He wants me to come outside but I don't anymore. I don't know what I'm going to do when school starts."

Classes were scheduled to resume right after Labor Day. Libby had already thought of a solution. "Once your grandmother finds out you're pregnant I can help homeschool you until after the baby is born. That way you'll be able to stay here until you're ready to return to your regular classes."

Ava nodded. "I . . . think I might want to keep my baby."

"You don't need to make that decision now. Think about it, Ava, think very hard, because there is a lot at stake here. It is more than your future; it's the future of your child, too."

"Lots of women do."

"I know, but it's hard work and you need to be prepared for that." Libby didn't feel she could say anything more just yet. She didn't want to influence the teenager, and at the same time she felt she needed to let Ava know it wouldn't be easy to raise this child by herself.

"Thank you, Libby," Ava whispered,

squeezing her hand. "I don't know what I'd do without you."

"Just let me know when your doctor's appointment is scheduled and I'll go with you." She glanced at her watch.

"Do you have to leave now?"

Libby sighed. "Sorry, yes, I have a meeting."

A very important appointment . . . with Martha Reed. The entire future of her own private practice was at stake.

Chapter 25

Libby had visited the home of Mrs. Martha Reed several times while she was working at Burkhart, Smith & Crandall. The mansion—and really, that was the only word to describe it—never failed to impress her. As the large wrought-iron security gates slowly opened to allow her passage, Libby sucked in her breath and whispered a silent prayer. A great deal hung on this meeting. While she was prepared to present herself to Mrs. Reed, Libby couldn't help thinking about her morning with Ava. She was determined to do what she could to help the girl, but her options were few.

The housekeeper answered the door, and although she'd admitted Libby to the house any number of times she gave no indication that she recognized her.

"Hello, Alice," Libby said.

Alice cracked a smile. "Good to see you again, Ms. Morgan."

"You too." Libby stepped into the large foyer. A round mahogany table with a dazzling floral arrangement rested in the center and a crystal chandelier hung overhead, the glass sparkling in the sunlight.

"Mrs. Reed is in the library," Alice told her.

"I know the way," Libby assured the other woman.

It didn't matter; Alice led her to the room, opened the massive pocket doors, and announced her. "Ms. Morgan to see you."

"Libby." Mrs. Reed held out her hand without getting up. Although she was in her eighties, Martha Reed remained a striking woman. She wore her thick white hair in a bun at the base of her head. Libby had never seen her in anything but a dress. In fact, she couldn't remember ever seeing the older woman unstylish. On a couple of occasions Mrs. Reed had taken Libby into her rose garden. She pruned the bushes herself and was inordinately proud of her prize roses. She'd worn an apron over her dress as she'd wandered through the garden, pruning as she strolled along the paved pathway.

"Sit down, please."

"Thank you." Libby took the wingback chair next to the family matriarch. Her husband, Bernard Reed, had died nearly twenty years ago. He'd devised some small part that had revolutionized the airplane engine and had been handsomely rewarded for his invention.

"I've asked Alice to bring us tea."

"That would be lovely." Past experience taught Libby that Mrs. Reed preferred to chat before discussing business. Libby guessed that Ben Holmes had been all business from the moment he walked in the door. Big mistake.

Alice rolled in an elaborate cart and

poured them each a cup of steaming Earl Grey. She didn't need to ask how Libby liked her tea, she remembered and added a teaspoon of milk without being prompted.

"Thank you, Alice," Libby said when the housekeeper handed her the delicate china cup and saucer.

"My pleasure."

The second cup went to her employer. The cart remained but Alice left the room, closing the doors behind her. The library was an impressive room. Floor-to-ceiling cherrywood shelves were filled with thousands of volumes. Some were valuable collector's items. Mrs. Reed had an impressive array of autographed books. Libby had held a copy of *Uncle Tom's Cabin* and seen Harriet Beecher Stowe's signature for herself. Mark Twain's signature was penned in *The Innocents Abroad* and Ernest Hemingway had autographed *The Old Man and the Sea*. That was only a small part of the older woman's collection. Row upon row of autographed books dating as far back as the early 1800s graced these shelves.

Libby loved this room, with its faint scent of leather. She knew that Mrs. Reed spent a good portion of her afternoons in here. If she wasn't in the library or attending some charity function then she was in her beloved rose garden. Libby was somewhat surprised the older woman had chosen to meet in the library, seeing that it was such a beautiful sunny afternoon. But then this was business and Mrs. Reed preferred to talk business in the library.

"How have you been, my dear?" Mrs. Reed asked as she stirred her tea, dissolving the single sugar cube.

"Very well. And you?"

Martha sighed. "Good."

"The children and grandchildren?" Libby asked.

The older woman's face lit up as she mentioned each of her four children, from the oldest to the youngest. When she finished she spoke of her nine grandchildren. Mrs. Reed was a woman who loved family. The vast majority of her estate was designated to charity, but she would leave a substantial sum to each of her children and had set up trust funds for each grandchild.

Libby knew all of Martha Reed's family members by name, although she'd never met them. Hershel had, she knew, but not her.

After she updated Libby on her family, Mrs. Reed focused her attention on Libby. "What have you been doing with yourself these past five months?"

Five months? It felt like so much longer. It would kill her to admit she'd been unable to find a position in all that time. Instead of focusing on the negative, she relayed the changes that had come about in her life.

"For one thing, I took up knitting."

Mrs. Reed rested her china cup in the saucer. "Really? I knit myself, but that was years ago now."

"You'd enjoy it, Mrs. Reed," Libby assured her. "I started out making preemie hats and then advanced to . . ."

"Preemie hats?"

Libby explained why these warm hats were so important to tiny infants and how the customers at A Good Yarn had taken it upon themselves to supply the warm, knitted hats for the babies in need.

"Why, I think I would enjoy knitting those myself," she said when Libby finished.

"I'd be more than happy to help you get started," she offered.

"Oh, dear, thank you but there's no need. Alice and I will be able to figure it out."

"I'll give you the name and address of the yarn store," Libby offered.

"That would be wonderful." Mrs. Reed seemed enthused and even a little excited.

"I've also volunteered at Seattle General Hospital, rocking the newborns."

The older woman's eyes widened with surprise. "I didn't think rocking babies would be of interest to you."

Libby smiled. "It came as a shock to me, too. Both knitting and spending time with the babies has helped me deal with . . . life's frustrations." Again she was determined not to mention that she hadn't found work with another firm.

Mrs. Reed went silent for a couple of

moments. "I suppose you heard that I've left Burkhart, Smith & Crandall."

"I did get word that you'd recently made that decision."

"Bernard trusted them with our business for many years. I never thought to question his choice. My husband was an astute businessman and Hershel was most helpful following Bernard's death."

Libby responded with a simple nod of acknowledgment.

"But lately I've grown displeased." She pinched her lips together for an instant before she continued. "I can't tolerate that young man Hershel assigned to my account."

"Ben Holmes is a gifted attorney." Libby felt obliged to defend her former colleague. "But he—"

"He's rude and arrogant and always in a dreadful rush. He told me he didn't have time for tea. I hardly had a chance to tell Alice not to bother before he pulled out my file and started talking business. He might not want tea, but I prefer it when discussing the details. I found him to be most unpleasant."

Libby recognized that to Mrs. Reed business was a delicate issue and should be dealt with in a leisurely manner. "I apologize for Ben," Libby said, although she knew Hershel had probably already offered his own regrets. "He's young and ambitious."

"Hershel said much the same thing and assigned me some other attorney . . . Oh dear, I've forgotten the name now. Ander, Anson . . . something like that."

"Jake Amber?" Libby guessed. She couldn't think whom else Martha might mean.

"That's it," she said, and sounded relieved. "It was the same thing. Oh, he had tea with me, but I could see he didn't enjoy it. Everyone is always in such a rush these days. Why, I can remember the time back in the mid-seventies when our son . . ." She paused and shook her head. "You don't want to hear the ramblings of an old woman."

Libby immediately recognized this was a small test to see if she'd changed from the attorney and woman she once was. "On the contrary," Libby said, and

settled against the back of the comfortable chair. "I'd like nothing better
than for you to tell me about your son.
Paul or Wade?"

"Paul. Oh, that son of ours—he's our
youngest, you know—was such a ras-
cal. He, too, was always in a rush . . ."

Libby relaxed and let the older woman
talk. Martha Reed was proud of her
family and it showed. Libby found the
sound of her voice comfortable in a
soothing sort of way. She'd never known
her maternal grandparents—they had
died when she was young. Her father's
parents had lived in Texas and Libby
saw them only sporadically through the
years. They both died when she was in
her early twenties, and while she still
had an aunt and two uncles, they
weren't part of her life. Libby mailed
them each a Christmas card every year,
but that was the extent of their contact.

What she loved about Mrs. Reed was
the close connection she maintained
with each of her children and grandchildren. How Libby envied that.

Hershel had told her she needed a
life; what Libby realized now was that

she needed family, too, needed that sense of connection that came from being part of a whole. In the months since she'd been let go, she'd started building one. Not a traditional family perhaps, but a family of the heart. She was closest to Robin, but there were Lydia and Sharon and Ava, too. Libby had hoped Phillip might become . . . She put a halt to that line of thinking. A sadness settled over her. Oh, how she missed him.

Mrs. Reed spoke animatedly for several minutes and Libby listened attentively, laughing now and again.

"I hope your children and grandchildren realize how fortunate they are to have you," Libby said, and meant it sincerely.

Mrs. Reed smiled. "You flatter me."

"I value family. As you may remember I lost my own mother when I was barely a teenager." Her thoughts drifted to Ava and her heart clenched. While Libby would never replace the mother Ava had lost, she fully intended to be a friend and mentor to the young teen.

"You still miss her, don't you, dear?"

"Yes, but . . ." Libby hesitated before speaking, wondering if she was doing the right thing by even mentioning Ava. "This morning I went to visit a young girl I met at the yarn store. She's a thirteen-year-old living with her grandmother, and she's pregnant."

Mrs. Reed gasped. "Pregnant?"

Libby nodded. "Her biggest fear is what will happen when her grandmother finds out. She hasn't seen a doctor yet."

"How far along is she?"

"We don't know. Possibly as much as eight months."

Mrs. Reed shook her head as Libby relayed a few more of the details, being careful not to say names.

"This girl is lucky to have you helping her. You have used this time away from the firm wisely," Martha said after several moments. "I'm proud of you, Libby, very, very proud."

Emotion swept over Libby and a lump formed in her throat at the words of praise from this wonderful woman who'd given so much love to her family.

They chatted for a few minutes more

before Mrs. Reed announced, "It's time we got to the matter at hand, my dear. Now, tell me what you have in mind."

Libby reached for her briefcase and brought out her notes. She had to work from memory as the files remained with the firm, but she had a good recollection of where they had left off in the estate planning. She wasn't presumptuous enough to assume she would manage the entire account, but she hoped Martha would be willing to allow her to take over everything that she had handled previously. She also made several recommendations and suggestions for moving forward.

When she finished she realized she'd probably said too much.

"These are all very complicated legal anglings."

"They are," Libby agreed. "The thing is, you don't need to understand it all but I feel obligated to explain it as best I can. I want you to see what will happen in the future to the funds you leave behind."

"That's why I would hire you."

"Exactly." Libby sincerely hoped the

other woman would consider bringing this aspect of her business to Libby.

Martha set her empty teacup aside. "As you can imagine there are a number of law firms vying for my full account."

Libby suspected there would be.

"Hershel has been in contact several times himself, looking to mend fences, but I fear it's too late for that. I told him before that that young man didn't suit me, but he refused to listen. I went so far as to request that you be reinstated at the firm. Hershel said he'd like nothing better himself but the matter was out of his hands."

Libby counted Hershel as both mentor and friend and suspected he had been outvoted by the other partners.

"Naturally my inclination is to continue with you," Mrs. Reed murmured thoughtfully.

Libby sat up straighter. "I can assure you that you would be my most important client. I would give you my undivided attention." What she failed to add was that Mrs. Reed, for the time being, would be her *only* client.

"As you can imagine this is a very important decision."

"I agree and I don't want you to rush. Take your time and think it over carefully," Libby advised. Bottom line, she wanted only what was best for the older woman and her family.

"I'll talk this over with my children. You have one advantage, but I do have to tell you, Libby, that the fact that you're a sole practitioner isn't in your favor. All the others competing for my business are large firms with support staff and resources. I don't know how they'd feel about me taking a part of this account elsewhere."

Libby had no argument. "But no other attorney will care about you as much as I do," she offered.

"I realize that, my dear." She stifled a yawn and Libby realized it was time for her to go.

Reaching for her briefcase, she inserted the legal pad with her notes. "Thank you for seeing me again, Mrs. Reed."

"It was a delight."

"For me, too."

As if by magic Alice appeared.

"Alice will show you out."

Libby stood and, holding on to her briefcase with both hands, smiled down at the older woman. Everything rested with Martha Reed now. Libby had made her case and now all she could do was wait.

"I'll be giving you a call soon," the older woman promised.

"This way, Ms. Morgan," Alice said and motioned toward the door.

Libby left the house and reached inside her purse to turn her cell back on and realized she had three messages, two of which had come from Robin.

She hadn't talked to Robin since Saturday night. She immediately pushed the button that would connect her to her friend's cell. As she walked down the steps to her car, she pressed the phone to her ear. She hoped she'd catch Robin out of court.

Her friend answered on the second ring. "Hi," Robin said lamely.

"Hi. You sound dreadful. What's up?"

"I called in sick with the flu."

That explained why she hadn't shown up at the gym that morning.

"Only I don't have the flu. I just couldn't face going into work today. I feel so wretched and miserable. I'm sure I won't ever hear from Roy again."

"Okay, that does it. I'm on my way over and I'm bringing chicken soup."

Chapter 26

Robin clenched a tissue and held it beneath her nose. If there was one thing she hated in this world it was emotional women. Three glasses of wine with Roy Bollinger and almost overnight she'd become a hysterical one herself. It was all so hopeless. She was hopeless.

Sniffling, she blew her nose and then rubbed the back of her hand across her upper lip. The tears only contributed to her misery. She felt weak and spineless and a wreck.

The doorbell chimed and it was almost more effort than she could bear to answer it. She wouldn't have budged from the sofa if she didn't already know it was Libby.

Libby walked into the condo, took one look at Robin, and shook her head. "You look dreadful."

"Thank you ever so much," she muttered sarcastically. She was still in her cotton nightgown and hadn't bothered to comb her hair or make the effort to put on makeup. She was a complete mess, inside and out.

"Okay, tell me," Libby insisted. "What happened?"

"I thought you were bringing me soup."

"I decided making an extra stop would take too long. You sounded—"

"Miserable . . . and I am." She returned to the sofa, jerking another tissue from the box with such force it toppled to the floor. She pressed the tissue against her face with both hands. Holding back a sob, she collapsed onto the sofa.

"Are you going to tell me what happened or are you going to make me torture it out of you?" Libby dropped her purse and joined her, sitting in the chair across from her.

Robin hiccuped in an effort to suppress a groan. She had brought Libby into this and invited further embarrassment, but she had to talk to someone or she'd go crazy.

"Stop," Libby said, "I want to get us something to drink."

Robin frowned and shook her head, dismissing the very thought. "It's too early in the day for anything alcoholic."

Libby smiled. "I wasn't talking about a Manhattan, Robin, I was thinking we could both use a glass of ice water."

"Oh." Robin felt all the more foolish, although at this point she was ready to drown her sorrows in just about anything.

Libby disappeared into the kitchen and returned in short order with two tall glasses of water.

Robin took a deep swallow. The cold liquid helped relieve the tenderness in her throat. In all her life, Robin couldn't remember being this emotional over anything. Maybe this was a symptom of early-onset menopause. She hadn't even been this upset when she went through her divorce. Really, she was being ridiculous. But everything felt so bleak, so impossible. She took another long drink; she hadn't realized how thirsty she was. Well, no wonder; she'd been having regular bouts of tears for the better part of three days.

Libby returned to the chair and patiently waited for Robin to start explaining. She didn't urge or pressure her and for that Robin was sincerely grateful.

"After you left us, Roy and I had another glass of wine. He refused to let me pay although I insisted I wanted to repay him for recommending you for the position."

Libby nodded without comment, which encouraged Robin to continue. She paused long enough to take another swallow. Again the cold water against her throat helped.

"That's just it. Nothing happened. Nothing's ever going to happen. I'm spineless and I hate myself."

"Oh, Robin, I think—"

"The minute you left on Friday I clammed up like a . . . a . . . clam," she said, cutting her friend off. "I don't know what Roy thought because he grew quiet, too. We tried to talk but every subject returned to his wife, Sally. It was Sally this and Sally that. I don't stand a chance; I'm never going to be Sally."

"Did you try to talk about the wine?" Libby asked.

Robin rolled her eyes. "I tried, but there's only so much to be said about pinot noir, and I'd . . . I'd said all I knew, which took up maybe thirty seconds. Do you know what Roy added? Well, of course you don't. His comment was to tell me that Sally preferred white wines."

"Could you bring up office gossip?"

Robin shook her head. "Roy isn't the type to gossip and I don't really know any. I tend to mind my own business at work."

"You and I are too much alike," Libby muttered, and leaned against the back of the chair, crossing her legs. Robin was glad at least one of them could relax.

Libby was right, too: they were a lot alike. Robin didn't take time at the wa-

tercooler to hear juicy tidbits; she had
work to do, meetings to attend, criminals to prosecute. Gossip simply didn't
interest her.

"Does he have children?" Libby
asked, leaning forward slightly. "I was
just with Martha Reed and she talked
nonstop about her children and grandchildren. You could always ask Roy
about his family."

Robin shook her head. Libby was
trying to help but all she was doing was
proving how utterly useless it was.
"Sally couldn't have kids." She wiped
her hand beneath her nose again. "By
the time I finished our second glass of
wine I realized that Roy will never view
me as anything but a weak substitute
for his beloved Sally."

"Robin, you're jumping to conclusions."

"What else am I to assume?" Libby
had been with them only a short while
and after she left everything had gone
so quiet . . . so awkward and uncomfortable. Every word out of Roy's mouth
had been about Sally. It must be nice
to be that loved. All the evening had

proven to Robin was that she didn't stand a chance with Roy. She couldn't compete with a dead woman.

Libby's eyes widened with what looked like disbelief. "He seemed happy enough to hear from you on Friday night. He was the one who suggested you meet, wasn't he?"

"Yes, but . . ."

"Robin—"

"I was there," she cut in a second time. "I'm not a complete dunce, Libby. I can read the signs. He isn't interested. He's polite and friendly, but the bottom line is obvious even to me. Roy respects me and thinks I'm a good attorney but he isn't interested in developing any kind of relationship."

Libby's shoulders sagged with defeat. "I've never seen you this distraught; I want to help."

"I know," Robin whispered. "I'm just so disappointed. I've carried this romantic fantasy around in my head for months. It's time I face facts. That's all it is . . . a fantasy. Make believe. And it will never be anything more."

They sat quietly for a few minutes

while Libby apparently mulled everything over.

"When was the last time you ate?"
she asked, glancing at her watch.

Robin couldn't remember precisely.
"Yesterday around lunchtime, I guess.
Why?"

"Because everything will seem better with food in your stomach." Libby
started for the kitchen.

"Good luck," Robin called after her.
"I haven't gotten groceries in weeks.
The milk is so old it has a picture of the
Lindbergh baby on the carton."

"Okay, fine, I'm going out to pick up
dinner for us. I'm famished. What
sounds good to you?"

Robin shook her head. "I don't really
care. You pick."

"Okay, I will."

After Libby left, Robin took a quick
shower and changed clothes. She was
combing out her wet hair when the
doorbell chimed. It certainly hadn't
taken Libby long to find dinner.

When she opened the door it wasn't
Libby who stood on the other side of
the threshold. It was Roy.

Once more she went completely mute. Robin couldn't have said a word to save her soul.

After a stilted, awkward moment, Roy asked, "Would it be all right if I came in for a few minutes? I promise I won't stay long."

Still unable to find her tongue, she stepped aside to allow him into her condo.

Once the blood returned to her brain, Robin gestured for him to sit down. Embarrassed by the stash of used tissues that littered the top of the coffee table, she immediately stuffed them inside the empty tissue box. The pillow from her bed and a blanket were sprawled across the sofa. She reached for the blanket next, intent on folding it.

"I came because I heard you'd phoned in sick," Roy said. "Your assistant gave me your address. Are you okay . . . ? I mean, you look like you're feeling better."

"I am better, thanks."

He remained rooted to the carpet just inside her front door, hands buried in his pockets. "I'm not good at this sort of thing," he murmured.

"What sort of thing?" she asked. She folded the blanket and held it tightly against her stomach.

He looked away. His gaze bounced around the room, landing here and there and everywhere—except on her. "I don't know what I did wrong on Friday night . . ."

"You didn't do anything wrong," she rushed to tell him. She stopped just short of saying she couldn't be Sally. He'd come to her and she needed to listen and not leap to conclusions or make rash judgments.

"I didn't do anything wrong . . . but," he hesitated, looking her way for the first time.

"But what?" she asked softly, her heart rate accelerating rapidly.

"But you grew so quiet and then you wanted to leave and I was sure I must have said or done something to offend you."

"You didn't, Roy, it's just that . . ."

"What?" he urged, taking one step closer.

She looked down, wondering how best to address the subject.

He moved slightly closer. "I like you, Robin." He twisted his head to one side and briefly squeezed his eyes shut.

"I . . . like you, too," she rushed to tell him.

"You do?" He sounded shocked.

She nodded.

"I mean, I really like you; I have for a long time, but I didn't know how to let you know and then I saw you at the fund-raiser and we talked and . . ."

"Roy," she breathed, hardly able to believe what he said. "Are you telling me . . . are you saying you're interested in me romantically?"

He didn't answer right away, and then he exhaled slowly. "Would it be all right if I sat down?"

"Of course."

He claimed the chair Libby had recently vacated.

Robin sat on the sofa across from him, the folded blanket still pressed against her stomach like a security shield.

"I married Sally when we were barely out of high school."

Sally again. Robin forced back a groan.

"I've only been with one woman my entire adult life. When she died I assumed that I'd live alone until I died, too."

Robin wasn't sure any comment was required of her.

"But I've been lonely. I'm over fifty . . ."

"That's not old," she blurted out.

"Some days it feels like it."

"It shouldn't," she added with a shy smile.

He offered her one in return and it felt as if her heart was melting inside her chest.

He exhaled again. "What I'm trying to say and doing a terrible job of . . . is that I realized I don't want to be alone for the rest of my life. I didn't think it was possible to fall in love again, but since being with you . . . I think it's a possibility." He looked down at his hands. "I'd like to date you, Robin. I . . ."

"Okay," she said, laughing at herself. He was talking about her now, not Sally.

"We can start slow . . ."

"Okay, whatever you want." It probably wasn't in good taste to show how eager she was.

"Do you play bridge?" he asked.

"No, but I can learn."

"I'll teach you," he said, grinning.

She nodded.

He smiled and she smiled back.

"How about Wednesday night? We can have dinner and then we'll have our first bridge lesson. I'll invite the Wainwrights over and . . ."

"The Wainwrights?"

"Yes, they were friends of Sally's and mine and . . ."

Robin stopped him. "Roy," she said, "I do think there's something I should say: I'm not Sally. If you're looking for a replacement for her, then it's not me." It amazed her that her spirits could rise and fall so swiftly. She supposed she should be honored that he'd chosen her as a replacement for his dead wife, but Robin wanted . . . needed to be loved for herself.

"Sally and I used to play bridge as often as three times a week."

"I'm honored that you have such confidence in my card-playing ability," she murmured.

"We used to dance, too. Do you dance?"

She shook her head. He'd talked at length about his and Sally's love of dancing.

Everything he said confirmed her worst suspicions.

"I believe I might have spoken too soon," she whispered. "The thing is, Roy, we really don't have that much in common."

"But you said you'd be willing to learn," he reminded her.

"Yes, I did, but at the time I didn't realize that you were looking for me to just play the role of Sally. You must have loved her a great deal."

"I did."

"There's probably someone out there who plays bridge and likes to dance and do all the things you did with Sally. I'm honored that you want to do those same things with me, but I can see right now, this relationship won't work. I'm sorry, Roy, so very sorry."

His eyes widened and it looked for a moment as if he was about to argue with her. "Okay, I can accept that."

He stretched his arm toward her as if to shake her hand. Robin smiled and walked toward him. She slipped her arms around him. Slowly his arms came around her, his touch gentle, tentative.

After a few moments he slowly released her. "I blew this, didn't I? I said all the wrong things."

"You were honest."

Robin stepped away from him for fear she would change her mind. Part of her was more than willing to be a stand-in for his dead wife, hoping against hope that he would eventually grow to love her, too. Quickly she changed her mind. The stakes were much too high.

Without another word, he reluctantly turned and left.

Surprisingly, after a few minutes Robin felt better than she had in days. Worlds better. The disappointment and frustration she'd carried on her shoulders was gone. She'd laid her cards on the table and it was a relief.

It couldn't have been easy for Roy to seek her out. She admired him for the courage it had taken to come to her condo.

The doorbell chimed again and Robin opened it to find Libby with a take-out bag dangling from each hand. "I got us Italian."

"I love Italian."

"Me too, and I worked out this morning, and you didn't," Robin's friend reminded her.

"I'll be there Wednesday," Robin said, and took one bag away from Libby.

"Hey, you're looking much better." Libby grinned as if she were solely responsible for the transformation.

"I feel better." But she didn't say why.

Opening a kitchen drawer, Robin removed two forks and handed the first one to Libby. They moved to the small kitchen table by the window. Robin had a view of the Seattle skyline. As she glanced out at the street she saw Roy standing on the corner across from her building. He had his hands in his pockets and he remained frozen, looking up at her floor. It was impossible for him to see her.

After a moment or two he removed his hand from his pocket, pressed his fingers to his lips, and blew her a kiss.

It was quite possibly the sweetest thing Robin had ever seen any man do. And he'd done it for her.

Phillip showed up at the gym right on time on Wednesday morning. Libby pretended not to notice, but to her surprise he couldn't seem to take his eyes off her. Every time she glanced in his direction he was watching her. By the time she finished her workout, Libby's mouth was dry and her heart was pounding. She knew this had nothing to do with her routine on the treadmill. Before Friday night she'd been desperate to make amends, if at all possible. But it hadn't been as easy to eat crow as she'd imagined. She lacked both opportunity and courage.

Then after seeing him with Ms. Bimbo—that wasn't fair; the other woman was stunning—Libby swallowed hard. His date had been lovely—in fact, she'd been perfect. Libby bet she wasn't forced to work out in a gym five mornings a week in order to sweat off an extra ten pounds. Okay, she was being hard on herself; she was no more than three pounds heavier than she'd been when Hershel called her into his office.

Despite the fact that Phillip couldn't take his eyes off her, he didn't make an effort to talk to her. If this was his way of sending a message, then she was too much of a coward to act on it.

Then later that same morning, Phillip stopped off at the nursery. He had to know this was one of her days to volunteer.

He nonchalantly walked into the room, and picked up a chart as though he was there on official business. When he looked up, he pretended to be surprised to see Libby there.

She sat in the rocker, a sleeping infant in her arms, and met his gaze head-on, afraid her expression might give her away. Seeing him again gave her hope she could redeem herself and resuscitate their relationship.

"You really shouldn't ever plan on being onstage," she told him.

"Oh?"

"You're a much better physician than you are an actor."

"Really?"

It appeared the conversation on his end was limited to one-word replies.

"You knew I'd be here."

"Did I?"

Okay, this was better. He was up to two words. "Yes."

"Not necessarily."

Okay, two could play this two-word reply game. "Why's that?"

He set the chart down and stepped toward her, crossing his arms. "You seemed pretty upset about missing that job interview. From what I remember you blamed the babies."

"No," she corrected. "I blamed myself." Libby hesitated and then rushed ahead, hoping to find the right words. "It shook me up pretty bad, blowing that interview. I was down on myself and I reacted impulsively. I . . . I do that sometimes, and then later I regret the things I say and do." Her eyes widened with an appeal for understanding.

He held his ground for several moments before he spoke. "Regret, you say?"

Libby nodded. "Quite a bit of regret, if you must know."

"I see."

Undeterred, Libby plowed ahead. "I was wondering . . . hoping, really, if you'd forgive that outburst and pretend it never happened. The truth is, Phillip, I've missed you."

He joined his hands behind his back, and then a slow, easy grin came into play. "Actually, I was hoping you'd come to your senses."

Libby glanced down at the baby in her arms. "I don't think you missed me nearly as much as I missed you."

"Oh?"

Libby thought it was only fair to let him know she'd seen him with the Beauty Queen.

"I saw you on Friday," she said. It was important that he know Libby had been out as well. She had social opportunities of her own and so she added, "I was out with . . . a *friend* myself."

"Any particular friend?" he prodded, with slightly narrowed eyes.

She wasn't about to go into details. They weren't important. "A very good *friend,* if you must know."

"Did you have a good time?" he asked.

"Very. You looked like you did, too." Okay, that was a slight exaggeration.

"Looks can be deceiving." He offered her a tentative smile. "The whole time I was wishing I was with you."

"Were you really . . . ?" Her heart went soft with emotion.

"There's something to be said about . . . friendship. I missed you, too, Libby, more than I thought possible."

"Oh, Phillip, I was such a fool. Forgive me, please."

The smile faded from his eyes and his look grew serious. His gaze held her captive. "It was a good lesson for us both. What we share is special, Libby. We've both had time to step back and think this through."

"I'm willing to give us a second chance if you are," she burst out, hopeful and at the same time afraid.

He hesitated and then nodded.

Libby held her arm out to him. Phillip gripped her hand with his own. Bending over, he kissed her knuckles. "Okay, tell me who you were out with Friday night."

"You first," she insisted.

Phillip grinned. "A blind date. One of my poker buddies set me up."

Libby looked away. "She was adorable."

"Was she?" he asked, as if he hadn't noticed. "You were with Robin?"

She nodded.

His grin grew wide. "Thought so. Why were you walking back to your condo alone?"

"You saw me?" Only now was he admitting that. She felt like she'd been sucker punched. Irritation flared but only briefly. Phillip was allowed that. He'd earned it.

"I saw you standing there on the other side of the street."

Libby looked up at him and rolled her

eyes. "I bet you were on top of the world to see me mooning over you."

"You were mooning?"

"Big-time."

"Good, that was what I hoped."

Sharon entered the nursery just then, and when she saw Phillip, the nurse's gaze instantly connected with Libby's. She raised both brows and her lips quivered with a vain attempt to suppress a smile. It looked as if she was about to comment when Phillip spoke. "I'm helping to organize the hospital's fund-raising dinner next week. Are you interested?"

Posters for the dinner were displayed all over the hospital. The tickets were $200 each, which was more than Libby could manage. But if Phillip was asking her, well, that was a different story.

"I could be," she said, playing it cool.

"I've got space at my table and an extra ticket if you'd care to join me."

"I'd love to."

His gaze held and warmed hers.

"Is there any chance we could go out on your sailboat later this afternoon?" Libby asked, remembering that the first time he'd kissed her had been while they were on the water together.

"That can be arranged," he assured her.

"If you two are looking for privacy there's a cleaning closet down the hall," Sharon piped up from across the room.

Phillip jiggled his eyebrows suggestively and Libby laughed. It felt good to laugh and she was excited that Phillip had been willing to accept her apology.

Libby walked on air for the rest of her shift. After she'd finished she met Abby Higginbotham for coffee. "You should attend the fund-raising dinner," she advised Libby. "You're looking for clients and I could introduce you to a couple of wealthy prospects."

"Phillip invited me to sit at his table, and you're right, it might be a good chance to network." She should be thinking about Mrs. Reed. The older woman didn't like to be rushed when it came to making a decision, even a small one. Libby could be patient. But it wasn't the possibility of getting the older woman as a client that filled Libby's mind. Instead all she could think about was Phillip. She hadn't wanted to admit how much being with him meant to her. Now that they'd made up, Libby's head swam with possibilities, hope, and a mixture of joy and happy anticipation.

Chapter 27

After leaving the hospital, Libby walked to the yarn store. Her step was lighter than it had been in a good long while. She'd be meeting Phillip later at Lake Washington and it was all she could do to keep her feet from dancing down the sidewalk.

She was only a block away from A Good Yarn when her cell chirped. Caller ID told her it was the firm, probably Sarah. Because she hadn't yet heard from the paralegal, Libby had made other arrangements after meeting with Mrs. Reed. Feeling positive and inspired, she'd leased a space in a nearby office complex that had the advantage of a receptionist. Her services, plus that of the other office equipment, were included in the rental fee.

Once Libby was on her feet, she'd hire a paralegal . . . and it wouldn't be Sarah. Despite all the years they'd worked together Sarah hadn't found the courage to be honest with her—she'd let her silence do the talking for her.

Only it wasn't Sarah on the phone.

Instead it was the managing partner, Hershel Burkhart. "Libby," he said, sounding friendly and upbeat. "How are you, my dear?"

Hershel was the last person she'd expected to hear from.

"Fabulous." Truth was she'd rarely felt better. While she wasn't overwhelmed with clients, they would come. She would keep her own hours and continue with her volunteering and knitting until then.

"I was wondering if it would be possible for us to meet for a drink this afternoon?"

Libby stopped walking and stood in the middle of the sidewalk like a large rock in the center of a river. People rushed past her, giving her space as she pressed her cell phone against her ear. Traffic noises came at her from all sides. Her mind whirled with all the possible reasons Hershel might want to speak to her. Only one came to mind.

They wanted her back. He'd managed to talk reason into the other partners.

Oh, sure, she'd signed a twelve-month lease and now Hershel was going to ask her to come back to the firm.

"Libby?"

"Yes, of course. What time?"

"Does four work for you?" he asked, and mentioned a downtown hotel.

"I'll be there at four," she managed to respond. Libby ended the call and dumped her cell back into her purse. She resisted the urge to contact Robin but she texted Phillip, explaining that she'd need to take a raincheck on their sailing date.

Her mind continued to whirl—if Hershel wanted her, then she wouldn't come cheap.

At four Libby sat at the bar at the Four Seasons. She straightened when Hershel walked into the dimly lit area. He hadn't changed much in the intervening months, she noticed. He grinned when he saw her, and wove his way around tables and chairs in order to join her in the far corner of the room. Libby had chosen the table that she felt would offer them the most privacy. She stood as he approached and offered him her cheek, which he kissed lightly. Then, setting his briefcase on the floor, he pulled out a chair and joined her.

Libby crossed her legs and relaxed, content to let him do the talking. The waitress came for their drink order and they both asked for a glass of merlot.

They exchanged pleasantries until their wine arrived. Hershel touched the rim of his goblet to hers. "I see you took my advice."

"Oh?"

"You're volunteering at the hospital, I hear, and dating that doctor."

So he knew about Phillip.

"Do you enjoy sailing?"

My goodness, he'd been keeping close tabs on her. No doubt through Sarah. Libby was determined not to reveal her surprise. "I do."

"Wonderful." He sampled his wine and nodded in approval.

Libby had yet to taste her own as she struggled not to give away her surprise. "You told me to get a life."

"Not everyone takes my words to heart," he said with a smile.

"I understand you've decided to open your own office," he continued, setting his wineglass down on the small circular table.

"I have." The ink had yet to dry on the office lease, but he didn't need to know that.

"Congratulations."

"Thank you."

Hershel leaned forward slightly. "I also understand that you recently met with Martha Reed."

Libby smiled, rather amused, although she was sure his source had been her former paralegal. "Hershel,

have you had a private investigator following me?" she asked, half-joking.

He grinned and shook his head. "I
have my sources."

"Apparently you do."

His smile faded. "I called because a
couple of the other partners are concerned about your visit with Martha
Reed."

"Oh?"

"They feel you're poaching our clients."

"Poaching?" Libby repeated, stunned
that he would suggest she would do
such a thing.

"The truth is, given your position, I
would have done the same thing. Unfortunately, the others don't see it that
way. They feel that Mrs. Reed is our
client."

"Was your client," she reminded him.
"She left the firm."

"I'm pleased with the changes you've
made since leaving the firm," he continued, ignoring her comment. "You're
doing exactly what I hoped you would
and I applaud that. I couldn't be more
pleased, but Libby," he paused and re-

garded her steadily, his gaze wide and sincere, "I don't want you to make a misstep now."

"Misstep?" He'd just admitted that given the opportunity he would have done the same thing.

"Martha Reed is a longtime friend. I knew, given time, she would eventually have a change of heart. The partners and I spoke with her recently, just after your visit, as a matter of fact, and she's decided to come back to the firm."

"Oh." Libby couldn't hide her disappointment. "And who will she be working with?" Hope sprang eternal; perhaps the firm wanted her back after all.

"We're assigning Linda Freeman to the account. The partners feel Mrs. Reed does better when she can communicate her needs to a woman."

Not Libby. Linda.

Again she swallowed the taste of disappointment.

"But—"

Hershel held up a hand, stopping her. "I know; she'd left the firm and you had every right, but it irritated the others." He left the words hanging, leaving her to speculate.

Libby had a good idea what he was telling her. Basically her chances of being asked to return to the firm had been dashed because she'd taken the initiative and contacted the elderly woman on her own. A sickening feeling tightened her stomach.

Hershel's eyes held hers. "I tried," he admitted.

Libby nodded, letting him know she understood. Managing a weak smile, she whispered, "Congratulations. I think Linda will do a great job."

Hershel smiled back encouragingly. "Starting your own practice is a big challenge, Libby. I don't doubt that you'll make it a success."

"Thank you."

"You're a good attorney."

Libby looped the purse strap over her shoulder. "My best to the other partners," Libby murmured.

By the time Libby was outside the Four Seasons she felt like kicking something. It was apparent that Sarah, the paralegal she had once considered a good friend, had been more than willing to relay information to one or more of the partners. No wonder Libby hadn't heard from her.

When she checked her messages later that afternoon, Libby saw that she had a missed call from Martha Reed. She phoned back right away.

"I'm so sorry to disappoint you, my dear," the dignified woman apologized. "I talked over the decision with my children. They all know how much I've enjoyed working with you. However, they're concerned, as I am, that you don't have the backing of a larger firm."

"I understand," Libby said, although it was difficult to hide her feelings.

"And then several of the partners and Hershel came to the house and made their plea."

"What made you decide to go back to the firm?" Libby asked, curiosity getting the best of her. She couldn't imagine what the partners could have promised. Mrs. Reed had been adamant that she was ready to move on. The firm had already failed her twice.

"Frankly, they made me a very attractive offer."

"Oh?"

"Yes, and really, they made it impossible to refuse. They agreed to cap my fees."

Libby had guessed that the incentive must have been something along those lines. Considering the money Mrs. Reed brought into the firm, the partners must have been desperate not to lose her. Losing clients was never good, especially influential ones like Mrs. Reed.

"I do wish you the very best, my dear," the charming lady told Libby.

"I know you do. And if you ever feel that you want my legal advice please feel free to contact me." Libby enjoyed Mrs. Reed and would do anything she could to help her.

Right away she called Phillip, but his cell went straight to voice mail. Thankfully Robin was available. She met her at the Starbucks closest to the courthouse. They each ordered a skinny vanilla latte and sat in the corner with their heads together.

Robin listened intently as Libby relayed the events of the afternoon.

"You've got to be kidding." Her friend was outraged on Libby's behalf when she told of the meeting with Hershel and what she'd learned about Sarah. "I hardly know what to say."

"I thought of her as a friend." Libby remained stunned. "Sarah's the only one who knew I intended to speak to Mrs. Reed. It had to have been her."

All Robin could do was shake her head.

Libby was tired of all this. It'd been a busy week. It seemed like more had happened in this one week than in the last five months combined.

"How are you?" Libby asked her friend. Her true friend. She knew it'd been difficult for Robin to return to work, especially when it meant seeing Roy Bollinger every day. Only later did Robin tell her about Roy's visit to the condo the day she'd phoned in to work sick.

"I'm okay," Robin said without meeting Libby's eyes.

Libby cocked her brow, unsure she should believe her.

Robin lowered her voice. "I saw Roy at the office."

"Did you speak?"

Robin shook her head. Her eyes softened as she spoke. "But I wish we had."

"Oh, Robin."

"It's better this way. I just never believed he'd be interested in me and now that he is . . ." She left the rest unsaid.

"Just remember what you've told me all through this long period of unemployment."

"What?"

"That eventually everything will right itself."

"I said that?"

Libby grinned. "Any number of times."

Robin smiled, too. "I didn't know I could sound so wise."

But she was wise, wonderfully so, and Libby treasured her.

Chapter 28

Libby sat in her small office and arranged her desktop. Everything was neat and orderly, just the way she liked it. She'd already gotten two business calls. One she'd rejected outright. It was from a friend of a friend who was looking for an attorney to get him out of a speeding ticket—his third that year. Libby happily referred him to another attorney.

The second call showed promise. The referral had come from Abby Higginbotham at Seattle General. Libby made an appointment to visit the cou-

ple the following afternoon to talk about
estate planning and setting up a trust
fund for their two grandchildren. They
had already talked to a number of financial advisers but were looking to
get advice from someone who didn't
have anything financial to gain from
their investments.

Libby phoned the hospital to thank
Abby.

"Hey, no problem. They're friends of
my husband's family. Really wonderful
people."

They chatted for a few more minutes
and exchanged a bit of hospital gossip.
Libby ended the call when she was
buzzed by her shared receptionist.

"Yes," Libby said.

"There's someone here to see you.
She said she didn't have an appointment."

"Ah, sure." A client was a client. Libby
left her desk and opened her office
door to find Casey Goetz sitting in the
waiting area. The teen flipped through
a magazine until she noticed Libby.

"Casey?"

"Oh, hi." Casey set aside the magazine, stood, and, with an I-told-you-so smile at the receptionist, followed Libby into the office. "Mom said you'd gotten your own office. Cool." She looked around the room and nodded as though she approved.

Libby had been talking to Ava every couple of days on the phone just to make sure everything was okay. Ava's doctor appointment was scheduled for early the following week—the earliest date the social worker had been able to get.

"Casey, this is a nice surprise. I understand you're here on official business. What can I do for you?"

Casey looked surprised, as though it should be apparent. "I've come to hire you."

Well, this was certainly interesting. Libby sat down and Casey took a chair, too. "Are you having legal troubles?" Libby asked, half-joking.

"No, I'm actually here on Ava's behalf."

"Of course." Libby was grateful that Ava had a friend like Casey. She knew they chatted nearly every day after Darlene Carmichael left for work. "How can I help you . . . and Ava?" Libby inquired.

Casey sat up straighter. "We talked and Ava has decided that she wants to give the baby up for adoption." She reached for her purse and took out her wallet. "Ava thought it might cost money. I have my allowance saved up so I told her I would pay you . . . if necessary." She held on to her purse with both hands.

"Has Ava's grandmother accepted the truth that Ava's pregnant?" Libby asked.

"Not yet."

Well, Mrs. Carmichael would be facing facts soon enough.

"Can you help Ava with the . . . adoption?"

"What I can do," Libby said, "is refer her to an agency." She'd thought the social worker might have brought up the subject, but now she realized that the woman wouldn't be able to do that until after Ava's condition had been confirmed.

"How much will that cost?" Casey had her hand on her wallet, ready to take out the cash and pay Libby a retainer.

"Actually, that service is free."

"Free?"

"Referrals are free," Libby emphasized. She was touched by Casey's resourcefulness.

"Oh." The teenager's shoulders relaxed, as though she was relieved.

"I can make a list of phone numbers for Ava or even make the calls myself on her behalf."

Casey nodded. "I think it would be best if you made the calls; Ava feels it's best for someone else . . ."She hesitated, and then added, "to take the baby."

Libby was relieved by Ava's decision. She realized it must have been a difficult choice for the young teenager. As Libby and Ava talked regularly, she was surprised Ava had asked Casey to approach her about this, especially in light of the fact that they'd even discussed Ava's options concerning the baby.

"How's Ava doing?" Libby asked. She'd talked to her the day before, but

Casey might have an entirely different perspective.

"Okay, I guess, although she doesn't leave the house now. She says you've brought her books and yarn and stuff and . . . and I think that's great. Ava needs you."

It was funny that Casey should say that, because Libby was thinking how much pleasure she got in helping the teenager. Ava reminded Libby of herself at that age—uncertain, lonely, and lost. They talked quite a bit about what it meant to be without a mother. Libby hoped to encourage Ava.

"Ava trusts you. She's hoping . . ." Casey looked away and didn't finish the sentence.

"What is she hoping?" Libby asked.

Casey squared her shoulders. "When Ava said she wanted to give her baby up for adoption she also said she felt odd giving her baby to strangers."

"I agree that it's a difficult decision." But certainly it was the right one. The teen was little more than a child herself. Taking on the responsibility of raising a baby was beyond Ava's emotional and mental capabilities, Libby believed.

"It was hard for her."

"I know." Libby would phone Ava again in the morning and together the two of them could go over the list of adoption agencies. "I'll talk to Ava about this myself," Libby promised. "She doesn't need to worry about her baby. She'll have the opportunity to read over the profiles of the families looking to adopt. The social worker will help her and she can actually choose the family."

"She can choose herself?" Casey's eyes brightened. "That's great, because she already has someone in mind."

Ava hadn't mentioned this to Libby. "Really?"

Casey beamed at her. "Can you call her?"

"You mean right now?"

The girl nodded.

"Is she expecting my call?" Libby didn't want to risk the possibility of Ava's grandmother picking up the phone.

"She was hoping you would call. She

asked me to talk to you first about the adoption because she was a little afraid of what you'd say."

That was odd, because Libby had tried to steer her in that direction as much as possible. The choice had to be Ava's, but Libby felt it was important for the girl to understand everything that would be involved if she decided to raise the baby on her own.

Casey stared pointedly at the phone. Libby reached for it and punched in Ava's number. She must have been sitting right next to the phone because she picked up on the first ring.

"Hello," came her tentative greeting.

"Ava, it's Libby."

"Is Casey with you?"

"She is."

"Did she talk to you about the adoption?"

"She did," Libby assured her.

"What do you think?" She sounded so tense, so uncertain, which was understandable, Libby supposed.

"I think that's a wise decision for you and your baby."

"Oh, thank you," Ava breathed, and it

sounded as if she was about to burst
into tears. "I was afraid, you know, that
being single you wouldn't want my
baby."

"Want your baby? Me? You're talking
about *me* adopting the baby?" Oh my.

"Yes," Ava breathed.

"Ava, there are any number of families who are eager for an infant. Remember how we talked about this?
Some couples have waited years for
the opportunity to adopt a child."

"You did tell me that, but I don't want
just anyone to have my baby."

This wasn't making any sense.

"They're strangers," Ava insisted. "I
want my baby to go to a good home,
to someone I know will love her. I think
of the baby as a her because I want a
girl more than I want a boy."

"Anyone who adopts your baby will
love her," Libby promised.

"Would you?" Ava asked.

The question gave Libby pause, and
she realized in a sudden rush of emotion that she already did. "Yes," she
whispered and she sincerely meant it.
She would love Ava's baby.

"Then I want *you* to adopt my baby."

The words should have rocked Libby's world, turned it upside down. But after the initial shock of it, Libby realized they hadn't. She remembered holding the Wilson baby and thinking that the baby could have been hers. The rush of regrets that had overcome her in those few moments had multiplied a dozen times when she'd realized that Baby Wilson was her ex-husband's son.

"You want *me* to adopt your child?" Libby asked, to be sure she understood Ava's wishes.

"Yes, you. I know you'll love her. I know you'd be a good mother because . . . because you've been such a good friend to me. You've been like a mother to me. I . . . trust you more than I do anyone else in the world, even more than my grandmother. Please, say you'll adopt my baby, Libby. Please."

Chapter 29

Libby didn't know how to answer Ava. The idea of raising Ava's child was obviously a huge thing to contemplate. Her first impulse was to explain how impossible it would be for her, especially at this juncture in her life. The objection barely surfaced before it quickly dissipated. On the surface of things this was an idea that made no sense. She was just starting up her own law firm and would need to devote her energies in that direction.

But slowly, gradually, her thinking came around to the place her heart had gone immediately. This baby belonged with her. She would love Ava's child and build her life around this baby.

Phillip phoned Sunday morning to ask if she'd like to take a drive up to Paradise on Mount Rainier. In all the years Libby had lived in the Seattle area she'd never once visited the national park or been to the lodge there, although she'd heard great things. Phillip told her he'd booked lunch reservations for them and that he thought it was time they talked. Libby agreed. The ride would give them privacy to discuss in more detail what had happened between them and how they wanted to move forward.

Instead they discussed Ava.

"You're sure about this adoption idea?" Phillip pressed when Libby admitted she was leaning toward raising this child as her own.

"Yes . . . and no."

Phillip chuckled. "Sounds like you really haven't decided yet."

"I have," she countered, and smiling added, "at least for now." Then, because she felt she needed to explain, she said, "One of the lessons I've learned this year has been that getting a life really means developing relationships. It's more than joining a bowling league or working out at the gym. It's about opening up my life and my heart to others."

"A baby?"

"A very special baby. It started the moment I held the Wilson boy. I realized that under different circumstances he could have been my son with Joe. My heart felt that need, that desire for a child, but deeper than any other emotion, the need for a family. When I learned the infant in my arms was actually Joe's son . . . it felt as if my entire world had imploded. That day was pivotal for me."

Phillip reached for her hand. He kept his eyes on the road, but the tightness of his grip told her he'd been affected, too.

"From that moment forward I started to build my own family. Now I have the opportunity to add a child to my life. I realize sacrifices will need to be made, but I'm willing to make them. Ava's baby will give me purpose beyond my work, and will help broaden my world. And I want to give this baby a home, and love." Already her heart was linked with Ava's child. It was almost as if this was meant to be.

"Is there room in that assembled family for growth sometime down the road?" Phillip asked. He briefly took his gaze off the narrow, twisting mountain road.

Her mind spun, and responded with a question of her own. "Would you like there to be?"

"Very much," he admitted.

Libby sighed.

They spent a wonderful day together. After a leisurely lunch at the lodge they hiked the trails leading up to the tree line, resting in a meadow filled with blooming wildflowers. They kissed and held hands on the trail on the way back to the car. As Phillip drove back to Seattle, Libby realized anew how much she wanted this incredible man to be part of the family she had formed for herself.

On Monday morning Libby felt great.

She was on her way back to her apartment after her regular morning workout, eager to shower and change clothes in order to get to her office. She wasn't in a rush, though, the way Robin always was, the way she'd been at one time herself.

Libby had to give her friend credit. The truth was, Robin didn't appear as driven as she had in months past, either. Libby wondered if those changes had been inspired by what was happening in her own life. She certainly wasn't the same woman who'd walked out of the law offices of Burkhart, Smith & Crandall last March. And frankly, Libby was glad of it. She'd gotten the butterfly tattoo on a lark and yet it had come to symbolize the profound changes taking place within her. It had come to represent the faith she had in herself to be a whole person and not just a driven attorney who used work as an excuse to avoid emotional entanglements.

Thinking back on those months, all her fumbling around in an effort to find herself, Libby realized that her old life was nothing like the new one and that was fine by her. Like the butterfly on the small of her back, she was undergoing her own metamorphosis. The fact that she didn't have any pressing cases didn't send her into a tizzy of worry. Clients would come with time. It felt good to be back in a groove, although that groove remained pretty shallow at the moment.

Another huge change was about to take place in her life. She'd discussed the adoption with both Phillip and Robin. They had listened and then asked serious questions that had caused her confidence to waver a bit. Caught up in all the possibilities, Libby hadn't been thinking clearly. Yet she still felt a deep sense of peace that this was the right decision.

"What about day care? Would you hire a nanny?" Robin had asked.

Libby knew she'd need to find someone and fairly quickly. She'd do her best to keep the baby with her for the first few months, she'd told Robin.

"You can't be serious," her friend countered. "You're going to bring the baby to the office and try to work at the same time? Are you out of your mind?"

Libby quickly revised her plans. Robin was right. She couldn't work and care for the baby at the office. She'd need to make provisions for day care.

"What about a father's influence?" Phillip had asked, giving her pause.

"There are plenty of single mothers in the world."

"A baby needs a father."

"Well, things don't always work out the way we want," she argued, but deep down she worried Phillip was right, especially in light of the fact that the adoption agencies were crowded with applications from married couples hungry for a family.

Regardless, Libby planned to schedule a couple of preliminary interviews with possible day-care facilities. She would keep the baby with her as much as possible when she wasn't at the office. There was also the matter of making her home ready for the baby. Robin had promised to help her shop.

As she exited the elevator, keys in

hand, Libby found Ava sitting on the carpet outside her front door.

"Ava?" She called out the girl's name and hurried to the teenager's side. "What's wrong?" Weeks earlier she'd given Ava her address and phone number and told the young teen to come to her if she ever needed help.

Ava clenched her stomach. "It hurts, Libby, it hurts real bad."

The girl was in labor.

It was too soon, although maybe not. Libby couldn't be sure because Ava hadn't even been to the doctor yet.

This had been one of Libby's biggest fears—that the baby would arrive before Ava had had any prenatal care.

Fighting off panic, Libby's hands trembled as she unlocked her front door and led Ava inside. Once in the front door, Ava yelped in pain and water gushed from between her legs.

As calmly as she could, Libby hurried to her phone and dialed 911. She had to get the girl to the hospital. Next she contacted Phillip.

After explaining the situation, he said, "Call an Aid Car."

"I already did."

"Have them take her to Seattle General."

"Okay." Libby's heart was pounding so hard that she could barely hear him above the roar of her own pulse. She had towels between Ava's legs and wrapped one arm around the girl's waist as she listened to Phillip's advice.

"Contact the guardian. The grandmother will need to sign release papers before we can treat her."

"Okay."

Libby disconnected the call. "Has your grandmother left for work yet?"

Ava, who looked pale and shaken, shook her head. "I . . . I don't think so. I snuck out of the house before she was awake. She didn't hear me, otherwise she would have stopped me."

Libby kept her cell phone in her hand. "I need to get ahold of your grandmother."

"No!" Ava screamed. "Don't, please don't."

"Sweetheart, I'm sorry, but it's necessary."

Darlene Carmichael answered on the

fourth ring, at the same time the para-
medics arrived.

"This is Ava's friend Libby. Ava is with
me . . . I've called an Aid Car to take
her to the hospital."

"What does she need to go to the
hospital for?" Darlene demanded.

"She's in labor."

The teen's grandmother gasped. "No,
she isn't. She can't be."

Libby didn't have time to argue with
her. "Listen, Mrs. Carmichael, I'm taking Ava to the hospital. She's in terrible
pain and needs to see a physician."

"I can't afford this."

"I don't want you to worry about the
expense; that isn't important just now.
Taking care of Ava and her baby is."
Libby was willing to agree to just about
anything as long as Ava's grandmother
cooperated. "You need to meet me at
Seattle General to sign papers in order
for Ava to be treated." Before the other
woman could complain she added, "If
there're any medical charges I'll pay
those, too."

"I can't be late for work," Darlene
cried, sounding like she was close to

tears. "I can hardly afford to feed these kids, let alone pay hospital bills."

Her own voice quivering, Libby carefully enunciated each word. "I'm sure your work will understand if you're a few minutes late. You need to get to the hospital and sign those release papers so Ava can be treated. Understand?"

"All right," Darlene muttered. "I'll be at Seattle General in fifteen minutes."

"Please hurry."

Because Libby wasn't allowed to go in the Aid Car, Ava was already set up in the labor room with Sharon Jennings when Libby arrived at the hospital. The admission papers, which awaited Darlene Carmichael's signature, were on a clipboard at the end of the gurney.

"Libby." Ava half rose from the bed and stretched her arm toward her.

Libby grabbed hold of the girl's hand and brought it to her lips. "I'm here. Everything is going to be fine."

Ava relaxed against the pillow and breathed in deeply. "No one told me it would hurt this much."

Never having experienced labor and

never having been with anyone who had, Libby hardly knew what to say to comfort her. She hoped the pain wouldn't get much worse. As it was the teen's face was pale and pinched, her eyes wide with pain and fear. Libby brushed the hair back from Ava's forehead. The teenager looked so young and vulnerable against the white sheets, far too young to be in this predicament.

Within a few minutes Libby heard Darlene Carmichael outside the labor room door. "Where is she?" Darlene called out. "What have you done with my granddaughter?"

Apparently someone pointed the way because Darlene burst into the room. "What is Ava doing in here?" she demanded, not bothering to greet her granddaughter.

"Ava is in labor," Sharon said and handed Darlene the clipboard for her signature.

Darlene penned her name and handed it back to Sharon. "In labor? Are you all fools? Ava isn't having any baby. She just eats too much."

Just then a pain contorted Ava and

she squeezed her eyes closed and groaned while twisting her head back and forth against the pillow. "Make the pain stop. Make it stop." As the labor pain eased, she exhaled and gradually relaxed.

"Tell them you aren't pregnant," Darlene told her granddaughter.

"Grandma," Ava said, her voice reed thin. "I'm having a baby."

Darlene gasped and cupped her hand over her mouth.

"Mrs. Carmichael," Sharon said, glancing down at the chart and Darlene's signature. "Your granddaughter is in labor. She is definitely giving birth within the next few hours."

"She's only thirteen," Darlene cried.

"Apparently she's old enough," Sharon replied calmly. She brought an IV bag over to Ava.

"What's she doing?" Ava demanded of Libby, watching Sharon.

She gripped hold of Libby's hand so hard that she had to pry the girl's fingers loose.

"I . . . I don't like needles."

"It's all right," Libby assured her

softly. "Turn your head away, and don't look."

Darlene stood by mutely, as if in shock, while Sharon inserted the needle into Ava's arm and then secured it with tape.

"I don't believe this is happening," Darlene cried, and started to weep loudly. "All this time I just thought she was overeating."

"I'm sorry, Grandma, I'm sorry." Ava started to sob now, too.

"It's all right," Libby tried to reassure Ava.

"I can't have you upsetting my patient," Sharon told Ava's grandmother.

Darlene Carmichael wiped the tears from her face. "What are we going to do? A baby? How will I ever be able to afford a baby?" Then, as if she suddenly realized Ava hadn't gotten pregnant all on her own, the older woman squared her shoulders. "Tell me who the father is." Angry now, she slapped the side of the bed. "I'll string him up by his balls, I will."

"Mrs. Carmichael," Sharon said again. "You're upsetting my patient."

"You don't think I'm upset?" Darlene flared back. "I just found out that my thirteen-year-old granddaughter is having baby." With that she gave a wail of frustration and shock.

"Grandma, I'm sorry, so sorry . . ."

"Mrs. Carmichael," Libby said, putting her arm around the older woman, "now isn't the time to demand answers. Ava hates that she disappointed you."

"I want to know who did this to her. Who's responsible."

Libby had guessed but she couldn't be sure. "There will be time enough later to find that out. Right now we need to do everything we can to help your granddaughter."

Darlene stared back at her as if she hadn't understood a word Libby had said. "If I'm late again for work, I could lose my job, then what will happen to us?"

Ava endured another contraction, thrashing her head back and forth against the pillow as she softly whimpered, "It hurts, it hurts." She clenched hold of Libby's hand in a grip so tight it left marks.

"Help her," Darlene cried. "Do something to help her."

It was easy to see that the grandmother would be more of a distraction than a help.

Ava must have felt the same thing. "Go on to work, Grandma, I'll be okay. Please, just leave, okay?"

Darlene hesitated and then nodded. "Okay, but someone will phone me, right?"

"Of course," Libby promised.

Darlene Carmichael patted Ava's shoulder. "Everything will work out, Ava. I'll find out who did this to you and we'll deal with what to do with the baby later. Don't you worry." Tears glistened in her eyes as she turned away and hurried out of the labor room door.

"Who's her physician?" Sharon asked.

"She doesn't have one," Libby explained. "She had her first appointment scheduled for later this week."

Sharon shook her head. "Okay . . ." Then, looking to Ava, she smiled and gently patted her shoulder. "Not to worry. Libby and I are here and we'll help you through this. I'll be with you as much as possible and will explain what's happening to your body. Everything is going to be fine. You, me, and one of our great doctors will bring this sweet baby into the world together, okay?"

Her reassuring voice was exactly what Ava needed. "Okay," she agreed, her own eyes bright with tears. "But I want Libby with me, too."

"You got it," Sharon said, and gave Ava's arm a squeeze.

Libby stayed with her as the labor progressed.

"Sing to me," Ava pleaded. "Sing to me the way you said you sing to the babies."

"Okay." Libby chose a Kelly Clarkson song and to her surprise Ava's voice joined hers after the first few words. The pure quality of it stunned her. Ava had mentioned before that she liked to sing, but Libby hadn't realized how talented she actually was.

"Ava, you have a lovely voice."

"I like singing . . ." She paused as another pain overtook her.

* * *

Ten hours later, with a staff physician attending, Ava delivered a four-pound, one-ounce baby girl. Libby had to admit, the teenager had been a real trouper. Not once had Ava given in to the pain and screamed. Instead she sang. Sharon had praised Ava several times for her self-control. Ava cooperated in every way, although she wouldn't let Libby leave her side for more than a few moments.

Phillip was in and out of the labor room and between pains Ava smiled up at him. "I know you."

Phillip cocked his head to one side. "You do?"

Ava's smile widened. "You were the doctor we saw in the elevator that day, the one Libby talks about all the time. She's hot for you."

"Ava," Libby protested, embarrassed.

Phillip winked and leaned forward and whispered to Ava, "Well, the truth is, I'm hot for her myself."

"Good. I'm glad." Another contraction came then and Ava focused all her attention on getting through the pain.

Following the delivery Ava was taken to a hospital room, where she promptly fell asleep. Libby took the opportunity to check on the baby . . . her daughter. The infant was incredibly tiny but she was a giant compared to another one of the babies, who weighed in at less than three pounds.

"How is she?" Libby asked when Phillip joined her. He stood behind her, his hand at her neck.

"She's relatively good. We're estimating that she's about thirty-five to thirty-six weeks. Early is never ideal but her vitals are strong and her lungs seem developed enough that she should be fine."

"She's perfect, isn't she?" Libby whispered, looking down on the small, sleeping bundle. "And so beautiful." Her voice cracked with emotion. This was her child, her daughter.

Phillip brought her closer. "She's a little lazy just yet, not sure she wants to breathe on her own. Would you like to hold her?"

"Can I?"

"Of course." Phillip reached into the incubator and tenderly lifted the newborn from her bed, placing the tiny bundle into the cradle of Libby's arms.

Libby sank into the rocking chair and was surprised when the baby opened her eyes and looked straight up at her. Their gazes connected and it seemed as if this tiny four-pound baby had found a soft place to nestle in Libby's heart. To her surprise Libby's eyes instantly moistened.

"I'd like to name her Amy Jo," she whispered. "My . . . my mother's middle name was Jo and I've always liked the name Amy."

"Amy Jo," Phillip repeated, standing behind her, his hand on Libby's shoulder.

"I know you and Robin raised some excellent questions about me adopting this child. I had a few doubts myself, but the moment I saw her, I knew making her part of my life was the right decision. I'm going through with the adoption, Phillip. This baby is my daughter."

His hand tightened briefly against her

shoulder. "You're going to be a wonderful mother."

His confidence in her meant everything to Libby. She crossed her arm over her chest and placed her hand on his resting on her shoulder. "Thank you," she whispered as the emotion clogged her throat.

Phillip leaned forward and kissed the side of her neck. "Congratulations, Momma."

Libby was grateful they'd had the opportunity to talk about the changes bringing this child into her life would mean. She needed his support, and his heartfelt reassurance was enough to send a fresh batch of tears rolling down her cheeks. For a woman who rarely cried the tears seemed to flow with relative ease. Emotion blocked her throat. It'd been quite the day and it wasn't over yet. She'd need to make all the legal arrangements necessary to start the adoption process and arrange for custody of the child until the adoption was formalized. Then she'd need to look into day-care options and prepare to bring Amy Jo home from the hospi-

tal. She had no crib, no stroller, no dia-
pers. In fact, she had nothing.

"You were wonderful with Ava," Phillip said. "Encouraging, supportive, helpful, and loving."

Libby had been so preoccupied with
Ava she'd barely noticed that Phillip
had been in the labor room several
times during the day. "I love Ava." And
Libby loved this baby, too. It astonished
her that she could experience so much
love for this tiny being when she hadn't
carried Amy Jo within her own body or
physically given birth to her. Yet the instant Libby had laid eyes on her, she
knew intuitively that this baby was hers,
and that she was going to love her beyond anything she could ever have
imagined.

Amy Jo's birth would be the turning
point for Libby. Her life would forever
be marked by this day, the day she became a mother, the day when her world
came to focus on this infant who'd been
entrusted to her care. She had to believe God wanted Amy Jo to be part of
her family.

Libby wiped the tears from her eyes

and smiled up at Phillip as he lifted Amy
Jo from her arms. He placed the baby
girl back inside the enclosed crib that
would help the baby breathe.

Libby left the neonatal intensive-care
unit. The first person she phoned was
her father.

He sounded surprised to hear from
her after eight on a Monday night. "Everything all right?"

"Yes, I know this is late notice but I
thought you should know I've made
you a grandfather today."

The returning silence was deafening.
"You're pregnant?"

"No, I'm adopting a baby girl. She
was born just an hour ago. I'm naming
her Amy Jo. The Jo part is for Mom.
She's tiny, just over four pounds, and
she'll need to remain in the hospital for
a week or so, but everything should be
fine."

"Adopting a baby?" he repeated,
sounding shocked.

"You're going to love her, Dad. Your
first grandchild."

"Yes . . . I suppose I will."

"Sorry to make this so short but I've got a zillion things to do."

"Okay, well, congratulations."

"Thank you, Dad."

This was probably one of the longest telephone conversations Libby had experienced with her father in the last ten years. She felt good; in fact, she felt wonderful. The next person she phoned was Robin.

"It's a girl," she cried.

"Ava had her baby?"

"An hour ago."

"Why didn't you text me?" Robin cried. "I would have come to the hospital."

Libby had badly wanted to contact her friend but she hadn't been able to. "Ava wouldn't let me leave her side for more than a minute. She did great, by the way. That girl has got grit."

"Are you ready?"

"Ready?"

"Do you have what you need to bring her home from the hospital?"

"Not a single thing." Libby started to giggle. "The truth is that for someone as focused and organized as me, I'm vastly unprepared. Obviously I had no idea she'd choose to arrive four weeks early."

"What time is it?" Robin asked.

"After eight," Libby said, checking her watch.

"The stores are closed; you'll need to go in the morning and I'm coming with you," Robin announced.

A workday and Robin was joining her? "You can do that?"

"I'll take a personal day. The two of us will head to the mall and buy out the baby store."

Libby could hardly believe that Robin would willingly take a day away from work, and then she started to giggle all over again.

Chapter 30

Robin held up a dainty pink dress and her heart felt like it was going to melt. It was incredibly cute. "You have got to get this," she insisted and draped it over her arm along with the ten other outfits she felt were absolutely necessary for Libby's daughter.

"Robin, I can't buy all this stuff. Remember, I'm on a limited budget."

"Maybe you are, but I'm not and I'm Amy Jo's godmother." Robin had been thrilled when Libby honored her by requesting she take on this special role in young Amy's life. She took the responsibility seriously. In due course, when Amy Jo could read, Robin would purchase the little girl her first Bible. She'd see to it that Libby got her daughter to Sunday school, too. If Libby didn't go then she'd escort the little girl personally. To Robin's way of thinking every child needed a secure foundation in faith. Even if she personally hadn't darkened a church doorway in years, she still considered faith important.

"I'm bushed," Libby said, her face beaming with happiness, "not to mention out of money."

Robin knew that Libby was anxious to get to the hospital to visit Ava and the baby. She'd already stopped by earlier that morning before heading out on their shopping expedition, and was eager to return. Robin didn't know what time Libby had gotten home the night before but she realized it must have been late. In all the years she'd known Libby, Robin had never seen her friend so joyful, so excited.

Robin was genuinely happy for her. The joy seemed to spill over onto her as well. How could it not? Despite the disappointment she'd felt after Roy's visit to her condo, she had become infected with Libby's happiness. It felt good to dwell on someone other than the judge. She just hoped his late wife had appreciated how much he loved her.

Robin left Libby at around two that afternoon. Instead of going to the courthouse she returned to her condo. If she showed up at the office she was bound to be bombarded with work. That was the nature of the beast, working as a prosecuting attorney. Working from home would be less intrusive than going into the office. Answering a day's worth of emails was sure to take her well into the late afternoon.

Once home, Robin kicked off her shoes and poured herself a glass of iced tea. After a couple of sips, she logged on to her computer. Just as she suspected, the emails started to roll in, filling up the screen. She tackled them one at a time until she felt fairly confident that she had a handle on the most pressing ones. Now, when she returned to the office on Wednesday, the list of demands wouldn't overwhelm her.

Her doorbell rang. Libby for sure. Barefoot, Robin hurried to the front door, finding it amusing that they'd parted only a few hours ago and her friend was already back.

Only it wasn't Libby.

For the second time, she found Judge Roy Bollinger standing on the other side of the door, clenching a white sack in his hand. He looked completely out of his element. Seeing her, the color seemed to drain from his face.

"Roy," she whispered, shocked to see him. Her eyes went wide until she feared they would fall out of their sockets. Since their last encounter they had passed each other in the courthouse nearly every day and both had looked the other way, pretending . . . she didn't know what.

"You're not sick?" he asked, and it seemed to disappoint him that she was obviously in good health.

"No."

"You weren't in court," he argued.

"I took a personal day."

"Oh." Roy thrust the white paper bag at her and seemed eager to turn tail and run.

Now that he was at her front door, she didn't want him to leave. "What's this?" she asked, delaying him.

He made a self-effacing smile. "Chicken noodle soup. I assumed you must be ill."

"As you can see I'm perfectly fine."

"I can see. And yes, you look just . . . fine." He paused and cleared his throat. "Actually you look more than fine. You look wonderful."

Compliments didn't roll off Roy's tongue the way they did for some men, but she couldn't help but blush. "Do you want to come inside?" she asked.

He hesitated. Now that she held the sack, he buried his hands deep inside his pockets. "You've . . . never missed a day without being sick. Well, other than recently."

"Until today," she amended, and then remembered she had called in sick following their disastrous date. "I was out shopping with a friend."

"A friend?" he repeated slowly, casting his gaze down to his feet. Apparently he assumed her "friend" was male.

"Libby Morgan, you met her the night we had drinks," she said, clarifying the issue. She didn't want to give him the impression she was seeing anyone else, because she wasn't.

Just as quickly his eyes came back to meet hers and he visibly relaxed. "Of course, I know Libby."

"She's adopting a baby girl and she asked me to be the godmother. I helped her pick out what she needs for the nursery."

"I didn't know Libby was married." His brow crunched with a perplexed look.

"She isn't." It seemed a little ridiculous for the two of them to be standing in her doorway chatting like this. "Roy, please come inside." She reached for his hand and gently brought him into her condo.

He glanced around as if seeing it for the first time. Robin resisted the urge to tell him that she hadn't changed residences in the last week.

"I'm grateful to hear you're not ill."

"Roy," she said, and hesitated. Neither of them seemed to know what to say. She certainly didn't and he seemed just as much at a loss for words, and so they just stood there staring at each other.

"I've . . . been doing some thinking," he blurted out.

"Oh," she said, just as quickly.

"About what you said about . . . you not being a replacement for Sally."

Robin's knees felt like they were about to give out from under her. She sank onto the sofa. As soon as she sat down, Roy did, too. He was so close to the edge of the chair cushion that for a moment she feared he might fall off. She waited for him to speak. He was the one who seemed to have something he wanted to say.

"Basically, you're right. I was looking for a woman who would step into Sally's shoes, someone who would make my life the way it was when she was alive."

"That woman isn't me," she said, and while it saddened her to admit it, she couldn't change who she was no matter how deeply she cared for Roy.

"I realize that now. It dawned on me that I wasn't attracted to you because you're like Sally. You're not in any way, shape, or form like her."

All Robin could do was stare at him.

"Sally would never get a tattoo."

So he'd noticed that. Instinctively she wanted to thrust her arm behind her back. Pride demanded she didn't.

"I admire you because you're decisive and direct," Roy continued. "You have a strong work ethic and you care about the law, about helping those who are willing to accept help. Too many of us have become jaded and cynical when dealing with the criminal element."

That was true. Her mother worried that that was happening to Robin, and perhaps it was. Robin had a reputation at the courthouse for being hard on criminals and defense attorneys. Her attitude toward those who broke the law was unyielding. She believed in stiff consequences. But she didn't care

what others thought of her, save one
man . . . Roy Bollinger.

"I came today to drop off the soup. I
assumed you were sick so I'm not really
prepared, you know, to talk about this."

Robin wasn't about to let him go so
soon. "You're here now, though," she
argued.

"That I am," he said, and stared down
at his hands. "First of all I want to apologize for being obtuse. I don't know
what I was thinking, but I promise you
I'll never ask you to play bridge or go
dancing unless that is something you
want to do."

"That's in the past, Roy. But if it eases
your mind, your apology is accepted."

"Thank you." His gaze connected
with hers. He actually almost smiled,
as if she'd lifted a heavy burden from
his shoulders. "I was hoping you'd be
willing to give me another chance." He
paused and seemed to be awaiting her
response.

"I'd be willing . . ."

"In that case, I'd like to ask you to
have dinner."

"Tonight?"

"Tonight," he echoed. "If you're free, that is, or tomorrow or the day after tomorrow—or any day you suggest." He smiled completely now.

"Tonight would work."

"Great." He stood and reached for her hand, bringing her to her feet. He frowned when he saw the tattoo. "What is that, anyway?" he asked.

"A Chinese character," which was the same thing she'd told anyone else who'd asked. She and the tattoo artist were the only two people who knew its meaning; well, other than those who were fluent in Chinese.

"What does it stand for?" he asked, and then glanced up when she hesitated.

"It's a little embarrassing, actually," she said, resisting the urge to pull her hand free. If she hadn't craved his touch, even in the most innocent of ways, she would have. Just being this close to him made her feel light-headed. In her entire life Robin had never felt this strongly about any man, not even her husband, as brief as her marriage had been.

"The tattoo embarrasses you now?" Roy asked.

"Not really."

"Then the meaning?"

"Not that, either," she admitted.

"Then what embarrasses you?"

She held her breath for several seconds before she was willing to tell him. "My feelings for you." Robin stared at him, unable to breathe, unable to even blink.

"Feelings?" Roy asked, his voice low and carefully modulated.

Turning her wrist so he could see her tattoo again, she said, "I haven't told anyone what this Chinese character means, but I'll tell you."

His gaze held hers.

"Libby and I had a bit too much to drink and decided we would each get a tattoo. Actually she wanted one. I didn't, but I went to the tattoo parlor with her anyway and helped her decide on a butterfly."

"So you got the tattoo when you were with her."

"Hers is in a place you'll never see," Robin added.

"Okay."

"While I was there I started looking at all the different designs. None of them got my attention or gave me the slightest desire to have something permanently placed on my body, until I happened upon this Chinese character."

Roy frowned slightly. "It must have a deep personal meaning for you."

"It does," she agreed, her voice weakening. "It's the Chinese character for hope," she whispered.

"Hope," he repeated. "Why that?"

"You gave me that, Roy. I didn't ever think it was possible for me to care as deeply for a man as I do for you. I've admired you for so long, and hoped that you might one day share my feelings." She stopped as she considered whether or not to bare so much of her heart.

His entire face seemed to go limp. "I had no idea. Since when?" he asked.

Having taken the conversation to this

point, it didn't make sense to turn back. "Ever since we worked on that political committee all those years ago. You were the most decent, kindest man I'd ever met. I dreamed of meeting someone like you for a very long while and it never happened. My problem was that you were married to Sally and so I said nothing. Did nothing."

"Oh, Robin . . ." He slipped his arms around her and brought her close, pressing his mouth to hers. His lips were warm and moist, gentle and persuasive.

He angled his head to one side and continued to kiss her until Robin was sure she would dissolve into a puddle at his feet. Her hands roved his back and she leaned into him. By the time he eased his mouth from hers, Robin was trembling.

He held her away from him but his hands continued to cup her shoulders. "I don't know that anyone has ever said anything more beautiful, or more perfect to me." He leaned his forehead against hers. "It would be very easy to love you."

Happiness stole over her. "Don't fight it, okay?"

He grinned. "I don't think I could if I wanted to."

"Good."

Chapter 31

Late Wednesday afternoon Libby hurried back from the hospital, changed clothes, and struggled into a pair of panty hose. At one point nylons had been part of her daily routine, right along with crisp business suits and high-heeled pumps. These days it felt as if she was stuffing sausage, trying to squeeze her legs into the control-top hose. How quickly one forgets.

She opted for a slinky black dress and her mother's pearls for the hospital fund-raising dinner. Phillip had asked her to sit at his table and, at Libby's suggestion, he had invited Robin and Roy to attend as well. Abby Higginbotham from HR had managed to find the extra tickets at the last minute.

Libby had spent the majority of the day with Amy Jo at the hospital. Ava had been released and was back at home with her grandmother. Darlene Carmichael had apologized through Ava, although the shock of the birth of her great-granddaughter had yet to completely wear off. She was grateful Libby had agreed to adopt the child, and that she wouldn't be responsible for caring for anyone beyond Jackson and Ava.

Libby's one disappointment was that she'd seen Phillip only briefly over the last few days. Today he'd been rushing down the corridor at the hospital when they happened upon each other.

"Tonight's the fund-raiser," he'd reminded her.

"Not to worry, I remembered."

"Good." They started walking backward, taking small steps, needing to be someplace else.

"You're ruining my reputation, you know."

Libby frowned. "Your reputation?"

"Yeah. They used to call me Heart of Stone. But ever since I met you that's all changed."

"I've changed, too." It was important that Phillip know she wasn't the same woman, either.

"You have," he agreed, "but not all the changes in you have to do with me."

"Don't be so sure." She pressed her fingertips to her lips and then held up her palm to him.

Phillip muttered something she couldn't hear under his breath and pressed his hand over his heart. "See, you're doing it again." And then he added, as if all this sentimental talk was uncomfortable, "Do you want to meet outside the ballroom?"

"Sure. See you tonight."

"Tonight."

His eyes held promise, promise that Libby fully intended to collect upon.

Sharon had seen the hungry looks Libby and Phillip exchanged and slowly shook her head. "You've both got it bad." Libby had flushed, embarrassed that her feelings for Phillip were so easily read by others.

Libby's mind whirled as she headed into the bathroom to apply her makeup. She was running late because Abby had asked to talk to her before she'd left the hospital.

"I know you've recently rented your own office and struck out on your own, but there's a position here at the hospital that you would be uniquely qualified to fill."

"Me? A job at the hospital?"

"We need another fund-raiser on staff. Robert Lopes, who heads the department, told me the young man who's been working with him has taken a job elsewhere. Robert is set to retire in a few years and we're looking for someone to step into his position when he does."

"You want me to apply?" Libby hardly knew how to respond.

"Having worked in trusts and estates you have access to several wealthy families who might consider making a contribution to the hospital. We need someone like you to reach out to the business community as well."

Instinctively Libby felt it wasn't the right position for her, but she was highly flattered.

"Give it some thought," Abby urged. "You'd be perfect."

"I will think about it," Libby had promised. More than anything Abby's encouragement told Libby that her people skills had vastly improved.

Not wanting to drive to the function, Libby caught a cab. If not for her high heels she could easily have walked. The hotel ballroom where the fundraiser was being held was fewer than eight blocks from her condo. Libby was anxious to see Robin and Roy, and of course Phillip, too. Apparently the other couple had decided to give their relationship a go after all. Libby was pleased for them.

The area outside the dining room was crowded for the cocktail hour. When Libby arrived, the first thing she did was look for Phillip, but she didn't find him right away. Robin found her, looking stunning in her own slinky black dress. Roy smiled and offered to stand in line to get their drink order.

"So how's it going?" Libby asked.

"So far it's been wonderful. We've been together every night this week. He doesn't need to work nearly this hard to sweep me off my feet, but I'm not about to tell him that."

They both giggled like teenagers at a senior prom.

Phillip found her just before the doors opened for the dinner. He couldn't seem to take his eyes off her. With his hand on the small of her back, he guided her into the dining room and to his table. Robin and Roy were seated close by.

As the tables were being cleared after the meal, Abby approached her with one of the staff doctors. "Libby, I'd like you to meet Dr. James Buckley."

"Hello," Libby said, looking up at the physician. She knew his face from the hospital but they'd never formally met.

"If you have a moment I'd like to introduce you to my parents," Dr. Buckley said. "They might want your help in some estate planning."

"Of course." Libby stood.

Phillip gave her hand a gentle squeeze and off she went. Dr. Buckley led her to the far side of the room. His parents, an elegant older couple, smiled as she approached. His father was in a wheelchair next to his mother.

"Mom and Dad, this is Libby Morgan, the attorney I mentioned earlier," Dr. Buckley said. "Libby, my parents, John and Wilma Buckley."

"I'm so pleased to meet you."

James held out a chair for her. "Please, sit down."

Libby did and the elderly couple leaned toward her. John spoke first. "I realize this isn't a night to conduct business, but Wilma and I would like to discuss some estate planning at a time convenient for you."

"I'd enjoy that very much."

"We've heard nothing but wonderful things about you from our friend Martha Reed."

"I'm honored to have worked with Mrs. Reed in the past," Libby said.

"Our estate isn't nearly as complicated as Martha's," Wilma went on to say, "but we haven't been happy with what's been done so far. We realize you've only recently started your firm but we're comfortable with that."

"Can I phone you tomorrow and set up an appointment?" Libby asked. "I'd be willing to come to your house if that's easier for you."

John nodded and patted the side of his wheelchair. "That would be helpful. Thank you for your consideration."

He made it sound as if she were making a huge concession on his behalf, when in actuality Libby preferred it that way. If the Buckleys were to come to her office with the shared receptionist, they might have a change of heart. At this point her entire office setup was extremely low budget, though in time that would change, especially if she was able to attract other clients such as the Buckleys.

"We have another family friend who might also be interested," John went on to tell her. "Would you mind if I gave him your contact information?"

"Not in the least."

When Libby returned to Phillip's table, it felt as though she was walking on air. The speeches that followed were filled with tidbits of hospital humor and good-natured joking. Although Libby laughed at the appropriate times her mind churned at the speed of light. One of the reasons Hershel gave as to why she was being let go was her inability to bring in new clients. Well, here was the potential for her to pick up one wealthy client, and if she worked hard she might be able to snag the Buckleys' friend, too.

When the event was over, Libby saw that Robin and her judge were sitting close together. The judge's arm was around Robin's shoulders. Phillip's gaze followed hers and he reached for her hand, intertwining their fingers. His grip was firm and tight, as though he couldn't bear the thought of letting her go. For her own part she wanted to hold on to him for the rest of her life. They hadn't discussed the future. For now it was simply one day at a time. Phillip was everything she looked for in a man, and he understood her and her drive to succeed. He'd helped her broaden her horizons and take hold of life in new and unexpected ways; the sailing, the trip to Paradise Lodge, the long talks they'd had gave her a feeling of expectancy and hope that they might, at some future point, build a life together.

The two couples went out for a glass of wine following the banquet. They chatted amicably for more than an hour, exchanging stories before Phillip struggled to hide a yawn.

"I'm not as young as I used to be," he complained.

"Tell me about it," Roy added.

"Is it past your bedtime?" Robin teased.

The two seemed to be getting along famously, Libby noted. For that matter, all was going well between her and Phillip, too. They parted ways in the hotel lobby and Phillip offered to drop Libby off at her condo rather than have the doorman call for a taxi.

She hesitated and then admitted, "Once I change clothes, I was thinking I'd stop by the hospital for a few minutes."

"It's late," Phillip protested. "Can't it wait till the morning?"

"I suppose, but I wanted to kiss Amy Jo good night and tell her what a wonderful evening I had with friends."

"Friends?" Phillip asked, arching his brow. "Friends? Is that all I am to you?"

Libby grinned. "Oh, honestly, you make *friend* sound like a four-letter word." The truth was, she feared suggesting anything more until Phillip claimed otherwise.

"I was hoping to be more than a *friend*," he said.

"Actually, I was thinking earlier we could enhance our friendship," she offered.

"Friends and lovers?" he asked. He cocked his eyebrows with the question, his gaze holding hers.

She smiled up at him. "Definitely. When the time is right."

He looked disappointed and didn't say anything for a moment. "Sounds fair. Let me see you up to your condo."

"Okay." She'd already told him she intended on visiting the hospital, but that could wait a few minutes, she decided. "Sure. Come on up." She hoped she sounded casual.

He parked outside the building and helped her out of the car. He stood behind her, hands rubbing the curvature of her neck as they rode up the elevator to her condo. Neither spoke.

Once inside, Phillip didn't wait for her to turn on the lights before he turned her in his arms and kissed her. This was hardly the first time they'd kissed, but she'd always felt restraint on Phillip's part . . . until now. Libby's knees nearly collapsed as his mouth devoured hers again and again.

She sucked in a deep, calming breath when she could and pressed her hand to her chest. "Wow."

"Wow," he repeated, pressing his forehead against hers as he stroked her arms.

"Okay, Phillip, I'm going to need a bit of direction here."

"How's that?"

"Exactly where are we in this relationship?"

She felt the cool touch of his lips against her cheek.

"I'm falling in love with you, Libby."

She smiled and wrapped her arms

around his trim waist. "Really? Just remember I come as a package deal."

"I can handle that."

She kissed the underside of his jaw.
They each came with the wounds of
old relationships, and while it was frightening to think of becoming vulnerable
again, she was willing and he seemed
to be, too. She accepted that medicine
would always be important to him and
he realized she loved the law. They
would help each other maintain a
healthy balance between work and
home.

His hands continued to stroke her
arms and then he kissed her again, and
again, before reluctantly breaking it off.
"When the time is right?" he repeated.
"And that isn't now?"

She pressed her forehead against
his chest and sighed deeply. "Not tonight."

He kissed the top of her head. "Okay.
I should go."

The temptation to keep him with her
was strong. Libby forced herself to re-
treat a step.

"I'll see you tomorrow," Phillip whispered and bounced his lips against her brow.

"Okay."

Phillip left. After changing into jeans and a sweater, Libby grabbed her car keys. She was headed to the hospital to visit her daughter. Even now, thinking those words took some mental adjustment.

Little Amy Jo had been doing well, and while keeping her at the hospital was a necessary precaution, Libby longed for the day she would be able to bring her daughter home.

Humming softly to herself, Libby walked into the nearly deserted hospital. Amy Jo had been moved out of NICU and into the regular nursery. As she walked into the lobby, Libby saw a tall, lanky young man pacing the waiting room, hands stuffed in his pockets, clearly agitated.

Peter Armstrong.

Libby recognized Ava's neighbor right away. While in labor, Ava had confirmed Libby's suspicions regarding the baby's father. Libby had explained that the state would require his signature before they could proceed with the adoption. Ava had seemed surprised that Libby had guessed correctly.

"Hello, Peter," she whispered.

He turned abruptly. "They won't let me see her. I'd like to at least look at her."

"She's beautiful," Libby whispered. "Let me see what I can do."

Libby found a staff member she knew and explained the situation so that Peter would be allowed in the nursery area.

"I didn't know Ava was pregnant," he said as they rode the elevator up together.

That didn't shock Libby, seeing as how Ava hadn't known herself until she was eight months along.

"She should have told me."

"It wouldn't have changed anything," Libby said, feeling sorry for the youth.

"I suppose," he murmured, but he didn't sound convinced.

The elevator doors opened and they stepped out. Peter went right away to the nursery window. His hands remained in his pockets. Libby noticed the sheen in his eyes. "Would you like to hold her?" she asked.

Peter looked away from the nursery and then slowly nodded.

Chapter 32

Peter Armstrong, dressed in a protective gown, looked strangely out of place in the nursery. He wore ragged jeans and beat-up tennis shoes with untied laces. Tall and lanky, the fifteen-year-old's prominent Adam's apple wobbled up and down as Libby had him sit down and then handed him his daughter.

The teenager looked down at Amy Jo for several seconds before he spoke. "She's so tiny."

"She's a fighter; she's already gaining weight."

"How come she's still in the hospital? Ava's at home."

Libby stood behind him and looked down at her daughter. "Amy Jo had a few problems breathing on her own at first; that's why the doctors are keeping her, to make sure her lungs develop more before she goes home. We can take her out of the incubator for short periods of time."

He twisted around to look up at Libby. "She won't die, will she?"

Life held few guarantees, but according to all the information Libby had received, the baby should do well. The fact that Amy Jo was an enthusiastic eater encouraged Libby. "She's doing great, so you don't need to worry."

Peter continued to hold the infant, although his arms were stiff and his back unnaturally straight. "I saw Ava. We didn't talk. I didn't know what to say."

"In time you'll find the right words." Libby hardly knew what to tell him.

Peter rocked for a bit longer. "You named her Amy?"

"Amy Jo. Ava liked it, too. How do you feel about her name?"

Peter shrugged one shoulder. "It's all right, I guess. I heard . . . you're going to adopt her?"

"I already feel that she's part of my heart." Libby placed her hand on his shoulder. She knew that the attorney she'd hired had already contacted Peter and his family.

"I . . . I didn't think I'd feel anything for her . . . but I do," Peter whispered. "I want her to have a good life with a family who will love her."

"I love her, Peter. With all my heart I love her. She'll be my daughter but she'll always be part of you, too." Libby felt it was necessary to assure the youth that she would tell Amy Jo one day about her young father and how she'd wrapped herself around his heart, too. Libby gently squeezed the teenager's shoulder. He held Amy Jo for several minutes, and then very sweetly bent down and kissed her brow. He lifted the newborn up and Libby took her daughter and gently set her back inside the incubator. When she looked up she saw that Peter had tears in his eyes.

Reaching out, she hugged him and patted his back several times.

"I . . . I should go," he said, sniffling. They broke apart and he ran his forearm below his nose. "I didn't tell my parents where I was going and it's past my curfew."

The irony of that caused Libby to smile. This young man was old enough to father a child and he had to hurry home because of a curfew. "I'll drop you off," Libby told him.

"You don't need to do that."

"I'm headed that way myself." Not true, but she wanted to see him home.

Once in the hospital parking garage, Peter climbed into the car and closed the door. Libby sat beside him and started the engine. They rode in silence for a couple of blocks before Peter spoke again.

"Before Ava could even tell me about the baby, her grandmother came over and started shouting at my mom and dad and said she was going to have the police arrest me."

"You don't need to worry."

"I know. My dad called a friend of his who works on the police force and he assured my parents that Mrs. Carmichael could threaten us all she wants but she can't legally do anything against me."

"Were your parents upset?" Libby asked. She could only imagine how they must have felt, finding out this way that their son had fathered a child at fifteen.

"My mom started to cry and my dad sat me down and we talked, you know, about really serious stuff. He said he regretted the fact that we hadn't talked like that a lot sooner."

"That's important."

"Yeah," Peter agreed.

"How's your mom doing now?"

He shrugged and lifted his shoulder in a halfhearted shrug. "She's still pretty upset. Most of the time she's been on the phone with her mother and older sister."

"Moms need time to process things," Libby told him, knowing how important it'd become to discuss matters with her own support system, especially with all the life-changing decisions she'd made lately.

"I guess. Her and Dad have been talking a lot, too, but they haven't said much to me. I guess I should be glad they didn't ground me or send me away to live with relatives, but, you know, I sort of wish they had."

"I imagine they have a great deal to think about. This news must have hit them pretty hard."

Peter kept his head down. "I never knew how bad I'd feel disappointing my parents. I . . . I feel like I let Ava down, too, but I honestly didn't know. I would have helped her if I had. I mean, I would have tried to help her."

"I know you would have."

She turned down his street and pulled up in front of his house. The porch light was on, while Ava's house was completely dark. Libby would have stopped to check on her if there'd been any indication anyone was awake. Ava and Libby had talked several times since Ava's release and the girl had revealed amazing resilience. She planned to

meet Casey at the yarn store the following day.

"Thanks for the ride," Peter said, before closing the car door.

"Not a problem."

Libby drove away and headed home.
It'd been a full, exciting day for her,
filled with promise and potential.

First thing in the morning, Libby
would schedule an appointment with
the Buckleys and see how she might
best serve them. She'd contact Martha
Reed, too, and thank her for the referral. While she had the older woman on
the phone, Libby would make sure
Burkhart, Smith & Crandall had held up
their end of the bargain and that Mrs.
Reed's expectations had been met.

Chapter 33

The following morning Libby woke with a feeling of expectation. She worked out at the gym, but Phillip wasn't there, which disappointed her. The slouch had either slept in or been called to the hospital on an emergency. She'd find out later. Robin didn't show, either, but she generally exercised only three times a week. Later, when she had a spare moment, Libby would catch up with Robin and find out how the rest of her evening had gone with the judge. From all outward appearances—at the fund-raiser and afterward—it seemed to be going very well. Very well indeed.

Libby arrived at her office and contacted the Buckleys and set up an appointment for later that same day. She was psyched. The Buckleys were eager to hear what she had to say and had already given her contact information for the friend they'd mentioned the night before.

Libby buzzed by the hospital an hour later and the first person she ran into was Phillip. He looked happy to see her, but no more happy than she was to see him.

"Hi," she said, and hated how her voice sounded whispery and out of breath. "Missed you this morning at the gym."

"You were there?"

She didn't want to admit that her main motivation for gym time these days was that he might be there, too. "Yeah, where were you?"

"I overslept."

"Likely story."

Phillip glanced at his watch. "Got time for coffee?"

"Sure. When?" She probably shouldn't sound so eager or so agreeable, but she couldn't help it; she was eager and he appeared to feel the same way.

"A half hour?"

She smiled. "See you then." Libby started to walk away when Phillip reached for her hand. He seemed surprised, as if he hadn't realized what he was doing. Then he smiled, and raised her palm to his lips and kissed her there.

He shook his head and grumbled under his breath, "Some Heart of Stone I am."

Libby stood in the middle of the corridor, paralyzed, staring at him. When she looked away she found Sharon Jennings studying her with her crossed arms. "I'm telling you, just seeing you two makes my heart beat faster. I'd forgotten what it was to be in love like that."

Libby opened her mouth to deny everything and found she couldn't. She was falling in love with Phillip. The problem was how busy they both were. They had to carve out a few minutes here

and there when they could. Fifteen minutes for coffee, a late-night phone call,
sailing when the weather permitted.

Even so, their relationship was moving forward, growing deeper every day.
Up until now they had both been cautious, careful for fear of getting hurt yet
again, of making a mistake. That had
changed.

At the prescribed time Libby met
Phillip in the cafeteria. He'd already
taken a table and bought their coffees,
waiting patiently for her to join him.
Libby slid into the chair and reached
across the table for his hand.

"I've had the most wonderful morning," she said, still on an emotional high.
The latest word was that it might be
possible to bring Amy Jo home over
the weekend. Libby could hardly wait.
She was more than ready to be a
mother.

"I'm meeting with the Buckleys at
three," she told him and glanced at her
watch, making sure she'd allotted herself plenty of time to get ready for the
appointment.

"Anything else happening I should

know about?" he asked, his mouth quirking sideways in an off-center grin.

Libby realized she'd been chatting nonstop for several minutes. "Oh, Phillip, I've done it again. I just can't seem to stop talking. I'm so sorry. How's your day going?"

He broke into a wide grin that made him look almost boyish. "Much better now that I'm with you." He squeezed her fingers. "Seeing how happy you are makes me happy."

"Can I call you later?" she asked. "After I see the Buckleys?"

"I'd be disappointed if you didn't."

"Can I fix dinner for you tonight?"

"You're on, sweetheart."

"Call me if you're going to be late." She took one sip of the coffee and hurried to her feet. Kissing his cheek, she rushed from the cafeteria and noticed that nearly everyone in the room had stopped to watch her go. It flustered her until she realized she wasn't the one who interested them. It was Phillip. Seeing Phillip with her.

The meeting with the Buckleys couldn't have gone better. Libby was thrilled to accept their retainer. The appointment with their friends was scheduled for the following week. Life was certainly on the upswing.

She had just gotten into her vehicle when her cell rang. It was Mark Williams, the attorney she'd hired to complete the adoption. "Where are you?" he asked.

"In my car, why?"

"I think it might be a good idea for you to head over to the hospital."

Libby swallowed hard and alarm gripped her. "Is everything all right with Amy Jo?"

"Yes, she's fine."

"Then what's this about?"

He hesitated. "I got a call from an attorney representing the Armstrong family."

"Peter is going to sign the paperwork, isn't he?" He'd certainly given her that impression the night before. Naturally he was confused and uncertain. What fifteen-year-old wouldn't be?

"That's what they want to talk to you about," Mark said. "It would be best if we talked once you get here."

Libby's heart slowed almost to a standstill. "I'm on my way."

Within a matter of minutes she pulled into the hospital parking lot and then rushed up to the maternity ward. Sharon caught her eye and then quickly looked away. Libby's pulse was already racing double time, as if she'd climbed three flights of stairs instead of taking the elevator.

The next person she saw was Peter, with a man she could only assume must be his father. Mark was there, too, talking to another man who Libby felt sure must be the Armstrongs' attorney. They stood outside the nursery. Looking through the glass partition, Libby saw a woman she assumed was Peter's mother with Amy Jo. She sat in the rocker and was cradling the infant in her arms.

As soon as she saw Libby she made eye contact with her husband.

"Hi, Libby," Peter said, and quickly averted his gaze.

"Hello." Libby stepped forward and extended her hand to Peter's father. "Libby Morgan," she said.

"Ron Armstrong. That's my wife, Marlene. We're wondering if we could all sit down and talk, preferably someplace private?"

"Of course. This floor has a small conference room; we could talk there if you'd like."

"That would work."

Ron, Peter, and Libby, plus the two attorneys, waited until Marlene joined them and then they all went into the conference room. Once inside Ron closed the door. He waited until everyone was seated around the table before he spoke. "Marlene and I asked for this meeting today because we wanted to talk to you about the baby." He looked to his attorney, who nodded for Ron to continue.

"Of course," Libby said. It was perfectly understandable that they would want to meet the woman who was adopting their granddaughter. "I'll be happy to answer any questions you have."

"We understand you were wonderfully helpful to Ava," Marlene said. "She told us everything you did for her and we want you to know how very grateful we are."

"Ava's a sweet kid, a bit lost since the death of her mother, and confused about life. She'll be fine given time." Because Libby felt it was important that they understand the emotional connection between her and Ava, Libby explained that her own mother had died when Libby was the same age as the teenager.

Marlene, Ron, and Peter listened and then Marlene spoke. "When we learned about the baby, well, you can imagine that we were more than a little shocked."

"Of course," Libby said.

"We understand you want to adopt the baby."

"Yes." She glanced at her attorney.

"We also understand that you're currently unemployed," Ron said, reaching for his wife's hand.

"I've recently started my own law practice," Libby said, stiffening.

"Do you have the financial resources to support a child?"

Libby could see where this was headed and she hesitated. Her savings account was dangerously low but she had investments. "I do," she offered without explanation.

"You'd be a single parent."

"Yes." She yearned to mention her budding relationship with Phillip, but they were nowhere close to making a full commitment to each other.

"I see." Ron and Marlene exchanged glances.

"As you can imagine, it's taken us a few days to get our bearings and make a decision about what is best for our son and his child," Ron said, holding her gaze.

Libby tensed, unsure of what was about to happen next, although she had a gut-wrenching feeling she knew. "And?" she asked, anxiety gripping her throat to the point she was barely able to speak.

She had every right to be worried.

Marlene looked to her husband, who spoke on their behalf. "My wife and I have decided that we want to raise Peter's daughter ourselves. This child is our child, too. Marlene has always wanted a daughter, and despite several attempts we were only able to have Peter. This baby is our blood. We have the financial resources to care for her properly and the advantage of a two-parent home. We've already spoken to an attorney, who has contacted your attorney. Legally you can't follow through with the adoption . . ."

The rest of what he said remained a blur. The bottom line was that Libby wouldn't be adopting Amy Jo. In fact, the Armstrongs had already decided on another name. A family name. Grace Jennifer.

No longer was this Libby's daughter. Amy Jo would go to another family who had chosen another name. Another mother.

"What about Ava?" Libby asked once the fog had cleared.

"Our attorney is working out the details with her and her grandmother now."

"It would be good if Ava had representation as well." Libby would see to that herself.

"I imagine this is a terrible disappointment to you," Marlene said sympathetically. "I'm sorry for that, but surely you can see that this is the best option all around. Grace will be with family, with those who love her."

"I love her," Libby insisted.

"We realize that," Ron said gently. "But she'll have both a mother and a father who are related to her by blood. You wouldn't want to deny Grace that, would you?"

"No," Libby choked out. "No . . . I want her to have the best of everything."

"We do, too," Marlene whispered. "We do, too."

Chapter 34

As soon as Phillip heard the news from Sharon Jennings, he left the hospital. He didn't know where he'd find Libby; the thought of Libby facing this alone undid him. She hadn't answered any of his calls, nor had she responded to the messages he'd left on her voice mail. When his frustration grew so much that he couldn't remain at the hospital any longer, he went directly to Libby's condo.

Phillip found Libby on the floor of the baby's nursery. She was huddled in a tight ball and sobbing so hard her entire body shook.

"Libby," he whispered, and got down on the floor next to her. He wrapped his arms around her and she eagerly sank into his embrace. "I'm so sorry, sweetheart, so very sorry."

She couldn't speak, and for a moment he wondered if she was even breathing as he held and rocked her. He didn't have any words of comfort, any words of wisdom to share. When pain was this deep he figured it was best to say nothing.

After a while she stopped weeping and simply clung to him.

"They want to adopt Amy Jo," she whispered brokenly.

"I heard."

"She's their granddaughter."

"I know."

"They didn't think I could love her as much as they would."

"They're wrong about that."

Her arms tightened around him. "How is it possible to love a baby this much and not be linked by blood?" she whispered.

Phillip had no answer to give her. "I don't know how it happens, but it does. I've seen it; I know it's true." He resisted the urge to kiss her for fear of where it would lead. He wanted her badly, yearned to comfort her, to show his love, to slowly sink his body into hers and protect her from the pain that consumed her. He would do anything to lift this heartache from her shoulders but felt helpless; all he could do was hold her and kiss her. Her response was strong and immediate. He realized he could make love to her right here on this carpet. His need was great but his love was stronger. Together they would get through this. He would help Libby as best he could.

"How . . . how'd you get into the condo?" she asked, rubbing the moisture from her cheeks.

"The door was unlocked. I rang the bell, but I don't think you could hear it."

"I didn't," she said, and blew her nose into the thick wad of tissues in her hands.

Phillip brushed the hair away from the sides of her face. Her nose was red and her eyes swollen and yet he could honestly say he'd never loved her more. His heart ached for her. If it were humanly possible he would absorb her pain, take it within himself rather than see Libby endure this emotional turmoil. He had never felt this way before. Never.

"What can I do to help you?" he asked, willing to do anything, make any sacrifice. Whatever she asked, he'd find a way.

"Just . . . hold me."

"I will." He kissed her crown, pressing her tightly against his heart.

"I . . . I went to the chapel after I met with the Armstrong family," Libby whispered. "I didn't talk to God . . . I spoke to my mother. I asked her—" She broke off for a moment and struggled not to break into sobs again. "I asked my mother," Libby said, trying again, "what I should do."

Phillip could picture her there in the hospital chapel, brokenhearted, reaching out to the one person in the world she knew for sure had loved her.

"My first thoughts were crazy," Libby

admitted. "I devised a plan to make off with Amy Jo and take her somewhere. I started figuring out how to do it, and had concocted all kinds of schemes before I realized I was being totally delusional. I love her. I would give anything to make this nightmare go away." She buried her face in his chest and broke into heart-wrenching sobs.

Phillip rested his chin on the top of her head and gently stroked her back.

"I so badly wanted to be her family."

"I know, my darling, I know."

"Abby was going to hold a baby shower for me at the hospital."

Phillip had heard all about that. In fact, several of the doctors he knew had planned to attend.

"I lost my family when my mother and brother died. My father . . . he just sort of gave up. It wasn't any better after he remarried. I always felt on the outside . . . like I didn't matter."

"You matter to me," Phillip whispered as he stroked her hair.

"I'm just feeling sorry for myself, aren't I? This is nothing more than a pity party."

"You're entitled."

"I called my dad and you know what he said?"

"No," Phillip whispered, although he had a good idea Libby hadn't gotten much sympathy from her father.

"He said that it just must not have been meant to be . . ."

The man might have tried to reassure Libby she could still have a family of her own one day, Phillip mused. Apparently it wasn't in the old man's heart to offer love and sympathy to his daughter. He hadn't been able to when Libby had lost her mother, so it made sense that he was equally incapable now.

She was silent for a long time. "I felt better after talking to Mom."

"Good."

"No one ever loved me as much as my mother."

"No one ever does," Phillip whispered.

The doorbell rang again and before Libby or Phillip could react, the front door opened and Robin rushed into the nursery.

"Libby, I got here as soon as I could,"

Robin cried. She paused when she saw Phillip holding Libby on the nursery floor. The crib was all assembled, with a cute mobile dangling above. In fact, everything was laid out and ready for Amy Jo to come home. Phillip knew Libby must have been up half the night putting everything into place, and it was all for naught.

"Oh, Libby," Robin said and sank to her knees. "I am so sorry." She stretched her arms around the two of them and hugged Libby, too.

"Who . . . who told you?" Libby whispered.

"Phillip. He called to tell me what happened and said you weren't answering your phone."

Libby lifted her head in order to look up at him. "You called me?"

Phillip had left no fewer than six messages before heading out to find her. He'd felt an irrepressible need to be with her.

"Phillip thought you'd want your friends around you."

Libby stretched out her arm and Robin grabbed hold of her fingers.

"You'll get through this, Libby. I know you will."

Libby nodded and seemed to find strength in her friend's confidence. "I will . . . it's just that it hurts so much right now."

Phillip realized this was just one more loss to hit Libby after so many others.

A knock sounded against the door and a voice called from the front of the condo.

"Libby. Libby, are you there?"

It was Lydia from the yarn store.

"Come in," Robin called out. "We're in the nursery."

"Oh, Libby," Lydia said, kneeling down on the floor with the others. "I'm so sorry. Ava told Casey that Peter's parents have decided to adopt the baby."

"Tell your friend Alix, the baker, she can cancel the order for the cake for the baby shower," she said, biting into her lower lip.

"Oh, honey, don't you worry about that right now. We'll take care of every-thing," Lydia assured her.

Now that Libby was surrounded by

her friends, Phillip could see she was in good hands for the time being. Slowly he released her and stood.

Libby raised her eyes to his, pleading with him not to leave.

"I'll be back in an hour," he said, and pressed his hand to his lips and then cast the kiss to her just the way she'd done for him so recently.

"Promise?"

"Promise."

By the time he returned with a quart of wonton soup her friends had left. Libby answered the door and she looked somber, but he could see that she'd pulled herself out of the first shock of the emotional crisis.

"What's that?" she asked, looking at the bag in his hand.

"Soup. I couldn't think what else to bring." It'd taken him the better part of an hour to decide what to get for dinner. It wasn't like menus offered suggestions for what best ails a broken heart.

"Soup," she repeated.

"Will that do?"

"I was going to cook you dinner," she whispered.

"I know. You can do it another time; tonight it's on me."

"Thank you."

He went into the kitchen and brought down two bowls. "I would have brought wine but I couldn't think of what would go with wonton soup."

"It's wonton?"

"One of your favorites, right?"

"Yes, but I'm surprised you knew that."

He couldn't remember how he'd picked up that small tidbit of information about her, but it was there in the back of his mind.

"Mom must have told you."

He smiled . . . perhaps so. It just might be that Libby's mother had steered him in that direction. He searched through the kitchen drawers until he found where she kept the silverware. Setting everything up on the breakfast bar, he joined her. They clicked spoons and then ate. Phillip finished first. Libby ate only a few bites.

"It's good . . . I just don't have much of an appetite."

"Don't worry about it." He rinsed off the bowls and set them inside the dishwasher.

"And you do cleanup, too."

"I'm multitalented," he said, wanting to keep the mood light. Drying off his hands, he joined her in the living room. It was still light out, the sun bright in the late August sky. It was a beautiful day as only late summer could be in the Pacific Northwest.

"What would you like to do?" he asked. "Do you want to go out? I always feel better when I get out on the water for a while."

She seemed to think it over, then shook her head. "Can we stay right here?"

"Anything, sweetheart."

"Would you hold me again?"

"Nothing would please me more."

They cuddled on the sofa. After a while Libby reached for the remote control and turned on the television. Phillip couldn't remember the last time he'd watched an hour of uninterrupted television. None of the programs were familiar.

He lost track of how long the two of them sat there. He laughed at some crazy sitcom joke and saw Libby break into a weak smile. Seeing her amused, however briefly, gave him such a strong feeling of love that he closed his eyes, unfamiliar with the richness of the emotion. Needing to respond in some way, he kissed the top of her head.

He wasn't a man who often sat and did nothing. Yet he was at complete peace, being here with Libby, sharing this time with her, knowing she needed him.

What amazed him, what he couldn't explain, was the knowledge that he needed her, too. Being with her was just as important to him. His reserve was gone, worn away bit by bit as their relationship developed. He'd watched her with the newborns and how she'd stepped up to mentor Ava. This was a woman he could love, a woman he could spend the rest of his life loving.

When the late-night news came on, Phillip knew it was time to leave. Yet he didn't want to go, didn't feel good about abandoning her. Not tonight.

"I should get home."

"Don't go," she pleaded, clinging to his arm.

"Libby . . ."

"I'm not asking you to make love to me."

"Trust me, darling, you wouldn't need to ask." If she only knew how tempting she was, red eyes and all. He'd never been more attracted to a woman than he was that very moment.

She looked up at him and smiled. "I need someone to hold me tonight. Nothing more. Can you do that?"

"For you, my love, anything."

"Am I your love?" she asked, frowning slightly with the question.

"Yes," he whispered and bent down to kiss her. Although it would have been easy to allow that lone kiss to become much more, he ended it quickly for fear he wouldn't have the fortitude to stop. "I love you, Libby. More than I realized it was possible to love someone. I'd mostly given up on falling in love." If he didn't love her he'd take her to bed and keep her up all night making love to her. He would do all that when the time was right, but that time wasn't now. Not tonight.

"Loving you frightens me a little."

He laughed softly. "Me too. We're a couple of hard cases, aren't we?"

In fact it frightened him more than a little, but not enough to give up now. With his arm tucked around her waist, he led her into the bedroom.

Chapter 35

Libby woke Saturday morning to discover Phillip asleep beside her. She blinked, thinking he might be an illusion, and then remembered that she'd lost Amy Jo to Peter's family. Phillip had been her comfort; she doubted if she could have made it through the night without him. In her grief she'd actually asked him not to leave her. Friday had been one of the lowest points of her life. Libby liked being independent. From the time of her mother's death, she'd prided herself on her ability to deal with the blows life tossed her. She was strong, capable, and resourceful, but yesterday, she'd badly needed Phillip. She'd clung to him, unable to face the night alone. How easy it would have been for him to make love to her. He hadn't—all he'd done was hold her close and whisper reassurances.

Although Dr. Phillip Stone enjoyed his hospital reputation of having a stone heart, that was a misnomer. He was actually tenderhearted, compassionate, and kind. Their romance wasn't based on sexual attraction, although that was definitely there. Oh yes, it was present and accounted for in spades, but tightly controlled on both sides. Neither one was willing to allow hormones to rule their actions. The pain of broken relationships had left scar tissue on his heart and on hers, too. Both had been wary of getting involved again, cautious—perhaps overly so.

The draw she felt for Phillip was beyond the physical. At one time Phillip had been trapped into thinking work was the solution to all of life's issues. Like her, his profession had fed his ego and allowed him to bury his problems behind a protective wall. But Phillip had broken free of his workaholic tendencies, and because he had she felt the hope and confidence that she could, too. Really they were kindred spirits, alike in so many ways.

He must have felt her scrutiny because his eyes slowly opened. "Morning," he said, stretching his arms above his head and releasing a yawn. He tossed aside the sheets and surged upright. It seemed that only then did he remember the reason he had stayed the night. He sat on the edge of the mattress and turned back to look at her.

"How are you feeling?"

"Passable." The pain wasn't nearly as raw as it had been the day before, but it was there, pressing hard against her chest, a heavy weight against her tender heart. For as long as Libby could remember, her cure had been to keep busy, to work harder and longer and ignore everything and everyone else. If she could occupy her mind with menial matters then she wouldn't dwell on her troubles. This was how she'd survived following her mother's death and how she'd gotten through her divorce.

"Good." He leaned down and kissed her forehead. "I'm sorry to rush out of here but I took weekend duty for a friend so I need to get to the hospital."

While she would have rather he stayed, she accepted that he needed to go. She walked him to the door and resisted the urge to hug him for fear it would make their parting even more difficult for her. "Thank you," she whispered.

"You're welcome." He placed his hand at the base of her neck and brought her mouth to his, kissing her gently. "Can I see you tonight?" he asked. "Would you like to go sailing?"

He'd asked her the same thing the night before, thinking, she was sure, that being on the water would help her deal with her pain. Earlier it had seemed impossible that she would ever be able to leave the comfort of her condo. This morning, she felt more inclined. "That would be perfect."

"I'll text you when I can." He hesitated as though it was difficult to leave her.

"Okay." She walked him to the elevator and he kissed her again, wrapping his arms around her, and holding her tight and close, so close that for a moment it was almost difficult to breathe.

Libby had a busy day. Robin stopped by shortly after Phillip left and packed up Amy Jo's room for her. Lydia phoned twice just to make sure she was doing all right. Her family of friends surrounded her with love. Later that evening, and on Sunday, too, Phillip came and they sailed across Lake Washington. The wind buffeted her face, drying her tears as she did her best to hide the fact that she was crying. Phillip simply held her as she worked through her loss.

Monday morning Libby found Phillip waiting for her outside Frankie and Johnny's. He draped his arm around her shoulders as they entered the gym.

He seemed to have a hard time taking his eyes off her. If they'd been anyplace else she suspected he might have kissed her.

Robin was waiting for her inside the locker room. "I wasn't sure you'd show," she said, watching Libby closely.

Libby sat on the bench and looked up at her friend. "The way I figure, I could stay home and feel sorry for myself, or get on with my life. I've decided to move forward." It wouldn't be easy, but Libby would ignore the hole in her heart and do her best to forget this abrupt and unwelcome twist in the story line she'd conjured up for herself. It was as if the universe had intervened and put the kibosh on her new, risk-taking, joy-seeking self.

"Anything I can do?" Robin asked.

"Not really, but thanks for offering."

"What are your plans for the day?"

Libby had given the matter some thought. "After the gym I'm going to talk to Ava about this adoption. I want to make sure, as Amy Jo's biological mother, she can have a role in the baby's life later even if she doesn't think she wants that now. My fear is that she'll change her mind at some point. Also, I thought I'd contact Peter's family and offer them all the baby furniture I purchased. They're going to need it."

"They should pay for it," Robin insisted.

Libby had briefly considered that. It wasn't like she could afford it, either. "No, it'll be my gift to them. They aren't wealthy people and they're already picking up the attorney costs for the adoption and making big changes in their lives for . . . Grace." She stumbled over Amy Jo's new name.

Robin shook her head. "You have a generous heart, Libby."

Libby wasn't convinced it was generosity as much as self-preservation. She didn't want the baby furniture at the condo any longer than necessary. It was a constant reminder to her of all she'd lost.

"Don't you have a second appointment this afternoon with those friends of the Buckleys?" Robin asked.

"I do." At three Libby was scheduled to meet with the Nyquist family regarding trust funds they wished to set up for their grandchildren's college education. After her initial contact with them Libby got the impression this could be the beginning of a long and fruitful relationship. She certainly felt that way about the Buckleys.

Following her meeting with the Nyquists, Libby stopped off at A Good Yarn. After everything Phillip had done for her over the past few days she wanted to find a special way to thank him. She decided to knit him a sweater.

They met for dinner on the waterfront that night. Phillip was full of stories from the hospital. She knew he was looking to distract and entertain her. They walked hand in hand along the piers and decided to ride the ferry over to Bainbridge Island for no better reason than to buy a latte and ride back. All the time she'd lived in Seattle, Libby had never taken a ferry for pleasure, and Phillip confessed that he hadn't, either.

* * *

Tuesday morning at the gym Libby stepped onto the treadmill and started her workout. She ran faster and longer than she usually did, struggling not to think about Amy Jo. She accepted that the Armstrongs had a claim on the baby that was their son's child, but that didn't make it any easier to let her go.

It was almost eleven by the time Libby stopped by the office and read over the adoption paperwork before driving over to Ava's to review everything. She purposely chose a time when Darlene Carmichael would be away from the house. This discussion was one she wanted to have without Ava's grandmother close at hand. Ava would do anything to appease her grandmother, and Libby wanted to take that additional pressure off her.

Ava sat on the front porch steps waiting for her. She stood when Libby parked at the curb in front of the house and ran to her.

Libby hugged her. "How's it going?" she asked, tucking her arm around the girl's waist as they walked down the cracked sidewalk toward the house.

"I'm feeling better every day."

Libby was extremely proud of Ava. "I knew you would."

"Peter and I talked. He told me how sorry he was and that he would have helped me if he'd known . . . only I don't know what he could have done. He wanted to tell me his parents will love our baby." She raised questioning eyes to Libby, as if seeking her approval.

"They will be good parents to Grace," Libby said, brushing the hair from Ava's forehead in order to get a better look at the girl's eyes. She nearly stumbled over the words, but she was determined to be positive for Ava's sake.

"I . . . I wanted you to adopt her." Ava frowned as though unsure what to think.

Libby swallowed against the tightness that gripped her throat. "I would have loved nothing better. But sometimes life throws us a curveball and we have to deal with it as best we can."

Ava lowered her head.

"What's important to me is that your rights regarding your daughter are clearly spelled out."

"I . . . I don't understand."

"Let's sit down and talk this out," Libby suggested.

The two of them sat on the front step. The concrete slab was narrow, so their hips pressed tightly against each other's. "Remember when I explained to you about an open adoption?"

Ava nodded. "Yes, but I think it might be easier not to see the baby again. Ever."

Libby wouldn't discount that. "The thing is, Ava, Grace is going to be living right next door to you. Of course, Peter and his family could move one day, but until then you won't be able to avoid seeing her." Libby suspected the family already had plans to make a change— for one thing, they would need a bigger house now that they were enlarging their family.

"I . . . guess you're right."

"You've already lost your mother," Libby reminded her. "I don't want you to look back someday and regret that you gave up your child without any provisions to be part of her life."

Ava considered Libby's words, a

thoughtful look scrunching her forehead. "This will allow me the chance to see my baby if that's what I want later."

"Exactly."

"Then I think an open adoption would be best if you do, too."

"I do. I'll contact the attorney as soon as I get back to the office and make sure everything is drawn up so you have that option. Before you sign anything, I want to read it over, understand?"

Again Ava nodded. "Okay."

Libby hugged her briefly. "I'm going to be at the yarn store later this afternoon. Will you be there?"

The teen broke into a wide grin and nodded. "Casey asked me to come to the shop today and I told her I would after I saw you. I thought I would knit myself a vest for school. I start classes on Monday."

"What color?"

"I like purple," Ava said. "Bright, bright purple."

"Purple is one of my favorite colors, too. I'm going because I decided to knit Dr. Stone a sweater."

"In purple?"

Libby laughed. "If that's what he wants. I'm going to let him decide on the pattern and the yarn."

"Cool. You must really like him."

"I do."

They spoke for several minutes and then Libby had to go. "I'll see you later this afternoon," she promised.

Ava nodded excitedly.

Once more Libby marveled at how resilient this teenager was, though she understood that Ava was far too young to fully appreciate what she was going through. That was why Libby found it important to protect Ava's interests with regard to her baby.

Libby returned to her office. She had a long phone conversation with the Armstrongs' attorney. Within minutes of hanging up Marlene Armstrong phoned to thank her for the offer of the baby furniture.

For the rest of the afternoon Libby worked on the Buckley account, and also on the trust funds for the Nyquists. After her meeting with them, Lois and Jamison Nyquist had given Libby a retainer. They were both in their mid-sixties, retired, and seriously looking at their financial future. As much as possible they were hoping to protect their assets and put something away for their children and grandchildren. Libby had proposed several options.

Phillip stopped by her condo and she fixed a Cobb salad for dinner. Actually they made it together, chopping and assembling the ingredients next to each other. Phillip brought along a bottle of merlot, which he deftly opened and poured while she set the table. He helped her with the few dishes afterward.

"I've decided to knit you a sweater," Libby said as Phillip dried the frying pan she'd used for the bacon and set it on the stovetop. "But if I'm going to put that much work and effort into the project, I want to be sure you're going to like the pattern." Margaret had been of the opinion that Libby shouldn't even consider such a time-consuming project without a ring on her finger first. When a woman decided to knit a man a sweater, the relationship had to be serious. Libby was serious about Phillip and growing more so with every passing day. Knitting a sweater for him felt right.

Phillip reached for his wineglass. "I don't have to go back to the yarn store, do I?"

"Would that be such a sacrifice?" She looked up at him and smiled beguilingly, or as close as she could get to beguiling.

"No, I guess not."

He didn't look or sound convinced.

"It would help if you chose the yarn, too."

Phillip folded the dishcloth and set it aside. "I hate to tell you this, but I know next to nothing about yarn."

"The color, sweetheart. I know you're partial to blue."

"I am." He frowned, bunching his brows together in a single jagged line. "How'd you know that?"

"You're not serious, are you? Nearly all your shirts are blue."

"They are?" He seemed shocked.

"Yes, and the color goes very nicely with your eyes."

He grinned then, accepting the compliment with ease. "Lots of women tell me so."

She jabbed his arm and he pretended to be hurt. "Come over here and sit down with me and we can look through a few patterns."

He dutifully followed Libby into the living room. She brought out the pattern book she'd bought and handed it to Phillip. It took him all of five minutes to choose a V-neck sweater.

"Now, about this sweater you're knitting for me."

"Yes?" She looked up and blinked at him several times, flirting outrageously. She felt better when she was with Phillip; the ache in her heart hurt less when he was at her side, and for a while she was able to forget.

"It seems to me knitting a sweater involves a lot of work."

"It is a huge undertaking. Margaret actually suggested I should have an engagement ring on my finger before I purchase the yarn. It's an investment, you know."

"The ring or the yarn?" he asked, and his eyes danced with merriment.

She smiled. "Both, actually."

Phillip exhaled as though giving the matter serious consideration. "It's a little soon for you to think about dragging me to the altar, don't you think?"

"Drag you to the altar? Oh, honestly, that's the most ridiculous thing you've ever said."

"Okay, okay. I just want to be sure we understand each other. Is this sweater your way of saying our relationship shows . . . promise?" He cocked his eyebrows with the question.

"Well," she murmured, hesitating. "Truth be told, I could easily see the two of us making a life together. We aren't kids. We both know what we want in life. Right?"

Phillip responded with an agreeable nod. "I definitely know what I want."

She waited for him to continue and when he hesitated, she prodded. "Well, don't keep me in suspense."

Smiling, he gathered her into his arms. "It should be obvious by now, Libby Morgan. I want you."

Chapter 36

The next day, Libby was busy at her desk when her receptionist announced that Hershel Burkhart was on the line for her. Straightening, Libby stared down at the phone, hardly able to think. Well, there was no time like the present to find out what he wanted. Libby reached for the phone. "This is Libby Morgan."

"Libby." Hershel greeted her warmly. "How good to hear your voice. I'm checking in to see how everything is going for you."

Though their last two conversations

had been strained, at best, Libby still felt plenty of respect for this man who'd mentored her. After a brief hesitation on her part, she updated him on recent events. She felt proud to be able to mention the two new clients she had recently acquired. She didn't mention anything about the failed adoption.

"I'm so pleased to hear how well you're doing," he continued. "Martha Reed was in recently and she told us how very proud of you she is."

Libby hadn't always thought kindly of her time with her former firm, but she was getting beyond the disappointment and bitterness she'd experienced when Hershel had reluctantly let her go. For one thing, she was a survivor. The last six months had proved as much. And for now, she had plenty of work and more coming in every day. Already she had retainer clients and more were sure to follow. Word of mouth had spread quickly. Her rates were more reasonable than those of the larger law firms with higher overhead. If she continued to take on new clients, then she would need to think about hiring a paralegal.

Knowing Hershel hadn't phoned to exchange chitchat, she asked, "What can I do for you?"

"Would it be convenient for you to stop by the office one day this week?"

This was getting all the more intriguing.

"For?"

"The other partners and I would like to have a chat with you."

Libby sat up straighter. "About?"

"I'd rather not do business over the phone. I think you'll be pleased, Libby. Now what day would be convenient?"

Libby hesitated and then, smiling to herself, she said, "Let me check my schedule." She placed him on hold and kept him waiting for a couple of moments. When she reconnected she said, "I could stop by Friday, say around five." She'd made it deliberately late in the afternoon so she could work for as long as possible.

"We'll see you Friday at five," he repeated. "As I said, I think you'll be pleased."

Libby replaced the phone and immediately contacted Phillip, who was out of town at a physicians' conference in Las Vegas. Unable to reach him directly, she left him a message on his cell phone.

Next she sent Robin a text. Thirty minutes later Robin texted her back and suggested they meet for a glass of wine. Libby agreed to meet her that afternoon. Robin came back with a location and time.

Three hours later the two of them sat sipping merlot in a wine bar off Fourth Avenue near Libby's office. "I think he wants to offer me my old job back," she mused aloud, holding her wineglass by the stem, resisting the urge to twirl it as her mind buzzed with possibilities.

"Clearly he needs you for something," Robin muttered, tapping her fingers while her eyes narrowed suspiciously.

"But why?"

"The answer is obvious," Robin said, relaxing against the bar stool. "Mrs. Reed. Would you go back?"

This was the same question Libby had been asking herself since Hershel's call. The very same question Phillip had posed in a text message he'd sent in response to her voice mail. Would she go back? "The truth is, I don't know," Libby admitted. She held the stem of the wineglass with both hands, as if she needed the goblet to center her.

"You'll go back," Robin said decisively.

"Really? And what makes you think that?"

"Well, for one thing, Hershel hasn't gotten where he is without a few persuasive skills. From what you've told me he's always been fond of you in a fatherly sort of way. Also, I suspect Mrs. Reed is still unhappy."

Libby had more or less reached the same conclusion herself.

"And," Robin continued, "because of the difficulties with Mrs. Reed, Hershel was able to convince the other partners that nothing would satisfy the older woman unless she worked with you."

"Do you think they might offer me a partnership?" Libby whispered, hardly able to believe the firm would be willing to go that far.

Robin sipped her wine, her look pensive. "They might. It depends."

Libby shook her head. They were both leaping to conclusions. She hadn't even met with Hershel yet. Still, the thought was there. Partner. Her heart beat just a little faster. Could it actually be possible they would want her desperately enough to offer her a partnership?

"Is this what you want?" Robin asked, leaning toward her slightly. "You've made a lot of positive changes. Are you sure you want to get back into the same old grind?"

Libby didn't need to think twice. "I do. I deserve to be a partner. I worked for this." In her mind everything would change once she'd achieved the goal that had driven her for the last six years. Being a partner would make all the sacrifices worth it. Besides, she was a different person now. She would balance her work life and her personal life and avoid the mistakes of the past. It'd be difficult, but she could do it, especially with the support system she had built over the past few months and with Phillip at her side.

"All you can do is wait and see what Hershel and the others have to say," Robin said as she glanced at her wrist. "Gotta scoot, I'm meeting Roy for dinner."

Libby nodded. Robin had changed from the career-driven workaholic she'd once been. These days she left work at six and spent most of her free time with Roy. The two were the talk of the courthouse, from what Libby understood. Seeing Robin this happy thrilled her.

Her friend left money on the table for the wine. "Have you talked this over with Phillip yet?"

"He's out of town. I left him a message and he texted back. We haven't actually talked yet." Smiling, she had to wonder just how much of the conference he was attending. Every time he phoned all Libby could hear was jarring casino noise in the background. He'd arrive back in Seattle on Sunday.

* * *

The rest of the week passed slowly. Finally, Friday afternoon, at two minutes to five, Libby walked into the familiar office. The receptionist, Lois, stood when she stepped off the elevator. "Ms. Morgan, welcome," she said, sporting a huge smile. "I believe the partners are awaiting your arrival."

Libby squared her shoulders.

Hershel's office was directly down the hall and although Libby was well aware of the location, the receptionist led the way and announced her arrival.

As soon as she entered the room, everyone stood and stepped forward to shake her hand. The other partners beamed smiles in her direction.

Libby blinked a couple of times to make sure she hadn't fallen into some fantasy. If this was a dream world, she didn't want to wake up anytime soon.

After two or three minutes of small talk, Hershel cleared his throat. "I know you're curious as to why we've asked to see you."

Libby nodded.

"Basically," Hershel said, "we'd like to offer you your old position back. Of course, you'd be working with Sarah again and we'd be willing to offer you a slight increase over your former pay scale."

Howard Smith spoke. He was a short man of only about five-six who wore his hair in a crew cut, most of which was gray now. "We're hoping you'd be able to start sometime next week."

Libby blinked. Hershel had told her she'd be pleased and she was, but hesitant, too. Why the rush? Next week?

She crossed her legs and after settling into the wingback chair she regarded them closely. "I'm sure you're aware I have my own practice now." Before she made a commitment Libby wanted more details. As for working with Sarah, the offer didn't hold as much appeal as it once had. She didn't feel the same about the paralegal since it'd become clear Sarah had betrayed her confidence with the partners, not to mention her failure to respond to Libby's job offer.

"We've taken the fact you've struck out on your own into consideration," Hershel spoke for the group. "You can keep that office if you wish and of course the firm would pick up the lease on your behalf or, if you prefer, you could take an office here."

"A bigger one," Howard Smith added.

Oh boy, they wanted her and they wanted her bad. Interesting, very interesting.

Glancing around the room, Libby took in the anxious looks on the partners' faces. She was about to speak when Hershel cut in.

"As I mentioned, one of the reasons we felt we had to let you go, Libby, was because you hadn't been able to attract new clients. You worked hard, supplied billable hours, and were an asset to the firm, but every partner needs to bring something to the table. You've since proven that you are capable of doing so."

"So you're offering me a partnership."

The men in the room exchanged glances.

Hershel answered, "That's definitely a possibility."

Howard Smith crossed his arms.

"When Hershel says a partnership is in the offing we want you to know it's a very distinct possibility. If the Buckleys and the Nyquists agree to transfer their accounts here then I feel I can speak for all of us when I say we'd be more than happy to put that on the plate."

"And if they don't?"

"Six months."

"Are you saying that in six months you'd be willing to make me a partner either way?" Libby asked. She wanted this clearly spelled out.

Howard grinned and nodded. "You've proven yourself, Libby. We'll give you a few months to get settled back into the office and go from there."

"Do we have a deal?" Hershel asked.

"I'll want to consider your offer over the weekend." She already knew what she was planning to do, but she wanted to talk to Phillip first. Robin, too. And she didn't wish to appear overly eager.

"Of course, of course. This is an important decision. Naturally we'd want you to think it over carefully," Howard said, favoring her with one of his rare smiles.

"We'll wait to hear from you Monday morning, then," Hershel said.

"Yes, Monday." Libby rose out of the chair. "One thing," she said in afterthought.

"Yes?"

"I'd like a new paralegal. I'm sure Sarah has made a smooth transition working with Ben Holmes. I would prefer someone new."

"Done," Howard assured her.

Libby waited until she was out of the building before she sent Phillip a text. CALL ME ASAP.

He phoned less than five minutes later. "What's up?"

"You won't believe what just happened," she said, speaking so fast the words nearly blurred together. Before he could ask she told him everything. "What do you think?" she said.

His hesitation came as a surprise. Libby had expected him to be as excited as she was, or nearly so. "Is this something you want, Libby?"

"Of course it is." No need denying the obvious. "I feel vindicated after all these months."

"You aren't worried that you'll fall into the same rut you were in when you left the firm?"

"No," she insisted. "I've learned my lesson. Oh, it might be intense the first few weeks while I train my new paralegal and get caught up with the Reed account, but I promise you, Phillip, I'll never go back to the way I was before. I have a life now, friends and . . ." She hesitated, her heart nearly bursting with joy. "I have you."

The silence on the line felt deafening.

"Say something," she whispered. She wanted—no, she needed—Phillip to be happy for her. Being made partner was what she'd longed for from the start. It was everything she'd strived for over the last six years and beyond. It was what her mother would have wanted for her.

"What would you like me to say?" he asked with a decided lack of enthusiasm.

"I want you to tell me that you're happy for me and will support my decision," she blurted out.

"The decision is yours, sweetheart—

yours and yours alone. I thought you were happy with the idea of your own practice, but if you want to go back with the firm then by all means, you have my complete support."

"Thank you."

"I'll see you on Sunday and we can talk more then," Phillip assured her.

"Okay . . ." Reluctantly she ended the call. She knew he was busy with the convention but wished they could have spoken longer.

Libby waited until Saturday morning before she called Robin. The two met to go shopping. Robin hated buying clothes but was running out of anything suitable to wear on her dates with Roy. Her one black dress had taken her about as far as it could.

"I hate this, you know," she muttered when Libby met her at the downtown Nordstrom.

"I know, but it will be painless."

Robin snickered. "Don't be so sure."

Libby had already given her friend all the details of her conversation with the partners earlier. Sitting outside the dressing room, Libby waited while Robin tried on outfits. She didn't appear to be having much success as the salesclerk was rushing back and forth with armloads of dresses.

"I look ridiculous," Robin muttered from inside the fitting room.

"I doubt Roy would say that."

"I wish now I'd paid more attention to my mother. She has a sense of style, which unfortunately completely escaped me." Having said that, Robin opened the dressing room door and stepped out in a bright red dress that looked incredible.

"Robin . . ." Libby's mouth sagged open.

"I know. I look like an overweight poinsettia."

"You look gorgeous." Libby meant every word.

"Really?"

Libby nodded.

Robin looked at the salesclerk. "I'll take it, the blue outfit, and the pink one, too."

Robin in pink. She probably hadn't

worn anything that wasn't blue, black, or brown in years.

After Robin paid and carted the garment bag to the parking garage, they decided to eat lunch.

Her friend waited until after the waiter had taken their order before she spoke about Libby's meeting with the firm. "Two questions."

"Ask away." Libby set her water glass down.

"What did Phillip say?"

Libby slowly released her breath. She was having a difficult time reading his reaction. He'd been encouraging, but not overly so. She sensed that he would rather she moved ahead with her own practice instead of returning to the firm, but he hadn't said so. "He told me he'd support my decision. He knows how important this is to me. I don't think he wanted to say anything to persuade me one way or the other. Besides, they offered me a terrific package and he knows I've practically gone through my entire savings. I need this. My bank account needs this."

Robin frowned as she reached for a

roll from the middle of the table, as if to say she knew this was about more than the money. The waiter appeared with their salads. She waited until he'd turned away before asking her second question: "Did you contact Martha Reed?"

Libby smiled gleefully. She'd been waiting all afternoon to share this news. "I did and I explained that Hershel had asked me to rejoin the firm, and Mrs. Reed told me that it shouldn't come as any surprise."

Robin set the buttered roll aside. "The sweet old lady decided to pull her account once and for all if you weren't the one working on it, didn't she?"

"Bull's-eye," Libby said. "Mrs. Reed told Hershel that upon reflection—her word, not mine—that upon reflection her rapport with me outweighed her history with the firm and their offer to cap fees."

Robin clapped her hands. "I love it. So they are about to lose her."

Libby was ready to burst with a deep sense of self-righteousness. "It was exactly the ammunition Hershel needed to convince the other partners they needed me. I still don't know that her children would have been comfortable with her bringing the estate part of her business to me, but it was definitely a concern." It didn't hurt that Libby had clients she would potentially be bringing into the firm, too.

"Another question," Robin said.

"That's three."

"It's important."

Robin had gone quite sober, which surprised Libby. Libby sat up a bit straighter, and gestured toward her friend. "Ask away."

Robin looked her straight in the eye. "Are you sure . . . are you absolutely convinced that your willingness to go back to the firm isn't an escape from the pain of losing Amy Jo?"

A rush of fresh hot pain shot to the surface and emotion clogged Libby's throat. She waited until it passed before she answered, waited until she was sure she could trust her voice. "I . . . I don't know, but what I do know is that this is the opportunity of a lifetime and I'm grabbing hold of it with both hands. This is my chance to vindicate myself."

"Then go for it," Robin advised. "Give it everything you've got."

"That's exactly what I intend to do," Libby said.

Later that afternoon, exhausted from shopping, Libby sat in her condo watching the sunset. Phillip would be back from Vegas the next afternoon. He planned to come over as soon as he landed. In mulling over his response to her news, she'd reached an insight. While Phillip might be unwilling to share his feelings, she could pretty much guess his thoughts on the matter.

He was afraid of what would happen to them as a couple if she returned to the firm. With her own practice the only person she had to compete with was herself. At the firm there were the partners who would be constantly looking over her shoulder, critiquing her performance and her ability to bring in new clients.

What Phillip didn't understand was that he didn't need to worry. She wouldn't allow anything to come between the two of them. She wouldn't fall victim to that treadmill mentality again. She'd found her life and she was determined not to repeat past mistakes.

As she headed for bed that night, Libby paused to look into the nursery. The room was empty now. The Armstrongs had come and collected all the furniture—they'd been grateful and appreciative. Libby stared at the empty space for a long time. Then, with a lump in her throat, she bounced her closed fist against the wall and turned off the light.

Chapter 37

Two months later Libby tore into her condo, unfastening the buttons to her business jacket with one hand as she tossed her briefcase to the floor with the other. She kicked the high-heeled pumps from her feet, and one flew onto the sofa and the other landed somewhere in the kitchen. She didn't care. She was already late and Phillip would be over to pick her up in a matter of minutes. Julie Busbee, one of the doctors' wives, was holding a surprise birthday party for her husband, Scott, and Phillip and Libby had been invited to attend. They couldn't be late—it would ruin the surprise.

The party was at the Busbee property north of Seattle, outside of Woodinville. According to the invitation there would be hayrides, a buffet dinner, and, later on in the evening, a bonfire. No way Libby could wear her suit and pumps. Jerking a sweater out of her closet sent the hanger into a seesaw rocking motion. While pulling the sweater over her head, Libby grabbed jeans and stuffed her feet inside slip-ons.

She barely had time to run a brush through her hair and put on some lipstick when the doorbell rang. Phillip!

Libby squirted on a quick spray of her favorite perfume and dragged in a deep breath to steady her pounding heart before she opened the door.

Phillip's eyes widened as he stepped into the condo. "It looks like a cyclone landed here," he said, looking past her. Libby's suit jacket was tossed on the floor, followed by her skirt, leaving a trail that led into her bedroom.

"I was running a bit behind schedule," she said, hoping he didn't hear the breathless quality to her voice.

"Libby, Libby," he said, kissing her forehead and holding her close for a moment. It seemed like he wanted to say more, but he hesitated. "Get your coat, or we'll be late."

"My coat," she repeated, opening the closet and grabbing her dark wool jacket. The weather had turned decidedly cooler over the last week.

With his hand on the small of her back, Phillip led her to the elevator. Libby didn't relax until they were inside his car. Then and only then did she breathe a sigh of relief.

"You weren't at the gym this morning," he commented.

"No, I needed to get to the office early." It was necessary if she intended to leave in time to make this birthday party. She need not have worried about missing out on gym time; she'd gotten a good workout on her mad dash from the office to her condo.

She'd tried; she'd made a genuine effort not to put in too many hours at the office, but all her good intentions had quickly fallen by the wayside. By the end of the day she was too tired to think, too tired to feel.

What Robin had said to her before she rejoined the firm had often come to mind over the past few weeks. Her dearest friend had asked her if, deep down, she was choosing to bury herself in her work as a way to forget about the baby she'd loved. At the time Libby hadn't been one hundred percent sure. She was now. Working unbelievably long hours felt comfortable. Inside the office she could block out the pain. She had purpose, ambition, and drive, and she was able to convince herself the firm needed her. Mrs. Reed needed her.

"Robin was at the gym."

Libby glanced at Phillip. "I called to tell her I couldn't make it." She figured Phillip would comment on her absence and held her breath waiting for his censure. None came.

"Robin mentioned your call." Phillip was quiet for several minutes while he maneuvered through the busy Seattle traffic, taking back streets to get to the

I-5 on-ramp. Once they were on the freeway he asked, "So how's my sweater coming along?"

He had to ask! He didn't berate her for all the overtime she'd been putting in; instead, he just asked pointed questions. The fact was that she hadn't picked up her needles all week. Not a single stitch. "The sweater's great. I'm up to the armholes on the back."

"Weren't you at the same place the last time I asked, which was when? Two weeks ago? Three?"

"Yes, well, it's been a busy few weeks." She hadn't gotten home before seven a single night. She hadn't meant for this to happen. With Phillip's help she'd even made up a list of rules, modeled after some of his own. These were guidelines that had helped him, and Libby had hoped they might keep her from falling into the same old groove of all work and no play.

Rule number one. She would never bring work home again.

Rule number two. She would keep up with her exercise program.

Rule number three. She would stay in touch with Ava.

Rule number four. She would make time for her newfound friends: Robin, Lydia, Abby, and Sharon.

Up until now her track record hadn't exactly been stellar. It didn't take a week for her to fall back into the pattern of bringing work home. She didn't feel good about it, and the only reason she did it was because of Phillip. He called her every night and if she wasn't home before seven she could see that it irritated him.

Phillip hadn't said anything negative about her return to the firm. Really, she hadn't been able to turn down that kind of money, and her savings account was so low it frightened her. Her credit cards were all hovering near their credit limits and she needed to pay them off as quickly as possible. The job offer had come at exactly the right time and for more reasons than she'd given Phillip and Robin. Because she felt she would rather work from an office at the firm, Hershel had negotiated the termination of her lease.

She had kept up with the exercise program . . . with a few skipped days. Before going back to the firm she'd worked out at least four times a week and more often five. That had quickly dwindled down to three, and this week she'd been to Frankie and Johnny's only once. Libby promised herself next week would be different.

Once she was done setting up the Buckley account, straightening out the mess Ben had made of Martha Reed's paperwork, and training her new paralegal, Libby wouldn't need to work these long hours. But for now it was becoming harder and harder to get work done in the office with meetings, conference calls, and other demands on her time. It was either arrive early and stay late or take work home with her.

As for keeping up with Ava, they'd talked at least twice this week. Ava was back in school. Everything seemed to be going okay, although the teenager didn't often mention her classes. Libby worried that there was something Ava wasn't telling her. This weekend Libby planned to take her to lunch so they could chat one-on-one. She suspected word had gotten out at the school that she was the mother of the baby Peter's family had adopted.

"You're frowning," Phillip commented, glancing away from the road. "Anything wrong?"

"Nothing; I was just thinking about Ava."

"What's going on with her?"

"I'm not sure, but something."

"When did you last talk to her?" he asked.

"Tuesday . . . I think." She'd meant to call her again, but the week had been hectic with one demand after another. Thankfully Libby's new paralegal seemed to be a good fit, but settling into a working relationship required time and patience.

"You're frowning again," Phillip said, chuckling softly.

"Oh, sorry . . . I was thinking about Sarah."

"The new paralegal is working out?"

"Melinda's great." Libby turned her

head and looked out the window to hide a yawn. Phillip saw it, though.

"You're exhausted."

"I'm fine," she countered. "Really."

"Close your eyes for a few minutes," he suggested. "It'll take another twenty minutes in this traffic. I want you to have a good time tonight." He patted her thigh.

Following his suggestion, Libby closed her eyes and leaned her head against the window. It did feel good to relax. Although she didn't want to admit it, she was bushed. It'd been a difficult week. She was out of practice with working these hours, and everything seemed to be hitting her at once. It'd taken time and effort to convince the Buckleys to come on board. The Nyquists had decided to take their business elsewhere. Despite Libby's reassurances that they wouldn't be lost in a large firm, and her promises to give them her personal attention, they'd decided against it.

Hershel, however, was a man of his word. In a matter of a few months she would be welcomed into the firm as a full partner. Every time Libby thought about seeing her name added to the letterhead, her heart did a small bee-bop of satisfaction.

Libby deserved to be partner and it gratified her that her role in the firm had finally been acknowledged. It'd taken the loss of Mrs. Reed's account to show them her worth. Well, they were making it up to her now.

The car slowed and Libby opened her eyes, shocked to discover that she'd slept nearly the entire drive there. They were in Woodinville, at the Busbee property. Because it was a surprise party, Phillip had to park his vehicle in a vacant field out of sight of the house and road. They walked toward the house hand in hand. Julie Busbee had arranged for everyone to hide in the barn. She planned to tell Scott his present was in the outbuilding. He'd assume it was the quarter horse he'd wanted. Julie had gotten him the horse, too, but when he walked into the barn all his best friends would be waiting there with the horse.

Julie's plan worked beautifully and

Scott was more than just surprised—
he seemed completely stunned. The
party was well planned. One of the
women Libby had met at the yarn store,
Bethanne Hamlin, Robin's former sis-
ter-in-law, owned a party business and
had assisted with the arrangements.

The buffet dinner was wonderful, followed by live music, and a hootenanny-
style songfest. After the meal the birthday celebration continued with a
horse-drawn hayride. Everyone was
having a wonderful time and there was
lots of teasing and laughter. As the evening wore on, Libby did her best to dis-
guise how tired she was. She knew almost everyone from the hospital and
mingled with Phillip and Scott's friends
easily. It was good to see everyone
again, especially Sharon Jennings.

Instead of the traditional candles on
the birthday cake, Julie had arranged
for a large bonfire in the middle of the
pasture. Everyone roasted huge marsh-
mallows in Scott's honor, with a lot of
good-natured joking about his advanc-
ing age.

After the traditional singing of the

birthday song, Libby swallowed another yawn, hoping no one noticed.

Unfortunately Phillip caught on right away. "I need to get you home before you fall asleep on your feet."

It was early yet and she hated to spoil his fun. "In a bit," she said, linking her arm with his. Without question they were considered a couple now, and there were several joking comments about when they were going to make it official. Phillip easily laughed off the good-natured teasing. Not so with Libby. She wanted to marry him, yearned to start a family. Once she achieved her goal and was made partner, she'd feel free to take the necessary time away from the firm. Her position would be secure.

After the first few couples departed Libby agreed it was time for them to go, too. On the ride back into the city, Phillip seemed unusually quiet.

"Tired?" she asked him, struggling to stay awake herself. The warm car, the fun evening, and simply being with Phillip had eased the tension from her shoulders.

He didn't answer right away. "Not particularly."

Libby sat up straighter. Then there was another reason for his silence and she had a good idea what it might be. "What's on your mind?"

Again he was quiet for several moments. She noticed that his hands tightened around the steering wheel and he stared straight ahead, not chancing a look in her direction.

"Basically I want to know how you plan to balance your work life and your real life. Because what you're doing now isn't working."

"My real life?" she repeated, amused.

"Libby, I'm serious."

"Yes, I know you're serious, and I am, too."

"You've fallen right back into the same old grind. This is exactly what I was afraid would happen if you quit your own practice. I helped you set up those rules only because you asked me to. As far as I can see they haven't done you a bit of good. You've almost given up on working out at the gym. You've only talked to Ava once this week and you can't remember the last time you picked up your knitting."

"Phillip, I know it looks bad."

"It is bad. We were supposed to meet for drinks on Wednesday and what happened?"

It wasn't like he didn't already know. "Okay, so I was a few minutes late." She'd been held up at the office.

"Thirty-two minutes, to be exact."

"I couldn't leave . . ."

"So you said." His mouth thinned to a hard line.

"It isn't just me who's changed, you know," she said. "It's hard to talk to you. It's like there's a concrete wall between us. You were like this when we first met."

"Like what?"

"I don't know: emotionally stagnant. We used to talk all the time, text, too, but if I text you, I don't get a response."

"Mainly because you're texting to tell me you're going to be late, again."

"That's not true." Libby didn't want to fight. Not tonight. Not any night. It'd been a long week and they were both tired. Finding fault with each other was far too easy. She wanted to talk to Phillip about the changes in him but she could see it would serve no purpose now.

Silence stretched between them like a barbed-wire fence, the barbs ready to draw blood if they dared attempt to climb over it. Finally Libby couldn't stand it any longer.

"It was a lovely party. Julie pulled it off; Scott couldn't have been more surprised."

"I was just happy you could spare the time," he muttered, not bothering to hide the sarcasm.

"Phillip, please, don't be like this."

"You'll always have an excuse, Libby. Just wait. It'll be the same next month and the month after that. We both knew this could happen, and despite your efforts and promises, everything has fallen apart within two months."

"Please, Phillip, I don't want to fight. Not after we've had such a good evening." Reaching over, she placed her hand on his forearm and gave him a pleading look.

He exhaled and nodded. "I don't want to argue, either."

The silence was a bit more comfortable until Phillip said, "You think that if you bury yourself in your work you won't have to think about Amy Jo?"

Libby bit down on her teeth, clenching her jaw in an effort not to give in to the hot surge of anger that instantly rose into her chest. She waited until her heart calmed before responding. His comment was a low blow and not appreciated. "You aren't going to leave this alone, are you?"

He exited the freeway and stopped at a red light. Keeping his gaze focused on the road, he exhaled a slow breath and said, "Okay, you're right. I apologize. I love you, Libby. I'd hoped that the two of us could build a future together."

She reached out and placed her hand on his arm. "I want a life with you, Phillip, and my career. I love what I do, and I'm good at it." She thought about Martha Reed and the Buckleys. "Just give me a few months and I promise everything will change." It would be a rough few months. She wouldn't lie to him. He needed to be prepared to accept the fact that she would be late a lot of nights and miss a few sessions at the gym. She would finish his sweater but it wouldn't happen before Christmas.

Phillip pulled up to the curb in front of her condo and then exhaled slowly, his shoulders rising and falling as he waged some internal battle.

"All right, Libby, I'll do my best to be patient."

"Everything will right itself soon," she promised, and pressed her head against his shoulder. "Come up for a few minutes, all right?"

He turned off the engine and together they rode up in the elevator. His mood lightened and she was grateful. While she picked up her discarded clothes and shoes, Phillip poured them each a glass of port.

They cuddled on the sofa. Libby was nestled in his arms and she pressed her head against his chest. She enjoyed the steady strong beat of his heart. Leaning down, he kissed her. His mouth lingered on hers and Libby raised her arm and gently stroked the back of his neck. They'd managed to avoid a major confrontation and she was grateful. Phillip was willing to give her the time she needed to settle back into a reasonable routine.

Everything would be different; it had to be. Libby wouldn't allow history to repeat itself.

Chapter 38

The second week of November Libby tossed back her covers and fell into bed. The firm had challenged her to prove she could be an effective member of their outreach efforts. As a result, in addition to her office duties, she was expected to wine and dine potential clients in the evenings, often not returning home until ten or eleven at night.

The last month had been an endless series of making connections and serving as a hostess at these special dinners. Her newly polished social skills had proved to be beneficial, as she'd brought in two new clients in the last three weeks. Her role within the firm was expanding, and while she was encouraged, she'd paid a stiff price in her personal life.

Despite his promise to give her time, Phillip had grown increasingly impatient with her schedule. She'd tried reasoning with him. He should be able to understand that this was a huge professional opportunity. It was vital that he realize how important it was for her to prove to the partners that they'd made the right decision in asking her to return. Like every other business, they wanted proof that their investment in her was going to pay the necessary dividends. It felt good to grow as a professional and see herself becoming skilled in the areas where she'd been weak before. But it was just so frustrating that there weren't enough hours in the day for all the things she wanted in order to live the rich, full life she hoped to have. Instead she was caught in a crazy balancing act, looking to reassure the firm's partners and at the same time maintain her relationship with Phillip and the other friends she'd made. She didn't want to believe it was an either/or situation.

Phillip had grown distant; the emotional walls were becoming thicker and harder to penetrate. He was often sarcastic and cranky and eager to start an argument. Libby tried to be patient. She bit her tongue so often she feared it had permanent teeth marks.

His own surgery schedule had increased after one of the other surgeons opted for early retirement. The hospital was hiring a replacement, but the interview process was taking far longer than anyone had anticipated. As a result, Phillip's workload had increased dramatically.

Phillip often phoned her between surgeries, asking her to meet him, to take time for a cup of coffee, to sneak away for lunch, or to just stop working long enough for them to connect. Each time Libby had no choice but to put him off. As much as she would have liked to spend time with him she couldn't just walk away from the office because he had an hour or less free. She had responsibilities, too.

Twice now they'd argued so bitterly that she'd had to walk away to cool down.

"What happened to the woman I fell in love with?" Phillip demanded.

"I'm right here. Nothing's changed," Libby insisted.

He laughed, scoffing at her. "Are you the same woman who took time to help a pregnant teenager?"

"Of course I am."

"When did you last speak to Ava?"

Libby clenched her fists at her sides. "She can call me, too, you know."

Phillip just stared at her and shook his head.

And that wasn't the end of his barrage.

"Sharon tells me that since you started work you haven't been to the nursery even once."

Libby had to acknowledge that she didn't have time now to rock newborns. "I haven't, and I miss it."

"Sharon misses you and so do the babies. You were wonderful with them.

I fell in love with you watching you sing to the babies." His eyes grew dark and sad, as if the woman he spoke of was forever gone.

"I was unemployed. I had time on my hands. I don't any longer; I have a job now, other responsibilities."

He just stared at her as if he hadn't heard a word she'd said.

"How's Robin?" he asked next.

The question gave Libby a reason to smile. "Fine."

"Really? When was the last time you talked to her?"

"This week," she shot back, although now that he asked, she wasn't completely sure. The days flew by so quickly.

What Libby didn't mention was the sarcastic comment Robin had made the last time they'd connected. They were supposed to meet up for a drink after work and Libby had canceled at the last minute. Robin hadn't taken kindly to being put off. It'd been the second time in as many weeks.

Now, tired as she was, Libby lay on her back, staring up at the ceiling, assessing the last few months. The days had flown, seeming to trip over one another like falling dominos. Scott's birthday party seemed like last weekend but it was almost a month ago. Soon it would be Thanksgiving and then Christmas would be upon them.

Phillip had invited her to fly to Arizona to meet his parents for Thanksgiving. It had broken her heart to turn him down. Ironically, he hadn't seemed the least bit troubled. He'd simply shrugged it off, almost as if he didn't care.

The sound of her doorbell startled her. Libby sat up in bed and glanced at the clock on her nightstand. It was nearly one o'clock in the morning. The only person she could think it might be was Ava, and the thought filled her with apprehension.

Libby had connected with Ava only a few times lately and the girl wasn't happy. She wasn't doing well in her classes and was fighting with her grandmother. Peter's family had put their home up for sale and had already purchased a house outside of the neighborhood.

Grabbing her robe, Libby stuffed her arms into the sleeves and tied the belt around her waist. Before she reached the front door, the doorbell chimed again. Checking the peephole, she was shocked to discover a disheveled Phillip standing in the hallway outside her door. He looked terrible. Apparently he'd been walking in the rain because what she could see of his coat was drenched. Rainwater dripped from his hair.

Unlocking the deadbolt, she tossed open the door and with her heart in her throat asked, "Phillip, what's happened? Are you okay?"

He looked at her and blinked as if he didn't know where he was or how he'd gotten to her condo. Running his fingers through his hair, he didn't seem to know what to say.

Taking him by the hand, she led him into her living room and helped him out of his raincoat.

"What time is it?" he asked before he flopped onto her sofa. He leaned forward and stared down at the carpet, his arms dangling between his knees.

"Almost one."

She sat next to him and took his hands in hers. They were shockingly cold. She rubbed them to start the circulation flowing back into his fingers. "What happened?" she whispered.

"Just let me hold you for a moment."

Libby had never seen him like this. She climbed onto the sofa on her knees and wrapped her arms as far around him as they would go. Resting her cheek against the top of his wet head, she gently brushed the thick strands of hair from his forehead while softly singing the way she had with the babies in the nursery.

It must have been ten minutes before he spoke. "I lost a baby this afternoon."

Libby had guessed it was something like that. Phillip took death personally, as if he were responsible, as if life or death was a decision he made instead of God. She yearned to remind him that he was only an instrument, but knew that he didn't want to hear it. At this point she doubted he'd believe her.

"This was a special child . . . long anticipated."

He paused as if every word caused him pain.

"The mother underwent five IVF attempts and the baby came early and with a heart defect. This child was their only chance for a family and she begged me to take every measure necessary to save her son." Phillip paused and didn't seem able to continue. Several moments passed before he spoke again. "He died on the operating table. We weren't able to resuscitate him. He lived less than five hours and . . . and I had to tell the parents." He rubbed his hands across his face.

By now Libby was so affected by his grief that her throat was clogged and she couldn't speak. She could only imagine how the parents had reacted to the news. All Libby could do was hold him the same way he had held and comforted her when the adoption had fallen through. She would have given anything to lessen his pain, to ease this horrific ache from his heart.

After several minutes, he broke out

of her embrace and stood. His eyes were more intense than she could remember.

"I can't do this anymore."

"Phillip, my love," she whispered, aching with the desire to comfort him. "The hospital needs you; these babies need you. The worst thing you could do now is to walk away. I agree that what happened would tear at anyone's heart, but you can't allow it to destroy you."

He stood and stared at her for several seconds. "I wasn't talking about the hospital, Libby, I was referring to us. It's over."

A cold chill whipped through her. "You don't mean that." He was in pain and he didn't know what he was saying.

"This isn't a spur-of-the-moment decision," he said, sounding calm now and completely reasonable. "Our relationship has been weighing on me for weeks. I thought I could do it, give you the time you needed to get your work schedule settled. If I could hold out, if I could be patient, then eventually everything would even itself out. I've waited and I can see now that nothing is going to change. If anything, it's gotten worse."

"It will change, Phillip. I promise it will."

Slowly he shook his head. "You're a fool if you believe that, Libby. A fool."

Her nails bit into her palms; she didn't take kindly to being called a fool. "You need to sleep on this. We belong together. You know it and I know it. Don't be so willing to give up on us. Not yet." Although it was difficult she did her best to remain outwardly calm. On the inside her heart was in a panic. She couldn't lose Phillip.

"I've watched what's happened, Libby. I've tried to be patient, but it's time to face facts here. This relationship isn't working for either of us."

She denied it with a sharp shake of her head. "That's not true. It's working for me. I need you. You don't know what you're saying."

"Are you telling me you haven't figured out why you've had such little contact with Ava?"

"In case you haven't noticed I've been busy," she snapped, surprised by the vehemence of her response.

"Ava reminds you of Amy Jo. You couldn't deal with what happened when the Armstrongs decided to adopt her. As a result you're avoiding Ava. She needed your encouragement and support when she was pregnant but she needs it even more now and where are you? At the office. You're always at the office because your work there gives you an escape. You don't need to think about what you lost. The same thing happened when your mother died and after Joe left you. You buried yourself in your work."

Every word was an accusation, each one flung at her as she stood defenseless and exposed. Stinging tears filled her eyes and she quickly blinked them away.

"You aren't the man I thought you were, either," she cried. "The man I love would never say such ugly, mean things, whether they were true or not."

Phillip rubbed his hand along the back of his neck. "I'm sorry."

She swallowed hard and because she found it difficult to speak she accepted his apology with a short, abrupt nod.

"I am sorry, but not for what I said, Libby," he qualified and although his voice was soft, almost gentle, his words pierced her heart. She squinted at him, not knowing what to think.

"I'm sorry because I really believe we could have been good together." He started toward the door.

For one paralyzing moment Libby stood frozen in the middle of her living room. Then she ran after him and grabbed hold of his hand, stopping him. She'd allowed Joe to walk away. She wouldn't let it happen again. Not with Phillip.

"Don't go," she pleaded. "Please, Phillip, don't do this."

He reached out to her, his hand at the base of her neck, and brought her into his arms. When he kissed her it was with a locked-up passion that was almost painful in its intensity. He released her so abruptly that she stumbled backward.

"It's over, Libby," he said starkly. "Don't make it harder." He left then, leaving her stone cold and in shock.

By late the following afternoon Libby had left no fewer than six messages on Phillip's cell. He didn't return her calls. When she couldn't reach him by phone she stopped off at the hospital.

"Dr. Stone took a few days of personal time," Abby told her after she found his office locked.

"Do you know where he went?" Libby asked, trying to pretend nothing was amiss and failing miserably. She stood with her arms crossed and her heart in her throat.

"No, sorry," Abby told her sympathetically. "We've missed you around here."

"I've missed being here," Libby said, and realized how true that was. "If you see Phillip, mention that I stopped by, would you?"

"Of course."

Libby left the hospital, and sat in her car for several moments. She knew she should go back to the office. She'd gotten several stares when she'd walked out without an explanation. They would expect her back, but Libby had somewhere else she needed to go. Someone else she needed to see.

When she parked in front of Ava's house she saw Jackson practicing free throws off the hoop in the Armstrongs' driveway. He paused when he saw her and stared as if she were an alien who'd stepped out of a spaceship.

Libby walked up to the front porch and rang the doorbell.

Ava answered and immediately her eyes brightened as she threw open the screen door.

Libby opened her arms and Ava walked into her embrace, hugging her so tightly that it hurt Libby's ribs.

"I've missed you so much," the teenager whispered. "I never see you anymore."

"I should have come sooner," Libby whispered as she ran her hand down the back of the girl's head. "I'm sorry, so sorry, but I'm here now. Let's go someplace and talk. Just you and me."

"Okay," Ava breathed on the tail end of a sob. "Just you and me."

Chapter 39

Libby didn't hear from Phillip all weekend, although she clung to the hope that he would return her calls. By Saturday night she was an emotional disaster. Convinced that she'd lost him the same way she had lost Joe, Libby cuddled up on the sofa, wrapped a blanket around her body, and hibernated the rest of the day, watching the Food Network and reruns of *Law & Order*.

Phillip was gone. He'd basically told her not to pursue him. For him there was no turning back; the decision had been made. He was through, and no amount of reassurances would change that.

Amy Jo was out of her life, too. Libby's dream of nurturing and loving that beautiful baby girl was over. Phillip had made what seemed like hurtful accusations, telling her she had hid her grief by burying herself in her work. At the time she'd denied it, denied everything. But now she could see that he was right. When the Armstrongs had decided to adopt Ava's baby it had felt as if the infant had been ripped from her arms. The ache simply wouldn't go away. The distraction she'd chosen was the same one she'd used for nearly her entire life. She studied, she worked, she did whatever it took so she wouldn't have to face the pain confronting her.

All she had left was her career. Libby had worked hard to prove herself, to make her mother proud. Yet despite everything she'd accomplished since returning to the firm, she wasn't happy.

How could she be happy when her personal life was in shambles? She missed her friends and the life she had

carved out for herself while unemployed. She missed Phillip and the
closeness they'd once shared. And yet
Libby could hear her mother's voice
from her sickbed telling her how important it was to make the most out of every opportunity because life held no
guarantees.

Molly Morgan had wanted Libby to
be a success, but suddenly Libby realized that her mother had wanted her to
be successful in *life*. Life consisted of
more than top grades in school or a
career in law. Happiness meant opening herself up to be with others, being
loving and accepting the love of others.

Her mother had wanted Libby to be
a whole person. For Libby that meant
strong relationships—a husband, family, friends, and work that fit with her
talents. She'd been so focused on making partner, as if the title alone would
fill all the empty holes in her life.

What she'd learned from Phillip was
that she needed so much more than a
title on a door and a place on the company letterhead. She needed the family

she'd found, the friends. Most of all she needed Phillip.

Here she was weeks away from achieving her goal and she was utterly miserable. She'd earned the position of partner, or she would very soon. She had it in the palm of her hand.

It meant nothing.

She felt nothing . . . nothing at all.

Not elation.

Not joy.

Not pride.

That hole inside of her should be filled up, overflowing. It wasn't. She'd worked and stretched and searched and sacrificed for nothing.

Because she'd dealt poorly with the failed adoption, Libby had let Ava down. Phillip was right; seeing the teenager reminded her of Amy Jo, of loss. It was more than the failed adoption. It was every loss Libby had suffered through-out the years: her mother, her marriage, her job. One loss after another until they became an insurmountable pile that overwhelmed her every time she was forced to confront it. She'd let that pile come between her and Phillip, between her and their future together.

No matter what happened from this point forward Libby was determined to stay in touch with Ava. She might not have control over much else, but this she could and would do. Because Libby knew what it was like to be without a mother, she could help the young teen navigate through the twisting, turning road of adolescence. She would be Ava's mentor. For years Libby had thought of herself as motherless. It suddenly struck her that that wasn't true.

Libby had a mother, a wonderful, loving, supportive, encouraging mother. She just wasn't here any longer. Molly was gone but she would always be with Libby, in the same way that Ava's mother would always be with her.

Darlene Carmichael loved her granddaughter, but much like Libby's father, she was caught up in her own grief. The older woman did the best she could with what she had, but that wasn't enough for Ava. Darlene didn't understand the emotional needs of her granddaughter in the same way that Libby's father hadn't understood hers. Libby was determined to provide all the encouragement and support Ava needed. No one had been there for Libby, but she would stand by Ava because she knew far too well what it was like to feel alone, isolated, and afraid.

Ava wasn't the only person Libby had abandoned since going back to the firm. She hadn't chatted with Lydia in weeks. The first time she'd seen Abby Higginbotham since Scott's birthday party had been when she'd gone in search of Phillip. Because she was distraught, Libby hadn't exchanged more than a couple of sentences with the woman she'd once considered a good friend.

Sunday morning Libby climbed out of bed after a restless night. She had tossed and turned for hours. As she sat on the edge of her mattress, feet on the ground, she realized she had a huge decision to make. She could either move forward and take positive action, or spend the rest of her life a failure in every way that mattered.

Unsure of what to do first, she

dressed and decided to attend church. Worship services were held just down the street from her condo. Libby wasn't sure which denomination it was, but she wasn't overly concerned. After losing Amy Jo she'd sat in the hospital chapel and ignored God, reaching out instead to her mother. Now she was willing to admit she needed God. Wanted Him in her life, guiding her.

The organ music greeted her as she ascended the church steps. She sat in the back pew and reached for the hymnal, hoping no one would notice her. Coming into the worship services her spirits were low, but gradually, as she bowed her head in prayer, a sense of peace came over her. It seemed as if God had been waiting for her to turn to Him all along. It'd taken these hits, these gigantic losses, for her to realize what she needed and how best to proceed with life.

Libby returned to her condo and sat down at her desk. She turned on her computer, and as she did so she noticed the withered plant sitting on the corner of her desk. The very plant she'd nursed back to health during her months of unemployment.

"You poor, neglected thing," she whispered. Picking it up, she carried it into her kitchen, set it on a plate, and watered and fed it plant food. Then she set it in the sun, determined to love it back to health . . . if it wasn't too late.

Chapter 40

Sunday afternoon, Libby typed out her letter of resignation to Burkhart, Smith & Crandall. How shocked Hershel would be. Actually, she was pretty shaken herself. It might be too late for her and Phillip, although she prayed it wasn't. This was something she needed to do for herself . . . for her future.

As soon as she was finished, she signed the letter and placed it inside an envelope, then contacted Robin.

"You want to go shopping and to a movie?"

"Libby, is that you?" Robin repeated

as if hearing a voice from the grave. "You aren't working? I thought you worked twenty-four/seven these days."

"Not anymore."

"Starting when?" Robin asked with a skeptical lilt to her tone.

"Starting today. Now, about that movie: I am absolutely craving buttered popcorn."

"Ah . . ." It seemed Robin was at a complete loss for words. "Sure, I guess."

"Great. I'll pick you up in thirty minutes."

The two spent a glorious afternoon together and then later Libby stopped by Ava's house and the two went out to dinner.

"I want to be a singer," Ava confessed over taco salads. "I think I'm good. There are auditions at school for a musical and I was thinking I should try out. What do you think?" she asked Libby shyly, her gaze focused on her food.

"Absolutely."

Ava smiled. "Then I will. Can I call you if I get a part?"

"You can call me anytime."

"Even if you're at work?"

"Of course. Use my cell phone number, though. Okay?"

"Okay." Ava's smile softened and she reached for her glass of milk.

Monday morning, Libby had never felt better. She strolled into the office and delivered coffee and doughnuts to the receptionist.

"Hershel would like to see you right away," Lois said.

"Perfect," she said, so happy it was all she could do not to waltz down the hall to Hershel's luxurious office.

He motioned her inside as soon as he looked up. "Libby, Libby, come in."

"Good morning, Hershel."

"You're certainly in a cheerful mood," he said, smiling now himself. "And I'm about to give you a reason to be even happier."

Oh, really? Libby doubted he could say or do anything that would match the sense of peace she'd had ever since she'd typed out her letter of resignation. It meant she was back to square one, but she would deal with that. Abby had mentioned a fund-raising position at the hospital some time ago; perhaps it was still open and she could apply for it.

"The partners and I have decided you've done such an outstanding job since your return that we're moving ahead and making you partner even earlier than we originally intended. You've proven what an asset you are to the firm. Two new clients in three weeks. Amazing. Martha Reed is happy and we all know how much that sizable account means to this firm."

Libby held up her hand, stopping him. "Before you say anything more, you might want to read this letter." Stepping forward, she handed him the envelope.

Hershel frowned and tore it open. He quickly scanned the contents and as he did his eyes narrowed. "You're resigning?"

"You said yourself I should go out and get a life, and I did. I really did, and I've discovered that I love my new life, the friends I've made, the family I've formed."

Frowning, Hershel leaned back in his chair and steepled his fingers beneath his chin. He motioned for her to take a seat, which she did. "What about your career?" he asked. "You're an excellent attorney. Are you sure this is something you want to give up? What do you plan to do with yourself? Go back to your own practice?"

"I don't know. I haven't decided. The hospital may have a job opening for a fund-raiser."

Hershel's frown deepened, as if he couldn't see her in such a position. "You'd enjoy that?"

Again she was uncertain. "I believe I would. The hours would be more reasonable."

"It would mean a substantial cut in pay."

She grinned and crossed her legs. "If nothing else, seven months of unemployment taught me how to live frugally. And you know what? It wasn't so bad. And Hershel, one lesson I've learned through all this is that money doesn't buy happiness. It really doesn't. I thought making partner was the end all, and yet I'm willing to turn my back and walk away without a qualm because of what it will cost me in other ways."

"I thought making partner was what you wanted," Hershel said.

"I thought it was, too. But it all goes back to March fifth."

"March fifth?" he repeated.

"That's the day you called me into the office and let me go. I was devastated and angry. You offered me advice. At the time I didn't want to hear it, but I heard enough and I'm grateful I did. You claimed it was an opportunity for me. I should broaden my horizons, make friends. Basically you told me how important it was to enjoy life. I took your words to heart, not right away, mind you, but soon enough. I volunteered at the hospital and fell in love and . . . and had the opportunity to adopt a baby. Unfortunately, that didn't work out." She faltered slightly when mentioning Amy Jo and paused long enough to regain her composure. "But she's with a good family who will love her. When I lost the opportunity to make the baby a part of my life, I reverted back to everything that was familiar.

The job offer from the firm couldn't have come at a better time and I did what I've always done: I buried my feelings and focused on being the best attorney money could buy.

"Working hard hasn't brought me fulfillment or lasting satisfaction. My career didn't fill that hole of grief and loss I experienced, no matter how many hours I put in."

Libby paused, half-expecting Hershel to comment. He didn't, so she continued.

"Stepping back into the grind had exactly the opposite effect. Instead of helping me forget it made everything ten times worse. I realize now how important my friends have become to me. I neglected my relationship with Ava because I thought it was more important to bring in another client to the firm and earn my brownie points with you than spend time with her.

"That was another mistake. Ava reminds me of the girl I was at her age: motherless, bereft, frightened, and alone. I consider it my duty and my honor to be a mentor and a friend to her."

"What about the young man you love?"

"It . . . may be too late for us. I don't know yet; I hope not, but if so, I'll recover and so will he."

Hershel straightened in his chair, seemingly deep in thought. "You're too important to the firm for me to let you walk away."

She loved hearing it, but his rare praise wasn't enough to convince her to change her mind.

"We can't take the chance of losing the Reed account. Would you be willing to continue working with her? She's difficult to please, and she's obviously attached to you."

Libby was fond of the older woman and she welcomed the opportunity to work with Mrs. Reed, but not if it would cost her everything that was important.

"And the Buckleys, if you wish, since you brought them into the firm," he added. "And the new clients, if you want."

"I'm not sure I understand," Libby

said, confused but eager to hear what he had to say.

"I come in at nine and leave at six every night," Hershel said. "I had to make myself leave the office because my marriage was at risk. My children didn't know me. I thought it was more important to work hard and give them the material goods they wanted than spend time with them. In the process I nearly lost everything I valued. I could see the same thing happening to you, Libby."

"But I don't know if I can slow down."

"You can and you will. I'll help you. From this point forward you aren't to arrive at the office before nine and you are to leave at six. Your workload will be cut in half and you'll still be a partner."

"What about bringing in new clients?"

"You already have your client load."

"Mrs. Reed, the Buckleys, and the new clients I brought in, but only if I want?"

"Exactly."

"What will the other partners say?"

Hershel smiled. "They'll be fine; I'll

make sure of it. I didn't fight hard enough for you the first time around and I won't make that mistake again. Besides, you've proven your worth. Go talk to your young man, have the family you want and your career, too. I'll help you find the balance the same way a good friend helped me years ago."

Libby sat in the wingback leather chair too stunned to respond.

"Oh, and Libby, congratulations, you're a partner in the firm now." With that he tore her letter of resignation in half and tossed it in the wastebasket.

He rose out of his high-backed leather chair and came around to the front of his desk. He stood directly in front of Libby and placed his hands on her shoulders.

"I wish you nothing but happiness."

Too stunned to react, Libby thanked him and then headed into her office. The first person she phoned was Robin.

"Did you do it?"

"Hershel talked me into staying. The firm is cutting my hours and responsibilities. Basically I only have Mrs. Reed and a few other accounts." It made sense that he'd want her to stay on for the Reed account alone. Martha Reed had already made her opinions clear. She preferred to work with Libby. If she left, then it was highly probable that the older woman would as well, and the firm couldn't risk that happening. Not again.

"You'll handle just a handful of accounts?" Robin made it sound too good to be true.

"Oh, and that's not all."

"You mean there's more?"

Libby couldn't have held back a smile for a million bucks. Her face actually ached with the joy that flooded her. "I was made partner."

Robin laughed outright. "Talk about having your cake and eating it, too. Congratulations, Libby."

"Don't congratulate me yet. I've still got to win back Phillip."

"You will," her friend said with utter confidence.

Libby sincerely hoped Robin was right.

Her next call was to Abby.

After Libby delivered her news, Abby

said, "A little birdie told me Phillip Stone will be returning to the hospital on Wednesday."

"Tell the little birdie that I appreciate the information."

Wednesday afternoon, Libby stopped by the hospital to rock the newborns. Sharon Jennings did a double take and then greeted her with a warm hug.

"The babies have missed you," the head nurse said. "And so have I."

Libby donned a gown and entered the nursery, opting for the infant who was crying the loudest. Gently picking him up, she settled into the rocking chair and looked down at the baby with the deep red face.

"Now, now," she whispered soothingly. "What has gotten you so upset?" She started singing to him as she gently rocked back and forth.

A little more than twenty minutes later, Phillip stepped out of the elevator. He walked directly past the nursery, glanced inside, and continued on for another couple of steps before he stopped abruptly and did a double take. He paused, continuing to stare at her and then after a couple of seconds, continued on his way as if he hadn't seen her.

Ten minutes later he was back. This time he stepped into the nursery and his gaze went straight to Libby.

"What are you doing here?" he demanded, sounding none too friendly.

Libby placed one hand on her hip. "Rocking the babies. In case you've forgotten I was here two or three times a week for several months."

"That was before you went back to the firm," he argued. "What happened? Did they lay you off again?"

"No," she said. "I made partner."

He frowned as though he wasn't sure he'd heard her correctly. "Partner?"

"Yes," she returned simply. "Actually, that came as something of a shock to me, too. I'd gone into the office Monday morning intent on handing in my resignation and . . ."

"You were going to resign?" He continued to stand several feet away from her with his back stiff and his shoulders tensed.

Libby returned the sleeping infant to his crib. "I tried to quit but Hershel talked me into staying with reduced hours. I'll be working on a few accounts, but that's it."

"Why would you be so willing to walk away from a career you love?"

She shrugged. "There were far more important goals I wanted to achieve."

"Such as?"

"Such as being a mentor to Ava and a good friend to Robin, Lydia, and Abby, and that's only the beginning. I'm not an accomplished knitter but I'm fairly good and I have this sweater I've been working on for the longest time. It's about time I finished it."

"A sweater?"

"For a man I know."

"A friend?"

"He's that for sure. A very good friend, but I would like him to be so much more."

Their eyes connected. Phillip's gaze narrowed as if he wasn't sure he should trust her. Libby's heart pounded so hard it felt like a sledgehammer slamming against her ribs, to the point that she pressed her palm over her heart. This was it. Crunch time. Phillip either accepted or rejected her.

"What will make it different this time?" he asked.

"There's a certain fulfillment in working with the law and being made partner, but I know what's most important and it isn't my career."

He raised his brows but didn't respond to the news.

"I've discovered I want so much more out of life."

"Like what?" He crossed his arms as though protecting himself, standing guard over his own heart.

"A husband, for one thing," she said, shocked at how low her voice dipped.

He cocked his head to one side. "That's a possibility."

"Children, too," Libby added.

Phillip's mouth twisted as though restraining a smile. "That's negotiable."

"Oh, Phillip," she whispered, "I couldn't lose you; I just couldn't."

Dropping his arms, Phillip took two giant steps toward her. He locked her in his embrace and lifted her two feet off the floor. Libby's arms circled his neck.

"I don't want to face the future without you. I love you, Phillip." Her voice choked with the sincerity of her words. "Nothing I've strived to achieve means a blasted thing if I can't share it with you."

He closed his eyes and nodded. "I didn't make it easy for you, did I? I convinced myself we were finished. I thought it best for us to have a clean break but I couldn't stop thinking about you, about the promise we have together. I love you. I thought I could walk away but it didn't take long for me to realize I couldn't leave matters the way they were. I couldn't stop loving you."

"Don't try so hard next time," she teased.

His gaze held hers for the longest time. "I love you," he whispered huskily as he brought his mouth to hers.

Libby gave herself over to his kiss, slanting her mouth over his and opening to him like a blossom in the warmth of the summer sunshine.

They broke apart when Sharon cleared her throat.

Libby pressed her forehead against his. "I'm ready to spend my whole life with you, starting now," she whispered.

"Funny," Phillip joked, "I was just thinking the same thing."

Epilogue

One Year Later

The John Adams Junior High School auditorium was bustling with students, faculty, and parents as the band members sitting to the far left of the stage tuned their instruments. Their discordant squeaks only added to the fun as Libby and Phillip made their way into the area of reserved seats. Libby entered the row behind Phillip, holding on to his hand. She did her best not to step on anyone's toes as she maneuvered past parents and teachers alike.

Robin and Roy followed her until they reached their assigned seats.

Libby heaved a sigh of relief as she settled into the folding metal chair. Not the most comfortable of seats but certainly adequate. She opened her program and felt a surge of pride when the first name she found was Ava's. She was playing the lead role of Maria in *The Sound of Music.*

Robin leaned close. "This is a bit ambitious for junior high, isn't it?"

"They have a wonderful music program." The group wouldn't be performing the entire show, but an abridged version. "Did you notice Ava is the lead?"

"I believe you might have mentioned it ten or twelve times," Robin joked, elbowing Libby.

"What are you two muttering about?" Phillip leaned close to ask.

"Nothing, darling," Libby returned ever so sweetly. Then, hoping Phillip had remembered, she asked, "You ordered the flowers for Ava, right?"

"Yes, love."

Libby relaxed.

The school principal appeared onstage and the chatter died down as he stepped forward. "Ladies and gentlemen, we're honored to present to you this evening the talents of our students. We couldn't be more proud of all the hard work that has gone into making this such a special performance. We're blessed by a number of exceptionally gifted singers and musicians. You'll soon see for yourself what I mean. Now, join me in giving these young people your attention and your applause."

Libby clapped long and hard. She was excited for Ava and at the same time nervous, too. Ava had desperately wanted the lead. Libby had played the piano when she was much younger and she'd helped Ava practice before tryouts. Even Phillip had thrown in a bit of coaching.

She looked around and was sad to see that Darlene Carmichael had yet to arrive, although she saw that Ava's brother, Jackson, was sitting with his friends.

The thick stage curtain parted and Ava stood center stage surrounded by pots of flowers. She threw open her arms and burst into song. *"The hills are alive . . ."*

Almost immediately Libby's eyes filled with tears. She couldn't be more proud of the young teen and how she'd braved through so many challenges over the last two years. Ava had grown another inch taller and was slim and beautiful. Her voice had matured and so had she. Libby had become more of a big sister to Ava than a substitute for her mother.

Libby caught a movement out of the corner of her eye and noticed the side door open. Darlene Carmichael sneaked into the auditorium. She stood mesmerized for several minutes as if she couldn't believe what was right in front of her. Not until a lady in a red jacket motioned that Darlene was blocking her view did the older woman move. Darlene apologized and then pointed to Ava, apparently bragging that the girl singing was her granddaughter.

The old woman had pulled through after all. Libby was pleased. Darlene needed to hear Ava sing onstage in order to appreciate what a talented grand-daughter she had.

As the performers transitioned into the second song, Phillip leaned close. "Are you comfortable?"

"I'm fine."

He cocked both brows.

"Phillip, I'm fine," she said with a bit more emphasis.

He dropped the matter. Forty minutes later the curtain closed as the entire group ended with the song "Edelweiss," and the audience was asked to join in. Phillip reached for her hand, intertwining their fingers, his rich baritone joining her soft soprano voice. Even Robin and Roy sang along.

When the curtain opened again, Ava and the young man playing the part of Captain Von Trapp stepped forward to a roaring round of applause. Libby clapped so hard her hands stung afterward.

One of the teachers stepped forward and presented Ava with the bouquet of flowers Phillip had ordered. The Von Trapps stepped behind the curtain once more.

The two couples remained seated as the auditorium emptied. As soon as she could Ava joined them, hopping down the side stairs off the stage like an eager rabbit. Libby hugged her first.

"You did a wonderful job. I was so proud of you."

"My grandma came," Ava said excitedly.

"I saw her bragging to one of the mothers that you were her granddaughter."

Ava beamed. "Did she really?"

"I'm not making it up, Ava. I saw her with my own eyes."

Ava looked to Phillip. "Thank you for the flowers."

Phillip looked surprised. "Did we send you flowers?"

"The card said they were from Grandma, but I know they really came from you."

Robin cleared her throat.

"And Robin and Roy, too." Ava studied the slightly round mound of Libby's tummy. "I can tell you're pregnant now," she said, smiling shyly.

"Oh, good."

"She started wearing maternity tops at two weeks," Robin teased.

"Robin," Libby cried. "I most certainly did not."

The good-natured teasing continued until Ava had to leave.

As the two couples left the school grounds, Phillip had his arm around Libby's shoulders. "She's going to do just fine in high school next year."

"I believe she will, too."

"We're destined to have a stellar year ourselves."

Libby smiled up at her husband. He was right. It would be a very good year indeed.

Knitting Pattern: Long-tail Hat

When a baby wears this hat, the long "tail" (aka, i-cord) will swish from side to side, just like the tail of a cute baby elephant. Use any two colors that grab you.

To find out where you can donate baby hats, please visit Debbie's website at www.debbiemacomber.com.

SKILLS REQUIRED

Long-tail cast-on, knit 2 together (k2tog), i-cord, joining new color, tassels

YOU WILL NEED
- Size 9 (5.5mm) 12- or 16-inch circular needles and set of 4 or 5 double-pointed needles
- Cascade Yarns Baby Alpaca Chunky (100% baby alpaca; 3½ oz/ 100g/108 yds), 1 skein each in 555 petal bloom (A) and 563 sapphire (B)
- Stitch marker
- Yarn needle

GAUGE
16 stitches and 24 rounds = 4 inches

SIZES
0–6 months (6–12 months, 1–2 years, 2 years and up)

FINISHED CIRCUMFERENCE
12 (14, 16, 18) inches

PATTERN
With A, cast on 48 (56, 64, 72) stitches, place marker, and join to begin knitting in the round.

Work in stockinette (knit every round) until piece measures 1½ (1½, 2, 2) inches from the cast-on edge. Note:

Stockinette edge will curl, so unroll for an accurate measurement.

Change to B.

Continue in stockinette stitch until piece measures 5 (5½, 6, 6½) inches from the cast-on edge.

Decreasing

Round 1: Knit 6, k2tog. Repeat to end of round.

Round 2: Knit.

Round 3: Knit 5, k2tog. Repeat to end of round.

Round 4: Knit.

Round 5: Knit 4, k2tog. Repeat to end of round.

Round 6: Knit.

Round 7: Knit 3, k2tog. Repeat to end of round.

Rounds 8–13: Knit.

Round 14: Knit 2, k2tog. Repeat to end of round.

Rounds 15–19: Knit.

Round 20: Knit 1, k2tog. Repeat to end of round.

Change to A.

Rounds 22–25: Knit.

Round 26: K2tog. Repeat to end of round.

Continue to k2tog until only 4 stitches remain.

Transfer these 4 stitches onto a single DPN and work i-cord for 4–5 inches. Bind off all stitches.

FINISHING

With B, create a small tassel and attach it to the end of the i-cord. Wrap a length of B around the base several times. Weave in all ends to finish.

ABOUT THE AUTHOR

DEBBIE MACOMBER, the author of *A Turn in the Road, 1105 Yakima Street, Hannah's List,* and *Twenty Wishes,* is a leading voice in women's fiction. Seven of her novels have hit #1 on the *New York Times* bestseller list, with three debuting at #1 on the *New York Times, USA Today,* and *Publishers Weekly* lists. *Mrs. Miracle* (2009) and *Call Me Mrs. Miracle* (2010) were Hallmark Channel's top-watched movies for the year. Debbie Macomber has more than 160 million copies of her books in print worldwide.

www.debbiemacomber.com